Lies About Truth

Paul W. Jackson

ISBN: 9798344450094 (sc)

ISBN: 9798344452333 (hc)

See more of Paul W. Jackson's works at www.paulwjackson.com

Website by Forge Ave | www.forgeave.com

Dedication

For my mother and her love for books.

Acknowledgment

Glory to God for conceiving rivers, each one as poetic
as change and endurance.
And thanks to Chris Pearson, fisherman.

Karen

J. P farmers are the

Best-

Paul Yoder

Chapter 1

Late July, two weeks before the primary election

He hadn't told his editor, but Garit West was taking the day off. She would not understand, but his sanity required it. He parked his Jeep in parking lot F.

A tall and thick double-row of Blue Spruce, donated by a local tree farmer 20-some years before, blocked his view of the hospital entrance and muffled sounds he hoped he wouldn't hear.

He cursed when he followed the sidewalk past the trees and saw the crowd. Still? These people were like fire or the grave. Never satisfied. Never knew when to quit. Didn't even have enough sense to come in from the rain.

He pulled his black raincoat hood over his Olde English D baseball cap and retreated to the Jeep, wishing he wasn't a reporter any longer. So much for time off. He retrieved his camera and tucked it under the coat, as much for stealth as protection from drizzle. Would his job never be satisfied? Somewhere in Proverbs, there was a list of three things that never had enough. Sometimes, he'd discovered, the Bible says things that can be applied to real life. How about that?

If he remembered, there were warnings in there about certain women, too. He'd have to look that up if he had time.

He sneaked around the crowd's edge to get one more photograph – sure to be clickbait – of Freedah's image as she prepared to address the adoring crowd. He was putting himself in danger, he knew. Still, Aspen – who was far more than just his editor – would express her unhappiness if she knew he was here and didn't shoot some photos for the publication's website and Twaddle, social media's hottest new platform and a bane to Garit's existence.

The Jovial World and Sasser used to be devoted to news. Award certificates on the wall testified to that. But Twaddle was all about image. The more clicks, the better. That's all Aspen seemed to care about anymore. Clicks. It was a slow creep. She used to be meticulous about the news. And even though she still had an uncommon devotion to news integrity, she was slowly letting money seep into her motivations.

Freedah's new nose ring would make lesser beauties look like heifers leaning through a fence in search of forbidden, luscious green grass. But in Freedah's nose, it worked. Maybe it was a bit too large for her petite form, but it was polished and shiny like the sparkle in her blue, crystal eyes that entranced men so completely.

He considered her beauty differently now, and not just because his privilege with her was long gone, never to return. And it was a shame, really. Like pearls dripping from a hog's snout, her neck tattoos made her look dirty, unlike when she and he were involved three years ago. Most people would gladly overlook her tattoos, blinded by beauty so encompassing that it could never end. But his eyes were open to her "truth," and he would not be deceived again.

***

A couple of TV guys who knew Freedah's image would improve their ratings shoved through the crowd toward her. They jostled Garit's eyes back to her, just like always, just like everybody's.

Her naturally tight form embodied covetousness, but as her melodious voice prepared for amplification into her bullhorn, she clanked it with the new nose ring, sending pig-like squeals through the PA system and into hospital rooms across the street. He'd never seen her that clumsy before, but only he, apparently, saw anything less than elegance.

As easy as getting free drinks from some schmuck in a bar, she let the sound die and smiled the smile that brought instant forgiveness from the rabble below her. Only Freedah could pull it off so smoothly. Undeterred, she cooed softly and gently as a newborn fawn, sniffing the air for the scent of agreeable opinions that excited her. The mostly male crowd around her responded with cheers and veneration.

Her eyes were painted dramatically to enhance their ferocity, though she didn't have the need. She was angry today.

She was always angry these days as if she was searching for people to offend her. She called it passion. She said it with such conviction and ferocity that argument was futile. Kind of like Twaddle. Emotion provided the highest moral ground because it was so fluid. Catch Twaddlers in a lie, and they changed the narrative. Without objective truth, nothing could be proven false.

His camera made him conspicuous in this crowd where only approved media types were allowed, but Garit had obligations. Even when he was off the clock, Freedah was his focus, his job, right now. Newsworthy events were not confined to 40 hours a week, no matter how much he wished. Her face was a guaranteed sell on social media. Out in California, Aspen had told him, images of Freedah were guaranteed to go viral, even when she was fully clothed.

His camera's whirling aperture would attract attention to what he was doing, and if the instigator of this protest saw him, he was in for more abuse, maybe even a beating. They had silenced him before, at least on Twaddle, where a majority of followers called him a propagandist and labeled him a hate-speech monger. It's what he'd heard. He'd so far kept his vow to never even look at that Twaddle, so why did he care?

He asked himself again how Freedah Forest could make people do her bidding so effectively, but he knew. It was that obvious.

One-on-one, sure. She could charm the pants off just about any guy she wanted. Including Garit. Not anymore. He was done with her. Once and for all. He'd been bitten once, long ago. And he'd warned Ty, the man he came to see in the hospital bed across the street, but he hadn't listened. Who would have? There was nothing any man could see about her that wasn't appealing. Her image was the baseline from which all other women would be judged.

It wasn't until he met Aspen that Garit's nagging regret over Freedah had been set aside. Besides, Freedah hadn't really caused his pain. People who stepped into bright, shiny, unhidden bear traps knew the consequences before they took that step. She was just Freedah. And she could fix any young man's pain as thoroughly as morphine could fix a broken hand. The regret would come when a young man realized he was addicted to her.

But now, she'd graduated. Her power over individual men had grown mundane. Now, she could manipulate entire crowds without even trying.

***

This protest was so draining and newsworthy because it was happening across the street from the Jovial Community Hospital entrance. That didn't happen very often, if ever. What's to protest at a hospital, where politics are supposed to take a back seat to compassion? Most people respected the sick and dying, giving them little space in the hospital. Freedah was not one of them. Passion was far more important to her than kindness, and the fruit she produced showed that plainly to anyone who wasn't stumbling around in the dark, waiting for her to emerge from the shadows and spread her light.

Even this gathering of activists, a combination of zealots, imported professional rabble-rousers, hangers-on, and in-the-way TV cameras, usually had enough respect to keep their baffling, dislocated messages near government offices, where they belonged. But this crowd had long since lost its focus on any issue, if it ever had one. Its focus was on Freedah.

He entered the crowd from the back because getting through the mob was the most efficient and the only way he knew to get past them and into the hospital's front door. He pulled down his hood in the light drizzle and cautiously stood behind a TV cameraman, waiting for him to become aware of his surroundings outside the viewfinder.

"What's the protest all about?" Garit had been asking the same question all summer and would keep at it until he got an answer, though he knew he'd never get one. He had to try. Again.

The cameraman looked at him, his blank expression revealing an emptiness that Garit considered as vapid as the footage scheduled for the evening news.

"Don't know and don't care," the surly cameraman replied.

"Have you asked anyone?"

"Nope. That's up to the on-air talent to figure out."

"Looks like the chick with the hair is pretty angry about something."

"Yep. Anger makes good TV. She makes the best TV."

"Got that right. She can sell just about anything."

"I'll buy that," the cameraman grinned and went back to work.

Garit spotted Freedah's trademark barn-red and forest-green hair and moved to the other side of the crowd after zooming in and taking a few closeups of her face and some shots of protesters with their signs. His quick calculations led him to believe there were about 25 people here, including reporters, just like it had been for two months. Fifteen professional protesters, four people who questioned their facts much less frequently than their trust-fund balances; two former members of Acrid Reins, still hanging on for the ride and publicity; four mob-approved reporters, and him.

Things had changed. Youthful idealism had turned to hard-boiled gang anger. Blind and senseless. No thoughts of tolerance, no backing down from the frenzy. If Freedah instructed them, they obeyed.

Freedah climbed onto a retaining wall that kept landscaping from eroding into the massive sign that faced the hospital's front entrance. Garit ducked behind the tallest TV guy.

"First," Freedah brayed into the voice amplifier, "Let me say something positive since we're so often accused by the local biased press of being negative. It was good that Ty Mooring was put out of commission. It's much better for all of society that one man die than the whole country falls victim to his anti-earth attitudes."

The protesters cheered as their training had indoctrinated them, then quickly turned their attention back to Freedah's face and form.

"Are we going to let one man's immoral, racist, capitalistic attitudes ruin our river?"

"No!" the fifteen professionals shouted.

"Have there been crimes against humanity and against Majestic Mother Earth done right here in Jovial?"

"Yes!"

"Has the truth maliciously been hidden from us all?"

"Yes!"

"Are we going to let them continue to ruin the environment?"

"No!"

"What do we want?"

"Justice!"

"When do we want it?"

"Now!"

Garit knew the nascent chant would be short-lived. Attention spans amid this group was slightly shorter than a big dog with a small treat in a yard full of squirrels. Garit was continually amazed that their chants were so predictable and lacked even a smudge of creativity, yet they seemed enchanted and invigorated by it all. Good pay could buy just about anything.

Careful to keep hidden behind the rabble, Garit's plan faltered when he looked away from his viewfinder and noticed the crowd had shifted like a large flock of birds in mid-air, exposing him. He saw Freedah fix her gaze his way, so he tucked the camera under his raincoat, turned and began walking toward the hospital.

"There's one of the criminals now!" Freedah shrieked through the bullhorn.

"There goes a man – a toxic earth-destroying white male – who will not tell the truth. What do we do with liars?"

"You bully them into accepting your lies!" Garit shouted back, instantly regretting it because it was all so useless. She would never accept or even consider his intended hurt anyway. He turned and walked, head high, to the hospital entrance, guiltlessly flipping up his raincoat hood in anticipation of the deluge.

The first thing he felt pelt his back was likely a tomato. Perfectly chosen to be just soft enough to ensure maximum splatter. Research on rotten fruit was as far as they'd gone. No curiosity about truth could penetrate them. They had Freedah, and Freedah's truth was good enough for today.

Garit thought himself fortunate that they weren't throwing rocks as he'd expected. Then came more, softer fruit, but he would not run. Some landed and splattered on his head; some struck his back. Most fell on the ground, missing the mark by yards. Then came the harder fruit. Apples. Pears. Some were newly purchased from local organic farmers, of course, and hard enough to leave a mark if they landed.

Garit reached the street separating the protesters from the hospital and walked across it to the institution's steps. They'd been warned by the police, who apparently thought a warning was a fine substitute for their presence, and so far, the protesters had been cowed into staying where they were, held back by Freedah's insistence that they were peaceful protesters.

"Come on, you bunch of wussies!" Garit had turned around to face the crowd and cupped his hands around his mouth. It was raining harder now, and the rotten fruit washed off his back as a few more tomatoes fell on the street's center line.

"Ain't got a decent arm in the whole crowd, huh, Sandra? Maybe you should have recruited some celebrity wacko athletes. At least they might be able to give you a little more bang for your million bucks!" A tomato hit the street's center line and spread upon impact to land a small portion of pulp near the hospital's lowest step.

"That all you got, Sandra?"

Garit saw Freedah, the girl who was named Sandra when she'd beguiled him, wind up and wing a small, hard apple his way, but it barely rolled to the street's center line.

"Still throw like a girl, Sandra!" he was grinning resentfully, yet still drawn to her eyes.

"Misogynist!" She shouted back. "Stop suppressing the truth, you planet killer! You're a murderer!"

Garit shouted louder: "Why don't you tell people your real name?"

He turned his back, flipped up the tail of his raincoat, undid his belt and tugged at his pants and underwear. Not knowing or caring if anyone was twaddling or recording, he wiggled his bare butt with gyrating hips like he was doing the happy dance, then pulled everything back up, calmly and slowly fastened his pants and belt, and walked up the hospital stairs. By the time he reached the doors and looked back, the protesters had become nothing more than a mass of disjointed, grumbling, milling, soaked-to-the-skin morons. The TV cameras had left with the first heavier rain.

Satisfied that he'd won, at least temporarily, Garit opened the door and took the most direct route to a fourth-floor room where Ty Mooring lay, tubes running both in and out of his pale, frail and weakened body.

13

Chapter 2

The previous February

Unlike other jails, the casino lockup featured top-of-the-line cells. Best Tyson Mooring had ever been in. Almost comfortable enough to forget about imminent threats. Thugs or lawyers – maybe both, since the two are interchangeable – were likely on their way, but nothing could be done. If only he'd have kept a low profile for two more weeks, he could pay his way out. Two more weeks, and he could buy and sell thugs and lawyers alike. But he'd been impatient. Story of his life.

It was the tribe's fault for sucking him in. The Indians' public relations department had promised opulence from basement to tower suites, and, well, when the jail was this nice, Ty knew their slick advertising wasn't just PR BS. They'd really done it. The cell doubled down on his desire to see the inside of one of their hotel rooms, though he'd never thought, before he received his letter from the state, that it could be within his reach. Luxury was what they called it, and the social media PR pitch emphasized it with an exaggerated U sound, as in luuuux-ury. And when he was comfortable and unguarded in the jail, what must a top-floor room be like? Only the rich and/or famous knew.

Not that Ty Mooring had wanted to see the inside of the casino jail, but now that he sat in a cushioned chair in a warm room with pictures of mythical tribal warriors bolted to the wall; and no restraints except the bars keeping him in his place, he was impressed.

There were four other chairs in the room just outside the bars, surrounding a metal table. Each one featured rainbow colors with the same style of cushion built into the metal seat. Likely a nod to the all-important 'diversity' the whole world seems to be chasing these days. It would all go out of style before long.

He pondered – in obedience to the huge tribal policeman's orders to think about what he'd done – where he'd made his mistake. Or was it a sin, what he'd done? No. A mistake. Failure to plan. Carelessness.

The chaplain who visited him in the last cell to which he'd been confined would have called it a sin, but to Ty, if it were a sin, it wasn't much of one. The local tribe had lots of money. Why shouldn't he have some of it? They wouldn't even miss it. They wouldn't have even questioned his winnings if he'd just remembered the last count of face cards he'd seen at the blackjack table. Taking from the rich was biblical, right? Take from the rich and give to the poor? It had to be in the Bible. But then, he hadn't read much. He was just getting started, after all.

All he planned to do was win two hundred bucks, enough to pay for a couple of off-season weeks lodging at the less-than luxurious riverfront hotel run by his friend and fellow fisherman Ernie Cook.

Two more weeks, and he'd be flush with cash. But no. He'd lost track. He'd gotten impatient. All because he'd gotten greedy and let himself be distracted. He'd already won $200. It was in his pocket. He was playing with house money. He should have been happy with that, but as he surpassed that goal, he found himself with visions of grandeur. Just a few hundred more and he could afford a night's stay in a casino room with a four-person whirlpool tub and shower/sauna that seated eight.

A little more than that would have been enough for some high-potency, fancy drinks before he settled into his hotel room. Maybe enough for dinner for two. Maybe even breakfast in the morning for a companion the casino could provide. But he'd lost count. It was that waitress. She'd rubbed her chest against his shoulder, stroked his arm and likely seen the tiny counter he was hiding in his left hand. And then she moved on to the next sucker whose head she could turn so incredibly easily.

He heard the lock in the door outside the cell, and it gently opened, revealing a big tribal cop. The Chief of Police. Ty felt special and studied him. He looked vaguely familiar. The cop pulled a chair out from the table, opened the cell door and directed

Ty to a seat. He sat across from Ty and placed his hand on top of a file.

"So, have you thought about what you've done? Because if you haven't, we can ship you off to the county jail in a heartbeat."

Ty looked away from the cop's face to his name badge.

"Oh, I've thought about it, officer." – He turned his head to see the badge.

"Summerhawk, Chief Summerhawk."

"Any relation to Cody?"

"My little brother." The chief straightened his shirt so Ty could see the name tag better.

"He and I used to play basketball in the rec league together. Great guy. Lousy point guard, but he sure could shoot."

The chief chuckled. "I always called him a ball hog. Never met a shot he didn't like."

"He tried to post me up one time. Spun around and elbowed me in the mouth. All accidental, of course. Never thought Cody was a dirty player, unlike some of those folks from the church teams."

"Is that what happened to your teeth?"

"Nope. That's all just pure me." Ty smiled to reveal the tangle in his mouth. "Genetics. Bad teeth run in my family."

The chief opened his manila file and looked at it. Ty couldn't tell if he was doing it for effect or really reading it. He leaned forward, trying to get a look at it, when the chief slammed it shut.

"I don't really think you're a threat of any significance." That was Ty in a nutshell.

"People try this crap all the time. I'm going to let you go, but your picture will be at the front desk. You'll be searched every time you walk in to gamble. If you have a counter again, you'll get a cell one floor below this one. And we're confiscating your two hundred bucks."

"Oh, I've learned my lesson. No more card counting for me. Wasn't very good at it anyway."

"Ain't it the truth. Sit tight. I'll process you out of here, but it may take a little while. Just relax. Need a cup of coffee? Cigarette?"

"Coffee would be great. And thanks, Chief. You won't have any trouble with me again."

Chief Summerhawk nodded and left the room.

***

When Ty heard the door handle shake again, he assumed it was the coffee delivery. But the door opened violently, slamming into the wall as it bounced solidly on its hinges. Two tribal officers and one county deputy shoved a man face-first into the room, where he planted his chin on the tight Berber carpet, raising a red rash on his cheek from the subsequent slide.

The door slammed shut again as Ty sat back in his chair and watched the man reaching for his wounds. He lifted his head and looked at Ty, his right eye already swelling enough to block his sight.

"Reverend!" Ty exclaimed, and rushed over to help him to his feet.

***

Two years before

Tony Finn was arrested at a hotel room near Tulare, California. The synthetic fox head hat that identified him as the prime suspect was lying on the cushy chair near the room's only window, with several small, smooth stones huddled inside it in a perfect circle as if arranged.

The next day, when an anonymous benefactor bailed him out, two deputies led him away across a pea-stone walkway between the courthouse and the parking lot. They called a cab for him.

Later that day, he told Kaley Carrumbo on the set of her television show that it was all a sign from the universe.

"I was walking out, as proud as I've ever been that I could suffer for the cause of the earth, and these little stones kept jumping up into my shoes like they were trying to escape their forced placement. It was then that I became convinced, without a doubt, that I was right all along. Stones have mystical properties. They have the power to heal, if we humans would only tap into it. Rocks and stones deserve our respect and protection just as much as rivers do. My new album is going to be about rivers, of course, but I think I have to give some love to rocks and stones, too. They're all a part of Majestic Mother Earth, after all."

That night, as Freedah Forest loaded crack cocaine into a large bong, the first tunes of Tony's new album seeped into his brain. He would call the song, appropriately, Rocks and Stones.

Chapter 3

Late July, 13 days before the primary election

Editor and girlfriend Aspen Kemp called Garit into her office at the Jovial World and Sasser. Several of his photos from yesterday's protest were on her screens, and his story was printed in her hand. She didn't appear pleased. The printed story was cluttered with red exclamation points, question marks and frowning cartoon faces. Funny how she was okay making faces on paper, but if she found them in a text or social media post? She'd erupt.

"We have some problems here." Their eyes met for a moment, long enough for Garit to understand that she was in her editor's mindset, which allowed her to separate her job from their personal, mostly troubled relationship. She applied both roles with equal fervor, although he preferred her eyes fixed on his in a romantic role, not this professional look. With Aspen, he took what he could get when he could get it. Things were easier that way.

"The copy doesn't seem to line up with what I'm seeing in the photos," she started. "Too much opinion. Needs a rewrite."

"This story is completely factual."

"Really?" she pointed to a photo on one of her three screens of a young man holding a placard that read 'Stop steeling our land!'

"You infer in this story – though I will admit subtly – that this man is obviously white and has no credibility acting like an Indian."

"So? It's true."

"It's not factual. First of all, how do you know he's not an Indian and that his land wasn't stolen from him?"

"First," Garit started, knowing that his defense wouldn't stand up to her scrutiny, "look at him. Blonde hair, blue eyes and about 20 years old. He has no land to steal – or even 'steel.' Besides, any land he claims was Indian land was not stolen. It was purchased legally more than two hundred years ago. It's all in hand-written, legal documents from the state, county and township archives."

"The natives have a different story."

"Hearsay. Would never stand up in court."

Aspen sighed.

"Ty isn't all white, either, but he looks it." She pointed at the photo in question. "I can't run this picture. The misspelling taints the reader's perception."

"No, the sign reveals the truth. If a man appears in public with misspelled lies on a placard, don't readers deserve to know what kind of moron is in the crowd of protesters? Stupidity taints the whole message like one fly in the ointment." Check him out, using Bible references.

"Did you talk to him, ask him about his background and opinions?"

"Didn't have to. He's been in the crowd for weeks. I've heard him spouting all kinds of stupid things. I've heard him agreeing with Freedah no matter what moronic things she said. He has a 'born to loose' tattoo on his arm. And, it was kind of hard to ask him questions when I shot this because I was fearful about my own safety."

"So it was out of fear for your safety that you mooned the whole crowd?" Garit, after all this time with her, still couldn't tell if comments like that were sarcastic criticism or her attempt at comedy. She smiled, and he knew she was out of editor mode. How long would it last?

"Either way, your sorry butt couldn't even go viral." She manipulated her mouse and pointed to what looked like a spreadsheet on her smallest screen.

Analytics from the Mother Earth Liberation League (MELL) burst onto the screen. In one column, under an 18-second video of his backside, titled "Biased reporter goes full Monty for MELL protesters," were the numbers. No written explanation with the photo. Hits to the MELL website were considerably up because of the video.

"My butt gained 1,200 new visitors to MELL? You better treat me better, Aspen. MELL hates me, and they still wanted to see my butt. Probably all of them women!"

"Don't get too excited. Your butt fell a few thousand clicks short of viral. Even Donald Trump's butt would do better." She shuddered for effect.

She straightened her smile and got back to business. She watched the video one more time and slid it into the background.

"You think that was a good thing to do?"

"I'll admit that wasn't the smartest thing I've ever done, but I've been out among these idiots for a long time. They're paid activists with no real passion except the money. Pay them a buck an hour more, and they'll take the other side."

"You don't know that."

"I do know that. They need to be exposed for their hypocrisy."

"Oh, so you're an activist now and not a reporter?"
Garit bristled.

"These activists are generally brain-dead. They're not even approaching the truth here. They make up their own truth depending on the day, the issue, and their mood."

"Your responsibility is simple: only to report facts. Let the readers decide what's true. Anything else is activism."

"Have you seen what they did to Ty? This is about reporting what's right, not just bare facts without context. And the context is lying in a hospital bed. Freedah's mob is responsible for his injuries, and that's a fact."

"You don't know that. The police reports haven't even been filed yet."

"They will be."

"Then we wait until then to report it." She scratched out three paragraphs from his news copy with her thick red pen.

"Your job is to report the facts, then find out if those facts are right."

"You mean my job is to search for truth?"

"No. Facts are our job. Truth is relative."

"You're wrong, Aspen. What about the media's responsibility to expose lies and reveal the truth? There is absolute, objective truth, you know. It's not based on opinion."

"And this piece is full of opinion! It's your opinion that this man is white, your opinion that the protesters are responsible for Ty's injuries, and your opinion that the sign doesn't mean stop trying to 'steel' the land – you know, protect it against attackers."

"Look at the context. That's ridiculous. For months, they've been saying white men stole their land, all without fact or documentation. And that's not even why they're supposed to be protesting. It's supposed to be about pollution, but these native American wannabes must have gotten the wrong text. The historical records shoot down everything they claim. And you printed their allegations. White folks didn't steal other white folks' land. Not in the way the state took it from the Indians, anyway. It's all obvious race-baiting. And even if it were true, this guy's ancestors were likely the ones who stole the land, not the victims."

"That's not our call. I think you've become too close to this story. You've lost your objectivity."

"Well, at least I haven't lost my ability to see through the bull. They almost killed a man, a man whose motives are a lot purer than theirs. And if I can expose them, that's good for the community. And if that makes me an activist, maybe that's what I should be."

"You just go ahead, then. But you're too good a reporter to change into an idiot-stick activist. Don't worry. I'll rewrite it."

"You'll make it stale and unfeeling and arcane." He regretted that and likely would regret it more. "But maybe you're right. Maybe from what I've seen the last few years, reporting it isn't enough. Maybe there's a higher calling to loyalty and relationships and truth."

"Again, with your opinions." She was out of the editor mode and into the girlfriend mode again, though not completely. "Now start writing the shooting story so it will be ready to go when the police reports come in. Oh, and on the good side, since these protests started back in May, our website hits have nearly doubled."

"It's because of my butt."

Aspen rolled her eyes, which were as beautiful as the deep, cold lakes surrounding Jovial. Garit knew as well as she did that the increased web traffic was all about Freedah.

Chapter 4

Back to the previous February

Ty grasped hands with the man commonly known as Grandy and pulled him off the prison room's floor. With a gentleness that surprised them both, Ty guided Grandy's imbalanced body onto a chair at the table. The reverend slid onto the seat, disheveled and injured, blood coagulating from a raised wound in his left temple. His right eye was swollen shut and seeped a cloudy liquid. There were bruise marks all over his upper arms.

The last time Ty had seen the Good Reverend Donald Grandersma – known to prisoners as 'Reverend Repent' – was when he pulled Ty up out of the water the third time. He'd seen the good Reverend's face, shook the water from his head like a dog and exclaimed his rehearsed line: "Hallelujah! I'm a brand new man!"

Grandersma's face had beamed as he passed Ty a towel and wrapped his thin arm around his shoulder. He quickly pulled away when he felt the water from Ty's dripping body soaking into his shirt. He raised his hands and his preacher's voice:

"Gentlemen, this is where you want to be before you leave here. Salvation will keep you from coming back. Tyson has made the right choice. Salvation is irrevocable. Once saved, always saved. God will never leave you or forsake you as long as you don't doubt him."

Ty had paused from his toweling off and spoke softly so the other prisoners couldn't hear.

"But Reverend, what happens if I leave or forsake him or have doubts?"

The reverend looked him in the forehead, a look of confusion on his face that Ty would never forget.

"It's never come up."

Thirteen days later, Ty was given his release. From what Grandy had said, he assumed that he'd walk out with freedom and a new outlook on life, but he didn't feel like a 'brand new man.'

When he started walking the long and frigid road to Jovial, he feared that nothing had changed. He knew he was saved, but he felt that in his heart more than he knew it in his mind. But from what had he been saved? No one had told him what was next or what Jesus expected of him. Maybe baptism was all there was to it. A one-time event that got him out of hell for free. Seemed simple enough. Maybe too simple.

He started walking southeast toward Jovial on a paved road. He'd gone about three miles when he felt a blister forming inside his right big toe, but he had no other plan than to keep going.

He stopped when he came upon a sign that said, "Prison area. Do not pick up hitchhikers." He removed his shoe, adjusted the sock and stood. He worked up a big wad of saliva and some gunk from his nasal passages and spat a large loogie, which stuck satisfactorily onto the sign's emphasized word 'Not.'

After another mile, when he could feel his hips complaining because of his limping gait, he watched a Ford F-150 zip by him, then slow and stop. Despite the pain in his foot, he began to run, hoping the pickup was owned by whom he suspected.

He was still a couple hundred yards away when the truck's driver-side door opened, and he knew he'd been right. Standing, waiting for him, was Coney Dogues, the leading farmer in Jovial and his former employer. There had been a lot of employers, but Ty had more respect for Coney than any other man he'd ever met. His parents had always spoken well of him, even during the peak picking seasons.

They shook hands when Ty caught up.

"What are you doing way out here?" Coney was grinning.

"Headed back home. Give me a lift?"

"It's why I stopped."

They drove off.

"Where have you been?"

"You hadn't heard? I been locked up."

"Oh, the lottery thing. That was some time ago."

"Yep. Served my time."

"So where you headed? Any plans?"

Ty looked out the window.

"Don't know. I have no long-term plans, no future to speak of."

"Everybody has a future. But first things first. You got a place to stay?"

"I have been talking back and forth with Ernie, and I can stay in his bunker for a while, at least during this special trout season coming up."

"Ernie Cook?"

"Yep."

"I thought that bunker was shut down."

"Well, technically, it is, but it'll do for now."

"You can work for me any time. I can get some heat into the old migrant housing if you want."

"I might take you up on that. But you know me, Coney. I just have to get back to fishing. I've missed that old river more than you know."

"You can make a living doing that?"

"Hope so. Haven't talked terms with Ernie yet."

"Well, Ernie is a pretty square shooter. Never seen anyone who could match him in fish cleaning. Only restaurant owner I know who could get a six-ounce filet out of a five-ounce fish."

They chuckled together.

"You may not have heard. There's a lot of crazy stuff going on with the Jovial now," Coney said. "Lawsuits, enviros and greeniacs, some state agency sticking its nose into things. Some big changes are coming if these attorneys get their way."

"I've made some changes too." Ty looked out the window again at the territory zipping by. Still unfamiliar territory, about 40 miles from Jovial.

"Promise you won't judge me?"

"Yep."

"I was saved in prison, Coney. Baptized."

"Wonderful! That's the best choice anyone can ever make. Welcome to the new."

"What does that mean?"

"It means that you don't have to live your old life, the one that got you put in prison. It's about a change, you know, for the better?"

"Ain't nothing better out there for me, Coney. I mean, sure, I can finally get to fishing again, but I can't survive on that for too long. I could work for you, but again, it's just a wage. How long can I do that? What's in front of me?"

"I have a feeling you're stuck in the middle, and you want to move into one lane or the other. There are a lot of things you're carrying on your back that you don't need anymore. I don't know what they are, but you do. Face them. You're a child of God now. Everything is changing. It's a great place to be, even though it might not feel that way right now. Be patient. You can figure it out, but first, you must decide who controls your life."

Ty fixed his eyes on Coney. "That makes no sense. I'm in control of my life, just like everyone else."

"But you're not like everyone else. You're unique. No one in this world is just like you. With salvation comes a unique mission."

"I'm not going to be some preacher!"

"Well, see, there's a good start. One less option to consider. Have you ever heard the Bob Dylan song 'You're gonna have to serve somebody?'"

"Yeah, I've heard it."

"Everybody is a servant of someone. Dylan said, 'It might be the devil, it might be the Lord.' I would add that it might be yourself. But that's a very small perspective. You're a servant of the most high God, and that's a very high position. It's like you're a cabinet member of the highest authority there is. There's no greater honor than serving the King!"

"An honor to be a servant? That's news to me. All I've been told all my life is that I must make my own way. You know, work for yourself, not for someone else. They even taught that in school. The best place to be – the successful place – is having control over my own life, right? I'm out of prison now, with a chance to control my own life. It's all up to me."

"And what about the man who saved you? Don't you owe him something?"

"Who, Reverend Repent?" Coney rolled his eyes, and Ty laughed. "No, I know the Reverend might think I owe him something. I suppose I owe Jesus for saving me, but how can he control my life? He's out there in the vapor somewhere, somewhere like heaven, I guess. What if he's just a story, a kind of fable that gives people a crutch? Aren't we better off, stronger if we handle things ourselves, in our own power and ambition?"

"Well, maybe that's the biggest decision you have to make if you're going to figure that out, Ty. Figure out who God really is. There are only two choices when it comes to Jesus. Either he is who he said he is, or he's the biggest fraud who ever walked this earth. You have to decide that, and you have to figure out who he is. If he is who he said he is, that is, if all this salvation and Christianity is true, don't you think you owe him?"

"Do you owe him?"

"Every day, for everything."

"But I just got out of prison, where other people controlled every minute of my life, every day. Don't you think it's time I took control of my own life again?"

"But it isn't your life! Your life has been bought at a very high price. Blood and death bought you, Ty. Ask yourself, if you believe there is a God, who he really is? You'll find the answer in the Bible, but it might not sink in if you think he doesn't exist or if you think he's kind of apathetic toward you. The point is, and this needs to sink in first, that you're not God. If you're not, then someone else is. But I know for a fact that it ain't you, or me, or anyone else on this earth."

"Okay. I believe I'm not God. But he's not going to make my decisions for me. That's up to me. And right now, I've decided that I'm going fishing."

"Seems like a good option to me. But read your Bible too. It will help you decide just who God really is."

"I don't have a Bible."

"No problem. Just stop by some evening after you get settled, and we'll give you one."

"If I come by, will Jenn feed me?" The thought started his mouth-watering.

Coney grinned. "I'll grill up some steaks. We'll drink a few beers."

"Agreed."

They rode into Jovial, and Ty asked Coney to stop in front of the casino. "This is where you want to be?"

"Temporarily."

"You're sure?"

"I got fifty bucks. Soon to be a couple, three hundred easy. I'd like to see what a luxury room is like."

"You can stay with us. Jenn's cooking is pure luxury."

Ty reached out to shake Coney's hand.

"I know. Thanks, anyway, Coney. I'll be by in a few days. There's something I'd like to get your opinion about."

"Anytime."

***

When Donald Grandersma left prison, a couple of weeks after Ty was baptized, he had five dollars in his pocket and chronic leg pain. He knew he had to take some risks if he were to boldly end the scourge of gambling once and for all. He'd told God it was his ultimate mission and never doubted that God agreed because God hadn't specifically disagreed.

A senior elder from the Church of the Commandment Keepers, Michael Nitholder, was waiting in his car.

The two shook hands after Grandy tossed his suitcase in the back seat.

"Well, that's finally over, huh?" asked Nitholder, trying to keep the conversation light, at least for a few miles. It was sunny but too cold to melt snow.

"God delivered one last lost soul yesterday on my last day in prison ministry, brother Mike." Grandy used his finest pulpit voice. "He's put me through a time of testing and trial, complete with intense and prolonged suffering for him. And now I'm free to continue my work for Jesus and to purge this sin from our community once and for all."

"Yeah, we need to talk about that. Things have changed. Your funds have been cut off for this prison ministry, and I'm afraid that what I've been assigned to tell you may cause you just a little more suffering."

"They can't cut off that money, Mike. I cried out to God, and his face shined on me. Besides this one yesterday, I brought five young men to Christ in the months I sequestered myself among the sinners, and at least a couple will join our church sooner or later."

"Anybody I know?"

"Maybe. One of my favorites was a young man whose name was Tyson Mooring. He was in because of this gambling scourge. A nice young man, really. A bit lost, but aren't they all?"

"I assume so. And so does the board of elders. In fact, we decided just last week that anyone who's harmed the name of our church is lost, and I'm sorry to say that includes you, too, Grandy."

"How can your pastor be lost, Mike? Sure, I suffered for the Lord, but it was to refine me and force me to focus on his mission for me, which remains as it always was. To rid this community of gambling."

"And our entire congregation agrees with you that it's a giant dog-doo stain on our Christian sidewalk," Nitholder said. "But they also agree that you stained our good name by the actions you took."

"So you think the best move is to shit on me? My actions were fully endorsed by the board of elders, Mike. You stood right there on the altar and gave me 100 percent support, remember?"

"You deceived us, though. You never said you were going to resort to violence."

"What violence? I destroyed some gambling machines, the very machines that would drag us down into addiction and steal all our money. It wasn't my fault that those two guards got in the way. I stepped in where the law – and the church – wouldn't. You'll never convince me that my actions weren't justified. I didn't think you, of all people, would be a doubter."

"But it didn't help, Don. The casino simply filed an insurance claim and moved on. That casino is packed all the time now with sinners trying to serve mammon and not God. Your bombs were all a waste. It was all for nothing. You should thank God that we didn't turn you over to the law way back then. We all supported you to go into the prison as a way to protect you, and to protect our church."

"It didn't change anything where the casinos were concerned because I was all alone in following God," Grandy spat with greater volume. "You had the chance but decided to compromise with the sin. I was the only one who stood up for the convictions of our entire church. Then God let me suffer at the hands of the very sinners I was trying to save. Just like Jesus. Doesn't that count for something?"

"I don't know how much it counts or how much bigger the list of things you've done for God is than your sins, but I know public opinion turned against us right away, and it's gotten worse these last three months. The rumors about you are just too strong, and they're growing. And let's face it. That limp of yours is hard to cover. We had to disavow any knowledge of what you did and set a policy that condemns your actions. Privately, of course, except that MOEIB knows. It was one of their conditions that stopped their legal crud. It was the only way we could survive. Attendance at Sunday services is getting pretty low, as you well know. The collection plate isn't hardly worth passing around anymore. We hired a public relations firm for a consultation, and we learned a lot in an hour of face-to-face conversation and instruction. We came away with one very clear situation. We had to take action or close the doors."

"So you folded?"

"If that's what you want to call it. We prefer to call it good public relations. Without that, no church in this modern world can survive. And it's worked to a point. Our social media comments have been more positive than negative since we started this PR campaign."

"Social media! Really? Are you involved with that now? So what does this all mean to me?"

"Well, I'm sorry to say it, Don, but you're no longer our pastor."

"What? This is the thanks I get for leading my flock to follow God? Let me talk to the board. They couldn't all have abandoned their stand against gambling."

"Oh, we're still against gambling, only we've decided to take a different route. The hard-line doesn't work anymore. Our protests outside the casino were getting us nowhere. You know that. The only thing being accomplished was to make us targets for rotten tomatoes and stuff. The board – and the PR firm – feared that bullets would be next, given the political climate around the country right now. We decided to get out of harm's way and put all our efforts into the legal battles. We've adjusted our battle tactics to meet the new reality. And we've decided that any member of our congregation that goes to the casino is to be severely disciplined. Internally. It's where we think we can do the most good."

"But we tried all that, Mike. We spent nearly our entire evangelism budget on lawyers before the Indians even put a shovel into the ground. It was all money down a rabbit hole. You and the board agreed we needed to change tactics, but not this way. Not by throwing money after lawyers."

"Explosives were not part of the tactics we agreed on, either, Don."

"I see. That's what you told the press, anyway." He stared at the passing scenery, sulking. "So that's it?" he said after several minutes of silence. "I'm out of a job, just like that?"

" No one told the press anything. But yes, you're out of a job. That's the long and short of it."

"What about Dads Against Gambling? What did you do with that money?"

"We haven't touched that money. Too risky to use potentially tainted funds. You're still the founder and president of DAG. You did the fundraising, and as far as we're concerned, you can do whatever you can with it to continue to fight gambling. But the church cannot be associated with it. So far, the press hasn't really connected the two, and we want to keep it that way. This Aspen girl – the reporter – is relentless and smart. She'll figure it out sooner or later unless we give her a different scent to follow, you know, get her on to another game."

"I'd sure like to talk to the board," Grandy said after his rage subsided.

"I'm afraid it won't do any good. It's been voted on. The decision of the board is final, as always. We'll let you stay in your house until you find a job and can afford to move on." Grandy stared out the window in silence for at least five miles.

"Dammit," he said, finally, smashing his hand on the car's dashboard. "This isn't fair! I suffered for the Lord – voluntarily – so you folks wouldn't have to! I did what anyone who really follows the Lord would do! I never looked back and never doubted God's mission for me. And I gave up a perfectly good leg for it. Our faith is a faith of action, but I seem to be the only one who's willing to take action. I volunteered to live in the prison until the heat died down. I did that for my congregation. I followed God. You didn't."

"We're following God now by saving our congregation. That has to be our highest priority. Better to lose one man than let the whole institution be dragged down."

"So I'm the sacrificial lamb?"

"If that's how you want to look at it."

"Stop the car!" Grandy slammed his clenched fist into the dashboard again. "Stop this damned car! I'll take nothing more from you hypocrites."

"But it's still 20 miles to Jovial."

"Don't care. If I can't be your pastor anymore, I'll find a place that supports the cause of God. Even if I have to make my own place."

The car stopped, and Grandy got out and fetched his bag from the back seat. Before he slammed the door with all the force he had, he shouted: "A curse on your church and you, Mike. I will petition the Lord to make it burn down into the hellfire where it came from!"

Chapter 5

Late February

"What are you doing here, Grandy?" Ty released his grip on Donald Grandersma's hand when he'd found some balance in his seat at the prison table.

"Same as always, young Tyson, God's work."

"God's work got you beaten up by the cops?"

"That's right. But you? I thought you were going straight and narrow. Has your baptism worn off so quickly?"

"Baptism doesn't pay the bills, reverend."

"I thought you had a big reparation coming your way."

"It's tied up in politics, apparently. Some lawyers sent me a letter saying it's coming, but the final documents haven't been signed yet. It will take another two weeks, he said. In the meantime, I need cash to find food and shelter."

"What about the fifty bucks you got when you were released from prison?"

"I had it turned into a couple hundred before they caught me trying to count cards." Ty grinned. A little rebellion was good for the soul.

"That's very poor stewardship of your money." Grandy pressed his hand to his throbbing temple.

"I intended to use the money for a hotel room and maybe rent some fishing gear. I have a friend who'll buy the fish to serve in his restaurant."

"Well, that's fine for now, but what about when you get your big money?"

"I've decided not to decide until it's in my bank account."

"Always good to plan. Have you learned about tithing?"

"Never heard of it."

"It's a command of God, started way back with Abraham, in which you give a tithe -- or ten percent-- of everything you earn back to God."

"That's quite a bit if I get the money they tell me I'm going to get."

"How much?"

"I'd rather not say until I know,"

"Well, whatever it is, I would advise you to obey God and give 10 percent to a worthy cause."

"How do you know what's a worthy cause?"

"You trust someone like me. I brought you to Christ, didn't I?"

"I thought you told me to put all my trust in Jesus."

"Jesus, me, we're all the same. At least we're both working for the same goal. We both hate gambling, and I believe you should, too, since it landed you in this jail cell. And the one before this. The point is that any money given to God will have a lasting impact. Everlasting. Don't make your decision now, Ty. Pray about it, and when you get the money, pray that God will direct you to send it my way so we can end this gambling scourge once and for all."

"I think no matter how much I think I'm going to get, the casino has a lot more. And a lot more lawyers."

"That's true, but remember, David was a lot smaller than Goliath, and he took him down with just a little stone."

"David and Goliath, huh? I thought that was like a Greek myth or something."

"No. It's in the Bible, and it's there to teach us all not to give up. To fight, even when the odds are against you. When the cause is righteous, God will fight the battle for you. Never doubt that, Ty."

"I'll look that up when I can afford to buy a Bible."

***

The outer cell door opened, and Chief Summerhawk walked in.

"You're free to go, Ty. Remember what I said."

Ty shook his hand, then turned to shake the Reverend's hand and walked out of the casino penniless.

As Ty walked out, Summerhawk said to Grandersma: "Get up, Grandy. We're taking you down to the county. And be advised. If our police force catches you within a mile of this casino again, you might never survive long enough to get to the county lockup."

Chapter 6

As he always did, Garit checked his phone first thing in the morning and discovered a text from an unknown number. The Reverend Donald August Grandersma had been taken into the county jail.

Garit's first call was to the Indian casino just south of Jovial and its young public relations spokesperson, Bethany Longarrow, who also was the spokesperson for the entire Donchawannnakissamee tribe.

"Hi, Beth," he said in his friendliest voice. "Garit. Remember you said you'd talk when Grandy popped up again? You said he was gone for good. Well, it's happened. What do you know about it?"

"We're aware that he was arrested. We've increased our security quite a bit. We're ready for him or any other terrorist like him."

"Seems like kind of a neutered terrorist, based on his history. And I can't put in print that you say he's a terrorist."

"Why not?"

"It would never get past Aspen." Beth laughed. On to more verifiable things.

"How have you increased security?"

"Two extra guards by every entrance during the day and four extra to patrol the perimeter at night."

"So Grandy is a great job-creator, kind of like the person who throws a brick through a window."

"I don't follow."

"You know. A broken window brings jobs for the window maker, the janitor, the window installers, etcetera."

Beth laughed. "I won't be quoted saying such things, but it's an interesting way to look at it. Officially, I'd just say the tribal leaders are wary and are committed to protecting our sovereign nation's interests against all threats, domestic or foreign. Grandy or any of his followers will be arrested immediately if he sets so much as one foot on the sovereign property of the casino."

"You really want me to mention his name? He was never arrested or charged in the bombing, if you'll recall. So you're targeting a person for his political views, not because he's a threat."

"Off the record, we both know he did it. Just because the cops didn't do their job doesn't mean our tribal police won't. You can remind your readers of that in your story."

"I'm not writing a story about it yet. I'm just calling to ask if you'll let me know if anyone sees him again. Don't think he has any followers left, if you ask me."

"You might be right, especially since the church board fired him."

"Good to know."

"We're still keeping our eyes open. Like always, if we see anything, you're my first media call."

"I appreciate it." Garit knew from experience it was a lie. "In the meantime, I'm going to check with his old church, see if he might have made his way back there."

"If he has no more followers, what would be the point?"

"You forget that the Commandment Keepers is a very forgiving group." They both laughed. The best joke of the day so far. "But someone with no followers can't really be a terrorist. What about the DAG group? Seeing any activity there?"

"You really think we follow what a fringe group like Dads Against Gambling is up to?"

"Yes."

"That's off the record too."

"And?"

"And no activity we can find since the day before Grandy fell off the radar. Our tribal police force is on its toes."

"How about an interview with Chief Summerhawk?"

"I'll see what I can do, but it's a long shot."

"Might be a good story, you know, security alerts to watch for the only terrorist – alleged terrorist – that's ever attacked the casino." Garit was baiting her again. He'd never thought of Grandy as a terrorist, just a zealot.

"We'd just as soon let it lie until something happens. You know, no need to panic our public. If the gamers thought there could be a threat, they might not show up."

"And with less income, you wouldn't be able to afford to pay for increased security?"

"Exactly." She giggled because she knew Garit's game. "Kind of a reversal on the broken window economic theory, huh?"

"Guess so. Anyway, thanks, Beth. Keep me in the loop?"

"Always."

Chapter 7

Ty walked five miles from the casino north along Riverfront Road, a winding ribbon of new asphalt that seemed out of place in late winter's gray landscape. To locals, the smooth ride was long overdue. To tourists, it encouraged high speed past views of the river as if it wasn't what drew them here. Without spring's colors, the river was like a movie star before her makeup and flattering camera angles.

Nearer downtown Jovial, the road straightened past the back doors and loading docks of the business district, home to almost any river-related business one could imagine.

Winter still browned the riverbanks like ground hamburger on low heat, though the snow was almost gone, leaving a smell that exposed winter's toll on frail plants and animals. Trees were still bare, waiting patiently for temperatures to signal their awakening like racehorses pressing against the starting gate.

Ty walked off the pavement onto the boardwalk, which was built to provide a pleasant, clean walkway between storefronts and the river if storekeepers kept their portion swept.

The atmosphere most desired by tourists who came north was to return to the earth, as long as it was swept, tidy, and organized. The boardwalk smelled pleasant, like new lumber, and Ty appreciated the replacement planks that overpowered smells from the river's last rotting winter cadavers.

He walked past several gaudy-signed rental places, including Kai Jackson's place, labeled Kayaks 'n Canoes, a name only attentive natives understood. Kai Jackson had married a Scandinavian girl, who pronounced his last name Yackson, thus Kai Yackson Canoes. Ty smiled at the inside joke and continued past closed jet ski rental storefronts, fishing guide come-ons, and candy and curio shops preparing for an influx of tourist money. He passed by five restaurants because they were dark and lifeless, nodded toward four open but customer-absent bait and tackle shops, and three marijuana mongers, open year-round.

In the middle of the district, he reached Ernie's Outfitters, which sported a new sign that said Ernie's place was an "Outfitter, Hotel and Fine Dining Restaurant." Ernie would try any opportunity for profit. Despite that, he could be trusted.

Ernie's Outfitters was a middle-sized business that lacked some of the fancier, showier things the bigger boys offered. Still, Ernie had better fishing advice and more honest pricing than anyone else in town. And, if Ernie knew you well enough, you could get a free lesson in freedom, the Second Amendment, individual rights, and the police state. If you knew him as well as Ty did, you could talk about the survivor's training school, a source of pain and frustration, and many discussions between them.

When Ty opened the door and its hanging, dainty bell sounded, Ernie Cook nearly ran from behind the sales counter to give Ty a lingering, firm-gripped, two-handed shake.

"My man Ty! I heard you were released. Got your debt to society paid after those trumped-up charges?"

"They weren't trumped up, Ernie. I did the crime. Never lied about it. I thought 18 months was a bit much for a $500 crime, but that's the way it is when prosecutors get involved." He said the word 'prosecutor' with venom despite his will to suppress it. "But it's all over now. No use looking over my shoulder. Time to start fresh."

"Good thinking, man. Bitterness never fed the bulldog unless you're a government bureaucrat who makes laws that guarantee it. So what brings you in?"

"I need you to set me up with everything I need to catch some brown trout if you need any. I hear the DNR is opening a special season day after tomorrow, and I need some cash. A room, too, for a while. Ain't got no money yet, but you know I'll be good for it in a couple of weeks. That's what some state-owned lawyers are saying, anyway. I want to use a spinning rod with a Mepps spinner, not a fly rod, and a couple of Rapala jerk bait lures. You pick a couple out for me. And waders. Maybe just a St. Croix or a

Shakespeare micro rod with a six-pound line, since I'll be going a ways upriver into those tangled tributary feeds; a creel, or maybe just a stringer; a Leatherman – the one with 18-19 tools on it – maybe, a net, and, first things first, a license."

"What happened to all your gear?"

"Sold it to pay for lawyers. Hardly scratched the surface."

Ernie hustled around the shop, muttering at first about the tyranny of state-mandated licenses just to get the right to hunt and fish.

"It's unconstitutional, you know," Ernie said. "If only we had a politician who had big enough balls to stand up to the corruption. And you know as well as I do that the environment government is richer and more corrupt than the legislature and Congress. Just like all the bullshit they pass year after year." He gathered supplies as he spoke, keeping an account of the cost on his phone's calculator. Ty followed at a short distance, approving of everything Ernie picked off the shelf with simple nods.

"Don't forget a nice long, strong rope. The way that current looks above the pond it seems like a good idea to tie myself to one of the property anchors up there by the fish farm. She's got a treacherous flow right now."

"Good idea. Only you would even think of that, Ty. It's why you're the best. How about a floater vest to keep all the lures and such?"

"Whatever you can think of that I might not regret carrying is fine, Ernie. I trust you, and that's becoming a pretty rare thing in this world."

"Don't I know it! If you can get me some good fish, I'll let you stay in the bunker as long as you're fishing."

"You just keep track of the trout, and we'll settle up when it all happens."

"Fair enough. You bring 'em in, and I'll buy 'em. The restaurant needs fresh trout now more than ever. I have a feeling tourists will start early this year."

"How much?"

"I'll give you five, no, ten bucks for anything of legal size, more for any whales."

Ty remembered but didn't mention, that a brown trout meal in any of the restaurants in this district would run $25 during the tourist season, with salad, side, and drink extra.

Ernie pulled out his license book and began scratching in it. "Remember that the limit for browns had dropped down to five a day."

"What idiot thought up that scheme?"

"You know the DNR. They keep listening to the fishermen's group lawyers. PFFF, or puff, as I call them. Sounds like a fart. Appropriate. Stupid bastards. They think only they should be able to fish, and they want everyone but them to throw them all back. Of course, the ones they throw back are butchered up by these rubes. You wouldn't believe it, Ty. These yahoos just yank the hooks out of their mouths and drop them back in, torn up so bad they probably can't ever feed again."

"I believe it. I've seen their carcasses floating down to the dam." He paused and sighed. I guess five a day it is. It kind of limits my income, but that's okay. Throw in breakfast for me once a day, and it's a deal. Oh, and let me use this address to forward my mail?"

"Fair enough. And if you miscount the fish at some point, I'll understand." he smiled and winked, and Ty smiled back.

"It's getting kind of late to get to the bunker. How about a room just for tonight? I'm supposed to go out to the Dogues' farm." Ernie agreed.

Ty's entire bill, license included, came to $560.

***

Ty put his meager belongings—one backpack full—in the room overlooking the river. He pulled a letter from it, stuffed it in his inner coat pocket, and walked back downstairs to the boardwalk. Ernie was busy painting the innards of giant stenciled letters on a large sign that read: "Alternative eco-friendly transportation, $20 per day."

"Eco-friendly?' What, Ernie, you've turned into a tree-hugger?"

"What sells sells. Tourists will pay to feel good about themselves, you know."

"Do I have to pay even if I don't really feel good about myself?" he smiled.

"I'll put it on your tab." Ernie tossed Ty a key to a padlock that secured a single long cable weaved through about 15 bicycles' front wheels.

Ty hopped on the first one and headed southeast toward the Dogues farm.

***

As he pedaled, he felt for the envelope in his coat. It represented his future, which was still so horribly uncertain. He'd be wealthy in a couple of weeks or less, and that possibility was beginning to demand all his attention. He tried to shake it off, think about fishing or girls or something, but it always came back, assaulting his brain.

What kind of life would $3 million buy him? What could he do with it? He imagined a large house looking over the Jovial, if there was any property available. Small plots on the river were in demand at very high prices, thanks to the influx of city folks from all over the Midwest who had money to burn and a vague desire to live in a clean place. The problem was that once they moved in, they demanded that the local government change this rural setting into a city. Didn't make much sense. Neither did his sudden wealth if it were true. That is why he had to speak with Coney and Jenn.

Before both wheels were on the driveway, two Great Pyrenees dogs, Pearly and Gates, began barking and growling. They rushed toward Ty, who slowed and let them recognize him. Within seconds, they bounced around his bike, sniffing and leaping joyfully, or so it seemed to Ty.

"What's up, guys?" He dismounted and tucked the dogs' heads toward his chest, one head under each arm. "You still remember me, huh?" They bounded away happily toward the house, where Coney Dogues and his wife, Jenn, were sitting on the porch. There was still a chill in the air, but the couple had several propane-powered upright heaters surrounding their picnic table and cushioned porch swing.

Jenn strode majestically off the porch, her arms open to prepare for a long, sincere embrace. Ty had always thought Jenn had the bearing of royalty. "About time you came back here." She hugged Ty tightly.

Coney left the porch, a locally brewed Indian Head beer in his hand, dripping water. It was ice-cold, having come straight from a cooler. Coney always had a beer on ice, though Ty had never seen him tipsy. Coney offered his hand, and Ty shook it warmly.

"Change your mind about a job?"

"Not looking for work right now, but I may be back a little later. I just got some fishing gear, so I'm going to see what's in the river first. Special trout season opens day after tomorrow. And I really won't need to work anytime soon." He pulled the envelope from his coat.

"I came here for some financial advice."

***

Coney opened the envelope and read it as Jenn did the same over his shoulder.

"Wow," they both said at once.

"We'd heard rumors about this, but I didn't think it was real," Coney said. Jenn agreed with a nod.

"I don't even know if it's real. I get these notices but haven't seen the money yet. And I don't really know why me at all. If it's real, what do I do with it? It's about all I've been thinking about, and I'd like to get it all out of my head somehow."

Jenn excused herself and entered the house, leaving Coney and Ty with the dogs.

"What do you want to do with it?"

"Spend it, I guess; what else is there?"

"There's responsibility and stewardship."

Ty leaned forward and frowned.

"What does that mean?"

"It means don't blow it. Put half of it away for retirement or a rainy day. That's stewardship. Invest it. But give a tenth away first."

"That's what Reverend Repent told me, but I didn't take it too seriously because he wanted me to give it to him."

"You can give it to whoever you want, just as long as you do it."

"Why?"

"Because of what you'll learn. If you give away at least a tenth as your first priority, it will help you keep your priorities off yourself and on people who need it. If you grip it tight, you'll turn into a miser, a money-grubber who only thinks of himself."

"Who else should I think about?"

"How about the person who saved you?"

"Jesus wants my money?"

"No. He's allowed you to have money. He wants to see how you handle it, how you use it to help other people."

"Seems to me that it's all my business. And why should I help anyone else? No one else ever helped me, except maybe you guys."

"Maybe that's the point. No one seemed to help Jesus much, either, but he still gave himself away."

"I can't live up to his example. I don't know much about being a Christian, but I know that much. I'm not perfect."

"None of us are, but that's not what it's all about. You said Jesus saved you, right?"

"That's what I've been told. Either him or Reverend Repent."

"It wasn't the good Reverend. What, you don't believe it was Jesus?"

"I believe that Jesus took my punishment and saved me from having to go to hell. Beyond that, well, I just don't know. All that saving is for after death, right? Hell and Heaven are both beyond this earth, so in the meantime, I have to live here and enjoy myself, right?"

"Jesus saved you from hell, sure, but there's so much more, and it's all on this earth. He saved you from nasty attitudes, like wanting to pay back people who hurt you, from being too proud to accept him. He saved you from thinking that this money should be all about you."

"But it *is* all about me!"

"Nope. It's about how you treat people around you. And the best way to do that is to put them ahead of yourself."

"What if they don't deserve it?"

"Mostly they don't. But neither do you. Or me. That's not our call. Loving others using Jesus' example is what defines your Christianity."

"I just don't get it."

"You will. Just keep trying to learn And try the tithe thing. It works. Give God 10 percent of whatever you earn, and see if he'll ever let you down. Doesn't mean he'll make you filthy rich, but he'll never let you starve or go without what you need. And, in many cases, giving 10 percent off the top helps the giver understand that money is a tool, a way to put your priorities into the right places. Money is a wonderful servant, Ty, but a horrible master. Give to God first – through charity to other people – and you'll better manage your money. Or your stuff or your talents."

"Ten percent seems like a lot. What if I need all of it?"

"That's why God makes it a challenge. Try it. No one I've ever known who tried it ever told me he went broke. It doesn't seem to make sense at first, but it works. Every single time."

"So, how do I know who to give that tithe to?"

"That can be tricky. There are all kinds of shysters and con men trying to take it from you and use it for themselves. So you have to be careful. My advice would be to give it to something you're passionate about, something you care about. If you care enough about this preacher, well, try it. Watch how he spends it. If it's on himself, then you know it's a mistake. If he uses it to help the poor or feed the hungry, then it's a good investment."

"That doesn't make it much easier." Ty took a swig of his second beer.

"Well, what do you care about? What do you think about most often?"

"Well, while I was in prison, I thought a lot about politics because I read a lot there. But I can't say I would ever trust any of those people. I also thought a lot about the river. I mean, it's been a lifeline for me and my parents for a long time. And all the environmentalists say it needs help. But the Reverend Repent needs help, too."

"You can split it up. Give a little to each, and see what happens with them. Good stewards will become as evident as bad ones in time. But be careful. Enviros are notorious for wasting donations on themselves. Sadly, so are many preachers."

Ty tipped up the beer as Jen came back outside.

"This is for you." She held out a cloth-covered book. It's a paraphrased Bible. It's not perfect, but I figure you'd benefit from something closer to modern language since you're just getting started. I suggest you read Proverbs first. It holds a lot of practical advice for living. And remember, the Bible isn't just something to read once and put down like some rookie's first novel. It's like the Boy Scout manual for living. It's your map to the Christian life, even like a mirror that shows you where you need help. You can use it as a kind of instruction manual and a challenge to help you question things and grow in your faith. Later on, after you've grown from a baby Christian to a toddler and beyond, we'll get you the Bible that's more accurate to the original languages. But this is a good start."

The Bible had a business card sticking out of it, and Ty looked at it.

"That's the name of our financial advisor. Good, honest man. He'll help." Jenn was nodding and smiling.

Ty thanked the couple, finished his beer, and scratched Gates's ears as he rose. Dusk was approaching.

"You call us or come over any time," Jenn said. "We're thrilled that you made this decision to be a Christian, and we want to help you grow in it."

"Well, I'm pretty confused at this point. My mind is full of stuff I don't understand."

"Like what?"

"Like what I'm supposed to do next. How am I supposed to understand I'm on the right path and not just floating through life without any destination?"

"Have you decided to change how you think?"

"What does that mean? I can't help how I think!"

"That's the first big lie you need to fight. You *can* change how you think. Force out the negative and invite in the positive. Pray."

"You need to renew your mind," Coney interjected. Ty looked at him, puzzled.

"Look up Romans 12:2 when you get home. Meditate on it. I know meditation sounds all churchy and mysterious. But all it really means is to think about it. Think it all through deeply, from every angle you can think of. Renewing your mind is something that all new Christians need to do. Well, even us old folks need to do it. Read all around it to get context. It will happen if you just trust God to renew your mind. We try to do it every day. It makes a difference in how you react to bad things and evil, stupid people."

***

Ty was one of only a select few so-called non-members who knew where to look for the well-camouflaged entrance to the underground lair of the small group of people—20 or fewer since the last he knew—he called the end-timers.

The next morning, with all his worldly possessions on his back, he walked from Ernie's place down to the soggy riverbank and followed it upriver. He noted Mother Nature's changes since his last trip this way. Growth. That's all it was, but today, Ty appreciated it more.

Before long, he could see the other side of the river and the obvious trappings of Olie Hansel's fish farm, although there was no printed sign, for many reasons. Activists were number one on the list because they had more than once opened his fish gates and released thousands of fish into the river. Once, after such action, they placed a sign facing the river that read: Keep your fish out of our river!" No one seemed to know what that meant, but the enviro crazies who released the fish weren't talking.

The place and people he was looking for was another half-mile up, through brush beginning to thicken. He could already smell the septic system.

By design, the group had no official name. Start letting society put a label on you, and soon it's all over, Ernie had said many times. Secrecy was important, and it amazed Ty how long this group had kept quiet. Ernie kept them all sworn to secrecy and loyalty, and he was an easy-going guy, one who people followed as much for his personality and generosity as for the services he offered.

As expected, when Ty reached the hand-carved tunnel entrance, hidden about 50 yards past a narrow pass no wider than a deer trail amid thickening wild blackberry plants, he heard a handgun's hammer pulled back right behind his ear.

He raised his hands. "Is that you, Todd?" He whirled around and looked at the gunman.

"Ty!" exclaimed a young man as he aimed the gun at the sky and eased the hammer back to a safe position. "When did you get out?" The young man holstered his weapon and pulled Ty close to himself in a bear hug. "Good to see you, man. About time we got somebody back here who knows what life is all about."

"Yep, first things first, Todd. Are you aware that your septic system can be smelled for about a half-mile off? Must be your drain field isn't working right."

"Yeah, we know. But with the spring being so wet, we can't get at it," Todd said. "Let's go in."

Chapter 8

The Reverend Donald Grandersma massaged his aching right leg as he waited for a consultation with a promised court-appointed attorney at the Jovial County Jail. When the door opened, a white-haired, white-bearded, overweight man dressed in a grey pinstriped suit – a thousand bucks if it was a dollar – stood before him at the cell door.

"Mr. Granderson?" Grandy looked up and turned his head to spit on the floor. He silently prayed, asking God why he was piling on to his misery.

"Grandersma. Sma! You know that! What do you want? Get the hell away from me, you scum."

"Now, is that any way to talk to the man who just bailed you out?"

"Never asked you to, and never will ask anything of you. You're not even worth my spit!"

"You might think differently when you hear me out," Grandy turned away, then quickly back as if he couldn't help himself.

"Snowmaker, you are the most evil, untrustworthy, corrupt son-of-a-bitch I've ever known in my life."

"Is that any kind of language for a preacher to use?"

"The truth is the truth."

"Come on, now, Reverend. My mother is not involved in this. Besides, what did I ever do to you?"

Grandy scowled. "Are you really that tone deaf? Let's see if I can remember them all. You tried to destroy my church on bogus racism charges. You kept us in court to ruin us financially. Then you went after our parishioners in court, trying to destroy us individually. You lied, cheated, broke the law, and used the press to try to take our property away. You destroyed our community by promoting the evil practice of gambling. Shall I continue?"

"I've read the papers. It was nothing personal. Just politics. Just doing my job."

"Your job is to destroy people?"

"Not at all. My job is justice," Snowmaker paused, his pride profound. "And equity."

"Your job performance will send you straight to hell."

"First things first. You want out of here or not?"

"Better to rot for the name of God than be free with the likes of you."

"But we're on the same side now."

"Impossible."

"In politics and the law, anything is possible. Even God uses evil deeds and turns them for good, don't you agree?"

"Not lately."

"I thought your greatest strength was you never doubted the work of the Lord," Snowmaker wasn't even trying to hide his mocking tone. "This is where I come in to help God work in mysterious ways. God can use us both to end gambling, it's just that I'm talking about a different kind of gambling."

"Gambling is gambling; It's all evil. Ain't no doubt about that."

"So why not fight gambling in an arena in which we can win?"

"Stop with the lawyer talk and state your business."

"First, you have to come to the realization that you will never win against an Indian casino. They have a whole squadron of lawyers almost as good as I am. I thought you knew that long ago. You can't beat them. These damn tribal lawyers hold all the cards, and they never lose. But you can win in the gamble with the planet."

"First, you are one of those damn tribal lawyers. And second, what are you talking about?"

"I'm talking about the Jovial River, specifically. The corporate interests are gambling with the health of the Jovial River, and we can stop them."

"What corporate interests?"

"The farmer corporations, the cruel factory farms. They're gambling with the health of this magnificent river in order to make money by growing food."

"And what does growing food have to do with a gamble on the river?"

"Pollution, my friend, pollution. These farmers dump tons of chemicals into the river every season with no repercussions. This food they grow can be gotten anywhere. Why should it be grown here when the future of the river is in peril? Farmers are an existential threat. That's a gamble the people I represent are not willing to take unless they can shift the odds in favor of God's glorious Jovial River."

"And what's all this got to do with me?"

"Despite our differences, reverend, I know you have a gift. You can stir people up. You can make them change their minds with your powerful, convicting speeches – er, sermons. You're a fighter. I had to work harder to get your church in line with the decrees of the state than anyone I ever dealt with. And after all that, the church survives. It was your personal charisma and your power to convince people that forced me to file so many suits before they started to stick. You're an influencer, and we need you to help us save the river."

"Why should I get in league with someone who nearly destroyed the church and did destroy me?"

"Money." Snowmaker smiled as if he'd just met an eager former lover. "Enough money to build a nice house on a bluff overlooking the river and look down your nose on the board of directors that pulled you down. Enough to start your own church. With your own rules. With your own passion. With your own parishioners. Enough people following you to really stick it to those former religious colleagues of yours and get a real ministry going." Grandy's leg endured a surge of pain, and he grimaced as he shifted his weight.

"Money isn't my main concern."

"It should be. Think of the work you could do for God for the rest of your life if you'd work for me for just a short time."

"How short?"

"A year, maybe two. No more than that. Make a sacrifice now, and God will reward you later."

"That's the first statement of truth I've ever heard from you."

"And I believe it, I swear." Snowmaker raised his pale white right hand in the air. "I'll sign you up as a registered lobbyist to the state legislature, working for a very powerful environmental group out of San Francisco. A very nice salary plus, if we succeed, a plot of land that would even make God envious."

"And what would I do as a lobbyist for – "

"MELL. Mother Earth Liberation League. All you would do is convince key right-wing religious politicians that gambling with the river is a sin. Convince them that the bills MELL supports will stop the gamble."

"And will they?"

Of course." Snowmaker grinned. "MELL is a non-profit. Dedicated to solid causes, financial security, and, above all, ending the practice of gambling with the Jovial River's future."

Grandy looked at Snowmaker, the disgust for him fading as the opportunity presented itself.

"I'd need time to pray about it."

"Sure, sure. Tell you what. I'll get the paperwork ready to have you bailed out in an hour or so; then I'll start working on the casino folks. If I get charges dropped against you, and maybe a few days or so to get the paperwork finished, is that enough time?"

Grandy looked at the suit Snowmaker wore, glanced down at the tassels on his shoes, and noticed the gold watch on his left wrist and a giant gold ring on his right hand.

"Yes. That's enough time. I won't guarantee anything. God will guide me. But just so I have all the facts, how much money are we talking?"

"I'll start you out with the lobbyist registration, which is all free. No expenses on your part, and $250,000 the first year. Plus, we have a nice apartment in Lansing, and if this will help you make up your mind, we'll get that leg fixed up. MELL has an amazing health plan. By the time you're walking around like a normal person again, you'll be making half a million bucks. If we stop this gamble, your pick of property, within reason, on the river, is yours."

"Get me out of here, and I'll start praying," Grandy said.

***

When Grandy was bailed out and back in the house the church had let him occupy, he was ready to see what God had to say about his decision.

He'd searched on his computer for stories the Jovial World and Sasser had written about his church's struggles with Snowmaker and the bureaucratic office he headed, and each one he found and read angered him. But at least now, he was reminded of all the facts before he began earnest prayer. Facts in the story of the church had been left out by Grandy's "friend" and board member, Mike Nitholder. During his time as a prison chaplain, he had no idea what the church board had been doing. Nitholder had held back information. But Grandy knew one thing: his leg hurt, and it hurt because of the work he'd done for God, without any compensation, so far.

He read Garit's most recent story about things that affected him and his former church:

A settlement has been reached between the Jovial Church of the Commandment Keepers and the Michigan Office of Environment, Inclusion and Bigotry (MOEIB).

Under terms of the agreement, the church can keep its present location at the edge of the tribal land of the Dontyawannakissame Indians and continue as a non-profit religious organization if it allows people of all colors and faiths into its congregation and disassociates itself with its pastor, Donald Grandersma, a well-known anti-casino activist. It must pay a $100,000 fine for "discriminatory practices" denied by the church, and it must never again "conspire to damage the reputation of the local casino."

The terms of where the fine money will go have not been disclosed, and such details are not spelled out in the settlement.

Church spokesman Michael Nitholder said the church was glad to have the whole legal battle behind it and is ready to continue as it has for the last 12 years since its founding.

"We firmly believe that our church was never involved in discrimination of any kind," Nitholder said. In the entire history of our church, we have never excluded anyone. In fact, our congregation includes several Hispanic parishioners, native Americans, and local white people. "We still feel that the way MOEIB went about its investigation and subsequent lawsuits was designed to target our faith, but we also felt it was time to move on and get back to saving souls."

As part of 'moving on,' Nitholder said, the MOEIB demanded that the church part ways with Grandersma. Grandersma was under fire from the state and MOEIB for his stand against the Jovial tribe of Dontyawannnakissamee Indians' casino. MOEIB director James Snowmaker told the World and Sasser that that stand alone was proof of discriminatory practices and bigotry.

Grandersma was a "person of interest" in the casino explosion several years ago that destroyed two slot machines and injured one casino security officer. Grandersma was never arrested or charged with a crime.

"During the course of our investigation," Snowmaker said in an interview with the Jovial World and Sasser, "we learned that, while the church board was largely supportive of Grandersma's bigotry, he was the driving force behind it. He went beyond church policy and railed against the casino, using racial slurs to attack the tribe and organizing protests outside the site before the ground was broken. We felt that, since Grandersma was given a sabbatical, voluntarily by the church, the board had seen the light."

Church records show that Grandersma had taken an extended break from the church to begin a total-immersion ministry in the Jovial County Prison. In this ministry, he moved into a furnished room and became a full-time chaplain, all paid for by the church.

In the newspaper's exhaustive perusal of each taped sermon from Grandersma cited by Snowmaker, no racial slurs were found in the pulpit. Grandersma often preached against the "sin of gambling" in all its forms and frequently identified tribal casinos as sinful places. But Snowmaker said his office is better trained to spot racism than a newspaper. Still, he would cite no specific words, instead repeatedly insisting that calling gambling a sin was racist and pejorative of the tribe's right to exist.

"He also called on the community, both in public and in several sermons which I witnessed, to take up radical positions – conspiracy theories, if you will -- in order to stop the casino from

establishing itself on its own sovereign territory," Snowmaker said. *"The hypocrisy was blatant, since the church building itself sits on Indian land."*

Title searches reveal that the church purchased the property from its legal owner and tribal member a year before it was built on the property. But Snowmaker said that's not legal when the tribe's land was given sovereign nation status two years before the alleged purchase.

"We still contend that all private land ownership, even by tribal members, became null and void with the federal government's recognition of the Dontyavannnakissamee tribe as a sovereign nation," he said. *"But the tribe was willing to overlook it, and because my department is nothing if not reasonable, we decided not to press the issue and let the church stay where it is."*

***

After reading the story, Donald Grandersma calmed himself with breathing exercises he'd learned in prison, but it didn't last long. Rage was like a low rumble in the back of his mind. He'd been conned. Deceived. God had set his face against him. He had to pray. It was all he had left.

He knelt on one knee because the other didn't work so well anymore, what with the shrapnel scraps doctors had never removed. He rubbed his right knee and appreciated it as a badge of honor, and started praying aloud in his pastor's voice:

"Oh Lord, you are holy and exalted above the sinners on this earth you made. You who know everything and resists the pride and evil of the world you created, this pain is your reminder to me, isn't it? A reminder of the great things I've done for you, the suffering I've endured, and for what? What else have I tried to accomplish for you, Lord, that you've taken on yourself to put down? I tried, Lord, to stop this scourge of gambling that you so detest. I took on this task you appointed me for without doubting and with divine fervor. But you didn't grant me success. Why have you fought me at every turn? Have you changed your mind? I tried to emulate your servant Elijah when he killed 400-some prophets of Baal, but I didn't kill anyone, unlike Elijah, and so I did not disobey your commandment to not kill. As my reward, you gave me this bum leg instead of victory. I don't understand that. Is it a reminder to endure pain for you and continue on this fight to defend your name? Or is it a reminder that I was wrong? That I never really heard your voice to begin with? It can't be. You only oppose the proud and unrepentant sinners. I've believed that without doubting, Lord, because your servant James said we should pray without doubting, or the wind'll toss us.

Doesn't matter, I guess, Lord. I'm still sure that you detest gambling, and I still think you anointed me to stop it in this part of the world you put me in.

But things have changed. And you've given me no answers. And you've given me a new situation to think over. But you haven't given me the strength you promised your other servants.

I'm beginning to think the changes, challenges, and opportunities that are before me now are a sign that you will change direction, Lord. But I'm not sure, Lord. Forgive me for that doubt and remove it from me. The messenger you sent is an evil man who tried to destroy me and the church that you gave me. I fought hard against him, Lord, but you didn't seem to care. You let evil prevail. And I know you can work through evil people, but I've seen no evidence that James Snowmaker is sent from you. Clear my head about that, please. I want clarity, Lord.

And then there's this challenge of money. I've never been a greedy man. But I sure could use some cash right now to continue your work. Sure, I have a house and enough food to eat, but I want out of there, Lord. I don't want to be beholden any longer to a church board that went behind my back and stabbed me. Don't hold the parishioners at fault for that, Lord. It's the board that turned their backs on me and you. I fought against the lawsuits. I led your congregation to seek your will as you've revealed it to me.

I led them to the property you provided and the modest church where so many people could worship. I may forgive them for what they did to me, but that will take time, Lord. They deserve punishment for what they've done, so do it, Lord. They abandoned the mission you gave me, and all for a little security, which we both know only you can provide.

Lord, you know all that. You know how badly I've been treated, and I guess I have to look at all that as a sign from you. Particularly after you've opened up a new door for me. A door in which you must have success waiting for me, or you wouldn't have closed the first one. You always provide, Lord, and this must be what you've been preparing me for.

Pollution is an insult to your creation, Lord. While I never have given much thought to it because I've been so zealous for your condemnation of gambling, what Snowmaker said is true. We sinful humans are gambling with your creation. And I know you want us to protect it since you gave it to us at the beginning of time.

You have provided me with an opportunity to prosper, which is what you want all your servants to do. This is pretty big money, Lord. Show me the ways I can use it for your service and be blessed personally at the same time. You've withheld your blessings from me, Lord, and the only thing I can think of is that you have reserved something better for me, your humble servant.

You've given me the talent of speech and persuasion, Lord. I need to use it. So bless me, Lord, in this new opportunity. You've shown me how to take away this leg pain, too. This is a sign that this offer is from you. I'm very tired of this pain, Lord.

Grant me success in protecting your planet from sinful people who would destroy your beautiful rivers. Grant me the right place on this river, where I can sit on a chair outside at night and take in its beauty. I can watch it to protect it in a way that shows your favor through the grandeur of local architects and builders. Make any structure I build a symbol of your favor and approval. And may my enemies in the church have coals of fire rain down on their heads.

Make my will your will, Lord, so I can continue in your service and in this cause that can still be accomplished. The casino cannot be stopped, Lord. There can be no doubt about that after what you've put me through. Sinful men have set up an institution against you, and you've made me impotent to stop it. The power of the gamblers is too powerful for me, Lord. That is evident. Forgive me for not seeing it before this. I was fighting a losing battle, and I didn't remember that you demanded surrender. Forgive me for being so stubborn and blind that I couldn't see it before. But you are faithful. You've opened my eyes by the hand of Snowmaker. And his offer of employment is by your hand.

Bless me in this new fight against gambling, against those evil people who would destroy your creation. Make me an instrument for your instruction and bless me with the money I can make, proof that you bless my decision here. May I never doubt your mission for me again, and increase my faith with a sign I already know. Real faith, Lord, is the absence of doubt. And heal my leg through the opportunities you've given me. I've suffered enough. Amen."

Chapter 9

Ty followed Todd as they walked, hunched under the low ceiling through a maze of barely-lit tunnels, complete with several dead-ends and false entrances. Todd even took a wrong turn once, and as they turned back to the main tunnel, a sulfur smell brought Ty a memory.

"Do you remember why this wing was abandoned?" Todd shrugged.

"It was that vein of dirty gypsum, too toxic-smelling to keep going. I can still smell it."

Todd preferred to keep his chatter about things they both remembered. "Remember that party behind the new McMansion development when the cops came three times? I sure wish we could go back and do things like that again."

"What were we, 15?" Ty responded. "Smoking dope and pounding moonshine. How did we survive? I guess we had some pretty strong guardian angels." Todd grunted.

After about 50 yards, the tunnel opened to a large room with bare cement blocks all around except for the glass wall facing the river. The glass was dirty but couldn't hide the thick, barely-budding undergrowth outside or great views of the river and woods. Small scattered clearings, visible through the glass this time of year, had a specific purpose: Spying stations were the best way to keep track of potential interlopers. During the days of the outdoorsman school, they held underground caches of potatoes and other root vegetables.

Ty's mouth watered when he smelled bacon and venison coming from the industrial kitchen behind the large room, and when he and Todd made their appearance, ten men and four women leaped up and surrounded Ty. They alternately hugged and patted him on the back, and questions began pouring from their lips, some in English, some in Spanish. He answered them all.

En masse, they escorted Ty to a 20-seat, round picnic table in the center of the room, and others came back soon with a plate of delicious game, potatoes and vegetables. He ate quickly, swallowed the large glass of homemade beer that had been brewed in another room just outside the kitchen.

Sated and relaxed, Ty took in the conversation while the beer flowed. Todd leaned toward him as if he were a disciple, guffawing at every quip from Ty. Suddenly, a door opened on the far side of the room, and a hallway led to a series of dormitory-style rooms. Out stepped Ernie, who smiled broadly and rushed over to grip Ty's hand long and firm, mostly for the benefit of the people there.

"Looks like our prodigal has returned, everyone." Ernie was beaming. "Glad you could still find your way in, Ty. Anybody follow you?"

"I'm sure no one did," Todd confirmed that notion with a thumbs-up.

"Let's be safe." Ernie directed three men, one a native Michigander and two Mexican, to lookout posts set high above the bunker in trees that most people who ventured this far into the woods would assume were benign tree-hunting stands, if they saw them at all.

"Have you changed your mind?" Ernie asked as more beer was brought out in large glass pitchers. "The invitation to join us stands, as always."

"I'm afraid not."

"It's an open invitation for people we trust." Ernie poured more beer into Ty's mug, then turned to address the crowd.

"Ty and I have an agreement. "He'll stay here as long as he wants, as long as he supplies fish for the restaurant." The gathering applauded as Ernie motioned with his hand and led Ty to the end of the dorm hallway, and opened a door to a spartan room with only a bed – no coverings except a pillow inside a pillowcase, and blanket on a coffee table. On one wall was a large gun safe.

His gear had barely hit the floor when the same group that had greeted him insisted he come out and drink beer and party with them. Amid the hubbub, Todd's voice became the loudest.

"This calls for a celebration." Todd raised his glass high above his head. "The good times are back!"

After most of the crowd had stumbled off, Todd had his chance one-on-one. He pulled Ty close, which he often did after his sixth beer, making him fall in love with almost anything.

"Well, old partner, looks like you have done and got it made. Ty, my man, you're set for life. And if I know you as well as I think I do, we'll all be living high on the hog for some time."

Ty hesitated, but the smiling faces and loud conversations took him back to a pleasant period in his life, when good friends and cheap liquor and weed were abundant, yet short-lived.

"Maybe." He turned to Todd. "I'm sure going to spend some money when and if I get it. But I also have to manage this money, or it won't last." Todd's expectations fell along with his smile.

"What, you won't help out your friends anymore? Is that what prison does to a man?"

"It's not that. It's just that I've been given this opportunity, and it's a big one. I'm not going to piss it all away. Just some of it." He smiled wryly. "I have to do something with it that helps a whole lot of people and maybe even helps me figure out all this God stuff."

"I'd heard that you got religion." Todd was talking louder than before.

"Oh well, that won't last. Sooner or later, you'll remember that you owe me. If it weren't for me, you'd never have been to prison and made that change."

Ty looked at him, incredulous.

"I owe you? It was you who got me arrested. You're the one who hatched that plot to make lottery tickets. I'm the one who kept you out of jail."

`"And I do appreciate your silence, man. But if not for me, you'd never have gotten the windfall."

"That had nothing to do with prison. This money would have come anyway, just based on who my parents were, I guess. Don't know all the details. I think God manipulated circumstances, and I don't know why prison was thrown in there. Doesn't make sense, other than the fact that I was saved in there by the grace of God."

Todd rolled his eyes. "And who got you in there?"

"The lottery police and the state government."

"No." Todd paused and slugged down the rest of his beer. "It was me. If not for me, you'd be back picking asparagus and blueberries and getting covered with black topsoil from the muck fields."

"I don't see it that way. My silence gave you another chance, and what have you done since?"

"I got a couple of things in mind." Todd reached out to refill Ty's mug.

"Such as?"

"Such as getting back to our celebration of your rich butt." Todd began, laughing in his hyena-like manner that only came out after seven beers or five cocktails.

"Come on, man. You can do what you want with your money. But you got so much now. I got nothing. A real Christian would help out his pals. But for the next few days, we got to celebrate. Let's go kill a few brain cells. C'mon, man. You used to be cool."

Ty hesitated. "Tell you what, Todd. I'm going to have a little party for the farmers and such pretty soon, if and when I really get the money. Why don't you round up the whole gang and join us? I'll let you know when and where."

"All on you?"

"Yep. Like you say, I can afford a few things now. I won't gamble, but we can celebrate. Don't think God has anything against that."

"Now you're on the trolley. Maybe the casino can find us a little companionship, too."

"We'll see," Ty said.

Not much later, the people went to bed, and Todd passed out, leaving Ty and Ernie to themselves.

After a few stories were exchanged, venting fans kicked on, bringing a whiff of the sewer system into Ty's nose.

"You know, Ernie, you really have to fix that septic system. I could smell it almost all the way down to Olie's fish farm. How long before some conservation officer paddles up here and smells it? They'll throw the book at you this time."

"It only smells because of all the rain we've had. It'll dissipate. And by now, most people in government have forgotten this place is here at all."

"Now's the best time to fix it. I helped you put it in, remember? It was designed in the permits for a single-family house, and you have 14 people here overloading it. It may be fine for a little while, and if there is one major rain, it will break and flow down the river. You don't want those kinds of fines, do you? They'll go after about ten thousand bucks a day."

"How do you know so much about it?" Ernie poured more beer.

"I spent 18 months in prison reading and researching things. I dug back into the history of the river, the regulations on it, and the attitudes around here. They've changed, Ernie, and they changed fast. Too many city people have moved here, and they only want what they've been conditioned to want by the media, which also knows nothing about what's really going on here. Or anywhere, for that matter. I don't think your septic system could have such a big impact on the old girl. She'll just keep on flowing. But you are in violation of a whole bunch of laws, and the environs will try to make an example of you. They have no interest in your financial situation or your excuses. They hate you to begin with for starting the survival training school. They got you labeled a gun nut and a far-right extremist, maybe even a white supremacist. You're already a target. Why invite more trouble?"

"For one thing, I don't have the money to fix it. Even if I did, they're not likely to approve the permits at all. So we're just gambling that the system holds, and they'll leave us alone."

"That's not a good bet. If it breaks, it's the end of this place and the survivor school, you know. I'll help you dig a new hole for a second or third septic tank if you want. Maybe install a pump to run it back up into your house's system. That would help for a while."

"Not a bad idea. We'll see if we have a good summer at the store. Maybe we could afford a new system then, but I can't ask for a permit. It would just alert the government that we're here."

"They already know the bunker is here. I mean, you operated the survival school legally for two years, and you did nice work. You provided a valuable service to people who want to camp and hunt and fish the way they're supposed to. Those people loved your school, and they learned how to survive in the woods. Then they went into town and booked vacations, canoes, meals, and hotels. I don't remember the locals having a problem with your business."

"Like you said, Ty, that's all changed. People talk about nature more than they ever did, but they participate in it a lot less. No. The less said about anything, the better. It's always the best course to keep politicians in the dark. Their corruption is getting worse, not better."

"Don't I know it. That's another thing I studied during my time in prison. I watched all kinds of political TV, read a lot about history."

"So you learned that I'm right to be wary of them."

"I learned that any idiot can be a politician, and mostly, it's idiots who make politics their career. Mostly greedy idiots. The lower the IQ, the more likely they are to rise to the top. Hell, Ernie.

I even became convinced that I could do a better job in government than these dufuses."

"So, run for office."

With that thought, Ty knew the conversation was going nowhere except to fantasy, so he called it a night.

Chapter 10

In the grey fog between sleep and waking, Ty's mind was fixed on the days just before his release from prison. A clean dream-like slate stood on a rickety tripod before him, dirty with misspelled questions about its reality. Would the whiteboard be clean when he arrived? He neared it with sodden legs and great effort and found a single dirty smear across it as if a bird had dropped its blackberry-colored business while flying over. And he had no rag to clean it, so he opened his eyes to his new reality and stark surroundings.

He shook the smeared vision from his sleepy head and realized he had choices. Could he build on his old life of drifting with currents he couldn't control? Control. That had always been the key. He'd had control when he relied upon himself. Even in the days when he'd routinely blown all his cash and became hungry, it was his efforts, his resourcefulness, that had seen him through. No one helped him then and likely wouldn't now. He had been smart enough to know where to go for food and other necessities, and he was proud of that. He'd even crashed a few family summer reunions, eating all he could before the hosts realized he wasn't Uncle John's boy from his second marriage. That lie was resourceful. That lie kept him independent. Funny, though, how when he'd done that and had used his cunning to make himself likable amid strangers, they usually didn't let him leave without a heaping plate of meat, beans, or salad or all three. And almost always, such folks asked him if he knew Jesus or told him they'd pray for him. But he'd been too independent to need such a crutch.

He'd been told by Reverend Repent that he had a new life now, but Coney had clarified that when he said he could depend on Christ, who is much more reliable than himself, but so far, Ty still didn't understand. He didn't see new opportunities in front of him unless he counted the promise of his reparation payment. He was anxious to get on with things and find a routine where he'd discover something more aligned with the mysteries of God that no one had yet explained.

He didn't know what awaited him, but he knew one thing. Money changed everything. It was the key to a better life, a comfortable life of ease and leisure, and a full pantry, which the entire world seemed to pursue. Seemed right to him. A billion people couldn't be wrong.

But the fear that this was all a scam, that he never would get the money, haunted him. If it was true, nothing about his old life would ever be the same except for fishing. That could not be anything but God's will. The old life was behind him, but the new lay within a dense fog before him. He needed plain language and clean slates, but did that mean abandoning all of the old? There was only one place he knew where he could clear that fog.

***

Ty had fallen asleep with his new Bible open to Romans 12, so when he was fully awake as the sun-splashed piercing blue sky against the river, his first clear thought was the first line of verse 2: "Do not be conformed to this world."

What was conformity, anyway? Going along with the crowd? He supposed so. Being like the world? Maybe. He'd heard somewhere that the world is dangerous, but as he thought about it, he considered that the world was only hostile to people who didn't have money. If he were to have it, he could live better than most. And that would make the world a great place to be. The world was a polluted, selfish place when he considered most of the people in it, but it was also beautiful, even majestic, when spring colors painted the earth's face. But that was still a little ways off.

He walked toward the bunker's dining room window overlooking the Jovial River. Perhaps she could help. He needed to look her over anyway, check out where she'd changed in the last 18 months, where she'd hidden her fish. She'd spoken to him before, and perhaps she would again. He never could tell. But he knew today would be a good day to see her since the fish wouldn't bite on a bright, sunny morning with no weather fronts coming in. Bugs wouldn't hatch today.

***

He walked to the top of Jovial's highest hill and stepped over the gate that forbade people from coming into the abandoned county park and scenic outlook.

The road into the park, which had never been much more than a narrow gravel path, had slipped into further neglect. Numerous potholes were too deep even for a four-wheeler to run through undamaged, and Ty felt grateful for that. A bad road would keep most tourists away from the park's view of the river, a view that very few of them deserved, and even fewer knew about.

After just a few steps amid the potholes, Ty smelled her, and he stopped, took several of the deepest breaths he could, and let them out slowly. The Jovial's favor is a narrow road, a hard-earned overflow of mystery and potential like lingering eye contact in a crowd of common flesh-pursuers. Her apathy toward tourists refreshed Ty's mind since, unlike them, she'd looked his way more than a few times. Nobody could receive that look or extravagance on a mere holiday or vacation. When she showed him – and no one else – where the fish were, it was as if she'd told him he was special, that he was privileged to discern the mystery and majesty of her benevolence. He'd also put in his time and done the work.

He was proud of that. The time he'd spent with the Jovial helped him avoid what tourists did. It was so common. They'd become spellbound with her loveliness, silenced by her song – but they'd forsake her when the bills were due. The spell too soon wears off. We can never predict when. But spells always do.

In the long run, it's better that way. How many young men had been on one of several narrow, rocky paths to the Jovial, only to fall with broken axles and ankles on the rocky path long before they saw her curves and attractions? They came to gawk at her, compare her to some other wild, brief acquaintance. Only persistent lovers like him saw more than her pretty summer face. Very few tourists or natives, he realized, could honestly say they'd touched or tasted the lips of pure, natural, liquid beauty. For most young people so favored with her smile and thus enamored, it was enough. Memories grow into legend and myth. A photograph becomes a trophy.

Trophy hunters were hurting themselves, filing lawsuits. It's why the county had this park gated with thick, ornate iron. It would be a shame to let anyone find this view, especially if they did it for free. Ty wondered if the county board had put the land up for sale yet. It had been rumored for years, but who could afford it?

The Jovial County Parks Commission had done well in choosing the acreage for the park. It had always rested on a wooded 10 acres far above the river and along the 4,000-feet river view bluff that geologists say the river once reached, where there is no bad view of the river valley. But Ty knew more. He used all his senses to draw himself to her.

There were times when he felt that the Jovial could only be appreciated by him because he'd put in his time. He'd loved her from the first time he saw her, way back about age seven, but it was deeper than the infatuation most men have for a pretty face. She would tolerate novices and sycophants, of course, since she was helpless to avoid them, but through her long spring and summer awakening, she'd favor men like him, who would not forsake her when she turned old, and her leaves turned brown and wrinkled, and her voice crackled and missed the higher notes.

He heard her and smelled her long before he saw her as he walked across the park's brown grass toward the bluff that would reveal what she offered. She had owned his infatuation long before, but it was time for renewal. Do not conform, but transform by renewal. Suddenly, the Bible passage made a little more sense. But it was her sound that fascinated him before he dared look down the cliff.

Despite her Jovial name, the river doesn't always laugh or chuckle as she rolls through rocks so massive that not even she can move them. Smaller rocks, which she moved when she was ready, evoked chords of power and gentleness, a paradox as the water's fingers crescendo through them, creating tunes that could never be written or played outside of divine insight. Sometimes, she buries those rocks under silt and muck and roil, and for a time, the chuckling seems drowned, but never carried so far downstream that she can't find Middle C again when summer finds its way to Jovial County, Michigan.

The Jovial, while singing her liquid songs, understands her power and helplessness to control herself, but as far as Ty knew, she never held a grudge or planned vengeance. She'd never resented the untuned rocks that clanked like one finger striking two keys into her song, even when the rocks surpassed the water's chords. She won't stop trying to move them downstream into a different key, although she often fails. She simply reacts, as materialist atheists would expect. She makes no choices. Her course had never been self-determined, nor had she ever behaved out of character. She's radically Calvinist, with all that fatalism implies.

She is the ultimate organism that "dances to its DNA." Nothing more, nothing less. She's neither happy with the dance nor does she ever plug her ears, sick to death of the maddening, catchy chorus. She does not understand her own mind. She just goes with the flow, like a conformist. But she demands nothing from Ty. She never asked for 10 percent of what he had. She couldn't use it if she wanted to. She didn't need people, didn't want money, and laughed when politicians and activists threw money at her as if she were a pole dancer. But as Ty lost track of time as he watched her flow, he had new things to think about. He had a mind to be renewed. As the sun crossed the Jovial, he wondered how long he'd been here. Soon, perhaps, he'd afford a phone, but until then, he was reluctant to leave the Jovial, even though he knew she'd be here when he returned.

Disparate voices, disconnected by the overflowing rush that was still trying to recede into its traditional path, would come together when the time was right. Knowing that patience was the best course of action at this time brought Ty peace. He didn't recognize it, even now, until he had fallen asleep listening to her. He wondered if that was peace, and if so, was it from God? All these things, including God, were so new to him. Coney and Jen would probably say yes, all peace comes from God, but he lacked their conviction and experience.

As her song repeated its chorus, Ty opened his eyes, trying to renew his infatuation with the Jovial River's deep water holes and shallow valleys. The pinnacle of privilege with which he contemplated her was something he wished everyone could experience with the same depth as he beheld her, but he would not share her. They'd have to work for it, just as he had.

He'd never told anyone about his special spot, just below the cliff's edge in a recess of rock, and he never would. So he climbed down and stared at her, followed her curve east to where she spread her legs and branched into two streams. At that moment, he felt like a stalker, but his eyes would not turn away from the audacity of her beauty.

Tourists would not see it this time of year. They coveted her when she fixed her face with a blooming canopy of yellow, orange, and blue, shades of green and brown. But Ty saw her as she was – an awakening beauty with strong, bare shoulders and a face that didn't need spring makeup. Mankind loved her when she was dazzling, but she didn't seem to know he loved her even in black and white. He didn't need her colors or sounds, but she fussed and sang anyway, as if one lover were not enough to hold her for long.

He examined her first wide bend above the stiller, wider waters leading down to the dam. She carried a bit of added weight from winter's inactivity, but she'd work that off soon enough. But right now, thanks to the time he'd spent, she revealed a new, cold area filled with fish. This was why he came back. Fishing was his immediate reality. By comparison, all this god stuff was mere theory.

So Ty planned to fish. Tomorrow, when a predicted storm was brewing and insects would hatch, there would be a feeding frenzy.

Only God knew which fish he could catch as he watched several trout breach the water as they fought the current to get deeper into her. But was God really real? Did he exist in the fish and the river? No, they're just fish, unaware of where the thought came from.

Suddenly, it all seemed so ridiculous. It was all just something people used to deflect from their own inadequacies. Did God really care about this river and all the life in it? Does he really care about some lost half-breed kid with no advanced skills and minimum education from Jovial High? Ty recalled Jesus's words from somewhere in the New Testament: He counts our hairs and sees every bird that falls. Seemed as far-fetched as a kid with a bobber on a pole catching a record-breaking salmon.

Frustrated, he shouted: "I need to know, God. Are you real?" He looked back at the river. "Anything, Lord. Just another fish jumping, maybe. That's all I need." He stared but saw no fish jump, no signs of the river's benevolence. Grandy would have chastised him for his doubt. Doubt, he'd insisted, has no place in the Christian's life. He could dig up a scripture verse to verify his theory if pressed. But Ty wasn't so sure. Plenty of people in the Bible had expressed doubts. Coney had told him that.

He shifted his weight, closed his eyes, and listened for God's voice, though the river could easily have muffled it. Unexplained tears burrowed tributaries down his cheek, and he thought himself a very foolish man. If God is so powerful, why can't he be heard above some rushing water he had created? All Ty heard was the Jovial. His brain cried 'foolishness,' but his heart felt something like a current that flows around or over everything in its way until it returns to join the flow again.

He remembered another scripture snippet. Some day, he'd have to read deeper and connect those snippets. Peter, Jesus's lead disciple, had said at some point that he was going fishing.

Ty examined the best route back down to the river. As he turned his back to her and pulled himself up on level ground again, he didn't see a huge trout leap majestically over a temporary sand spit.

***

Spring planting was to begin soon, and it would, right under Ty's feet, just as soon as the river receded and the soil dried enough to hold, and not swallow, heavy farming equipment.

Ty slid carefully down the steep bank, finding handholds in the rock that were still as solid as he remembered. He walked downstream to where the Jovial widened and formed what locals called "the pond" and slowed in preparation for its trip toward the Jovial dam. He said, "Thank you, Lord," for the sun on his face, grateful that it was already heating his arms and turning his skin a darker shade.

Walking downstream along the water's edge to the 100-acre miracle of flat, black, rich soil, he stepped on something stiff just under the inch or so of organic debris left as the Jovial receded from the spring rains. He found the edge and pried it with his fingers. The effort produced a six-foot-square sign printed on hard corrugated cardboard and laminated. The colors on it were still bright. He pulled it out, washed it off with a little river water, and read it.

"Join MELL," it said in bold, large letters. "Liberate the planet, one river at a time." Ty kept scraping. In smaller print, near the bottom, it read, "Won't you contribute today?

"What do you folks know about the river?" Suddenly, a thought grabbed him. Do these folks deserve part of my tithe? Is God so obvious as to give him a real, man-made sign? Maybe that's the only thing that could get through his thick mind, dumb as it was, as a pile of rocks.

Chapter 11

Ty could feel, somehow, the gathering storm system that promised a healthy spring rain. He didn't know why or how, but he had a sixth-sense or something like that. He couldn't remember when he didn't have it. Because of his time away from the Jovial, he'd lost some of his confidence, so he consulted local television meteorologists and watched the barometer in Ernie's store, but mostly he relied on his gut. It rarely failed him. But it was good to consult a higher authority sometimes.

The pond was slightly higher than usual, but few people could tell. It was odd that it was high, because the city had for the last few days opened a couple extra gates to let water through. The power company had repairs to conduct, and while they worked, the water still flowed, filling in the gaps that coal, wind and solar could not.

The pond had been created more than 100 years ago when the dam was built, and despite efforts to destroy the dam – mostly from wild-eyed greenies who insisted that the only solution to climate change was to restore the entire region to "pre-settlement days," the land around the pond was thriving with lush flora and volunteer maple trees. He'd tapped a few of those trees while jumping from job to job, although it wasn't allowed anymore.

As the pond slowly narrowed where the river was pouring in, he walked past the landmark huge rocks that had been placed there as a kind of reminder of where the Jovial submitted its wild natural surroundings for the excavated pond. They still protruded, but the current washed over them.

Ty walked about a mile farther up the Jovial. He found the tributary he'd identified from his perch on top of the bluff the day before. It was spilling clear, cool water from the winter melt. Combined with the natural springs that always flowed into this spot, the water was cool and deep, and trout loved it. It was easy to find once he got there. The Volkswagen-sized rock stood out, not just for its size, but because it offered multi-colored mineral veins that seemed to have been painted there for his own delight.

He cast lures onto that hole for about 15 minutes when the bugs started hatching with the first drops of gentle rain. Before the surface began swarming, he'd caught his limit and carried the large browns back to Ernie's. Each was well above the minimum size Ernie wanted. Seventy-five bucks would be fair, and he knew Ernie would agree.

***

As Ernie filleted them with his quick, expert hand on his large butcher-block table, Ty checked his mailbox, which was no more than a small square covey along the wall behind the restaurant counter. He'd been expecting his mail to be forwarded from his prison address for days now, and finally, this was the day.

In his mailbox was a letter from the Michigan Office of Environment, Inclusion and Bigotry. His hands trembled as he tore it open, as if his entire future was inside the envelope. He read it and shook his head. Nothing made sense. He picked up the landline phone behind the counter and called the only attorney he'd ever known.

Botsdorf told him to come on in. "I've been doing my research since we met a couple weeks ago. Interesting stuff."

When Ty walked into Botsdorf's office, the attorney was huddled behind a large stack of papers.

"I still don't understand what I did to deserve this," Ty said as he sat at a small round table in the attorney's office.

Botsdorf didn't look up but continued to read the contents of the new letter.

"That's the whole point of reparations, Ty. It goes to undeserving people based on wrongs – alleged wrongs – that were done to other people. You were just caught in the undertow of logic that no reasonable or sane person understands."

"Sure sign it was written by politicians," Ty said, and Botsdorf smiled. "By not understanding it, it proves your sanity. Ask any shrink." Botsdorf smiled wryly, and Ty reciprocated, understanding the sarcasm, though not completely.

Botsdorf scanned some of the other correspondence Ty had brought in, all tied neatly by an old shoestring inside a boot box. Botsdorf consulted the notes he'd made since Ty first called him.

"How do you know this James Snowmaker?"

"Never met him or heard of him other than that his name is on all these letters from this state department that I also never heard of – MOEIB. I have no idea why he wants to give me lots of money. Five million bucks, right?"

"Well, that's what they started out with." Botsdorf shuffled papers until he found one and pulled it out. "After costs, administrative fees, taxes, and other unnamed contingencies, including Snowmaker's $400 per hour fee for legal consultation to his own department, it's about $3 million. What do you plan to do with it?"

"Hadn't really made any plans. I guess I'll spend it."

"I think you need a better plan than that. Have you consulted anyone about this? You know, accountants or stockbrokers?"

"The only people who know – most of them, anyway, told me how lucky I am. A few told me I never have to work a day in my life again, but that doesn't really appeal to me."

If there was any sin he was sure was indeed sin, it was laziness. He could still hear his mother telling him that.

"Spend what you want, but be smart, young man." Botsdorf's face suddenly seemed intense and somber. "Don't go spending this on stupidity. Set up an investment account that will pay you six percent or more. If you do that with a million bucks, you'll earn $60,000 a year in interest. Have you ever made $60,000 in a year?"

"Nope."

"Well, now you can. Don't touch it. Let it grow because if you start spending, you can blow through it pretty fast, especially if you like to party, like I'd heard. Remember that most lottery winners are broke in just a few years. So beware. Be a good steward."

"What does that mean?"

"It means that you have responsibility now. Have you ever heard of the parable of the talents?"

"Nope."

"It's in the Bible. You've told me you're a believer now, right?" Ty nodded uncertainly.

"You have an opportunity here to be smart and to ensure that you won't go broke, but you have to set some aside. Listen to me about this. I've seen sudden money ruin families and even lives. Don't ever go into debt. You don't have to. I'll give you the names of some trustworthy financial advisors right here in town who will help you manage your money. But there's something more valuable here. You own about a hundred acres of riverfront property."

"That's impossible. I never bought a piece of land in my life."

"But your parents did."

"Nope. Never."

"Actually, they did. For a dollar."

"Right. What's the scam?"

"Well, back 20 years ago, when you were just a baby, your parents were part of the migrant workers who sued the Jovial Farmers Association for better housing. Actually, your parents and the other workers didn't know anything about it. It was the Migrant Advocates Watchdog (MAW) group, a bunch of lawyers who made lots of money settling disputes over housing that they said was inadequate and cruel or whatever. They'd cry racism and bully farmers into paying rather than going to court, not to mention the publicity it would bring, true or false."

"Was it bad housing? I don't remember ever living in anything but a double-wide. I remember vaguely the one mobile home that overlooked the river, but my folks moved on to the subdivision up on Widow's Hill before I was even out of grade school."

"That's where the name Snowmaker comes in. When you were a little boy and before that, before you were born, your parents lived in seasonal migrant housing every year. They'd come in spring and start harvesting asparagus. Then they moved on to work blueberries, onions, celery, all that. Sometimes, they stayed for cherries and peaches and apples. The farmers up here took care of their seasonal workers better than any other farmers in the country, and your parents were among the most valued workers. Records show your parents and most of the others in their group were better paid, got better benefits, and had better housing than any other state in the country. That's one of the reasons folks like your parents kept coming back. The farmers built well-insulated block houses in a grove of trees with relatively large rooms, showers, and toilets. Then, they bused them to the fields as each farmer needed them. This was long before MOEIB was created. The farmers, by request of the workers, separated the families – people like your parents with small children – from the single male workers. Gave young families security. The buildings were cool in the summer, naturally, and farmers provided propane heat for the colder nights and hot water. By all accounts – and I was here then and remember it because I represented many of them in various disputes – the workers were happy with their accommodations.

"But then, when the MAW group decided to visit, uninvited, they noticed that a couple of window screens had been damaged – mostly by the single men who cut them to run satellite TV lines in – and sued. It was quite a large population of migrant workers then – a couple hundred anyway, who worked for about 50 farmers around here, and the suit MAW filed caught the attention of the American Civil Liberties Union, who sent a young lawyer out here named James Snowmaker. Even back then, he was the biggest horse's ass since the Clydesdales were colts."

"Isn't that true of all lawyers?"

Botsdorf smiled. "Present company excepted, right?"

"I didn't mean you," said Ty.

"Don't worry about it," Botsdorf said. "Well, Snowmaker started filing lawsuit after lawsuit against the farmers until one day he told them he'd stop the legal action if they'd just dedicate to the migrants a piece of land – by the river -- and build new and expensive state-approved housing, which was a real moving target because of MAW. The farmers were told they'd just have to give small lots to the migrants – about a tenth of an acre per trailer, and that seemed okay to the farmers who could never win against MAW with their high-priced lawyers on board. Seemed like the housing rules changed nearly every year. The farmers were beyond frustrated. They just wanted to fix the screens and follow what the state inspectors told them to do, because that had been approved and adequate for years, and that was okay by the workers, too. They were happy enough in the block buildings, in the shade, in a protected place with a gate into the community. But by the next spring, when the workers came back – and they didn't know anything about all this legal stuff – they found they had new double-wide trailers just below the river bluff. They mostly liked their old housing better, but they moved into the trailers, not knowing that MAW had seized acres and acres of the riverfront farmland in their names, claiming just compensation for past sins. They didn't have the legal authority to do it. But no one challenged it in court, so MAW went to the workers and had them sign a deed – all written in only English -- to give them ownership. But MAW never owned it to begin with. MAW took a rather sizable real estate brokerage fee for their trouble, even though no legal transactions had taken place. Most of the workers, including your parents, I assume, thought they signed up to own the trailers, not the land. MAW never told them the details. I remember the workers complaining that they had to move from shaded, cool houses to trailers that were out in the hot sun so close to the river that their entrances were underwater most of the spring."

"So, how did I come to own any of it?"

"Snowmaker filed suit again, claiming unpaid back wages, which wasn't true, but because a few farmers hadn't kept good records, it was cheaper for the farmers to pay bogus wages than to keep fighting in court. So, the farmers signed off on the trailers, giving them to the workers. They thought they settled the whole back wages thing and got them off the hook for repairs and maintenance. And it did. The original documents the farmers signed were for just that. But when the state hired Snowmaker away from the ACLU as a staff attorney, he made - very quietly – an amendment that gave the migrants title to the land the trailers sat on all the way to the river. Of course, very few of the workers, including your parents, knew about it. Neither did the farmers. They thought what they signed was only the last formality, which brings up a question for you. Your mother was Mexican, right? But I thought your dad was a U.S. Citizen?"

"He was, but he was also illiterate. And when he met my mom while working on a farm, he decided he could make pretty good cash in the migrant camps and be with my mom at the same time."

"Makes sense, I guess. Anyway, by that time, many of the farmers were so sick of lawyers and their bills that they signed the documents without consulting an attorney. Not all of them, of course. Farmers who did consult with lawyers mostly didn't sign, but just enough did to give possession of about a hundred acres to people who didn't even know what they had. It was all illegal, of course. I assume your parents fell into that group. Like them, most of the workers had long before moved into the Jovial community and gotten year-round jobs and built themselves houses and lives. By then, they didn't want anything to do with the sun-baked trailers, so they moved on."

"That's right. Dad worked in construction until his accident, and Mom died of cancer before I got out of high school."

Botsdorf nodded. "The farmers, thinking things were settled, kept farming the properties as if they owned them, not knowing that they'd signed their deeds over to the migrants, who also didn't really know that they owned the land. So in ignorance, things kept on going as they had for years, except that many farmers mechanized operations and eliminated about half of the migrant jobs."

"So what about the reparations?"

"Well, a few years ago, when Michigan established MOEIB, they set up Snowmaker as executive director. He filed suit for back pay for migrants, based on today's pay scale, rather than what they got paid 20 years before. All he asked – and put it in writing – was that MOEIB get one percent of the money as attorney fees. That suit was settled out of court and was kept very quiet. The farmers, who knew very little if anything about Snowmaker's tactics, thought he'd go away if they paid money as back pay. Again, it was cheaper than going to court. They kept farming the land just like they're doing now. When Snowmaker was established as head of MOEIB, he decided to start a reparation project for all the former migrants. In essence, it formed a fund he could use to buy the land from the migrants who knew they owned it, if any. The political climate being the way it was got pushed through, again, without many people talking about it."

"That can't be all legal."

"It's not legal. But because of the high cost, it never went to court. I'm sure the farmers would win in court, but that hasn't happened yet."

"So, where do I come in?"

"You're the turd in the punch bowl. Snowmaker couldn't just take the land legally, so he did a search for any ancestors of the original migrants, who, despite the illegality, owned it. On paper, anyway. You, apparently, were the only one they found. So you are the beneficiary of the land, as the sole surviving heir, and reparation money."

"But how does all this help the state and Snowmaker seize the riverfront? And why does he want it?"

"It's very valuable land, and he's trying to buy you off. Expect him to come calling. In the meantime, I'd advise you to talk to the farmers who farm the land. Be upfront with them. Let them keep farming. Charge them rent if you like, but don't soak them. Keep them on your side because they can be a valuable ally. And beware. Snowmaker is coming for you and them."

Chapter 12

Tyson Mooring walked out of his new financial advisor's office with a stack of papers representing several investment funds. The advisor assured him they would be best friends as time went by.

As instructed, Ty went to the bank and opened a savings account and a checking account with what the advisor called his "liquid" money. He applied for and was approved for a new credit card but couldn't wait for it to be sent to his mailbox at Ernie's Outfitters and activated. He wanted to spend. If it was liquid, it must flow.

He rented a Cadillac Escalade, drove around Jovial County just to drive in luxury, and ended up at the casino. He parked the Escalade in a back parking lot. He looked back as he reached the casino's revolving doors and decided it was too much. He was no Cadillac man. He wouldn't flaunt his money.

He inquired about long-term rent and signed up. Thirty days of living well beyond what he ever thought possible, paid in cash. But he would not gamble. Somehow, he knew that would not be good stewardship, whatever that meant. He couldn't explain why, but he'd lost his desire to gamble. Perhaps it was fear, but it felt strange to him. As he melded into the room's whirlpool tub that overlooked the edges of Jovial, a sense of peace assured him he was on the right track.

***

The same day, Donald Grandersma pulled up to the Lansing Towers, his new home, in a rented pickup truck, courtesy of James Snowmaker.

He resisted the urge to spit at the thought of Snowmaker because he had others to spit about now. How can God reverse things? Once his worst enemy, Snowmaker had been the only one to understand his potential. He spit forcefully on the sidewalk as he thought about Nitholder and the other board members at the Commandment Keepers church. They and Snowmaker were alike despicable, but the church had disrespected him. Snowmaker had shown respect. Snowmaker knew and appreciated his talent. The church board did not. He spit again, even more forcefully. Snowmaker probably couldn't be trusted, but then, he was a lawyer, and lawyers could not be trusted unless they were on your side. They had to take an oath. Maybe he was playing with Snowmaker, the devil, but at least Grandy knew it. The church board had been snakes in the grass. That was what hurt the most. The only proper revenge was success. Show them what they'd refused to see. His talent. His insight. His devotion to God. They'd be sorry when they figured it out. He'd like to be in that board meeting when they did, but he would not give them the satisfaction of coming back even if they begged, as he prayed they would.

The two-bedroom apartment was furnished with white, overstuffed chairs and couches, and the stainless steel refrigerator was full of fresh meats, fruits, and vegetables, along with several kinds of craft beer, wine, and soda.

He sat tepidly in the comfy chair that faced the 76-inch television and prayed that he could defeat those devils back in Jovial. There had been a time when he'd prayed for victory over Snowmaker, but it hadn't happened. Now he saw why. God had wanted him to work with Snowmaker all along. To save the river. To stop the gamble on the fragile earth. How had he not seen it before? It was the church board's fault. They'd blinded him with their judgment. They were blind guides. But his eyes were now opened.

The failure of his efforts to stop the casino had been a part of God's plan. He'd been prepared through that failure to succeed on a bigger scale. How typical of God. Go big, or don't go at all. And as he walked slowly around the apartment, he resolved to feel no more guilt. God had favored him with this luxury, and God's favor was something he dared not refuse. He'd been corrected by God through his rejection by the church, not punished for his so-called misdeeds. Attempted mayhem? It was righteous judgment. Casinos, well, all gambling, was of the devil, and he was a warrior against the devil. But punishment would certainly follow unless he earned his keep this time. So he sat down to work at a marble-topped desk in a room that was set up, apparently, just for office work. He'd have been happy with a kitchen table, like in his church's house, but it didn't take long to realize his resources here lacked nothing. This internet was the fastest he'd ever seen. Another sign that he was doing what the Lord wanted.

Lobbying was far from pastoring, but it was all for the best. God had led him to a new opportunity, and he could not only help save the river, but maybe expand into larger fields of earth-saving, and perhaps even save a soul or two in the bargain. God was blessing him now since his eyes were open, and he wouldn't disappoint the Lord, even if it meant working for the world – full of lost souls – and putting off spiritual matters for a time. God worked in mysterious ways, but this was even more mysterious than his appointment as lay pastor of the church many years ago.

He reviewed his research. It was surprisingly easy to become a lobbyist. Almost as easy as becoming a lay pastor. Back then, all he had to do was know his Bible better than the next guy and maybe sin a little less. Maybe even to spot sin in others more quickly than mere congregants. To be a lobbyist, no special education was required beyond a bachelor's degree, and even lacking that wasn't a deal-breaker, as was evident in his recruitment by Snowmaker. There was no code of ethics to study, at least that he could find. MELL's website promoted no ethics, either. It contained story after story of how close the planet was to extinction, and even more about water, rivers, the perils of "factory farming," and tributes to just how much work there was still to do for altruistic groups such as MELL. And he'd fallen into it without even trying. God's will, after all.

He made a sandwich from the cache in his kitchen, and as he finished, he got a call on the new cell phone Snowmaker had given him. As far as he knew, only Snowmaker had the number. And, indeed, it was his new mentor.

"Hey, Grandy. How do you like your new digs?"

"Fantastic. But it's too much. I've never had this kind of luxury, and I really don't know what to do with it all."

"Welcome to the MELL world, Grandy. You've earned it. Stop looking at a gift horse in the mouth and enjoy it. You're just now seeing the difference between the real world and that churchy-world of yours. Let me guess, because I've seen the house you've been living in. An old farmhouse, right? Needs paint and windows? I bet you fought with mice a lot. And how could you ever bring a woman back to a house like that?"

"That's not been my concern. I gave up women after I gave my life to the Commandment Keepers."

"Well, that's all changed now. Did the church offer you better than what you have right now? You have almost everything now, and you can have women, too. What else could you possibly want?"

"I have no interest in any woman except the one God has ordained for me."

"The point is, I came through for you, Grandy. The church didn't. Did they promise you heaven? And did they come through? What could be better in life than having the best? It's why they call it the best! And you don't have to wait for heaven to get it. God wants you to have it here, and he's using MELL to make it happen. MELL offers you money and women, sure, but if you're stuck on finding 'the one,' why shouldn't she be the hottest, most gorgeous woman you've ever seen? If you need to fall in love, fall for a fox, man! Why not you? Think about this! You can have luxury accommodations wherever you go and freedom. You won't have to be a slave to that pittance of a salary from the church. You're free from that. And all you have to do is work as hard for us as you worked for them. But for a much better reward. How long do you think you'd have to work for the church to make a quarter mill a year?"

"It was never about the money."

"Well, now it is! But it's more! You can leave a legacy for the world here. What did the church do? Abandoned you. You can be in the history books with MELL. You can change the world. This world. Right now. Not some dream-like world after you die.

Look at the difference between what that church offered you and what I'm offering. There's really no comparison, and I think you'll learn that soon enough. It's something you can think about on your flight."

"Flight?"

"That's right. Tomorrow morning you'll be on a flight to San Francisco to get a week of training on MELL's philosophies and goals. But the best part is, you'll get to meet Freedah."

"Who's Freedah?"

"Oh, you'll appreciate her, Grandy. Every man does. She's God's Own Beauty. Almost makes me believe in a creator. No one is put together like her by accident."

Soon after Snowmaker punched out, Grandy received an email with his flight details, along with the hotel where he'd stay in San Francisco, and, in a secure side e-mail for which he needed a password, a generous expense account for his stay there.

He clicked his way back to the MELL website and saw pictures of Freedah. There was no denying Snowmaker's truth. She was God's Own Beauty. She would complete God's blessing on his new life abundantly. But who could hold her? Could she ever be his? A union blessed by God because of his obedience? Could she have been meant for him all along? It felt right to him as he tried a dark beer. He was on the right track. Don't turn down God's blessings. Appreciate them. Remove all doubt.

Chapter 13

March 1

Fish were apathetic on the last day of the special trout season as if they didn't know or care that a millionaire was trying to catch them.

Ty knew his chances were slim, but he appreciated their attitude. Everyone who cast a line was created equal to the fish. Equally inept, unobservant, and drifting. It's why he liked fish, most days, better than the people he'd met.

A storm had passed just a few hours before he set out, carefully choosing his steps amid the slippery rocks and sodden, shallow mud. It was unseasonably warm, too, but a northern wind demanded at least a spring jacket.

He cast into a deep pool about a half-mile farther upstream than he'd fished the day before, but trout had seen him coming and were lethargic after their storm-prompted bug feast. He gave up and walked downriver past all kinds of wealthy citified novices, nodding at them as they hurried to catch fish before the special season ended. They congregated in random spots where it was easy to stand or even put out a lawn chair. He'd seen their kind all his life, and very few of them ever caught anything worthwhile unless by accident.

Ty patiently made his way downriver past the bluff on which he'd spent many hours watching the Jovial, appreciating her every curve and song he could see and hear. He went behind the abandoned county park and climbed up a rising ridge where he could see the 100 acres of rich black soil he now owned, though it didn't seem possible. He was certain that this all would come crashing down before long, and he'd see the prime farmland – the best in Jovial County – escape him like the ace that could make him a winner.

He shook off the rambling thoughts. That was his past. The valley of black muck stretched out before him. The higher ground was drying out nicely, and he almost could see the new, rich nutrients spring flooding had left behind. It would contain spring's first planting, and farmers – his tenants, whether they knew it or not – had put out their soil monitors, wind-borne scab and other disease monitors, and rain gauges. Never too early to get data. The state appreciated an annual baseline.

The top field's drains were carrying streams of gently flowing water, as they were designed, into small tributaries that separated the 100 acres into five distinct fields. The multi-functioning drains had been dug by farmers generations before. Farmers called it the Fish Drain, although no one remembered why.

Not many years before, the DNR had declared all the ditches streams, and farmers knew why. It was so the state could regulate them and prevent farmers from dredging without expensive permits. But when drains filled with debris, farmers generally dredged anyway, knowing that a plugged drain could ruin an entire season's worth of onion, celery, radishes, potatoes, and, in some years, late-planted sweet corn. Better to ask forgiveness than permission, after all. It was the code most people he knew lived by.

He stopped to examine the rocks, some hidden, some proudly prominent, a few hundred yards upstream from where the Jovial spread into the pond and appeared placid. But there was a hole in the narrows where rocks had drifted in over the 100 years since the dam was built. The Jovial had carried them and piled them as if a bulldozer had shoved them into the center, creating undercurrents far more dangerous than the surface. In another day or two, the water would recede, and many of the smaller rocks would reveal themselves. But today, they were hiding just a few inches below the surface, except for the boulder, which protruded at least five feet above the water. It was the rock that he and his friends had used as a target hundreds of times. They'd shot BB guns toward it, threw baseball-sized pebbles at it, and even tried their hand at lassoing it.

These rocks were treacherous as a lawyer, Ty thought, but at this point, they were relatively harmless unless someone was in a boat and didn't know they were there. It was for that reason that the DNR, which was now a division of MOEIB, discouraged boaters from getting on the river this time of year. At least someone in that department still knew what they were doing.

As the ground leveled off when he approached the water's edge, Ty saw the first signs of green sprouting along the filter strips farmers had planted. Though Ty knew a late winter storm would damage new growth temporarily, the strips were already doing their job, preventing drenched soil from flowing into the river. They'd worked well for years at keeping nutrients and crop protection products in place, mostly because farmers had learned long ago when to apply only the necessary amounts. Losing expensive chemicals to the river was an economic disaster.

Ty walked along the filter strips until he saw the remnants of migrant housing trailers. In less than 20 years, nature had usurped what was left. In a few more weeks, as spring bloomed, few people would know where to look for the ruts and leveled areas left behind when the trailers were hauled away. They'd been sold by the state, which put the money into a slush pot called the Environmental Contingency Fund. Very few people knew what happened to the cash after that.

Near a favorite illegal tourist fishing spot – not because anyone caught many fish there, but because it was flat and remarkably beautiful when foliage bloomed – he found plastic bags, Styrofoam coolers, fish bait containers, and fish rotting with hooks in their mouths and lines wrapped around their gills. He looked across the river when his foot stubbed something hard. He dug just a little and uncovered a relatively new metal fence post, a nice eight-footer. He picked it up and pounded it with an old piece of metal that was protruding nearby, likely part of a ruined boat motor.

The stake hit something stiff, just under the inch or so of soil debris left as the river receded from the winter. He found the edge and pried with the metal post. It was a sign identical to the one he'd found earlier, printed on hard corrugated cardboard and laminated. The colors on it were still bright, just like the other one. He pulled it out, washed it off with a little river water, and read it.

"Join MELL," it said in bold, large letters. "Liberate the planet, one river at a time."

***

Ty was almost finished pounding the stake until only about three feet were exposed. It was as solid and secure as he could make it. As he tied one end of his rope to the post, he heard a small motor chugging upstream, struggling to make headway against the relentless current that could only be truly experienced by fish. He waved to the man in the small boat, a white-haired, middle-aged person decked out in all that would have been left of last year's outfitters' inventory. Hunting coat, hat with ear flaps, and binoculars, but no life jacket.

"Get out of the middle, and it'll be easier," Ty shouted through cupped hands.

With difficulty, the man maneuvered toward Ty as the outboard motor struggled to work harder, and when nearer the edge, he made more progress. When he was close enough, Ty stepped into the river as deeply as his boots allowed and pulled in the boat.

"If you stay near the edge, your gas will last longer." The man stared at him but said nothing until Ty asked, "Where are you headed?"

"Upstream." The man's voice was raspy and gruff. "How far to state land?"

"You got about two miles to go, but with this current, you'll never make it. "Got extra gas?"

"What for? If I run out, I'll just drift back." He pulled the motor rope and fired up the outboard.

"Watch out for hidden rocks and tree limbs and stuff," Ty shouted above the noise. "Especially coming back. That current will carry you places you won't want to be."

"Don't tell me what I want." The man opened up the small boat's engine to full throttle. He slowly pulled away upstream as Ty watched.

Sometime later, as Ty was stacking debris into one growing pile, the same man in the boat came floating with the current, spinning out of control, the motor silent. Ty watched as the boat hit a large hidden log about a hundred yards upstream of the central pile of rocks. The boat lurched, almost tipping.

"How do I get out of here?" the man screeched toward Ty.

"Throw out your anchor."

"Don't have one!"

"Try to get to a bank! This bank!" Ty knew that without a paddle or motor, the effort was futile. He tested his rope's security around the fence post, tied the other end in a lasso loop, and flung it toward the target rock, well ahead of where he assumed the man in the boat would end up. The current was fast, although Ty had seen it faster and deeper and more treacherous.

As if by a hidden hand, the rope flew perfectly, opening wider as it flew, then landed and looped around the largest rock. Though the rock was visibly slippery, it caught just above the water line and held as Ty tugged it taut. He knew it could slip off as quickly as ice could spill a skater.

"Grab the rope when you get there!" Ty pointed to a couple of heavy logs that were being held against the current by a colorful rock that just barely peeked out of the water. The boat was still turning, and the man inside was whirling in the boat, counter to its clockwise spin. By providence, another log brushed the side of the boat, pushing it away from the center of the water and toward shore.

"I see it!" the man yelled and leaned out to reach the rope, rocking the boat toward one side, and it was perilously close to capsizing. The man dragged his arm through the water up to his shoulder, and when his forearm caught the rope, he leaned a little more just as the boat smacked a hidden rock, and the vessel overturned, pouring the man into the water as he frantically tried to get a feel for the rope. He went under the current twice and bobbed back up to gasp for air. Ty could see the man trying to yell, but the water he was swallowing left no sound in his lungs.

Ty grabbed the rope near its attachment to the post and tried pulling. It slipped off the slippery target rock, but Ty could feel no weight from the other end that might indicate that the man had found it. Keeping the rope in one hand, Ty slipped out of his boots and jacket and leaped into the river, swimming with great difficulty against the strong current.

As he neared the floundering man, he could see between swimming strokes that the target rock that had capsized the boat had also held it, although the water was rushing fast enough to splash water into and over the boat. Ty let the current take him until he found the rope's end and wrapped it around his left wrist. Then he swam hard toward the rock. As his strength and stamina were about to give out, he grabbed the boat's stern just as a stray log smashed into it and dislodged it. He ducked under the water to avoid the debris as he felt the rope tighten. He was at the end. But where was the man?

Just as the boat was about to be pushed over the rock, Ty could see him. The man was holding onto the boat, not the rock, and with his last ounce of strength, Ty reached out and grabbed the man's pant leg as he nearly flowed past him. He tugged the man back toward the rock to which Ty now clung and reached out to grab any article of clothing near the man's head. Finding the jacket collar, he jerked the man's head above the water, heard him gasp, and felt his panic. He tied the rope onto the man's wrist and fell back onto the rock, hanging on with all the strength he had left.

The man went under. Ty took a deep breath and pulled again, as hard as he could, and felt the man's body coming back to him like a 40-pound salmon, fighting with everything it had. Finally, he caught the man's collar again and pulled him onto the rock. He was unconscious.

Ty flipped the man onto his stomach and began pounding on his back. Water had to escape from the man's lungs. After about five hard smacks, the man gurgled and lurched, spitting out far too much water. He gasped and lurched again and finally took a desperate, gurgling breath.

As the man came to his senses, Ty looked him over. His white hair and beard were disheveled from his ordeal, but Ty could spot a $100 haircut if it was a dime. His hands were soft, his jacket torn. His arms were bruised and scratched from what was under the river's surface. He carried a bit of a paunch, typical for a man Ty estimated to be in his early 50s.

The man's eyes were beginning to focus again, and he glared at Ty as he reached for a secure hold on the rock. The rope around his wrist had left burns nearly up to his elbow, and Ty removed it and replaced it, tighter this time, around the man's coat sleeve above the elbow.

The man coughed and turned to speak.

"You hurt me," he gargled. "I was doing just fine until you capsized my boat."

Ty looked at the man in disbelief. "You were a goner, sir. You have no business on this river right now. No one does. No one with any sense, anyway. If not for me, you'd be floating face down toward the dam right now." He took a deep breath, and his heart calmed a bit. "You were a dead man floating."

"I've been taking boats up this river every summer since the best parts of you were dripping down your momma's leg."

"A nice calm summer trip is way different than right now. It's still at least a month until even the conservation officers will dare put a boat in this water. You obviously don't know what you're talking about."

"Oh, I don't, don't I? Who are you to tell me anything? Now get me out of here so I can sue you for all this pain and suffering in my back and legs."

With one quick thrust of anger, which pushed aside any altruism and replaced it with instinct, Ty pushed the man off the rock. He watched him thrash, reaching vainly for a hand-hold, and spun as the current pulled him under. But even before Ty saw the rope snap taut above the water, his new heart overcame his emotion. "Sorry, Lord."

He leaped into the water, grabbed the rope, and began pulling himself toward the bank. Once he found some footing near shore, he pulled the rope and himself to dry ground and started reeling in the man, fist over fist on the rope.

When the man had been pulled up, he lay flat on his face for a moment, then slowly sat up, got to his feet, and removed the rope from his arm. His breathing heaved his whole body into a convulsion. That done, he fell, butt first, into the soft soil, leaving a rather large impression.

The two sat on the ground for a moment, eyeing each other.

"Perhaps I've been a bit hasty in my judgment," the man said, reaching out his hand. "My name's Jim Snowmaker." Ty shook his hand reluctantly.

"What are you doing out here? It's kind of early for tourists."

"I'm here checking out sites for my new house. Lots of great building sites out here. I'd like to own a whole lot of them."

"More power to ya. But right now, it sure appears that the river owns you."

Snowmaker slapped Ty across the face.

Ty immediately slapped him back harder and grabbed him by his shirt collar and belt. He tugged him to his feet and snarled: "I should toss your sorry butt right back where you came from." But he stopped as Snowmaker repented.

"I'm sorry, son, I'm sorry. I shouldn't have done that. I'm cold and tired and hungry, son. Don't do anything rash after you've done the good deed of helping me!"

Ty loosened his grip and let the man slip back to the ground as his anger subsided.

"What are you really doing out here? Ain't no building sites around here, and there ain't nothing for sale. And if you really come here every year like you say, you should know better than to get on the river when it's rolling this fast."

"The truth is, property is only part of why I'm here. I'm looking for someone. Maybe you can help. You from around here?"

"Born and raised."

"Maybe you know him, then. A Mexican fella just got out of prison, name of Tyson Mooring."

"Never heard of him."

"Never hurts to ask. What's your name, son? I'd like to reward your kindness."

"Jorgan," said Ty. "Hugh Jorgan."

Chapter 14

Aspen's responsibilities – and her commitment to them – had prevented her from attending one of her favorite events for years. But when publisher Botsdorf told her she needed to take time off, she became eager for the time away from work. She thought a couple of Garit's stories she'd submitted for awards were good enough to win high honors, and she wanted to be there if they did. Being seen at such conventions was good for her visibility. Networking could lead to contacts in better, more prestigious places, which she certainly deserved. Secondly, she hadn't seen her college roommate, Anne Hathaway, in years. They had it all arranged. Attentively attend educational sessions that could make their respective publications better during the day, then catch up over drinks every night.

They had ordered their third Long Island Iced Tea when Garit's name came up in conversation.

"You mean to tell me you're living with this guy? Your employee?"

"He's not really my employee. I just get to edit him. We were hired together, a package deal, after we bounced old Wally East out of town."

But Garit is the same guy who won three writing awards here tonight? Why didn't you bring him?"

"Because I'm stuck in a situation I can't figure out. I'm not even sure I'm going to tell him about the awards. First thing you know he'll get a big head and leave for someplace better. I can't have that. The stuff I post on social media is the only thing holding us there. Ad revenue is not great, but it's growing, and all because of him. If he left, we'd be up a creek."

"People move on. Why would you hold him back?"

"Because he's my boyfriend. I don't want to lose that. If he's gone, I don't know why I would stay there. I've been very patient about my career, and we're doing great work. But we're probably not as good apart as we are together."

"But it's just a small-town pub, Aspen, even if it is one of the best in the region. No doubt about that. You're too good to stay there forever. Your talent is bigger than Jovial. Remember what the guy from Senate Communications said during his presentation? Fact-checkers are in high demand. High wages, good perks, a chance to put your finger on the heartbeat of something a lot bigger than Jovial. And you've always been the best fact-checker I've ever known."

"That doesn't solve my problem, though. I mean, together, Garit and I turned this pub into a well-respected, money-making deal. Sure, I'd like to move on if I got the right offer, but I'm not sure Garit would go with me. I mean, we've been living together for a little more than a year, and we've never yet said that we love each other. We have no plans to go further than where we are now."

"Well, it sounds like you're stuck in someplace you don't want to be."

"That's not it. I love it in Jovial. But is it enough? I'm stuck, but not hopelessly, Anne. If things just stayed the way they are, that would be fine, I suppose. But how soon before each of us gets dissatisfied with it? I mean, the publisher probably won't give him a raise for those awards, although more pay might help keep him around. But how long can small-town pay keep him from moving on? Sooner or later, someone's going to come headhunting him. The only thing he's weak at is social media. He hates it, for some reason, and refuses to change his style for it. Says he won't kowtow to some word limit and shock-jock headlines. Says it's all too shallow. Very bullheaded."

"Sounds like someone else I know."

Aspen smiled sardonically.

"So let's get back to me. How much more money could I make someplace else?"

"Lots. Think of the money and men you'd attract in someplace like Washington, DC. Don't give away your chances for the sake of one man, Aspen. Someone as good-looking and successful as you? Men are a dime a dozen."

"But he's my dime."

Anne laughed. "All I'm saying is that you should think about your professional potential before you think about a man. You're better than that. Remember, you always said when we were in college that this journalism career is the best way to make an impression on the world. Can you make an impression from Jovial?"

"I think we already have. I mean, you saw the award entries. Not to brag, but I think the Jovial World and Sasser blows away the pubs I've seen."

"No doubt that. Hey, if it makes you happy and you can be satisfied there, stay. I'll be on your side no matter what. Nothing can break our bond."

It had been good to talk these things out with Aspen's dearest friend, but when she went back to her hotel desk and tackled Garit's stories about the reparation coming to a Jovial resident, a chill ran up her back. Garit's reporting was solid. His research had been patient and thorough, and he'd fact-checked and double-checked. His writing was tight. As good as anything he'd done before. She was stuck between girlfriend and editor, and she didn't know, still, how to balance the two and still keep herself and Garit satisfied.

She stayed at the conference in Chicago an extra day so she could shop with Anne, although they abandoned that when they saw how dangerous it had become to walk down the Magnificent Mile and went to the hotel bar. Tuesday, as usual, she was back at her desk promptly at 8 a.m. Garit would be in later since he'd been at a Jovial City Council meeting until 10 the night before. When he came in from their apartment above the Jovial World and Sasser, at about 9, she called him into her office.

"I don't know how to tell you this, but this is some fine research. A well-told story. A few edits here and there, and any leftover holes, can be filled in as you continue following it. It's not over yet, right? I just have a feeling."

"The only hole I can see is motivation," Garit said. "Snowmaker was a tough interview. He's a very deceptive man, and he wouldn't bite on a couple of those questions, even after I asked them several times from several different angles. But I think that very soon, MOEIB will issue a press release. It will be deceptive, of course. That's how his PR team works. They'll want to have a big scene, present a giant check, have some Mexican community leaders who've been hand-picked by MOEIB on hand to pat each other on the back."

"That's how all public relations teams work," she interrupted. Garit continued: "But Snowmaker's ego is too big to let a three-million-dollar reparation and deed to 100 acres of top farmland go to waste. Well, five million, actually. He took a pretty big cut, but I don't think money is his motivation. He thrives on his ego. And I fed it. Enough to get some answers, anyway."

Aspen paused. "While I don't like you manipulating sources that way, it's still a good story."

"Have you been in your editor's mode so long that you've forgotten that sometimes you have to manipulate people – bureaucrats and politicians in particular – into telling the truth? You'll never get it just by asking."

"I'm not criticizing your methods. When people are that deceptive, and it comes out in the story like it does here, you do what you have to do. Nothing unethical about it, I suppose, when the search for truth and facts is the primary goal. But here's what I'd like to do. Let's split this up into a few sidebars. One will be the interview with Snowmaker and the background on MOEIB. Then, the main story is about the legal settlement, and later in the week, after people start talking about it, the profile of Ty. By the way, how did you know it was Ty who got this settlement? And, can we get his picture?"

"I won't reveal my sources about how I knew," Garit smiled in the sly way that made Aspen's affection soar. She'd missed him during her four days away. Even longed for his touch. Was it enough?

"And about the picture? Doubt it," Garit said. "Ty wants to keep a low profile at this point. He's left open the possibility of a follow-up story when he decides what to do with his money. And he's a little sensitive about his teeth. Told me he's never smiled for a photo."

"Well, keep at it. You'll be following this story for some time. The greater question readers will want answered in time is, what will he do with the land?"

"He's doing his research. In fact, he's asked me if you could do some fact-checking for him in that regard once he speaks with all the people interested in it. And he's more than happy to pay you well for your time and expertise."

"If the pay is good, tell him I'd be happy to do it."

***

Here are the stories that ran later that week in the Jovial World and Sasser:

Main story:

Headline: Jovial man gets $3 million 'reparation' from state

by Garit West

A Jovial resident has been given a 'reparation' for alleged wrongs done to migrant workers who lived and worked on Jovial farms 20 years ago, according to the

Michigan Office of Environment, Inclusion and Bigotry (MOEIB).

The recipient, who is not being named in deference to his wishes, is the sole living heir of migrant farm workers who allegedly squatted on a 100-acre parcel of land as they worked on an estimated 35 Jovial-area fruit and vegetable farms for more than 10 years, according to a press release from MOEIB.

"All we know at the time we put out the press release is that there is only one living descendant of the 75 known migrant workers who were kicked out of their on-farm housing and forced to live in trailers down by the river," said James Snowmaker, director of MOEIB, in a telephone interview with the Jovial World and Sasser. "We know his name but have not yet been able to contact him to pay him back for all the injury and racism his family and others were subjected to from area farmers."

The reparation payment, made possible by an executive order three years ago by Governor Titus (Tidy) Holmes, entitles the descendants of migrant workers to collect a lump-sum payment for back pay and penalties for "any and all economic harm" done to them. That same executive order established the new office to investigate the case, among others, named it MOEIB and named Snowmaker director of the office.

"In this case, the living descendant will receive a payment of about $3 million and deed to 100 acres of riverfront land where his family lived after being evicted from their former housing," Snowmaker said. "We feel that action will settle the case once and for all and bring equity to the migrants who suffered so much at the hands of greedy and selfish farmers."

An investigation by the Jovial World and Sasser shows that the migrants were not evicted from their housing by farmers. It also uncovered that the reparations budget signed by Governor Holmes was for $5 million. Snowmaker *billed the state for nearly $2 million for legal fees from his law firm.*

The investigation turned up reports from various newspapers, which were confirmed by legal documents on file in the state archives, and interviews with an attorney who fought for the farmers in the case.

"The Jovial Farmers' Association (JFA) still believes this was a contrived case meant to enrich the lawyers from the Migrant Advocates Watchdog (MAW) group," said attorney Delbert Skinner, who represented the JFA in the original case. "The farmers had spent significant cash building housing for their migrants, and it was regarded at the time as the best in the nation. The housing was built under shade trees and remained quite cool in the summers, and they provided propane heaters for hot water showers and heat during colder nights."

Records from the JFA and the Jovial Community Bank confirmed that the farmers' association helped secure funds for the farmers for the buildings' construction, a loan of more than $100,000. All was paid back before the 10-year terms of the loans expired. Workers lived in the buildings for three seasons.

Then, records from the state migrant housing authority show, the buildings were given a failing grade by two first-year inspectors who noticed, in an inspection conducted five weeks before migrants were set to arrive for the first work of spring (asparagus season), that the propane tanks were empty, water was not turned on, and screens were in disrepair.

"That got the attention of MAW," Skinner said. "And that group filed a complaint with the American Civil Liberties Union (ACLU), who assigned one James Snowmaker, then a fresh-out-of-school lawyer, to the case. He pressed for condemnation of the housing and threatened severe financial penalties on the farmers."

Snowmaker, in the Jovial World and Sasser interview, admitted to being employed by the ACLU at the time but said he had little recollection of the particular case.

"But," he said, "It sounds right. Racist farmers at the time were really sticking it to the migrants all over this country, and Jovial County, one of the richest fruit and vegetable growing regions of the country, were undoubtedly abusing these people due to their race."

When asked for documentation of that accusation, Snowmaker said ACLU documents are sealed due to the sensitive nature of the allegations, and due to privacy concerns. The Jovial World and Sasser put in several Freedom of Information Act requests with the ACLU and MAW, which were all denied. Legal action to get such documents is pending.

As part of the settlement between MAW and the JFA 20 years ago, the farmers were forced to cede the title of 1,000 square feet of river-view property to each migrant on record working for members of the JFA at the time and to provide double-wide manufactured homes for each family, records show.

"The recent settlement proposed by MOEIB seemed innocuous since the people who lived in the double-wides were all gone, and each of them had signed agreements ceding the land back to the farmers," Skinner said. "As I recall, those workers didn't see much value in owning 1,000 square feet of wetland that flooded every spring and stunk with dead fish and debris. They took their proposed payments of $1,000 each and moved on."

But the MOEIB decided, with the power of the ACLU and MAW behind it, that the migrants were entitled to much more. And so, in what Skinner described as an illegal land grab, MOEIB seized 100 acres. Skinner said that land is still being fought in court.

"At this point," Skinner said, "the farmers are considering their options, but they don't have the money to pay for the legal filings needed to fight this. Their other option is to lease the land from whoever the owner now is, and hope they can keep farming the land. In some peoples' opinion, those 100 acres, if lost for farming, could bring real economic damage to the entire Jovial agricultural community."

Members of the JFA will bide their time and slowly collect money to pay for legal action, said JFA president Coney Dogues.

"Our members unanimously view this as theft of their land," he said. "The argument about the migrants having squatted on the property long enough to be legal owners has already been struck down in court."

That statement was confirmed in court filings and by Skinner, who said the squatting argument had no legal merit, a statement confirmed by both lower courts and appeals court rulings. You can read those decisions here (click on this link).

Sidebar 1: *What is MOEIB, and who is its leader?*

In the first three days after Governor Titus (Tidy) Holmes's inauguration, he signed 26 executive orders (EO).

The Capitol Press Bureau, according to a review of press clippings of the four most widely circulated news outlets during those three days, lavished praise on the Governor for "strong leadership," "decisive action," and "bold confidence" but ignored mentioning the one department that brought a Jovial man his newfound fortune.

In EO number 19, the Governor established the Michigan Office of Environment, Inclusion, and Bigotry

(MOEIB) and named attorney James Snowmaker its director.

The Governor's office of public relations said the office was "sorely needed as a way to consolidate the three offices that now exist to ensure environmental justice to all the under-served people of this state who to this point have not been privileged to enjoy this administration's efforts to truly bring the beauty of this pleasant peninsula to everyone, and not just the farmers who have for generations selfishly used their proximity to the great outdoors for their own profit-seeking ventures."

Farm groups were among the most vocal in opposition to the new office and pointed out that it did not consolidate anything but simply added new bureaucracy.

"We already have an environmental and natural resources department, and we already have the state civil rights commission," Jovial Farmers Association President Coney Dogues was quoted saying in an article in the Detroit Presser. "And disparaging the farm sector, the number two economic driver in this state, by calling farmers selfish for feeding the population, shows the true nature of the Governor's agenda," he reportedly said. A follow-up interview with Dogues by the World and Sasser confirmed that his quote was accurate.

"The recent announcement of the settlement with MAW (Migrant Advocates Watchdog) proves that their agenda is anti-farmer and pandering to activist groups with a goal of taking land from farmers and distributing it to wealthy campaign donors," Dogues said. "There has never been a governor so ignorant about agriculture or an administration more hostile toward farmers," he said.

While the reparation recipient, who will be named later, certainly does not fit that anti-farming description, James Snowmaker does, and several farmers agreed during recent telephone interviews. His appointment to head the new department is proof, Dogues said.

The local man is the recipient of the reparation, he told the Jovial World and Sasser, even though MOEIB did not reveal his name.

The beneficiary of the 'reparation' said a PR worker at MOEIB told him his name would not be revealed until MOEIB could arrange a press event, but he agreed to speak exclusively to the Jovial World and Sasser. See the sidebar story later this week.

Snowmaker, according to records from the Secretary of State's Campaign Financial Searchable Database, contributed the maximum personal donation of $3,400 to Governor Holmes' campaign and was the campaign chairman for a San Francisco environmental group named Mother Earth Liberation League (MELL), which contributed the maximum of $34,000.

Snowmaker also worked on Holmes' campaign as a "volunteer" fundraiser for other environmental groups, minority political action committees, and migrant advocacy groups, including MAW (Migrant Advocate Watchdogs), a so-called non-profit group whose board of directors includes six lawyers and one former migrant, who also is an attorney. At the time, Snowmaker was not on the board, but he is now in a position that pays $100,000 per year, according to records from the Internal Revenue Service.

In a telephone interview with the Jovial World and Sasser, after MOEIB announced the reparation to the as-then unnamed descendant of migrant workers, Snowmaker said his appointment was not a political favor.

"I was and remain the most qualified person in this state for the position," he said. "Campaign work and contributions had nothing to do with it. No one has worked harder for the rights of migrants or for the environment, which are intertwined."

When asked how they were intertwined, Snowmaker declined to answer.

Snowmaker's qualifications include his early work with the ACLU, which included several lawsuits against the Jovial Church of the Commandment Keepers and its then-pastor Donald Grandersma. The ACLU sued the church after a lengthy undercover operation in which Snowmaker accused the church board and pastor of excluding minority groups from its membership, a charge the church denied then and now.

"Our church has a policy that was established from the very beginning of welcoming anyone and everyone who wants to join," said church spokesman Michael Nitholder. "We've never turned anyone away. It's not our fault or desire that the majority of our members are white. That's merely a reflection of our community, but we do have members in good standing who are of both Mexican and Native American ancestry."

Even earlier in his time with the ACLU, Snowmaker was a key attorney working with MAW to begin the process which now has made a young man a millionaire and owner of some of the most prime agricultural real estate in Jovial County. (see background in the main story in this series here.)

Sidebar 2, two days later:

Tyson Mooring didn't feel lucky. Trying to make his own luck landed him in prison.

But today, he's free. And wealthy. More importantly, he said in an exclusive interview with the World and Sasser he has a deed to 100 acres of the richest farmland in the country. It's also some of the most scenic properties in the nation.

"I haven't been to too many places in this world," Mooring said, "but I've talked to people who have, and

they tell me there's no place more beautiful than the Jovial River Valley in Jovial County."

That beauty – and the richness of the thousand-acre plot of which his land is a fraction – makes Tyson Mooring feel a deep responsibility for his new-found wealth.

"When I accepted Jesus in prison," he said, "I started to get free from a lot of things. But in place of that freedom from my anger and hatred and desire for revenge came a weight of some sort. I didn't know what it was all about until I understood what was going on with these strange letters from a state department I'd never heard of. MOEIB. I thought it was some sort of scam. I kept waiting for the hook – you know, where at the end of the pitch, they promise to make you rich, but you have to give someone most of your savings. But the pitch never came."

Soon after his release from prison, Mooring consulted a local attorney, who told him it was true. He was the sole recipient of a reparation meant to absolve someone – and it's still not clear who needed the absolution – from guilt over what had allegedly been done to keep his parents in poverty.

"My parents never bought into all this victim crap," Mooring said. "My dad was an American – though illiterate – who met my mom while he was working in the fields on some of the same property I own now. She was a seasonal worker from Mexico. Her family came here every year to work because the Jovial farmers treated them well, paid them a hell of a lot more than they did in other states, and provided pretty nice, comfortable housing. They both taught me that you have to work to get what you have in this world. I believe it now, and I believed it all my life, for the most part. But there was that one get-rich-quick scheme that I couldn't resist. And that cost me 18 months of my life in prison."

It started, Mooring said, when he reconnected with an old grade-school friend who had just invested in top-of-the-line, computerized printing equipment.

"It was state-of-the-art," he said. But being unknown and without connections, he was having trouble getting work. So, one day, just to keep up with the technology, he tried his hand at reproducing some official documents. He ended up doing some fake identifications – you know, passports, driver's licenses, stuff like that until he tried his hand at lottery tickets," he said.

The pair, Mooring said, took their time and perfected the tickets, a task he said was much more difficult to reproduce than identification documents. But before long, Mooring passed a $10 winner at an out-of-town party store.

Emboldened, the pair began producing $25 winners, then a $50 winner.

"It wasn't much, but it kept us in pocket spending money," Mooring said.

Then, feeling that their craft had been perfected, Mooring tried to pass a $1,000 winner. He walked out of the store – the site of a sting – in handcuffs and was quickly sentenced for fraud and got 18 months in prison, although the prosecutors, records show, demanded much more. He would not reveal the name of his partner, nor would he ever, he said.

"That was something the judge commended," Mooring said. "I guess the judge felt there was something redeeming in me."

About a year into his 18-month sentence, Mooring said, the man the inmates called Reverend Repent moved into the prison and began proselytizing. That man has been identified and confirmed as Donald Grandersma, former pastor of the Commandment Keepers Church in Jovial.

"I hadn't thought much about God, and my parents were devoted to work, not religion," Mooring said. "But chapel services were a way to break up the boredom, so I started going. As I started thinking about the reverend's message, it began to make sense. I learned that life is not all about me. And I learned that if I stopped being so selfish all the time, I could become blessed by God. I didn't really know what that meant until I realized that God, through the state and its efforts to pay back my parents and their community for the supposedly bad things that were done to them, had given me a great gift and a great responsibility.

As of this writing, Mooring has not decided how he can be a blessing to the people around him. But he wants to use the money for the good of humankind – and spend a little on himself besides.

"That decision will take lots of thought, consultation, and prayer," Mooring said. "I know that Reverend Repent's church will get a sizable donation, but beyond that, I haven't decided. I'd like to have a nice house and maybe a nice car, but I know I have a real responsibility to serve God and man with this windfall. I've been counseled to follow what God puts in my heart as a passion. I don't know what that is yet, but I know I'll be praying about it."

At the time of the interview with Mooring, he said he was leaning toward giving money to something that can help the river.

"I don't really know if it needs saving or if a million bucks or more could really help it," Mooring said. "But that's my goal. Whatever I do, it must be worthwhile to make a lasting difference in the world. I want to do the right thing."

Chapter 15

When Donald Grandersma disembarked from the plane in San Francisco, he was met by a short, stout, black-suited Arabic man who held up a sign that read: "Mr. Granderson, MELL." After telling the driver his name is Grandersma, Grandy and the driver retrieved his luggage —one suitcase which had been provided by MELL – and arrived at an aging black stretch limo. Despite the driver's protests, Grandy insisted on carrying the bag himself.

Waiting for him on the sprawling back seat was a thick packet of information about MELL, along with some alarming facts about river pollution. It included a prediction from MELL's own on-staff environmental scientists that the Jovial River was in dire need of cleanup and would be irreparably polluted with farm chemicals within two years at the present pace. Unless, of course, the farmers were stopped from doing their dirty deeds. Now. The words' tipping point' were spun throughout the documents like dull blades in a lawnmower.

They arrived at the hotel, the Four Seasons San Francisco, and the driver told Grandy that he was only a half-mile from MELL's office building in Salesforce Towers, one of the most exclusive office buildings in the city.

"Don't get too comfortable," said the driver as he looked Grandy up and down, making him uncomfortable in his classic black but worn wool suit, the only one he owned.

"I know that won't be easy. These rooms cost about 500, 600 bucks a night, but don't fall asleep. You're expected to meet with Phoenix Tippin at 3 p.m. Sharp. And you are to walk there. Cutting down on carbon emissions, you know." He handed Grandy a map to the office and sped off, leaving Grandy coughing as exhaust fumes rose like an off-balance jump shot and invaded his lungs.

He arrived at the office building at 2:45 and breathed deeply of the building's cool air, trying to rid his lungs of the foul smell of the city. He took the smooth and quiet elevator to the 17th floor, well below the peak opulence of the 61-story building, the tallest in the city. Still, it was the grandest thing Grandy had ever seen.

MELL's reception desk was about the size of a vintage Oldsmobile, he estimated, and the lovely almond-skinned young woman in the center of it greeted him warmly.

"Mr. Granderson?" she cooed as she walked from behind the desk.

"Grandersma," he corrected.

"Well, I'll make a note of it. Mr. Tippin has been looking forward to meeting you. You'll love him. Not only does he share your passion for the river, but he's a whiz at all the science. And even though his mind is constantly burdened with all the horrible things farmers and other polluters do to the rivers, he manages to keep a very cheerful attitude and a winning smile."

The young woman escorted Grandy past an elder-wood paneled wall into a massive expanse of offices, each one separated by glass. At one end of the space, Grandy could see two young Latino men, one on a ladder and one below, washing the windows with squeegees and rags and wearing backpacks filled with what Grandy thought must be window cleaner. Straight ahead was one office that was at least three times bigger than all the others, and in powdery blue lettering – Sanskrit – it read "Office of the President Phoenix Tippin."

Grandy was instructed to sit in a leather chair facing the office, through which he could see a portion of the city before his eye led outward to the San Francisco Bay. Closer in, he could see a man, maybe 40 years old, with slick black hair, full as any Hollywood actor. Obviously fit, the man sat at a desk larger than the receptionist's, and to one side was a treadmill. On the other side was a hot tub.

Phoenix Tippin pulled a headset from his face and rose, beaming as he welcomed Grandy with a warm smile and outstretched hand.

"Mr. Granderson," he enthused, shaking Grandy's hand. Grandy was disappointed that Tippin's hand was moist and limp-wristed.

"Sma."

"Excuse me?" Phoenix's smile revealed perfect lines of white that Grandy had never seen inside a man's head before.

"The name is Grander SMA,"

"You're sure?" Tippin gave Grandy's shoulder an athletic bump with his hand. "Just kidding. Mr. Snowmaker told us it was Granderson."

"It's okay. I usually just go by Grandy."

"Well, isn't that just dandy?" Phoenix grinned as if posing for a movie closeup. "Grandy is dandy." He laughed. "Either way, it's a pleasure to meet the man who will bring our passion for rivers to Michigan so we can start to turn things around over there."

"To tell the truth, our rivers are in pretty good shape. The Jovial River, in particular, is one of the most beautiful places in the country. It's clean, except in the spring when it floods. It has to if it wants to carry the winter's debris out to the big Lake."

Tippin offered Grandy a seat in a leather chair that was even softer than the one outside his office, then lifted himself onto the front of his huge mahogany desk, where he crossed his legs.

"That's where you're wrong, Grandy." His smile quickly turned into a serious, closed-mouthed grimace. "It's not your fault. Things aren't always what they appear to be. Our research shows that there are tons of agricultural chemicals being dumped into that river every year. It's sometimes the things you can't see that are the most dangerous."

"I understand," Grandy replied, feeling the softness of the chair as he caressed its arm. "So, what is my role as a state lobbyist?"

"I like that. All business. Getting right to the point. Your background is as a fighter against gambling, right?"

"And as a pastor."

"Perfect. We want you to leverage your reputation as a fighter for the right things and convince your state legislators that if they don't take action quickly, they're gambling with the future of the pristine Jovial River. We've already got the ball rolling for you."

"In what way?"

"Mr. Snowmaker is about to file a series of lawsuits against the farmers, the state environmental agency, and the natural resources department, demanding that all agricultural activities be stopped immediately. With any luck at all, we'll get a cease and desist order. That's where you come in. We want you to convince lawmakers there that strict new controls should be put on any farm activity within two miles of the river. If we can't get that, we'll keep fighting. I understand that's your strong suit, Dandy Grandy. You don't stop fighting."

Grandy nodded. "So what's my first move?"

"First is your training. You'll spend the next week in the capable hands of our finest and most passionate environmental fighter. By the end of the week, you'll be prepared to hit the ground running there in Detroit."

"Lansing."

"What's that?"

"Michigan's capitol is Lansing,"

"Right." Tippin pointed his finger at Grandy as if it were a gun. He lept off his desk and hit a button on an office phone.

"Shania, will you send Freedah in here please?"

He motioned for Grandy to stand and turned him away from his desk.

"Be prepared. This girl is more than most men can handle."

Immediately, Grandy saw people in the glassed offices looking up from their computers and staring down the hall. Men and women alike watched until Freedah promenaded, inviting as a summer smoothie, past them. Some of them tried to turn their eyes, but it was impossible to look away. It was like watching a rainbow out of place in a clear blue sky. Who could break their gaze from such unusual beauty?

Soon, the door opened, and Grandy swallowed hard. God was indeed good. Freedah entered softly, delicately, as if her entire being were silk sheets waving gently in a cool ocean breeze. She reached out her hand, and Grandy took it, gulping. His heart quickened, and his hand was moist as he felt blood rushing away from his neck.

"Mr. Granderson?" Her voice was like the first bluebird of spring. "I'm Freedah Forest. Pleased to meet you."

"Call me Grandy." His voice squeaked as if he were in ninth grade. "The pleasure is mine." He'd never uttered a more sure truth in his life.

Chapter 16

When Botsdorf merged the Sventon Sasser with the Jovial World, he knew he couldn't make it a credible publication without Aspen. He gave her the title of managing editor in place of the deposed and disgraced Wally East and made Garit the senior reporter. But there was still something missing. The pair had turned the formerly competing pubs into one fine, reputable local news outlet, but it lacked something about which he had no knowledge or interest. There was no social media presence.

Aspen had started pulling the new publication into the present by establishing a daily e-news feed sent out to everyone who had a subscription to the paper version and an email account. Now, nearly two years after the merger, they had enough email subscribers to attract a few local advertisers, but social media was a low priority and a whole new ballgame. That could not continue. It was becoming clear that to survive, the Jovial World and Sasser needed to be on the web or be left behind, its solid reporting and upper-Midwestern tone lost in the flood of unhindered and sometimes irresponsible voices.

Motivated by the educational sessions she'd attended at the Midwestern Press Association conference, Aspen was determined to make it all happen. She had long before put Garit's best story links on Twitter, Instagram and Facebook, but, with Botsdorf's permission and investment, she started to file things on the newest, hottest social media platform, called Twaddle.

Since she started doing that, the Sasser had been getting fast exposure. In the first two weeks, more than 200 people had become followers of the Sasser.

She'd learned that Twaddle had been launched in San Francisco, but her nascent skills at digging deeper online stopped there. She couldn't yet tell who was the power behind it, or how to find such information, but she'd figure it out. She could figure anything out, given enough time and effort. Time was the problem. Another important duty on an already overloaded schedule.

When Garit came into the office, all three of her screens were filled with analytics, statistics and reports. She was frustrated that, despite their presence on popular social media platforms, the number of followers was ticking up too slowly to really call it growth. But Twaddle was the only one that didn't seem lethargic.

"Garit," she demanded, "how can I get you to create content for social media? How many times do I have to ask?"

"At least once more." His tone was defiant, as he intended. "I will never tweet, twat or any of the other words you can make up to describe inane, vapid activities like trying to stir things up with idiotic, incomplete statements. If you want credibility, you cannot be on Twaddle. Period. You're the fact-checking guru here. You know you can't get the truth out of social media. There's nothing credible or substantial about any of it. Nothing can be trusted, so why should we get involved?"

"The point is to drive traffic back to our website. That's where they'll get the credible news."

"Most social media followers only read headlines, then form their opinions from that. Social media is not designed to help people dig deeper, to educate themselves or to examine both sides before they form opinions. It's shortened attention spans. It makes the whole world dumber."

"We're the exception, I hope. Without it, we'd never get out info beyond our own few followers. Just do it. It's not that big of a deal."

"Then you do it. I won't. The World and Sasser is for a few thousand people right here in Jovial, and I aim to serve them. The rest of the world doesn't care much, so why should I? We can keep our community well-informed, but why do we care what some idiots out in California think about us?"

"Because if they care, we get hits and followers. And if we get that, we get more advertising revenue. You've done better lately at writing headlines that have our keywords, the ones that draw people in who normally wouldn't care about the Sasser, so keep that up. But we need you to write inflammatory opinion pieces on Twaddle. And if we get that, you and I might get raises."

"If I want a raise, I'll ask Botsdorf. I want nothing to do with social media. Especially that twaddle thing. Anything that got that popular that fast, I will resist. Popularity is the death of truth, especially on Twaddle, where opinions don't have to be well thought out. It's just a bunch of spew. Following the crowd is a horrible thing, and I want no part of it. I work for print and online publications; that's it. I don't work for corrupt teenagers who control information for their own egos. You, of all people, understand the manipulation going on, so you should be on my side."

"I'm as dedicated to facts and truth as you, but I also understand the real world. We have to use every platform at our disposal, or we'll die on the vine."

"I'd rather die with integrity than live with inanity," She rolled her eyes. Garit set his jaw, and his face turned red.

"You're such a hypocrite, Aspen. You go over all my copy with tweezers and a magnifying glass just to be sure the stories are beyond reproach, but yet you want some 140-character twat to go out that would destroy our credibility in mere seconds."

"Social media has nothing to do with facts. It's meant as a teaser to bring traffic to our website. Its credibility doesn't go beyond that."

"I agree, but far too many social media users don't understand that. What do we have here?" He reached over her shoulder and scrolled until he found the statistic sheet for Twaddle. "We now have one thousand, eight hundred and two followers on all our social media. About two hundred of those are not from around here. So why do we care about people who aren't part of our community?"

"All I know is one thing. It's all about the numbers. Doesn't matter where they come from. I think it's exciting to go beyond Jovial. We're getting more followers every day on Twaddle from

San Francisco. Don't know why, other than they found us when they searched with the words 'river' and 'pollution', but that doesn't matter. We need more traffic so our sales staff can pitch it. We can't make a go of this publication with just our website's news feed, with its twelve thousand subscribers. Sure, that's a lot for a pub our size, but it's not enough. We need more. You *will* begin to participate."

"No, I won't. My job is to report and write the truth about what's going on in this community and to inform people right here about how local, state and national politics affects their lives. Aside from that, some twaddle about my opinion has no place here. I thought you cared about being unbiased. I thought you cared about integrity."

"Integrity doesn't pay the bills. And bias is inherent, no matter how we try to squelch it. Humans are biased. Period. And that includes reporters. Besides that, aren't you interested in whether people like your stories or not?"

"Why should I care if they click on something for two minutes? My job is to report without bias, not to make people like what they see. And I really don't care what some yahoo out in Twaddle land thinks or says about me. I answer to a higher calling."

"Oh, boy, here comes that 'Christian worldview' crap again. You know, I could fire you right here and now."

"What's stopping you?" She looked down at the statistics but said nothing. They both knew what was stopping her.

"By the way," she said, ending the argument. "You won two first-place awards last week."

"For writing?"

"Yes."

"And did social media likes help?"

"No."

Garit smiled and went back to his desk.

Later that day, Aspen came to Garit's desk.

"I have an idea that might be good for the Sasser and prove something to both of us. I propose that, at some big event, maybe the election rallies coming up, you write a first-person account. I'd post it on the website and then run it on social media. I will guarantee that I can find a bias in your story, no matter what the subject matter is. I'll remove your bias before I post it on Twaddle."

"Like the old-timers used to do? First-person observations without personal bias? Sounds like a good challenge. Have you ever tried it?"

"No, but then, I understand my biases and don't let them get in my way."

"Neither do I. As much as humanly possible, of course."

"I don't think you do. That's why I'm giving you this challenge. I think it would be a good draw for our readers, and maybe I can convince you that it's impossible."

Garit thought a moment but was steadfast in his commitment.

"Challenge accepted. But on my terms. I pick the event?"

"Accepted."

"Wow, you're sexy."

***

Garit went on with his day, and Aspen, when her reporter's curiosity kicked in, decided to dig a little deeper into 200 Twaddle followers from the West Coast.

She dug about four layers deep, learning with every new level, then did a search for common characteristics among the 200.

What she learned didn't really connect with her because she knew nothing about the new followers except one thing: Everyone was already an active participant with one of two activist groups: The Pure Fly Fishing Federation and the Mother Earth Liberation League.

Chapter 17

Within hours of his first one-on-one instructional session with Freedah, Grandy carried a list of names into his lavish hotel room. Her scent lingered on his suit coat, so he left it on as he loosened his tie and spread the list in front of his computer.

There were 11 members on the Michigan House of Representatives Agriculture Committee, six of whom Freedah said might dare vote against House Bill 616 and thus bring the consequences of their sin upon themselves. The others, she'd insisted, were in MELL's back pocket and of no concern to him. His job was to learn background voting records and personal proclivities in preparation for convincing them that gambling with the Jovial River was evil and could cost them their seats in the next election.

Such threats might convince a couple of them. George Gratzyk, from the Kalamazoo area, had a lot of farmers in his district, but he also had the filthy Kalamazoo River so polluted that the state didn't dare approve permits to disturb the bottom. Two committee members represented people in the metro Detroit area and so could be convinced, with little effort, that pollution was the fault of farmers, not the city's leaky wastewater treatment system.

The two toughest nuts to crack, Freedah had said, were two farm-area representatives: Boyd McCockert of the farm counties south of Lansing and committee chair Peterson Fectid from the Jovial area. Both faced reelection in the fall if they got past the primary, but that was a foregone conclusion. The two had won primaries before by margins large enough to forego campaigning this time around.

Fectid, in fact, had vowed repeatedly, when he visited his district, to fight against HB 616, which is what polling told him his voters wanted.

Grandy was checking for Fectid's vulnerabilities when he heard a knock. A flamboyantly gay man with inch-long, multicolored fingernails carved into the shape of native American spearheads was at the door, his hair greased up into a five-spiked blonde crown.

"Orders from Miss Forest," the person said, waving his hand in the air as if it were a wand. "And I can see she was right." He giggled like a little girl and pulled out a cloth tape measure. "You absolutely need her fashion touch, honey. Well, and my tailoring expertise." He knelt in front of Grandy as he unbound the tape measure with one hand as if it were a yo-yo.

Although uncomfortable the entire time, Grandy allowed the person – who told him his name was Yum Yum, to measure him, even though he took too much time feeling around the crotch. At one point, Grandy nearly pushed him away, but he was in San Francisco, and he'd been warned about offending anyone. Lobbyists needed to be amiable, not preachy. It was one of Freedah's first commandments.

The next morning, Grandy was in the conference room, waiting in his new suit, which he had to agree looked good and was very comfortable, considering it had all been hastily tailored overnight.

While he waited, he continued trying to absorb the statistics MELL provided him about the pollution in the Jovial River, and he compared them with the official Michigan and EPA statistics, which stood in a pile on his computer screen. They told vastly different stories.

Freedah arrived 20 minutes later than the appointed time, and Grandy, though tempted, did not look at his watch when she walked in. Instead, he stood and gazed at her aura, forcing himself not to stare. She wore a form-fitting salmon-colored blouse with the shoulders cut out, revealing tan and toned shoulders that could have been manufactured in the gym but probably were natural. It's how she was made. Her short, tight skirt was thigh-high, and her legs were long and lean, with no blemishes such as freckles or bug bites.

She flashed her perfect teeth in greeting and sat across from Grandy, beaming at him.

"What were you studying?" Her inflection assured him that she was divinely interested.

"Just going over the stats from the Jovial River. MELL and the Michigan DEQ numbers don't seem to match up."

"Well, there's your first rookie mistake." She smiled and patted his hand across the table. "Our statistics are beyond reproach. That's the message you have to get through to your legislators."

"And what if they believe the DEQ instead of ours?"

"You convince them that ours are better. We're a non-profit and, therefore, have no agenda. The state departments always have conflicts of interest. To keep their tax dollars rolling in, they have to please the big industrial polluters, the recreation industry, and the farmers, who are the worst of all. We collect real data using real people. The state used scientists whose salaries are paid by taxpayers. Some of them think they deserve some sort of deference just because they live in the state and pay their taxes on time every year."

Grandy showed her a questioning look.

"I'm one of those people. And my experience with the Jovial River is that it's pretty darn clean. And none of these government reports shows anything different. Yours sure do. Sorry if I disagree with you."

"Our stats are true. And I like that you stood up for yourself. , but you're still wrong." She flashed her melting smile.

"Why?"

"Because we are beyond reproach. We answer to the rivers that are part of Magnificent Mother Earth, not the taxpayers. We dig deeper until we find the information that supports our theories. We know the truth, and we know it's hidden under a layer of deceit and wrong thinking. But more than that, we *are* the truth. It doesn't matter how we bring the earth back to perfection, only that we do.

That takes lots of work, and we're dedicated to doing that digging. We don't shy away from it, and neither should you. We use the scientific method. It's a lot tougher job than just taking samples and reporting the findings. We go the extra mile for the sake of Magnificent Mother Earth."

"But what if I can't convince the elected officials of that?"

Freedah shook her head and smiled, moving half of her green and red hair from behind her back across her breasts. "I can see you have a lot to learn. Always go with your strength, and your strength is to convince them that gambling with the river is wrong. Any type of gambling is wrong. That's why we need to go with a zero-tolerance policy. No gambling means no risk, and no risk means a clean river forever. That's what people want."

"I'm not sure everyone wants zero risk. Just getting up in the morning can be a risk."

"That's not a good argument. We're talking here about the future of the planet, a planet that would be a lot better off if a lot fewer people were around to get up every morning and spread all that risk around like it's some sort of pandemic."

Grandy paused as he wrote down that philosophy in his notebook. "So any risk aside from zero tolerance is unacceptable?"

"Now you're on the trolley." She smiled, patting his hand again.

"Seems like a pretty hard sell back in Michigan," he said.

"Don't worry. You'll be ready when the time comes. But if you have doubts, Grandy, are you sure you're worthy of our philosophy? We offer you personal blessings. Like that new suit, which, by the way, you look fantastic in, and your new apartment in Detroit --"

"Lansing."

"Whatever," she continued. "What about your nice salary? How about the chance to make a difference in the world, the chance to be influential? You really can be a savior of the world, you know. But you can't doubt at this point. It's up to you. Just keep studying with that in mind. Your god has a mission for you. Would you turn him or her down?"

"Of course not," he said, checking her eyes to see if she could really see his doubt. Her eyes had already bored into his soul, exposing many things, but it would be worth it. God didn't give her to him for nothing. With obedience came blessing.

"Well, then, let's move on. Now that we know our statistics are far superior to all the others, let's talk about the atmosphere in Jovial. What's the community like? What issues do people who live there have with the river? And how can we get them on our side? What can you tell me about it since you've had your boots on the ground there for so long?"

Grandy paused, wishing to appear thoughtful and perhaps a little deeper than he felt.

"Maybe you and I could start with these three stories that were just published during the last week in our local paper. They kind of summarize what's been going on with the reparations and such. I assume the reparations are key here since they came from Snowmaker's office."

Freedah rose from her side of the table and touched Grandy's arm as she took his phone when he'd found the links. She sat beside him instead of going back to the other side of the table.

"Would you be a dear and get us each a latte' while I read these?"

He obeyed, which was fortuitous, because when he saw Garit's byline, her face went pale.

She recovered in time to write down the name Tyson Mooring on her notepad in big, bold letters at the top of the page as if he were to become a new chapter in her book.

Grandy returned as she finished.

"So," she said, her pinkish glow returning. "Do you know this Tyson Mooring?"

"Yes. I led him to salvation while he was in prison."

She nodded. "When you go back to Detroit and start your lobbying –"

"Lansing."

"While you're doing that, I'm going to see if we can convince Tyson Mooring to join our efforts."

"Could be. He's really a good-hearted young man. Wants to do the right thing. The only thing I have against him is he sent money to my former church when I specifically asked him to send it to me. I couldn't have been more clear about that. Sometimes, the kid just won't listen."

"Good." She fell silent for a moment as she scrolled the stories on his phone.

"How about this Garit West?"

"I talked to him a few times for stories about the church. But I don't really know him except for his byline."

"Hmm," she said, nearly singing as she tapped a perfectly manicured finger against her lips. Her voice was always a song; one Grandy longed to learn.

Chapter 18

March 10

Having no experience with abundant money, Ty had not yet formed an understanding of its power. But, determined to learn when he awoke in the bunker, he retrieved his clothes from the long and winding clothesline outside the building. They were dry but still smelled of the water. To him, the smell was not unpleasant. Besides, they were the only clothes he owned. He packed up his other belongings in his tattered backpack, picked up all the fishing gear, for which he had not yet paid Ernie, and followed along the river to town.

His fuzzy memories from last night, after consuming too much alcohol with his old gang, reminded him that Todd had actually made sense for once.

"Why are you staying here, anyway?" Todd had demanded. "You should go to the casino and get a really nice room. You can easily afford it now."

"I could stay in Ernie's hotel a lot cheaper, and he doesn't have goons there watching for me."

"The casino cops won't even look twice at you. They let people with money do anything they want. When they see you, they'll know about your money just like everyone else after that story in the Sasser."

Because Todd was often wrong but never unsure, Ty decided, as he walked, to try the safe route first.

Ernie was not in the shop when Ty carefully arranged the fishing gear in a closet behind the restaurant's cash register, but there was a note in his mailbox. It was from Coney.

"Call me ASAP when you get a phone," it read. "It's about your property."

Ty pulled out his list of phone numbers, still damp and flimsy from the water, and wrote Coney's number to his list before he called on the store's land line. Jenn answered and told him he was invited for lunch at Fulton Gray's greenhouse complex.

It was still early, but stores were starting to open. Ty walked half a mile to the bank and got two blank checks with his account number hand-written on them by the clerk. His personal account checks had not yet been printed.

After another half-mile walk, he went into the Verizon store and bought a new iPhone. Actually, he bought a two-year plan that included the phone, for which the company would benevolently bill him every month until it was paid off.

With the phone uncomfortably stuffed into his back pocket, Ty walked up the hill to what the locals called Auto Alley. As he approached, a brand new Camaro caught his eye. He walked between it and the Corvettes, and he had to admit, he wanted one. Either one. Didn't matter. As long as it was brand new and fast. Or maybe a pickup was more his style.

As he peeked into the windows, his hands around his face to block the window reflection, a young man in a wool suit came behind him.

"I think what you're looking for is out back there," he said, smiling.

"I think this 'vette might be just what I'm looking for."

"I think you could much more easily afford something in the used category," the salesman pointed to the back.

"You think I can't afford this?"

"Let me ask you. Do you have a job?"

"No."

"Then how do you think you can afford monthly payments that could be as high as four-five hundred bucks a month, depending on your down payment?"

"How do you know I wasn't planning on paying cash for the whole thing?"

The salesman laughed. "No offense, uh, what was your name?" he reached out his hand, but Ty did not return the shake or say his name.

"I would love to put you in a car, sir, but I don't want to see someone like you getting underwater on payments. If we have to repossess it, nobody wins. You're out a vehicle, and we have to resell it for a lot less than we can sell it for now."

"So you think I can't afford anything but the junk out back?"

"Again, sir, no offense, but, well, people who look and smell like you generally buy a car for about two grand. This is upward of eighty."

Ty paused and looked at the man's name tag.

"Tell you what I'll do, uh, Billy. I'm going to walk across the street to the Ford dealer. You just stand here and watch what I drive off their lot. You just lost a big commission, Billy."

As he walked across the street, the Ford sales crew was sitting in the showroom window. It had been a very slow month, and by the looks of the young man walking toward them, it appeared that slow sales would continue. Damn, looky-loos.

Suddenly, one of the salesmen looked up from his phone and gasped.

"Do you know who that is?" No one did.

"That's Ty Mooring!" The sales crew looked with blank expressions.

"That's the guy that got three million bucks from that reparation!"

All five salespeople jumped up at once, fighting each other to get out the door, creating a kind of log jam in the door frame. The four men and one woman approached eagerly as Ty walked toward the pickups.

Ty, suddenly knowing he had power in the palm of his hand, looked past the four men and grinned at the woman, a 30-something brunette in a tight flower-patterned dress and large breasts.

"What's your name?" he asked. It was Brandy. She smiled and touched his arm, held it there.

Forty-five minutes later, Ty got a long, tight hug from Brandy and drove off the lot in his Ford 350 King Ranch pickup four-wheel drive. He'd written a check for $82,000, which Brandy told him was a steal.

He drove straight across the street and honked long and loud in the parking lot at the Chevy dealer until he saw Billy walk outside. Ty waved to him, sneered and drove off to Fulton's farm.

***

It was not yet noon, so Ty walked into the greenhouse and started picking up seed trays from a stack and placing them on a roller line. He was packing dirt into them, preparing the seeds for celery seed, when Coney called to him.

"Didn't call you to put you to work, but if you want, you can," he grinned. "But first things first. Come with me."

They went into the big pole barn's break room, where they found four large pizzas, salads, soda and plastic silverware. Already there, seated and eating, were Fulton Gray, Olie Hansel, Botsdorf and Noah Brenner. Each stood and shook Ty's hand, telling him to eat all he wanted.

When the pizza was about half gone and the salads a fifth gone, Ty was trying to understand his role. He understood little about the conversations going on, which were filled with statistics, acreage estimates and a common complaint of having too few workers.

Ty got up and took another slice and sat next to Coney.

"So, why am I here, Coney?"

"Because you're an owner, Ty. These folks are the executive board of the JFA, and they want to know what your plans are. Fulton is the only one here who has a lease on part of your ground, but these guys will all go back and fill in the rest. You're one of us now, Ty, whether you like it or not."

Ty pondered his new responsibilities, still confused when the door opened. A fit and thick, precisely proportioned woman with a button nose, sharp blue eyes, short dark hair and a wide, beaming smile stepped in.

"Hi, Melanie," Coney said, but her eyes were fixed on Ty. He smiled at her, and she turned away.

"Everyone, this is Melanie Swann, the head of PR for the state farmers association. She's here to brief us on this bill. And then, Ty, if you don't mind, we'd like to know your plans for that 100 acres of cropland. But first things first. We have a quorum of the board here, so it's an official meeting. Is that right, Bots?"

Botsdorf nodded and turned to yield the floor. "Melanie?"

She stood at the head of the break room table, capturing all their attention.

"Your old friend James Snowmaker is back," she said, holding a thick folder above her head. "He's suing you for polluting the river. See, as you know, according to House Bill 616, which we doubt could make it through the legislature, all he needs to seize the land is two filed lawsuits. Doesn't matter if they have any merit or if they ever go to trial. That's all written into the bill. This is his first suit, and we can all but guarantee he'll file another. It's what he does. He's trying to get ahead of the game. He's a very proactive man."

A low rumble moved through the farmers like distant thunder moving closer.

"He's also suing the state environmental agency and the Department of Natural Resources, and that may play to your advantage. All the state's statistics and data are on your side, and if this ever gets to court, they'll have to be on your side unless the

137

governor wants to back off and kick his own departments in the hind end."

"If there's one thing we know," said Olie Hansel, the fish farmer, "it's that this braying jackass of a governor will throw anybody under the bus, even his own staff. So none of those facts gives me a lot of confidence."

"Understood," Coney interjected. "But we have documented evidence from the state departments that have control over pollution – or think they do – that we've not contributed so much as a speck of dust to the river pollution in at least 10 years."

"They just make stuff up anyway," said Noah Brenner, a top-notch dairy farmer.

"But they can't do that in court and get away with it," Coney said.

"How do you know?"

"Because we have the evidence on our side," Coney said. "We can document with the state's own data that the Jovial River is one of the cleanest in the world, and it's been that way because we've been farming there, not in spite of it. The buffer strips have worked very well at keeping topsoil out of the river. Our precision farming methods and state-of-the-art weather stations all along the river have kept pesticides and fertilizer out of the water. If there is anything seeping in, it's too low to measure, and you all know that the state's standard on that is extremely low, like finding an eye-dropper of oil in a swimming pool. Our contribution to that kind of pollution is so low it can't even be found, and that's even after they moved the target to go to parts per million instead of parts per 100 thousand. Snowmaker and the MOEIB haven't got a leg to stand on."

"But it's still suing us," Fulton said as the rumble came back up. When it did, Ty felt an acrid pit in his stomach, though he didn't really know what it meant.

"We still have to spend our money to fight that shithead in court. Isn't there some kind of nuisance report we can file?

Botsdorf rose as Coney turned to him with an outstretched hand.

"We used to be able to do that, but in the governor's order that established MOEIB, he also made it immune to any lawsuit from anyone."

"That can't stand up in court, can it?" Noah asked.

"No, I don't think it could, but I also don't think you folks have the financial resources to fight it for the next 10 years. No, I think our best tactic is to try to get it all thrown out of court when we show that our statistics, along with the state's, match up and prove that how we farm does not contribute to pollution in the river. It should be easy to prove with the government's own statistics if we get a fair judge. And we all need to double down and be more careful than ever this year and not let the slightest particle of fertilizer seep into the river. They'll be watching us like cats at a mouse hole."

The rumbling resumed until Fulton stood and raised his hands to quiet the group.

"I believe we have to deal with the more immediate problem here," he said as he brushed back his long straight black hair. "We don't even know if we can farm the land this year or not since Snowmaker has given it all to Ty Mooring here." He gestured in a way Ty knew meant that he was invited to speak.

"First off," Ty said, wishing his knees would stop shaking as he stood and tried to steady his voice, "I had nothing to do with this. I was as surprised as anybody when I was informed that, for some reason I still don't understand, some state bureaucrats gave me 100 acres of riverfront property. I don't think I deserve it, and I sure never asked for it. And I worked for some of you when I was a kid. My mom and dad worked for some of you. I have nothing against any of you. At the same time, I love this community and this river. You gave my parents jobs and pretty good pay, after all. I still consider all of you and several other farmers to be my friends, not just employers. You've always treated me with respect and fairness, and I don't want to do anything to get in the way of that. I've driven sprayers. I've planted buffer strips. I've picked blueberries and strawberries and tree fruit. I've seen what this land can produce when it's taken care of this good. It's what I understand is called sustainability. And I respect you all for doing what you do. If it were me, heck, I'd probably have ignored all these state regulations and just gone and done things the way I wanted to. But you didn't. You followed the rules and spent the money even when you didn't have it. You went above and beyond the rules. So, I have no intention of taking that land away from you. I've spoken to both Coney and Botsdorf and have decided to honor the leases in place and keep you on this land for this year. Botsdorf has already started to draw up new lease agreements in my name with everyone who has farmed this property, and I won't increase the prices. As long as you keep this river clean, that's all I ask. I want to keep this river clean. Heck, I've been making my living fishing from it since I got out of jail, and I wouldn't harm it for anything. And I don't want to harm any of you, either. So go ahead and do what you need to do to plant this spring, and don't worry. I will honor every lease that's already in place. That gives me time to evaluate the impacts on the river. Then we'll talk next year when the leases are up. I'd like to strike a good balance between farmers and the river because you're both very valuable to me. And in case you didn't know, I'm doing all this on advice from Mr. Botsdorf."

The farmers stood as one and applauded.

"And as a token of my good faith," he said when the applause died, "Next week Friday, I want to invite you all to the casino bar for dinner and drinks. All on me. Invite your friends."

**

The day before he was to take a plane back to Lansing, Grandy had Freedah on his mind. He tried to expel her, but she wouldn't go away. Maybe it was her perfume, which he could still smell and hoped would never evaporate. He knew someone like him could never dream of being with someone like her, but it didn't hurt his mission at all to make her happy. Her influence was to be coveted, unlike wanting her beauty. One was a sin. One was not. At the moment, he didn't know which was which.

Too many times during their time together, he had to confess. He found himself looking into her eyes too long. He'd always broken the gaze first, his shame over being unworthy of her attention, much less affection, winning the day. He imagined that she probably thought how creepy he was, but she was too professional to let it show.

Still, it was her eyes that made him a believer. Those crystal-blue windows would always sparkle, even when a few laugh lines appeared in time, and she would look even better. If that were possible.

He shook off the longing. He knew idiocy when he saw it, especially in himself. But she could take him places if he'd continue finding favor in her eyes. Places God wanted him to go. All the evidence pointed to that. His expulsion from the church, his new plush apartment, and this trip to the other side of the country. That could be nothing more than God's favor and approval of his decision. Even if hearing her say 'well done' was all he'd ever get from her, it would be enough. Enough to motivate him to do God's work, to help Him fix the planet with all his heart. His mission was as pure as her beauty, and he was blinded by it; A blissful blind man whose eyes had been opened. And Freedah was the first thing he saw when he blinked. Her eyes seemed to flow like northern lights, shifting blue to green, an unpredictable wildness in them that exuded wisdom and mischief in one enigmatic magnetism.

He wondered what it was like in the Old Testament when conquered kings had their eyes put out after seeing their children killed. He wondered if any were ever given a choice, by benevolence or begging, to see something beautiful as their last sight. He would pick Freedah, even if she were dressed in a winter parka, as long as he could remember the unbroken gaze into her eyes as he died.

He'd learned fast under her watchful eye. And while some of the tactics of MELL were a bit distasteful at first, she'd convinced him. The rivers were at a tipping point. All the MELL statistics said so, and no amount of contrary evidence would change that. The ends justified the means, just like God, who could save people by hurting them. He told himself he believed that, but it still didn't make sense to him.

His best tactic right now was to make an impression on MELL and Freedah.

So, knowing that fundraising was not his job but not prohibited, and knowing he was as good a fundraiser as anyone else, Donald Grandersma made some calls back home and found Ty Mooring's new mailing address. The day before, with all this in mind, he'd picked up some extra packets of information about river pollution, full of statistics and carefully worded information, and now, he sent one to Ty's address in Jovial. With it, he sent a note saying: "I saw that you generously gave to my former church. I asked you to send it to me. All is forgiven. But with your future philanthropy, consider MELL. I know you love the river, so put your wealth to good use and a worthy cause. Here are some hard facts about the dangers of gambling with the river. – Reverend Repent."

Chapter 19

Freedah's plane landed in Detroit, and she bypassed the luggage claim and went to the rental car desk. She hadn't flown with anything but a single carry-on bag for more than a year, mostly because she rarely stayed in one place too long, aside from San Francisco. Part of her job was to be ready to go at a moment's notice when abrupt thrills and challenges came along. She'd earned the confidence the MELL board had in her when they sent her drifting from fire to fire, stomping on smoldering embers or stoking them into multi-colored flames, whichever she deemed necessary. The board of directors at MELL trusted her to know which action to take at which time. She'd put out fires in every division MELL had, from real estate to public relations to lobbying. She was best at public relations, but good at them all.

"I'm sorry, ma'am, but all the Teslas are already rented," the clerk said, hoping this woman's attitude was as pretty as her face.

"I ordered one yesterday!" She stared at him and pouted, "I only drive Teslas. Because of the planet, you know? Do you understand that? Or don't you midwesterners know about Majestic Mother Earth?"

"I do understand, but it's out of my control. There just isn't one available. We'd be happy to refund your money."

"That's not the point," she shouted, then waited dramatically as every head within 25 yards turned to hear, then focused to see her. "I've never been more betrayed, inconvenienced, and disgusted. You corporate bosses will hear about this!"

When she'd calmed down, Freedah settled for the only vehicle available, a monstrous Dodge Grand Caravan that rode like a tank. She got in, slammed the door, and fumed as she began her four-hour drive to Jovial.

Majestic Mother Earth would never recover from human excess as long as such vehicles were allowed to roam the earth like rampaging herds of elephants destroying whole villages. Damn elephants. Too cute not to use them for an effective environmental message, but too stupid to know they should have died out with the dinosaurs. One of God's biggest mistakes, if she believed in such a thing. Her faith had been taken away by soft but exploring clergy's hands, and she wouldn't ask for reparations. They were for the weak.

Of course, the elephants' biggest problem, the one that would lead them to extinction, was they lacked a solid public relations campaign. If only the elephant sycophants had come to her sooner, she could have shown them the way to a thriving life. She could have made people really care about elephants, enough to pay for the emotion, but it was too late. They would go extinct, no matter what the statistics said about their continued survival.

Her mind settled on a familiar train of thought. She was underappreciated back at MELL, but being overlooked because of her looks was nothing new to her. She assumed her attractiveness made even the progressives at MELL believe she was all beauty and no brains. Misogyny was ingrained into male society. She'd proven people wrong about her talent her whole life, but few would admit she was as smart as she was attractive. But she was more determined now than ever before. There was a lot to prove, and not just to MELL. There were still many things she needed to prove to herself, even after all the rewards she had earned. One thing about Majestic Mother Earth was that she was ambivalent sometimes. Not God-style ambivalent. No, more human than that. Her mistakes were what endeared Freedah to her. And her inability to forgive. She could be just as stubborn, were prizes given out.

She pulled into a gas station somewhere in the middle of barren, useless farmland to fill up, take a break, and buy some bottled water. This rural scenery, still and cold as winter finally faded away, was disgusting. Wasted land. If she'd learned anything from her life in the city, it was that food could be gotten anywhere, so farmland was just a wasteland waiting for development. Open spaces were obsolete, but these rednecks held on to them as if they owned them.

A McDonald's restaurant was attached to the fueling station like so many bad things were tied to necessary things in America. If she had anything to say about it, someday soon, there would be no need for gasoline, that planet-destroying slave driver. But that wasn't her greatest concern. During her early days at MELL, before she'd proven her loyalty and avoided a firing by changing her name to Freedah Forest and dying her hair editors ink red, she'd been a rising star in the fight to eliminate farming from the nation. Animal agriculture, in particular, was loathsome to her, and she was about to enter its world and immerse herself in it for the first time. Sometimes, things had to be handled from the inside, and no one had yet denied her entrance into various worlds.

Though she'd never been on a farm other than her community's sparse urban garden, she knew they were inhumane. She'd seen the edited videos, and she edited them more for optimum impact. No sense in giving her MELL supporters wiggle room for empathy toward farmers. Rich Republican bastards. Planet killers. She'd read all the literature on both sides of the issue, as diverse as Huffington Post to PETA. They all agreed. Farmers are hateful, conservative, gun-toting, ignorant hicks. That much was evident. She didn't have to actually meet a farmer to understand that. She didn't know any elephants, either, but she knew they needed her help.

As she ate her McDonald's salad – the only thing remotely vegan on the whole corporate money-grubbing, planet-destroying, greed-mongering menu, she reread the article that had lit the fire that brought her here.

It had taken little effort to convince Phoenix that she could manipulate the writer Garit West. Freedah had a long list of reporters she'd spit out like sunflower seed shells. But he couldn't be the same one she'd known. It was too common a name. Besides, the Garit she knew grew up in Illinois – or was it Ohio? And he had never struck her as the kind of man who moved too far from home permanently. His sense of adventure had never even come close to what she longed for, and her time with him had been a complete waste. They'd just never seen eye-to-eye on things. That was why she'd left him.

She shook his memory out of her head when she realized he had left her, and that realization, even after these two years or so, was still unacceptable. He was the only blemish on her record. She sneered at the thought. She'd not given him much thought when he'd left her. The high life had been much more important then. But now, thanks to a little patience, she was about to meet him again, and that required long-dormant vengeance. The score needed to be tied and then turned in her direction. She smiled as she finished her salad. Many a successful PR campaign had vengeance as its foundation, its motivator, as it should be.

The smell of burning animal flesh brought her back to the present. It was making her sick. Cannibals.

She got back into the van and looked at the notes she had made during the four-hour flight. Her strategy was pretty sound unless this Ty Mooring was gay, and no one with teeth as tangled as his could be gay.

She pulled into Jovial as the sun was lowering itself into the lake. Which lake, she didn't remember. It was big, anyway, but it smelled different than the San Francisco Bay. She selected a room available on the top floor, among the priciest they had, and checked in. With the printed article in hand, folded so it showed only Ty's somber but pleasant, unsmiling face, she walked through the slot machines, knowing that recent windfall recipients often could blow it all in a very short time. The timing here could be crucial.

She walked by the craps tables. Nothing. The blackjack tables. No one even resembled a snaggle-toothed, skinny young man who would be putty for a girl like her. Nothing at the slots.

She slipped into one of many casino rest rooms and checked herself in the mirror. Her hair, now a bright red in the casino's artificial light, was perfect, accented by streaks of forest green. Her petite clip-on nose ring looked like the real thing, showing that she'd endured pain for the cause of her righteousness. Her tight t-shirt, plain and white, clung to her unbridled breasts.

Perfect. The MELL leaders would be proud, as always, that she was on their team. Her arms were long and tanned and smooth. Her jeans shorts were also tight and allowed her already tight buns to lift into an irresistible shape. She was ready. But where was this idiot millionaire?

The weariness of flying was catching up to her. She wanted, as much as possible, to always be alert and at the top of her game. But as she headed back to her room to shake off the jet lag, she passed one of the casino bars and heard a loud celebration going on.

She stepped into the room, and as her eyes adjusted to the light, she saw a large gathering in the center of the room, six or eight tables pulled together and full of happy, likely oblivious people, both men and women, drinking freely from the six or more pitchers of beer spread across the table.

She sat at the bar and observed. Every guy in the place looked her over. Normally, she'd have taken a few photos on her phone. Postings about farmers getting drunk and carrying on in a casino could be used against them, and Twaddle – the newest and growing social media site that she'd launched – was the perfect platform. But now was not the time. She was too irresistible to take photos or videos without someone noticing. She watched as a waitress set two more pitchers on the celebrants' table, and she watched a young man slip a $50 bill into her hand. And then he turned, the last one at the table to do so amid the whispers from his male friends, and did a double-take at her. She focused on his eyes, knowing that was her easy access to any man she'd ever wanted, and, without breaking his gaze from hers, she lifted her bottle of water. He lifted a full mug of beer back at her and hid his smile with his other hand. Then he turned his attention back to his entourage. She was in. Just a matter of time. No one resisted her for long.

Chapter 20

James Snowmaker was growing impatient, as was common during the staff meetings he mandated every Friday morning. But it was worse today. He had a plane to catch, a plane back to San Francisco and away from this swampy, soon-to-be mosquito-ridden Michigan, the place that had so gullibly yet smartly granted him so much power.

The last agenda item, however, was of particular interest, and he was anxious to get Ty Mooring on the calendar.

"Okay," he said, looking at his watch. "Last up. Have we contacted our reparations guy?"

"His name is Tyson Mooring, a descendant of migrant workers, of course, but the last one – and only one – we could find," a staffer said. "That makes it all quite easy from an accounting standpoint. He's kind of a poor young man who has spent time in prison."

"I already knew his name. But I'm glad you got the background on him. He seems perfect. A downtrodden Hispanic who's already suffered under the slavery of migrant labor and the racism that got him put in prison."

"No, he was legitimately in prison," another staffer said. "Tried to scam the lottery system."

"Perfect again! Just a little brown man trying to make it in a Lilly-white system that's so stacked against him that he has to gamble. He's a victim. The perfect profile of who we want to showcase. Good job, folks. Now, do we have the press event scheduled with Mr. Tyson Mooring, Mexican con-man?"

"Not yet," said a senior PR staffer. "We finally got hold of him through snail mail to a bait shop, but he moves around a lot, apparently, being natural for him because of his migrant past, but he told us he doesn't want any big press event."

"I don't give a damn what he wants. If he wants our money, he's going to have to play by our rules."

"You can't force someone to appear," the staffer replied humbly.

"Bullshit!" Snowmaker rose from his chair. "This is not about some scrawny Mexican who got lucky. This is about MOEIB and its very survival. We don't just give away five million bucks and let it be quiet. Hell, half the reason he got the money was to keep our department in the public eye. Why would he refuse it?"

"We don't know, but we'll keep working on it," the staffer said.

"You do that. I have a plane to catch. When I get back, I expect to see a giant check and a date when we can get this jackass on the stage in front of the press. We don't do *everything* in this department in secret, you know. The public has the right to know about the good things we do."

As Snowmaker waited to board his plane, he made a call to Phoenix Tippin.

"We're delayed in our press conference for the reparations Mexican," Snowmaker said. "Apparently, this kid needs some convincing. Shy. Typical stupid Midwest fake humility."

"Don't worry. He'll change his mind soon enough. We got Freedah working on him."

Snowmaker chuckled into the phone. "That eases my mind quite a bit. I'll be in town by tonight."

Chapter 21

March 14

Freedah sat alone at the bar, her back to the raucous crowd at Ty's table of benevolence. Wonderful invention, the bar mirror. She could keep track of things behind her without appearing interested and, at the same time, check herself often to be sure she was perfect before she made her move.

She finished the bottled water she'd brought from the San Francisco airport and ordered an ice water. What would Michigan water, polluted as it must be by farm chemicals, taste like? Before she'd gotten three sips from it and noticed no adverse effects, the bartender set down a fancy purple drink with a straw and umbrella in it, separating three kinds of fruit wedges on the glass edge.

"Compliments of some smitten fella over at that table." She smiled, and the bartender, too, found himself smitten.

Without tasting the drink, she turned to face the table of revelers. Garit's stories had made her certain that Ty was shy. She'd read them all several times, just to be sure. And, dammit, Garit was better than ever. She had this knack of reading between the lines to see what was real. Especially his prose. He revealed himself to her through his pen years ago, and he still couldn't hide.

"This would be easier than she thought. She could conquer demurity with a furtive glance or less. Instead of Ty, however, Todd raised his glass of beer toward her and smiled as if she were a bet he couldn't lose. She didn't respond. Todd got up and approached her, stumbling forward as his companions started a quick gambling pool. Five minutes was the longest he was expected to last with that girl.

"Hey, gorgeous. I sent you the fanciest drink they serve here because you are the fanciest woman I've ever seen. It's also the most expensive and strongest drink in the house. But yet, you don't seem to like it. What's wrong?"

"Depends." She looked away from him and fixed her gaze on a distant object. "Who paid for it?"

"I did, of course."

Doubt it. You're here mooching off someone else."

"C'mon, little hottie." Todd reached his hand to her, and Freedah smirked. Todd's bravado was slipping fast. "What does it matter? I can show you the best time you've ever had."

"Doubt it. You don't look capable of showing me even a bad time, and you'll never get the chance. I buy drinks like this for a warm-up, a palette cleanser."

"Oh, so you're too good for me?"

"That's right."

"Ain't you stuck up!" She didn't respond as he expected. It was his best line, too. She didn't respond at all. She didn't even look at him. Most women would try to prove they weren't arrogant, but this babe was different. Her confidence was like hardened mud, and Todd knew she was unattainable, though he'd never admit it.

Todd slinked away as she turned her back to him. He returned to the table and the friends who had watched him fail and were now passing money between them.

"She's stuck up. Thinks she's all that."

"Well, she is," said a person at the table. "She's way out of your league, Todd. The only thing that influences a girl like her is money. What else could she possibly need? Look at her, Todd. Do you think she needs guys like you to buy her drinks? She's probably never had to buy her own drinks in her life. That makes her mysterious, which makes her even hotter. The proof is that your money ain't nothing to her." The young men at the table laughed at Todd's expense, and Todd wanted to change the subject fast.

He suggested that the gang he'd brought along go into the casino and try to make some money. When they filed out, Freedah turned to face the smaller crowd enjoying Ty's largess. It was an older crowd now, and Ty was in earnest conversation. Freedah called the bartender over and ordered three pitchers of beer for the table. When it got there, Ty protested.

"I didn't order another round."

"Complements of the lady at the bar." the waitress pointed.

Ty turned around to see Freedah, and to his surprise, his first thought was that God was an amazing artist. First sunrises, then fireflies, and now her.

As his eyes watered at her aura, he calculated the odds of lingering in her company. He lifted a glass to her, hoping she wouldn't notice that his hand was shaking as his other hand covered his mouth. Adrenaline warmed him like the sun on a calm stretch of river. She lifted her fruity drink, still untasted, set it down, and sipped her water.

Encouraged mockingly by a couple of giggling females at the table, Ty turned again and waved. She feigned cluelessness, looked behind her and then back at him, pointed to herself, and mouthed, "Me?"

Ty nodded and waved her over. She smiled and sashayed to him, sat down next to him, and introduced herself, gripping his hand in both of hers and holding them gently long after the appropriate time.

"I thought that guy would never leave." She touched Ty's arm.

"You mean Todd? He's harmless enough."

"I like to play it safe. And it's you I wanted to meet, but to tell you the truth, you're not what I expected."

"What did you expect?"

"Oh, I don't know." She pulled the newspaper article out of her small, stylish purse and handed it to Ty.

"I guess I expected a Hispanic, but that doesn't really matter. I like interesting people, unique people, no matter their race. People with passion intrigue me."

Ty glanced at the article, knowing all about it.

"You mean you like interesting people who have money?"

"What are you talking about?"

"Come on, girl. The article clearly points out the millions I just got."

"First," she smiled, "You'll find out soon enough that I'm no girl. If I were, I'd be looking for a man to make me a woman." Ty blushed. She didn't, but at the moment when his face was reddest, she knew exactly which pitch was coming down the middle, belt high.

"Second, money doesn't matter when a man is interesting, and I'm a collector of interesting people. I promote them. I make them famous."

"Believe me, I'm not all that interesting. Not worth collecting."

"What do you mean? A man who's been in prison, turned his life around, and then is the first person in this state to get a reparation payment? That's interesting. Especially when the reparations, as I understand it, are supposed to go to a Hispanic."

"But I am Hispanic. Half, anyway. Dad was an American, and Mom was Mexican.

"How interesting." Freedah leaned closer to him. "But there was something else if I remember. Your passion for rivers."

"Not really a passion. I just like the Jovial. Grew up fishing it, living near it. I could sit and watch it and listen to it all day."

"Me too. There's something about rivers that make me almost believe in a higher power, you know? But we all know that rivers need help sometimes."

"Really? I always thought rivers could take care of themselves."

"That's an interesting conclusion but ill-informed, Tyson. Rivers need our help, and the best help is from interesting, passionate people who understand and act when it's in their power to do something. You have that power."

"You think so?"

"Of course you do. You mean you've never even considered that a man like you, with an opportunity, maybe even a duty, to help the river, can do great things? Powerful things? Things that restore our environment the way it was supposed to be?"

"How is it supposed to be?"

"Interesting," she said, smiling again. Each smile was becoming more irresistible. "And clean. And perfect."

"Perfection is a pretty tall order. Unless we're talking about beautiful women, and you sure fit that description."

"Does that make a difference to you?"

"Attraction? Sure. And that's why I have to wonder why you think I'm so interesting. I'm not exactly in your league."

"I live in a league of my own." She reached under the table to gently pat his knee. "But you can join it. Because it's my league, I can invite whoever I want."

"And you're inviting me why? Because I'm so interesting?"

"Exactly. You have something to offer this world, and I can bring that to the surface."

"How?"

"You'll just have to wait and see. I've never met an interesting man yet who I couldn't bring out the best in if he'd let me. Let me prove it to you."

Ty gazed into her eyes, mesmerized by their clear beauty and sincere, perfect blue irises in a pool of fresh, thick milk. Suddenly intimidated by them, Ty broke the trance and looked up. He stood and shouted toward the bar entrance.

"Garit," he shouted. "Over here!"

Freedah looked up and immediately turned her back to the door and reached straight between Ty's legs. She gave his crotch a slow, gentle stroke. She leaned to whisper in his ear.

"I'm a little jet-lagged. Let's continue this conversation in private. Come on up when you're done here. I'll be waiting. I'll leave my room number and key card at the front desk." Keeping her back to the front entrance, she slipped away, sailing on a breeze that only she could create.

***

When the party broke up, and Ty and Garit had discussed a few things, Ty still had a lilt in his step. Knowing Freedah was waiting was enough to make him run a hundred-meter dash and win it, if it were true. If she was really waiting for him in a high-end hotel suite. Must be some kind of pig event, he thought. Hot girls didn't go for guys like him unless they were on a bet. He'd been a victim before. The ugliest date wins the prize for the girl who brought him. But something drove him on. Her aura, her smile, her body. It would be worth it to be humiliated if he could spend one hour with her.

He took the wide, winding stairs down to the lobby and inquired at the desk.

'"We have a message waiting for you, Mr. Mooring," the clerk said and retrieved a hand-written note and a key card.

"Room 1212," it said. "Freedah."

***

The top-floor suite was more than Ty had imagined. His key card slid in, and the door popped open to a massive space, larger than any he'd been in before. The drapes had been pulled back, and in the morning, the massive window would reveal a stunning scene of forests, the river, and part of Jovial's southern edge. The place was spotless except for pieces of women's clothing that seemed to make a path or directional arrows toward another room. It was even better than he'd imagined. He'd expected opulence, but this was closer to decadence. And he liked it.

He walked in. She was waiting on the bed, holding a satin sheet to her chest, letting it fall between her legs so that only her thighs were exposed.

Freedah leaned forward, holding the sheet just so, revealing skin so close to paradise that Garit was dumbstruck.

"So, how do you like the suite? I had a feeling you might like the best of the best. That seems to be the kind of guy you are."

"How would you know that?"

"I know you deserve the best after some of the things you've been through. But maybe you're still afraid to go after it. That's why I canceled your little one-bedroom room and upgraded you. You never would have done that on your own. I know that much."

"I don't deserve anything."

She adjusted herself, then sat cross-legged on the bed.

"You deserve the best. You don't just deserve a car; you deserve a Cadillac. Not just a room but this suite. Not just some girl, but me. I'm here to push you to go after what you deserve."

Ty reached to the nightstand and retrieved the newspaper article Garit had written.

"You think you know me from one article?" Freedah sensed defensiveness in his voice, which challenged her and excited her.

"I'm a very perceptive person. I'm very selective. I knew from the start, from the minute I saw your story in the local paper, that you're the kind of man who can make a difference in the world. And I'm never wrong about such things. You want to make a splash, to make the world better somehow. You want to make a difference. So do I."

"So it's not about the money?"

"Money is just a tool." She pulled him by the hand down to the bed, where she placed her hand on his chest. "It's how people use it that makes it better."

"I think my world is better already, and I haven't spent a dime." He stared into her eyes, which contained promises he never thought he could imagine, things that he could never earn.

"I will admit I've always wanted to see one of these penthouse suites, though. Never thought I'd share it with someone like you without paying a big price."

"Awe, you're sweet," she cooed. "But you know, there is a cause that really does deserve the best. It's bigger even than me."

"Are you talking about God?"

"The river." Ty adjusted himself to sit more upright, his back against the pillows and headboard.

"What about the river?"

"It's endangered, you know, just like all rivers. But this one is special. It's so clean, so much the lifeblood of this community."

"I guess it's pretty obvious if someone who's only been here a few hours can see it."

"Very obvious. And I know you have passion for it, too."

"Always have." Ty suddenly felt confident now that his feelings really could be described as passion. Having spent just enough time in Freedah's passion to know he wanted to go deeper, he knew a lot more about passion now than he did just an hour earlier. She deserved all he could give her already, so he began trying to exude confidence and commitment.

"I grew up on it, fished it since before I can remember. Its value is way beyond economics. It just is. It exists and seems happy to just be, to trust in its Maker that it will live in glory and fury and peace and anger, sometimes all at the same time."

"Sounds like you've thought about this river for a long time."

"Yep. It's given me a lot. It's given a lot of people more than it knows or that mere mortals can ever imagine. No matter how much people try to change it, it just keeps rolling on. It knows what it is, and its content just being a river. And, apparently, to fulfill its purpose."

"You're so … poetic," she cooed. "But eventually, she will need human help to keep on rolling."

"Doubt it. Kind of arrogant, don't you think, when a person thinks he or she has power over a river?"

"It's not a power thing, Ty. It's more like a helping hand. A preemptive action, like restoring a battered piece of antique furniture before it loses its solid bones. It needs to be preserved before people try to change it. You know as well as I do that even if they can't change it for the better, they sure can screw it up."

"Can't argue with that," he said as she pulled him up for a gentle kiss.

"You have the power to prevent people from screwing it up."

"How's that?"

"Your money. It's power. But only if it's used wisely, as an influencer."

"All the money in the world won't stop people from doing stupid things. But I have been thinking a lot about how to use it. The only thing I know for sure is that I'm not supposed to use it for myself."

"And that's why you have such power. Did you ever wonder why it was you who got the money instead of someone – anyone – else?"

"I do believe I was given a huge responsibility by getting so much out of the blue, and I sure don't want to shirk that responsibility. I owe God all that and plenty more."

"So you're into God?"

"Well, yes, I suppose I am, but I don't really understand him."

She lifted her head from his chest. "Who can? That's why I left him. He's too demanding. We're supposed to worship him and give him our money. Why? Is he so insecure that he craves attention from little puny humans?"

"Never thought of it that way. But again, I'm just getting started. I can't understand most of what I've read in the Bible."

Freedah sat up straight, unembarrassed by her nakedness.

"I can help you with that. I can show you things in the Bible that might help you understand why I think Majestic Mother Earth is the better god."

"You know the Bible?"

"Oh, god, yes," she said, grinning. "I was raised up with all that malarkey. Don't get me wrong, there are some really cool things in there. Some good poetry and even some good stories, although they're likely untrue. There's even a bunch of stuff about romance."

"No kidding. Like what?" He asked to be polite, but he was caught between patience and lust and felt like an ox being led to slaughter, yet anxious to get on with things he couldn't control. He was ready to give control to her.

She got up from the bed and checked the drawers in the room's polished oak furniture. "I'll show you a passage that talks about me and you particularly, and ways that show me that God – or the universe or karma or whatever – smiles on a new relationship like the one we just started." She found a Gideon bible and paged through it as she returned to the bed, smooth as the sheets in this high-end room.

"Let's see," she said as she sat facing Ty. "I think it was in Song of Solomon." She turned to Proverbs 7 and skipped verses 1-13.

"Here it is." Her cadence slowed. "This is why God will bless our relationship: Solomon describes a young lover saying: 'I have peace offerings with me; today I have paid my vows, so I came out to meet you, diligently to seek your face, and I have found you. I have spread my bed with tapestry colored coverings of Egyptian linen. I have perfumed my bed with myrrh, aloes, and cinnamon. Come, let us take our fill of love until morning; let us delight ourselves with love.'"

She stopped reading, paused, and looked heavenward. "See? This is profound poetry. And it all means that God loves lovers."

"And you've chosen me? And if I choose you back, it's what God wants?"

"That's right. You've been chosen by the cosmos to be the one to use all these things you've been given. That includes me, your money, and your passion for the river. I'm just the messenger. You have the power. You have responsibility now. It's interesting. You are the chosen one, whether you believe it or not. I believe it."

"And I'm a little embarrassed by it all. I didn't do anything to deserve it, and now that I have it, people treat me differently."

"Where? On social media?"

"I don't care one bit about that crap. Never been on it and never will be. But maybe I can change local minds about me. By giving something back. So what do you suggest?"

She sat up, excited. "Come to San Francisco with me." She rubbed his shoulders with her soft, salving touch. His eyes never left her gently bouncing breasts.

"I don't know. What's there?"

"What's not there? The whole world is there. And I have a job I have to get back to, you know."

"And when are you coming back?"

"That depends. If you go with me, maybe I can convince you that when we come back, we'll be in a position to change the world."

"With the money!" Ty said, as a statement, not a question.

"Oh, I don't know. She feigned hurt or betrayal, whichever would work best. "Maybe a small donation to help get things started with MELL. They're the right people to save this river before it's too late, and we can be major players in this river, for sure. Probably a whole lot more. We can save rivers nationwide."

"With a small donation to start." His sarcasm took Freedah off guard. By now, her touch and sensuous moves, her kisses, and her eyes would have exorcised a man of his cynicism. She'd thought this would be quick and easy. She had not expected this snaggle-toothed hick to be a challenge, but it thrilled her. It had been a long time since she was truly challenged.

She turned away from him as if offended. When she turned her face to his again, she appeared hurt, and her eyes contained just a hint of mist. He was instantly saddened and repentant.

"Is that what you really think of me?" Her voice broke just enough to begin melting his guard. "Look, I'm not after your money. I'm going to give myself to you, and that's not an accident or a common thing. I didn't ask you for anything before you came up here, did I? You're just a generous, passionate, interesting, and handsome man, and sometimes I think even you don't know the power you have. You – and only you – can make a difference in the world. You're in the right place at the right time. That's providence. That means the universe has chosen you for a task and me to help you begin and end that task. We were both put in this time and place for a reason, you know. At least, you should know it if you're a Christian, like this article says you are. And the Jovial River is just the start. You can save rivers all over the world if you want. But start here."

"I definitely want to make a difference." He nestled her face in his hands. He wiped the slightest tear from her left eye. "Especially if it means you'll be with me."

"I can be. You and I, together." She sat up suddenly as if extremely excited. "Come with me and we can take your message to the whole country." She leaned down again and pressed her breasts against his side. "Join with MELL. They have the resources to get things done. And believe me, they need it. Even a small contribution from you could really make a difference. They – and me – can make you a star."

Ty frowned. "MELL can take your message all around the nation," she said. "You – you with your handsome face and altruistic, interesting message – can be the face of the Jovial River.

"Don't know that I want fame. But I can make a donation. The farmers who have been taking care of the river so well for generations could use a fund to keep up with the costs. Rivers and farmers are the best cause I can think of right now, but then, all I've been thinking about since we met is you. You don't leave a fella much room for anything else."

"You deserve the fame, Tyson. It's yours for the taking. Not everybody in this world gets that chance. And some people have fame for the wrong reasons. But you and your cause are pure, unadulterated. You can be a positive influence, and doesn't God want that for you? Besides, good causes don't just market themselves. They have to have a face, a spokesperson, and you're perfect for the role. I can help you get a little more polished, maybe. Get you a little dental work. Definitely new clothes. But I believe this is your destiny. I know you believe in God. Don't you think He would want you to be a champion for God's natural environment? You're destined for greatness, Ty. I know it without a doubt. I'm never wrong about interesting people. I have a sixth sense, a real talent for things like this. And I can help you, not because of any amount of money but because I believe in you. I wouldn't have come all this way from San Francisco if I had any doubts. And, not to be too prideful, but as a statement of fact, I'm damn good at it. I might even be the best PR person who ever lived. How can you turn down a chance like this?"

"I'll have to think about that for a while. But in the meantime, I guess it wouldn't hurt to check this MELL out a little. How much do you think you'll need?"

"Let's talk details later." She moved close enough that he could feel her heat as she began to unbutton his shirt. They didn't speak again about money until after she confessed her blasphemy.

Chapter 22

March 15

As her breathing returned to normal, she rolled toward him and forced a heavy, overstuffed hotel pillow under her elbow. She tossed her shoulder-length bi-colored hair behind her face with an elegant flip of her sleek neck and leaned, her head like a bookend, on one palm. The other hand rested on his smooth, hairless chest as her fingernails made circles on his skin.

"So you say you're a Christian. What's that like?"

"Don't really know quite yet." He took a deep breath and turned his face to hers. "I'm new to all this. Still learning. But I guess it must work because a week after I was baptized, I got a letter from the state saying they wanted to give me three million bucks. And then, not long after that, I find you. It's all working out pretty well, I'd say. What about you? You said you're a 'mana'?"

"Yes, but that's just an old term from the Polynesians. You know, culturally appropriated by capitalists and Westerners? There's no English word that can capture the whole philosophy. It's different for everyone, kind of like people. No two are alike. And since no two are alike, I believe people need to develop their own individual morality and truth, don't you? You know, believe in themselves? Like me, being a real earth person requires a lot of self-reflection. And even your Christian God says to work out your own salvation."

"That's in the Bible?"

"Yep."

"I guess that makes sense. I mean, we all have to follow our hearts, right?"

"I'll tell you a secret." Her voice turned to a whisper. "This might be blasphemy, but sometimes Majestic Mother Earth is an unreliable, two-faced bitch." She paused, inhaled deeply and moved her face closer as if apostasy was a precious, stolen morsel. "It's why she needs people like me, to keep her image polished and even scrape off some crust and crud now and then. But when it comes right down to it, we're all out here, fending for ourselves, making our own way."

"And what's your way, Freedah?"

She pulled herself up to a sitting position.

"I'm a public relations expert." Ty instantly recognized her increasing enthusiasm. "It was a path I found all by myself, and if I do say so myself, I'm very good. I've made politicians change their minds and their votes. I can be very convincing."

"I can see that, yes."

"I've turned run-of-the-mill musicians into rock stars. I can do it for anybody. Their only obligation is they must really want it. I don't tolerate hypocrisy or less than full effort. If someone gives me everything, I can give them everything right back."

"And how do you do that?"

"I make it a point to only represent people and causes that know just how important they can be. And I think you might be just on the edge of knowing that the universe has chosen you. I know it all seems random right now, but look at the evidence. Money. Me. Your freedom. It's not really a coincidence. Some force somewhere – maybe it was Mother Earth, maybe it was karma, maybe it was even your God, I don't know. But I do know that together, we can make a difference. C'mon, Ty. Let me prove it to you. We can go on one hell of a ride, you and me."

"Leading where?"

"That's up to you and me. Mostly me. The only thing I know right now is this feels right." She kissed him quickly.

She leaned back and looked into his eyes, which were fixed like a rusted lug nut on her perfect face.

"I have to admit, you feel pretty good."

She felt better than anyone he'd ever known, but he wouldn't let her know. Not yet. "Imagining life with you sounds pretty good, too, but I don't know about all this earth-person stuff. I don't want to turn into some crazy activist or something."

"Activists aren't made, they're born. My job is to make them more effective. And what greater cause is there than the earth? I mean, three million bucks doesn't mean a thing to Majestic Mother Earth. At least not right now. But it could mean a lot to her in the end when she's rescued from the clutches of polluters like farmers who stuff their animals into cages and beat them just for fun."

He pulled himself up and rested his back against the walnut headboard.

"First, farmers do believe in caring for their animals and the earth, and they don't beat animals for fun. What possible profit could there be in that? Farmers are the original and still only practical environmentalists. But I still don't get your philosophy. I mean, you've been talking about it for hours now, and I still don't understand. Where's the objective truth, the foundation? Where's the evidence?"

Her eyes sparkled away from him with contemplation, and she shifted her gaze back to him like a patient cat that spotted sudden movement. "Funny, a Christian asking for evidence. At least, I admit there is no evidence of God. Truth is never objective. It can't be. Truth changes from day to day, you know, just like people's moods. And Majestic Mother Earth, despite her moods, is less confusing than your so-called Christian truth. She's a lot less judgmental than Jesus. I mean, you gotta admit that, right?"

"Don't try to convert me." He was trying to appear less pliable than she'd already made him, and couldn't know if it was working. But he was caught between two philosophies, both strange and new to him.

"Truth is the ultimate goal, right? It's something I've been searching for since my baptism without much luck. I'm just not sure the earth is where we can find truth. At least not all of it. It seems kind of, I don't know, fleshy to me. The earth doesn't even seem to know that people are taking advantage of it for their own greed because the earth is a physical thing, not a spiritual one. But now that I know you have doubts, too, I guess we have more in common than I could have guessed."

"Doubts are not uncommon. I've been tempted more than once to turn my back on the crazy earth aura thing. Happens when I get in one of my moods. Not that Majestic Mother Earth doesn't deserve rejection now and then. Keeps her on her giant toes, you know. But it isn't her fault she's been tangled up in the bear traps humans have set out for her. She needs our help, whether she's worthy of it or not. Sometimes, she doesn't even seem to notice. Ungrateful old witch."

"So why are you so faithful to it?"

"Please." She removed her hand from his chest as if offended. "She is not an it. But I'm faithful because Majestic Mother Earth doesn't care if she has a following of human sycophants." She continued, her whisper now normal spoken volume. "In fact, she'd be better off without humans. She has it all and is above it all. Her ways are a mystery, and they compare favorably with other confusing religious fallacies, like Jesus dying for his weird and indoctrinated children and then leaving them to fend for themselves. They have this illusion that they're in some sort of exclusive, secretive club that will save them from something no one can understand as they stumble around in the dark. Christianity offers some pie-in-the-sky mystery. Majestic Mother Earth is, well, down to earth, kind of like you. All she needs is a good public relations plan if she's going to keep her polish, her image. And that's where I come in."

She gazed into his eyes and rested her delicious hand on his bare chest again. "Think of what we can do together, Ty. Right now the earth and public relations is all there is, and not necessarily in that order." She kissed his lips gently. "Well, except for you and me. We've chosen each other. First things first."

She rolled over as if content with her mission.

"You really think I'm special?" He watched her until her breathing retreated into sleep, and his eyes grew heavy. He wanted an answer, but he supposed it could wait. For now, he'd enjoy the view. There was no part of her that wasn't excellent and flawless, except perhaps for her snoring. That was merely cute.

12 years earlier

Men's heads turned when Freedah walked by ever since she could remember. When she was a girl with a different name, a pastor warned her that she had a gift that was rare and, without careful management, could be misused. He'd said it was her decision to make, her choice between good and evil. He'd compared her to Esther of the Bible, but that, she'd already been convinced, was fiction. Despite her pastor's warnings, she'd read several books in which intelligent, rational, self-aware men – why were they always men? – contradicted the Bible. She hadn't the nerve to tell Pastor Mike that, though. It would upset him, and she didn't want him angry during those months when he often slipped his hand under her shirt and squeezed her training-bra-encumbered breasts.

"You are a temptation to me, girl, and you're going to be an irresistible temptation for thousands of men," he'd whispered in her ear, then took a deep breath, inhaling her soft, early-teen scented hair.

That day, as she was about to find the courage to cringe and pull away, he stopped and withdrew his hand. "You're as beautiful as anything mother nature could imagine. But it's time you took your place on the earth; let people pick the fruit you produce."

She wished she could wash the stickiness of his "fruit" from her memories of his large, too-soft hands. "What does that mean?"

"It means you're growing up, and like Esther, you've been placed in the world for a specific time and purpose. It's time you moved from Sunday School and youth services to the adult worship services."

"Will you be there?" She forced herself to stare into his pale eyes until he turned away. She'd won again.

"No, but that's okay. You don't need me anymore. Your beauty was made so you could benefit the whole world, so use it wisely."

He genuflected and rose slowly from his cushioned seat beside her. She watched him until, near the entrance, he looked back at her, then walked out and shut the door.

"I knew you couldn't just walk away." No man ever could. She'd tested her theory many times since. Never failed. Her eyes could hold a man still whenever she wanted, as long as she wanted. But like Majestic Mother Earth, she didn't know what she wanted. But she was a fast learner.

March 16

The next morning, Ty was up before the sun. He left a note for the sleeping Freedah that he was going fishing, and would think about her proposal. But they both knew all he would think about was her.

When she awakened, Freedah called San Francisco around noon and got MELL Chief Operating Officer Phoenix Tippen on the line.

"Haven't seen a check yet," Tippen said before saying hello.

"Be patient. Let me handle this, and we might get more than a one-time gift. I want to make this boy a media sensation. Get people to donate because of him. I'd like to bring him out, maybe get him on Kaylee Carrumbo."

"So let's do it."

"One problem. He needs some dental work. Fix his teeth, and we'll have women sending crypto our way like he was Tony Finn or something."

"So, get his teeth fixed."

"More complicated than that. I'll need time to convince him of his value to the river. And he's got this little hitch in his swing. He thinks farmers are good people who are doing good things for the river. We have to show him the light. I'll work on getting his teeth fixed. Give me a week to convince him to come to San Fran. Once he's all in, we all cash in."

"And get the land so we can fix the river for our friends," Tippen said. "Oh, yeah. I'm on it. Our mission is important to all of us who love Mother Earth. And that's the most important thing, right?"

Tippin nodded, hung up and went back to his financial statements.

Chapter 23

A moment before Ty and Freedah's flight touched down at San Francisco International Airport, Freedah received a text from Phoenix Tippin.

"We're all set for your boy," it read. "We'll impress the pants off him. You take it from there."

Tippin had arranged for Tony Finn to play a few songs in MELL's elaborate and new-smelling giant meeting room, decorated with abstract paintings that Ty suspected were meant to be rivers and a printed plate that noted that the room capacity was 200. All available employees were required to attend.

Freedah entered the room with both hands gripping Ty's left arm, and she kept her hands on him, either shoulder or neck or chest or arm, during all the warm introductions. But when she saw Tony, she rushed from Ty's side like a dog, leaving one bone to guard another. She embraced Tony warmly, and he kissed her cheek as he ran his palm across her posterior.

She pulled Tony by the hand and led him to Ty.

"So, you're the rural farm boy bloke who wants to save the Detroit River." He gripped Ty's forearm with his hand, Roman style, and pulled him in for a man-hug.

"Bloke?" asked Ty. "I didn't know you were British. Or is it Australian?"

"Neither, mate. I talk this way in an effort to embrace all cultures. Tomorrow, it might be an African accent, and then, maybe, something from the Greek. I'm trying to pick up a few phrases in Mandarin. You have to stay fluid in this world."

Ty looked over the murmuring crowd and wanted to break away from Tony's wild and wide eyes, but Tony had been instructed to wow the young man with his celebrity.

"Ever see any rocks in that river over by Detroit?"

Ty shook his head. "No, never."

"Don't tug my leg. Blimey. Everyone has rocks in their lives. They can either be embraced and teach us things, or they can be treacherous. It's all about your attitude toward them."

"Sorry. It's just that the answer is so obvious. There are rocks all over the place."

"Ever make love on one?"

"No, I prefer a nice pile of straw in a barn, maybe with a pig or steer watching." Tony didn't notice the sarcasm.

"Do the rocks ever talk to you while you're on the river?"

Ty's face took on a blank expression. Tony continued.

"You really should listen sometime, you old sod." He playfully nudged Ty's side. "Once, I spent 24 hours straight listening to rocks in the rivers out here, learning their language. They're quite wise. I slept a night on a bed of pea stone. They told me that no matter how big or small the rock, they're all important. They told me they deserve a place of honor, and they're upset that human animals don't give them more respect."

"Really. Can't say a rock ever spoke to me."

"Well, I'm blessed, Ty. I'm dedicated to the earth. I obey her whims and go with her flow. And she rewards me, just like God rewards his followers, you know, forgives them when they obey, if you believe in that sort of thing. In fact, my next album will have some songs dedicated to rocks and stones. It's not all written yet, but I'll get my guidance from them." He patted his hands on his jeans pockets. "I carry rocks in my pockets all the time. They help ground me."

"What does that mean?"

"They protect me from the negative aura people attack me with. They're full of positive energy. See, rocks provide my chakra – you know, keep me and Majestic Mother Earth on speaking terms. Oh, sure, there's a negative vibe here and there, but that's just because rocks get angry with how they get no respect. But they always balance me with the good. Do you know how many times

I've had a young fan ask if he or she can see what's between the two rocks in my pockets? I take things like that as a sign from the universe that the girl who asked and is most attractive is meant to be mine that night. And I really need those people – and it's usually girls – when I go on tour. Another blessing. See, I don't play anywhere but outside venues. It's so the earth can be blessed by my talent. Because of that, I spend a lot of time in rural areas, where farmers are out there trying to destroy the land that produces these sage old rocks. And they offer me their protection."

"Farmers are destroying the earth? Where did you come up with that theory?"

"It's not a theory. I've seen it. I've released imprisoned animals. I've earned the privilege of hearing rocks. Rivers, too, but it's the rocks in the rivers and fields that call to me most right now. They have a message, and we all need to listen."

"How do they speak or listen? They're rocks. Inanimate objects."

Tony gazed at Ty. "You're a real agitator, aren't you, bloke? I like that. I still think I'm right because of my intuition and experience, but sometimes even the right-side thinkers, like these chaps and birds here at MELL, need to look at things a little differently. But we'll set your thinking aright, eh, gov'ner? In the meantime, here's a backstage pass. You can use it at any of my shows if you want to be enlightened. My trademark is a fireworks show after each concert. You don't want to miss those. They're the dog's dinner." He handed Ty a thick, laminated card that said "Backstage VIP" with his photo on it. "I like people who challenge me, even if they're wrong. Eventually, they all see things my way."

***

Freedah and Phoenix approached, each looking at their phones. Research that included focus groups had revealed that fans of Acrid Reins desired fifteen minutes minimum time together if they ever met the handsome and charismatic singer/songwriter Tony Finn, and that time was up.

"Let's all settle down a little, folks, and take your seats." Phoenix raised his hands and smiled the pretty-boy smile that still captivated female employees. "We'll all get to hear Tony's latest song soon enough. But first, we're here now to welcome our newest and most esteemed member, Tyson Mooring, who, I understand, has had a passion for the Jovial River –that's up in the green state of Michigan – since he was a youth."

Ty leaned over to Freedah and whispered: "When did I become a member?"

"Your first hundred grand entitled you to a free membership," Freedah whispered back into his ear and licked his lobe gently, unperceived by the crowd, before pointing Ty's attention back to Phoenix.

Ty looked around the room. There were decidedly more women than men in attendance, and Ty could not see a single woman who wasn't well-dressed and made-up, with short skirts and tight blouses. MELL employees were required to conform to a dress code.

Phoenix was summing up his speech in his typical fashion with a call to action.

"Now I know all of you here agree, or you wouldn't be employed here. But let me assure you that your work here is the most important work on this planet. Rivers cannot continue to be polluted by corporate greed and racism." The crowd's members nodded to show him their enthusiasm.

"These corporate fat cats with their opulent offices and slush funds will be taken down and punished, and, thanks to our special guests here today, we will make sure our rivers are safe again, flowing freely without human-animal interference. Ladies and gentlemen, may I introduce our new benefactor and right-thinking man from the heartland, Mr. Tyson Mooring!"

The assembled crowd stood and cheered as Ty, who had not been told he was expected to make a speech, stood and was pulled to the podium by Phoenix's wet-fish handshake.

"This is all so overwhelming and so undeserved," Ty said when Phoenix had stopped egging on the crowd and hushed them. "I mean, I didn't expect a reception like this. Heck, I didn't even know MELL existed a week ago." The crowd murmured amiably. "Frankly, I'm a little embarrassed by it all. I sure never deserved any of this. Yes, I have been passionate about the Jovial River nearly all my life. I never knew it was a passion until Freedah helped me get my head together." The men in the audience nodded to each other.

"As you know, the Jovial has been named by some magazine out here in California as the cleanest river in the country, and that's because of good management over a long period of time. I didn't have anything to do with it. I'd always been way too poor to contribute to a cause as large and, well, grand – as this. But now that I have a little money, I know I can do something good for the world. I got it by luck, or as I'm learning, by the grace of God, not by some revelation from rocks that Tony was just telling me about. I mean, I'm sure I've never worked as hard as a musician of Tony's caliber must do. So I think I really need to know more about what you do before I'm put up as some kind of hero. I'm just a lucky S.O.B. But I am lucky by the grace of God, they tell me, and my only goal is to use it for His best purposes. If He wants to save some rivers through me, that's what will happen. So I look forward to learning more about MELL and, of course, to helping rivers in any way I can. And to help the farmers who want to save it and have done a good job so far."

The crowd, absent any cue from Phoenix about such a blasphemous statement to which Ty seemed oblivious, sat in silence. "I think I have enough money to make a difference in this world," Ty said, "and rivers are certainly a worthy cause."

Phoenix leaned over and placed his lips close to his secretary's ear. "Isn't that cute? He thinks five million is a lot of money." She grinned.

***

Ty stepped away from the podium to tepid applause and another wimpy handshake from Phoenix, who then introduced Tony Finn. He stepped up front with his guitar and a chair.

"Tyson here says he's lucky, but you blokes and birds here are just as lucky," he said as he ran his hand up and down the guitar's neck. "You get to be the very first people in the world to hear me perform my newest hit – well, it's destined to be a hit – and it's entitled Go with the Flow."

Finn played his mournful, albeit dulcet tune – a departure from his usual deep, driving base – deliberately and with the passion that had turned his only other big hit – It's All the Same – into personal wealth that dwarfed Ty's fortune.

Ty thought he'd heard a few riffs that were copied directly from It's All the Same, but he said nothing. Tony's lyrics spouted popular diatribes about the environment ("no clean air to breathe,") warned of impending doom for the planet ("we wheeze with earth's last breath") and crescendoed with climate change ("open your eyes, deniers, before it's too late to feel a cooling breeze").

"All-in-all, I thought it was boring, depressing and vapid," Ty told Freedah the next morning as they ate a sparse lunch of green and yellow things at their five-star hotel. "I never liked Acrid Reins anyway. Head-bangers bore me, just like his song about halfway through."

Freedah was about to defend Tony when her phone announced a message. The limousine Phoenix had arranged for the couple was waiting at the hotel entrance.

***

Freedah had arranged a full, busy day designed to show Ty exactly how MELL was making a difference in the world. From what he knew so far, he hadn't decided if MELL's influence was positive or negative, but when he looked into Freedah's eyes, he resolved to wait and see. Patience, he had learned from the Bible and Coney, was one of the fruits he could and should cultivate. That conflicted with what he'd heard all his life, that 'he who hesitates is lost.' But the world hadn't exactly proven its fidelity toward him, so he decided to try it God's way for a change.

They walked into Phoenix Tippin's office, with Freedah's hands never leaving contact with some part of Ty's body. She was generous that way, especially in public.

***

They were discussing river cleanup events that had been arranged for him when James Snowmaker arrived at the giant receptionist's desk and saw through the glass that Phoenix was meeting with Freedah and someone else.

"Who's in there with Freedah and Phoenix?" Snowmaker asked Tippin's executive assistant.

"Oh, that's our new member, Tyson Mooring."

"No way." Snowmaker stared at the young man's back. "How in the world did Freedah pull that one off? I've been trying to get him to be at a giant check presser, and he's turned me down every time."

"It surprises you that Freedah can get things out of a man that you can't?"

"Well, that's a separate issue." Snowmaker smiled at her. Just then, Phoenix checked his Patek Phillippe watch, rose from his desk and pointed Ty and Freedah to the door.

"Time to get back in the limo and begin the tour of San Francisco."

When Ty turned toward the door, Snowmaker's face turned instantly red like a boy caught with a spontaneous erection. He rushed through the glass door of Phoenix's office.

"This man is a fraud," he shouted, flailing his arms. "This is not Tyson Mooring. He's a fake. Look at him. He's not even a Mexican!"

"Now, just hold on, Jim," Phoenix said. "This is Tyson Mooring."

"No way," Snowmaker shouted louder than before. "This is some little pissant white-trash boy from Jovial, Michigan, that swampy piece of crap out in the middle of nowhere. I've met this guy. His name is Jorgen, and he's trying to con you out of your money."

"What makes you think he's not Ty Mooring?" Freedah asked.

"Because he tried to kill me in that god-forsaken river less than a month ago." Snowmaker ranted, his face turning redder with every syllable. "I forced him to tell me his name after he tried to drown me. It's Jorgen, I tell you. Hugh Jorgen."

Freedah looked at Ty and smiled. He grinned back. She had underestimated the young man's cleverness. She turned and smiled at Phoenix, who also was smiling.

"Think about it, Jim," Phoenix said. "Listen to it. He told you his name is Hugh Jorgen? Say it aloud a couple of times. Hugh. Jorgen. Hugh Jorgan?" He grasped his crotch and did a little bounce. "Huge Organ?"

Snowmaker's face was turning orange, and a neck vein throbbed from the base of his hair down to the top of his shoulder.

"You son of a bitch." His face had turned radish-red, and he moved slightly forward, his chest puffed out like a gorilla.

"Take me for a fool, will you? You're nothing but an impostor. How dare you claim to be Mexican? We can all plainly see that you're just a poser." He lunged forward and, with a quicker-than-expected right hand, punched Ty in the mouth, just below his nose. He struck again with a left, knocking Ty to the ground before Snowmaker leaped on top of him, smashing his face with the heel of his hand. Ty landed a knee into Snowmaker's lower torso, creating a guttural wheeze from the older man, but the unexpected blows and Snowmaker's heavy fat held him to the floor.

Phoenix's voice was calm and steady as he stood at a distance behind the shelter of his desk.

"Come on, guys, break it up," he whined without any attempt to step between them. Freedah began screeching for Snowmaker to stop, but she, too, stood her ground. Phoenix's assistant yelled for help, and three other assistants rushed in and pulled Snowmaker off Ty, but not before he'd left Ty's nose flat and bleeding and his mouth with at least two fewer teeth than before.

Snowmaker was pulled up and held by a newly arrived security guard, but it wasn't easy. Snowmaker apparently wanted more revenge. Before Ty got to his feet, Freedah had grabbed a box of tissues and was holding a wad of them to his mouth. She dabbed and looked, then applied pressure. When the bleeding had subsided, she turned to Phoenix.

"Who's that oral surgeon who fixed you up?" Phoenix blushed, his secret now known to more employees than he wished.

"Call him," she said before he could answer. Now! He will see us now!"

Ty's adrenaline drove him to his feet, enraged. His anger burst forth like a football star crashing through a paper sign. He didn't consider anything or count to 10. He did what was natural and rushed forward to throw wild punches at Snowmaker. Two of them landed on Snowmaker's granite jaw. Ty shook the pain from his hands as Snowmaker's blood flew out onto three employees, who stood now, aghast.

"I'll get you for this, you bastard!" Ty shouted. "I'll have you arrested before you get out of this building. Then I'll cut your ears off and paste them to your ass!"

"Calm down," said Phoenix, feigning an attempt to get Ty stabilized while doing his best to keep blood away from his suit.

"I want him arrested for assault!"

"Let me take care of it," Phoenix said.

"No!" Ty shouted. "I'll see that son of a bitch rot behind bars!"

The security guard wrestled Snowmaker out of the office.

***

The oral surgeon was waiting on instructions from Phoenix when Freedah led Ty into his office. He was immediately sent to a chair and administered some heavy anesthesia. Before he lost consciousness, he heard Freedah:

"Take good care of him, Doctor. Stop the bleeding and get him prepped. I'm going to see the plastic surgeon on the third floor. This guy's a real mess."

Ty didn't remember the trip to the plastic surgeon later that day, but he knew Freedah's influential charms had succeeded when he awoke, his nose bandaged heavily.

He was still groggy, but he heard Freedah's melodic voice.

"I just love your new face," she said. "Once the swelling goes down, you're gonna be a looker!"

***

Two weeks later, his mouth still sore and swollen and his hand still stiff, the last of Ty's mouthful of new teeth was set in place. Freedah picked him up at the oral surgeon's office and was instructed to keep him resting for a day or so. He was a quick healer, the surgeon had said, and should be fine and able to eat soft food, at least.

Freedah grasped his arm as he walked out of the office.

"This is all a good thing," she cooed into Ty's ear. "You're a real hottie now. You were before, but now, with straight, white teeth? Youza. And your nose is straight and perfect. We're going to get you on the Kaley Carrumbo show."

"First things first," Ty mumbled through his swollen face. "I've going to file an assault charge against that braying jackass Snowmaker."

Freedah thought she had talked Ty down from his sweltering rage against Snowmaker during their long stay in the hotel, in which he was bored to death. Despite the lavish room service and more television stations to choose from than he'd ever imagined, he'd spent most of his time planning his plot for justice or revenge. He didn't know the difference.

"Just let MELL take care of Snowmaker," she said. "We'll see that he's reprimanded. Besides, you're not thinking clearly because of all the mouth pain and anesthesia." He nodded weakly, and she tucked him into the hotel room's high thread-count sheets as gently as a dog licking her puppies. She kissed him softly.

"You need your rest, and I have some work to get to at the office."

When he heard the door close, he called the San Francisco police department. Later, an officer knocked on his room door.

It took about an hour, but Ty detailed the assault and gave the officer a count of how many people had witnessed it. The only names he remembered were Tippin and Freedah, but three secretaries and a security guard also saw it, he said.

***

The next day, a San Francisco police officer arranged for interviews with anyone who may have seen the incident.

Tippin was given a heads-up when the officer entered the building, and as he slipped out the back way from his office, he made a call on his cell.

"Jim, you'd better get out of town and fast," he said. "Our Michigan hick has filed assault charges."

"I'll just counter-sue him for kicking and punching me," Snowmaker said.

"Just get out of here and don't make any headlines for a while. "I'll soften it with the cops, but let's all lay low for the next few weeks."

Freedah and Tippin's assistant corroborated Ty's story, and before Tippin could make the call to the chief, a warrant had been issued for Snowmaker's arrest. After Tippin's call, it was given a low priority.

Chapter 24

All traces of swelling in Ty's face were gone, and just in time. As he looked at himself in the hotel room's bathroom mirror, he smiled. For the first time since Snowmaker had knocked out several teeth and broken his nose, Ty could smile and contort his face without pain. Also, for the first time, he liked what he saw, as if he had been transformed into someone else; someone more likable, more attractive, more empowered, more influential.

Freedah crept up behind him and slipped her hands across his chest. He looked away from the mirror, embarrassed by his nascent satisfaction.

"Keep right on looking." Her eyes caught him in the mirror. "That's right, Ty. You are a very handsome man. You're more than that. You're gorgeous, and that's what this PR campaign needs. But don't look at yourself too long. We have to put that face to work."

Freedah was enthusiastic as they climbed into the back seat of the MELL limo, exposing the distinct yet faint smell of diesel exhaust. His discomfort in the tightened, striped tie that he was told smartly matched the tailored suit, was obvious to her. She'd never seen him so quiet and sullen. It was Freedah's job to make him upbeat and likable, and his attitude needed adjusting to match his pretty new face.

"This is a really big deal for you and MELL, you know," she snapped like a cornered turtle as she pulled up the local TV show's website on her phone. "This appearance could make you the talk of the West Coast. Put on a smile."

"And why would I want to be the talk of the west coast? It smells funny out here. I like the smell of cows and pigs a lot better than this asphalt and smog."

"It's all about the cause, not your nose." She softened her tone and stroked his arm. "It sure looks good, though. Snowmaker did you a favor, truth be told. He broke the window, but now it's been replaced with a new, better one. But we need to focus now. In order to save rivers and the planet, we have to have a major PR push, and your face is the first step. Kaley is the PR agent's dream."

Ty looked at Kaley's publicity photo on Freedah's phone. She had a face made for television, and it reflected the complexities of the diverse local populace. Her blonde hair fell over one of her broad, toned, tanned and bare shoulders. Her eyes were sparkling green and slightly angular, just enough to suggest an oriental, perhaps Middle Eastern heritage. Her lips were thick and lush, painted with a just-off natural dark color. She smiled seductively as she stared into the camera.

"Yep, she's a looker," Ty said. "But I would like to get one thing straight here after this. Yes, I believe in preserving rivers. And I'm willing to help any credible effort. But just once, I'd like to know what I'm scheduled to do before I do it."

"That's my job." Freedah leaned closer to him. "I know PR, and at the risk of sounding immodest, I've been told I'm the best that's ever been." She smiled her heart-melting smile and leaned into Ty. "All you have to do is look good, which you do now; answer a few questions, and we'll move on."

"I guess I never really understood before what you did for a living. You're an agent, a promoter, a PR hack?" His former reticence was returning.

"Hack is not a very pretty word, Ty." She was offended and spoke like she'd been a target. "My title is public relations liaison, plain and simple, and as I'm sure you can see, I'm good at my job."

"Sorry to say it, Freedah, and maybe it's just my nerves talking here, but it doesn't seem like a very honest profession to me."

"Honesty is a relative term," she said, pushing down the accusation that she'd wondered about herself more than once. "It's what we believe that is honest. There is no absolute truth, after all, so we have to create truth that's designed to benefit all of mankind.

You're just nervous. But with a face like yours, there's no need to be."

"Me doing a local TV interview will help mankind?"

"Yes!" Her hand cupped his chin. "This face will raise awareness, first, but better is that we can – and this is any PR agent's most effective tool – put a face on this issue. A very handsome face. And there are fewer better faces than yours to help rivers. Ugly faces don't help. Yours will."

"Why not just have Phoenix do it? He's the pretty boy."

"Don't tell me you're jealous of Phoenix," she smiled with what appeared to Ty to be satisfaction at the thought.

"Not jealous. Just skeptical."

"We'll talk about that after the show. Phoenix will probably be here later. He's proud of you. He thinks, like I do, that someone like you who's looking for purpose has to be able to grab hold of it when he finds it. This is your purpose."

"How can you be so sure?"

"I just am. I don't know how. I have a knack for this kind of thing. It's why I'm so good at PR. I know what talent is before anybody else. I was on the ground floor of Acrid Reins, fresh out of college. I rode them right to the top. And I see a real passion hidden inside you, whether you do or not. So focus! First, we have to get you ready for the interview. Now I just want you to relax, pretend the cameras aren't even there, and talk honestly about your passion for the Jovial River."

"I can do that, but how is anyone from here going to understand my river? What difference will it make?"

"It's about promotion. This is just the first step, but it's the most important thing there is. There is nothing greater than an image. Nothing is more important than public relations. It controls the entire world's attitudes. But it doesn't always last very long. That's why you have to grab it and hang on while it does. You get a good image here, and we could leverage your money into even more money for the cause. We could have rivers all over this country saved, one by one, if we have to. And that's what will endure beyond our lives. Isn't that what all of us really want? To leave something for the world? To make our names known for the good we've done for Majestic Mother Earth? Isn't that what gives us purpose?"

"I'm not sure they all need saving. The Jovial River is in great shape thanks to the farmers there. I'd like to tell the truth."

"Without a public relations plan, who would know what truth really is? That's why we have to define it for them."

"But the truth is that the Jovial is clean and pure. Can't I talk about that?"

"If you want, but I think the river's dangerous future will be more important to the audience. And it's your purpose to keep the most important things in people's minds. Why won't you see the same potential here that I do? This is your destiny, Tyson. Someday, you'll be in the history books as the single greatest savior of rivers this country has ever seen!"

"Well," Ty said, feeling like a supplicant, "I have been looking for a way to make a difference."

"Start out talking about that. It makes you seem driven, truthful, and humble. Kaley will love that! And so will all of America who sees such a good-looking young man with such a nice smile, with such a passion for your mission to this world. Besides, you're already a celebrity. You're the first person in the nation to actually get a reparation. That's news. That's your starting point. The launching pad is your face. Take off with it!"

***

Kaley Carrumbo greeted Freedah first with a quick hug and a kiss on the lips. Ty's first thought was that Kaley's persona was as plastic as her breasts as she pulled him close and embraced him just a bit too long. She stepped back half a step and left both hands on Ty's shoulders.

"So you're the river saver," she said, smiling. She was indeed pretty, and her origins were hard to figure. Elements of Caucasian, Asian, Latino and African American were all easy to see, and they blended together in a very pleasing package. But she was quite a bit different from her publicity photo. Her Roman nose was slightly crooked in person, and her eyes were brown, not the piercing emerald green from the publicity photo. Her shoulders were much narrower than he'd expected, and her breath smelled of sugary, light-brown coffee.

"You just relax, Ty," she said, patting his arm. "We're all on the same page here to save our nation's rivers from the polluters. I'll start out with some softball questions, but be prepared. I will ask you a tough question or two."

"Like what?"

"Now, now, a good reporter doesn't show what's up her sleeve. But don't worry. We're taping this for later, so if you get stumped, we can work wonders with editing." He discovered later that 'reporter' was a self-proclaimed title.

***

After some time in a chair getting makeup put on, Ty's face was at least three shades darker than his natural complexion. Freedah assured him it was just standard operating procedure for television.

Ty sat on an oversized couch on the set, the lights already on and heating the place beyond his comfort. He was instructed, rather harshly, by someone who seemed to have authority on the set, to never look directly into a camera. Stay focused on Kaley, he was told. Answer her. Look at her. It shouldn't be too hard to do. Like Freedah, Kaley attracted his eyes like a jumping trout and a singing line.

Kaley walked on the set and told Ty to just relax. This would be painless. She began her intro when the same man who'd instructed Ty pointed her way.

"We're here today with a man whose passion for rivers – and fishing, I've been told – has really caught the attention – or should catch the attention – of everyone who loves and cherishes the earth. He's the newest board member of MELL, and as my loyal viewers know, the Mother Earth Liberation League is doing wonderful things to preserve this nation's rivers before they go extinct. And they work throughout the country, not just here in sunny California. Ty Mooring, of Detroit, Michigan, can explain it all."

She turned her attention from the camera and back at Ty, but waited for the cameras to move to capture her face.

"So, Ty, let's start with the basics. What makes someone as gorgeous as you so passionate about rivers?"

"Well, I don't know if passion is really the right word, Kaley. I've always thought of passion in the context of a romantic relationship. I mean, I've never hugged a tree or a fish. In fact, I'd rather gut and eat a fish right out of the Jovial River than hug it." Kaley laughed too hard, tilting her lovely head back toward the camera. Still, Ty noticed a bit of revulsion in her face. He expected her to follow the romantic metaphor, but she looked down at her note card, her eyes darting quickly as if she had no time left.

"But you do want to save the rivers, right?"

"Sure. Who doesn't? Rivers are amazing things. They start with trickles and end up sustaining life for humans, wildlife, amphibians, and a whole bunch of other things. Personally, I could sit by the Jovial River for hours, just watching it flow. It's never the same, yet always the same, you know?"

"That sounds like mystery and passion to me," Kaley said, smiling into the camera. She motioned with her left hand, low under the camera's view, and the cameraman knew what to do. He made the lens hone in on Kaley's eyes as she widened them as if coming to a unique revelation. "Sounds like you've been influenced by a certain song."

Ty had no idea of her reference, and just stared at her.

"More about that later," she said into the camera. "So tell us," she said, turning back to Ty, "what got you started on your mission to save the rivers?"

"It's a mission now? Well, maybe it is now, thanks to my friend Freedah over there."

The camera flipped around to look at Freedah, standing in the wings. The cameraman, stunned by her as most men were, held it on her face until Kaley cleared her throat. Immediately, the camera view came back her way.

"Come on up here, Freedah," Kaley said, waving her toned right arm. "You're very pretty. I'm sure our viewers would like to look at you."

Freedah feigned sheepishness better than any actor Ty had ever seen as she came forward to the small audience's applause. She sat hip-to-hip with Ty on the couch. Ty resumed:

"See, even if I had a conscious passion for rivers, and not just the Jovial River, there wasn't anything I could do about it. I mean, I picked up junk along the banks when I could, and I really appreciated the filter strips the farmers had installed. Not just because they look good, which they do, but because they're effective. They save topsoil, stabilize the banks and catch any small bits of stray fertilizer that may be on the soil. But I never thought of it as a passion or a mission until I came into a little money and Freedah convinced me that God had given me the money for a purpose. She guided me to MELL and has just about convinced me it's a good cause."

Kaley leaned over her desk to address Freedah. Her voice changed from impassionate (and incurious) reporter to breathless and feckless promoter.

"So Freedah. What happened here? How did a beautiful girl like you ever even know Ty was alive way back there in Detroit?"

"I'm not from Detroit," Ty interrupted. "I'm from Jovial, a very far cry from Detroit."

"Don't worry. We'll edit that out," Kaley said. "Freedah?"

"I used the power of the internet, and, of course, our newest and fastest-growing social media platform. Twaddle. Find it at ..." Kaley frowned outside the camera's reach and swiped her right index finger across her throat. Freedah had been warned about pushing for free publicity. She continued.

"See, as part of my job as public relations liaison with MELL, I keep my eyes open to any potential damage to any of our nation's rivers. A key word search of rivers, something that I pay attention to every single day, led me to Ty, who was featured in his local newspaper on line. He was trying to save this river all by himself, and I thought he could really use MELL's resources in his passionate work."

"Funny," Ty said. "I thought you learned about me because of the money."

Freedah laughed and giggled and grasped Ty's arm, putting her head on his shoulder to hide her nails digging into Ty's flesh. The audience expressed brief joy.

"You know, MELL's first obligation is to the rivers, but yes, I'll admit that we need money to finance our worthy cause. We wish it weren't true, but it is. But even though that's reality, the money has always been secondary to us. We wanted to help Ty not only to preserve the endangered Jovial River, but to help him manage his wealth for the benefit of all mankind, which is what I could see in his eyes even through the pages of a newspaper online."

"So tell us, Ty," Kaley said, turning her attention back to Ty as she gave Freedah the old evil eye, "I understand that your wealth is a story all in itself."

Ty told Kaley his story of imprisonment and release, adding that it was still a mystery to him how he was selected for reparation.

"Mostly, I'm afraid that the whole thing happened because of my race. My mother was a Mexican national who worked picking fruit and vegetables, and my father was illiterate. Me getting this money and land was all so unlikely that I have a hard time understanding the idea that my fortune was an act of God, just like the river is an act of God." Kaley feigned rapt attention, then looked at the camera.

"Amazing," she said. "So you think some divine deity did this for you? Made you rich?"

"Not some generic deity. God Himself."

The audience gasped.

"Don't worry," Kaley told the gaspers. "We can edit that out for clarity. Let's move on. So Ty, what spurred your passion for the Jovial River near Detroit?"

"First, the Jovial River is nowhere near Detroit. But I guess Freedah convinced me that rivers need human help. I didn't really get that at first. I mean, rivers are so powerful and so uncontrollable that humans, even if we think we have some kind of power, have very little power to impact a river. I don't think there's anything humans can do to save rivers. That's all in God's hands. But, that being said, it's clear that humans should be good stewards of what had been given them. The Jovial River is a good opportunity to practice that stewardship. Farmers in the valley there in northern Michigan have been extremely careful to preserve what they can. They've planted filter strips along miles of the river where they plant their crops. It's an area that contributes big time to the nation's supply of vegetables. In fact, Michigan is second only to California in several kinds of vegetables and fruits. Farmers couldn't do that if they were polluting the river. It's a lifeline to them, and they would never do anything to damage it."

"But they're doing it because the state mandates it, right?"

"Not necessarily. The state offered them a chance to be in a voluntary program with some minimal cost shares to put in filter strips, but many of them were doing that before the law passed.

"And now the state pays them to be, as you call them, 'good stewards?'"

"The state offers incentives, yes, but it doesn't pay the whole tab."

"What I'm hearing is that the government is really the impetus behind preserving the river," Kaley said. "Without it, farmers would continue to pollute?"

"I don't believe that. In fact, the government is more a hindrance than a benefactor if you ask the farmers. They put sometimes ridiculous restrictions on things, trying to tell farmers how to farm. Well, the government, as is obvious there, and probably all over the country, knows nothing about farming. They get in the way, adding costs that aren't necessary."

"We all know that farmers are on the public dole," Kaley said, icily. "Don't try to tell me it's not that way in Michigan?"

"No, it isn't. Most farmers I know – and I know a lot of them – could do their job better and preserve the river better without government interference. Government paperwork alone forced a lot of them to hire people just for that one job."

"So the state is a job creator?

"Maybe, if you want to look at it that way. But farmers see it as an unnecessary burden."

"But you have to admit that without the state as overseer, the Jovial River would be closer to extinction?"

"It's nowhere near extinction at all." Ty was getting excited now. "In fact, MELL's own magazine has named it the cleanest river in the United States."

Freedah interrupted. "Actually, to be accurate, the Pure Fly Fishing Federation put out that ranking. Go ahead, Ty."

"I reject the entire concept of extinction," he said, but his increasing passion was not what Freedah had groomed him for. She made a quick note to change the course of his mind. She hadn't expected him to be so independent. Most men would do whatever she wanted as long as they got what they wanted from her. But Ty barged ahead, refusing to look Freedah's way for visual clues.

"Human activity cannot endanger a river," Ty continued. "Sure, way back before I was born, there was a lot more pollution, but even then, rivers were polluted more near cities where wastewater systems were mismanaged and dumped raw human waste. But we've learned a lot. And maybe the first thing we all have to learn is that rivers cannot be controlled by humans. Rivers cannot be made extinct. It's beyond human power."

Freedah raised her hand, and Kaley allowed her to interject.

"I think that Ty here just needs his world expanded a little," she said. "Sure, in his world, the Jovial River is recovering, but much more is needed. Ty will learn as he takes this journey with MELL that there are many rivers in this country that need his help. We can cite his precious Jovial River as an example to all the others. But it takes money. And more than just Ty's money. It will take a village that consists of every person in this country who believes rivers are our lifeline. The pollution has to stop!"

"Well said," Kaley enthused. "But to our in-studio guests and viewers who are home, we have a special treat for you. Please welcome to the stage a real warrior for rivers, a man who you all know and soon will know as the voice for America's rivers, from the Acrid Reins; here's Tony Finn!"

Finn started playing his river dirge, and Kaley turned to Ty and Freedah off-camera and absent microphones.

"This was a tremendous waste of time," she spat. "Next time, be better prepared. This is not a show for debate. We're advocates here, not some idiot truth seekers." She turned and walked off the set. Freedah sent Ty a murderous look, and then the two were escorted by armed guards out the door.

Chapter 25

Donald Grandersma was ready to settle down for the evening in his upper-crust Lansing apartment when his phone alerted him to an email message. It was from Phoenix.

"Grandy: I don't know if Freedah had time to get you up to speed on Michigan House Bill 616. We've been very patient with it for years, knowing that the farmers there would create a big stink. Get the pun? But I've learned that the Farmers Association lobbyist who always got in our way has retired. The new person is a greenie who just out of school a few years ago. Likely doesn't know the issue. It should be easy to run over him if he even gets wind of it. Don't alert him to anything.

I suggest you visit Rep. Al Montenegro out of Detroit. He's the only one sympathetic to the river/gambling issue on the ag committee and will vote our way. But we need more than just him. Convince him to attach the bill to the budget appropriations bill for funding state money for environmental cleanup. Maybe we can run it through and change the pollution standard to something more palatable to our cause. Presently, there is no standard that tells the state enviro workers when to assess monetary penalties. And we need that to put these polluters out of business. -- PT"

***

Grandy looked up the bill, first introduced three years before as a standalone bill. By legislative standards, it was short and to the point. It changed the standard for measuring pollution – and assessing fines – from one part per million to one part per trillion.

He did more research. One part per million is one drop in 10 gallons. One part per billion is one drop in 10,000 gallons. One part per trillion is one drop in 20 Olympic-sized swimming pools.

193

But if that's what the scientists said was needed to create a zero risk to the river, he wouldn't doubt it. Doubt was a sin, one that he fought harder than any other thing in this world.

The bill mandated a fine for each part per trillion $10,000 per day per violation as long as the pollution remained. And it did not define the pollution's source. Farmers would be responsible for bird, fish, animal and factory manure.

But one thing still bothered and confused Grandy. The bill's language talked about fining farmers for their "potential" to pollute.

He called Freedah. When she called him back, her voice was like gentle rain on a brown spring hay field, refreshing and absorbing, making everything he could see grow and thrive. And her answer was just as refreshing.

"The 'potential' to pollute is basically PR language," she said, "but it's a result of MELL's efforts to be proactive, not reactive. See, if the state can fine a farmer for pollution, that's not enough. The pollution has already done its damage and washed on down the river..."

"Where it becomes diluted and benign."

"Maybe," answered Freedah. "Our statisticians haven't been able to disprove that yet, but we know it's not true. Pollution will eventually catch up with the people downstream, but that's not the point. We advocate a zero-tolerance policy because even a drop of pollution ruins the river's perfection. Kind of like one sin keeps you out of Heaven. That's part of being proactive too. We believe that we must stop pollution before it starts; before it even occurs. That's the only way to keep the river clean. Zero pollution from any source at any time. That's a victory for us. Nothing less."

Grandy wasn't sure he understood all that or bought the whole idea, especially the sin part. What did Freedah know about salvation and forgiveness, or even sin for that matter? A girl who looked like her was too pristine to sin all that much. And he found it just a little odd that Freedah would bring up biblical concepts. Still, he admitted, without Jesus, one sin would keep a person out of Heaven. His silence prompted Freedah.

"Grandy, remember your mission. Any speck of pollution is a gamble. And your God-given mission in life is to stop gambling, isn't that so?"

"I guess so."

"What? Don't go all half-assed on me now, Grandy. Any doubt at all ruins your conviction."

"Well, then, yes. Absolutely. God's given me a mission to end the scourge of gambling, and he's put me on a course that's much larger than just one Indian casino." Just saying it made him feel better as if his sense of purpose had been restored,; that his prayer had been answered.

"And what better cause is there than Majestic Mother Earth?" Freedah asked. "Extremism for the cause of justice is not a fault; it's a duty."

He longed for her touch but had to settle for the memories of her hand on his arm, her smile reaching from his heart down to his kneecaps. He melted. "You're right, Freedah. I'm an anti-gambling crusader, but I never knew before this that God had bigger plans for me than I could ever have dreamed on my own. I'm all in. Have to be. Anything less would be disobeying God. Thanks, girl. You're my rock."

Oh, how he longed for her to be more than that. But he'd settle for completing his mission for God successfully. Whatever that meant. Maybe Freedah would help him figure that out. If only he had more patience and more dedication. He had a choice to make, and it was easy. Freedah could be the only choice.

Chapter 26

"You embarrassed me!" Freedah shouted and smacked Ty's shoulder when they were a good distance from the Kaley Carrumbo set. "Here I give you the opportunity of a lifetime, and this is how you repay me?"

"I'm sorry," he said, unconvinced of his sincerity. "I thought you wanted me to be genuine. You know, truthful and honest."

"That's the problem. You don't know what the truth is. Maybe it's my fault, although that's unlikely. Maybe you just aren't ready for this kind of thing. You have to understand that it's not just the Jovial River we're concerned about. You need to see the big picture as I do. We're a nationwide organization. We have our hand in just about everything on this planet. Or we will have, eventually. It has to be an all-or-nothing proposition. No PR campaign can succeed without all hands on deck. MELL has all its affiliates involved, from the pure-earth activists to the website to the Twaddle launch to the real estate company. Why do you think we need all this money? This is not about some backward town in Michigan. It's about the health of the world. It's about the good of the company. It's about showing the least little bit of respect for Majestic Mother Earth. It's about making sure the world is a better place and giving you a legacy. It's about restoring perfection. If you can't see that, you need a real education!"

"Restoring perfection," he parroted. "There is no perfection on earth." He'd not been sure of that and hadn't searched for it in the Bible. Some TV evangelists said it and made a pretty good case.

"So, I'm not perfect now?" Freedah sulked. "You told me I was."

He looked into her eyes, and his defiance fled like cottonwood floaters in an early summer storm. "You're about as close as this world can come. And maybe I do need more education. But so do you." She bristled but recovered quickly.

"Education costs money, and I'm already educated," she said. "I've graduated to teacher, but teachers need to get paid."

"I'm happy to pay my own way. But have you ever considered that the MELL influence, the MELL education, has not told you the whole story?"

"Impossible. MELL does its homework and knows what's right for Majestic Mother Earth.

Her tone took away Ty's recalcitrance.

"Your homework is all from your desk in the middle of a smelly city. Have you ever thought about what your work really does to people?"

"People aren't as important as Majestic Mother Earth!"

"Really? How do you know? You say you love the earth, that you're dedicated to it. But have you ever looked Ma Nature in the face, smelled the spring rain or dug into the soil?"

"My job is to see the big picture. I don't have to smell her in order to understand her. And don't you ever disrespect her again by calling her ma. It's degrading."

"Maybe you need the smaller picture. I think you need to go camping with me if you really want to relate to people outside San Francisco. You're going to need the common man if you want to succeed in your goals, don't you?"

Freedah's first thought was no, she didn't need anyone, but she was in danger of alienating Ty and his remaining funds.

"I'll consider that, perhaps."

"So let's get out into the woods. Get some dirt under your fingernails."

"We don't have time. I have to get back to work. I have at least a week's worth of stuff I haven't done because of you and your surgeries!" She touched his hand, then slapped it harshly.

"So if it's waited a week, it can wait one afternoon. At least take the rest of the day to take a hike in the woods with me. I've seen online that we can catch all kinds of trails and scenery in the Mount Sutra Forest, and it's right here in the city." She paused, pursed her lips as if in deep contemplation, like unseen creatures in the forest. She checked the time. His flight took off in six hours.

"I'll do it, but only for you," she said.

***

The fog had burned away by the time Ty and Freedah disembarked from their Uber ride, but after only a few steps onto the South Ridge trail, it became dark and musty.

Freedah had changed into shorts, running shoes, and a shoulderless blouse, and she was immediately uncomfortable.

"I guess I should have told you that the guides say it's always damp and cold in here," he said. "I supposed you would have known that."

"How would I know? I've never been here before."

"You should have." Ty stopped to peer up at the 200-foot-tall trees. "This is one gorgeous place."

Freedah suppressed the urge to point out what he was apparently overlooking. How could he look past her to dark woods? The place stank of musty mildew. Her arms and legs already carried goosebumps, which she knew was not a good look for her, and she shivered as she forced herself to look up into the trees. But she saw nothing but darkness and heard nothing but pesky insect sounds. If they were quiet enough, she thought, perhaps they could still hear the sound of the giant city for which she longed.

She drew closer to Ty and pressed her chilled body next to his. He took her hand and slowly led her down a trail that contained flowers differently colored than anything he'd ever seen.

They walked in silence for perhaps two hundred yards until the path narrowed and led up a steep rise.

"I can't believe an earth-lover has never been here before," he said. She said nothing, and Ty sensed her displeasure. She checked her phone again, and he knew they would never walk the entire trail. Still, he wanted to try. Perhaps, if he were patient, something would show itself to her, give her the epiphany he knew she needed.

As he stepped up the narrow, slippery path, her hand in his, he felt a dramatic 110-pound pull. She slipped and fell directly on her tight buns, pulling him, laughing, on top of her. But she wasn't laughing.

"That's it!" she shouted as he pulled her back up. "I've had more than enough of this."

"But this is part of Mother Earth," he said.

"Majestic Mother Earth to you," she snarled. "And yes, she is majestic. Too majestic to be defiled by humans. People shouldn't even be allowed in here. Look at this path. All stomped down by human boots. It's profane. I'm cold and now all dirty and muddy, and I will have to throw these clothes away. I'll never wash the stink out of them. Let's get out of here. I have work to do."

The ride back to his hotel featured silence and brooding. He had a plane to catch, and she gradually softened as they parted.

"Next time, be more prepared, and we'll go out into the woods where I know the territory," he said. She grunted noncommittally. "It means you can buy a bunch of new clothes!" No response.

He pushed her back to arm's length while still holding onto her wide yet subtly feminine shoulders.

"Don't you think something like that would make you more relatable to the cause?"

"We'll see. I suppose, after all, it didn't hurt me too much, except I have this big lump on my butt."

"Want me to massage it?" he smiled.

She curled her lips into a forced smile. "We both need to get back to work. Don't worry. I'll be back in Jovial before you know it."

They kissed on the sidewalk, and she watched him enter the hotel as she climbed back into the Uber car, which would take her to her apartment.

She was a mile away when she remembered, so she texted Ty:

"Forgot to tell you that I had all your old clothes thrown out. You'll find two full suitcases with new clothes, which will make you even hotter. Also shipped a closet full to your room at the Jovial casino. Wear them. Trust me. Luv U."

Chapter 27

Ty's flight east fled the pestilent odor of San Francisco, and as the plane reached its cruising altitude, he wondered at the shame of it all. Such natural beauty. How could they have let it become polluted by stench, like a florid suburban backyard with a failing drain field?

The seat belt signs went out, and people began walking around the plane. A flight attendant, a short redhead with a pretty face and squat-thrust lifter's legs, smiled and leaned over until her face was inches from his.

"People have been asking me about you." She smiled with toothy charm and touched his hand with hers. "Are you on television?"

Ty felt a twinge of embarrassment.

"I was on one show, that's all."

"I got it!" she snapped her fingers. "You were on Kaley Carrumbo!"

"Yep."

"You and that total hottie Tony Finn, if I remember right. But I don't care what anybody says. You're much hotter than he is. Look, I have a lot of work to do here, but when we land, would you maybe let me buy you a drink?"

"I'm changing flights in Minneapolis," he said, noting a look of disappointment on her face. She reached into a pocket and took out a notepad. She scribbled something, tore it off the pad, folded it and handed it to him. "Let's see if we can do something soon." She smiled and walked away, heel to toe, which wasn't easy in the narrow aisle. He unfolded it and saw a name and phone number written.

Maybe it was the new suit, the first one he ever owned; maybe it was the new teeth and nose. Maybe it was this new life.

God apparently was opening new doors for him, and he had been too stupid to understand what was going on. He had fame and fortune now and, apparently, the chance to play against the house with the upper hand, a chance he'd never had before.

He looked at his dark reflection in the seat-back video monitor that he hadn't yet turned on. He hadn't let himself admit it before, but he liked what he saw. He wished he had a mirror. Freedah was right. He could be in demand, like some movie star with powerful looks but atrophied brain.

Straight teeth were something he'd not dared dream about, but he'd also never dreamed that he could look this good, even with a new face. He'd never even thought about a nose job, but he was glad Freedah had pushed the oral surgeon to take his time.

He'd been fighting the anesthesia when he heard her tell the doctor to "add a little flair to his broken nose, as long as you're here." And now? Thanks to her and the surgeon, he might have just been promoted into her league. Maybe he was worthy of her after all. She was the mountain peak of beauty. But now, he was in demand, even without her, and she had started all this in motion. He was unique. People – at least the ones he'd met in California – seemed to crave his opinion like no one anywhere had before.

Another nice-looking young woman passed in the aisle and smiled, keeping eye contact until she passed. He was an emerging celebrity, as Freedah had told him more than once, and with that came responsibility.

"People who throw away the chance for fame and impact aren't worthy of the air they consume from Majestic Mother Earth," she'd said.

Something in his talks about the Bible and God with Coney made him think that attitude was as crooked as the steep bank the plane was making, but when Freedah said it, it seemed so right. And it didn't matter at the moment just how attractive he was to amazingly attractive women. Freedah was still hotter than all of them.

***

When he arrived in Jovial in his pickup after a long day of travel, his first stop was the bank to withdraw some cash. His second was to Ernie's Outfitters.

He walked into Ernie's place soon after the peak dinner hour, and Ernie's wife, Betty, was working on papers at the restaurant counter.

"May I help you, sir?" she asked, looking him over like he was a thousand-dollar bill.

"Betty," he said quizzically. "It's me, Ty."

"Ty Mooring? Can't be." She emerged from behind the counter, reached out to hug him, then stepped back. "It *is* you," she said. "But you don't look like yourself." She held the hug longer than she ever had before, and he knew why.

"I've had a little work done." He smiled broadly. "No more snaggle tooth."

"Well, I suppose it's up to you how you spend your money," she said dismissively. He paid his bill for the fishing gear in full and was waiting for his receipt when Ernie walked in.

"Wow, Ty," he said. "You look as good as the best man in a twenty-five dollar wedding," Ty told Ernie he'd get his stuff out of the bunker before the day was out.

"Getting a room in the casino, huh?"

"A suite."

"Nice. So what changed, except your face?"

"Well, I guess it's all about a higher purpose. My girlfriend Freedah opened my eyes to the opportunity I've been given, and it's a higher calling than just catching fish."

Ernie stared a moment and shook his head. "I take it Freedah is a looker?"

"You can't even imagine," Ty said, grinning. Ernie grinned back.

***

When Ty had cleaned out his tiny bunker room, the contents of which all fit onto the truck's passenger seat, he went to the casino. He expected his room to be gone, rented to someone with more power, influence or money, that it had all been a dream. But the suite was waiting, a twelfh-floor expanse already cleaned and ready to be occupied at long-term rates in his name. He counted out cash to reserve the room for six months, signed some paperwork and stashed his gear into one of the three walk-in closets. The other two were already filled with his new wardrobe, shipped in from San Francisco. Then he opened the curtains to see the view of Jovial and a small glimpse of its river valley and thought it was time to thank God, as Coney had said was a habit that should be cultivated. He sat in an overstuffed chair and did just that.

"Lord, I don't know why you've decided to smother me with all this, but thank you. Help me to enjoy the ride as long as it lasts." The hotel suite was a good start. He could get used to opulence. He opened a large window and looked at the river valley, inhaling deeply. There was the smell he had coveted.

But there was something missing in his good fortune. He knew that between the money, the clothes, this room and Freedah's apparent reciprocated love for him, he couldn't ask for much more on earth, but Freedah's coolness to the last idea he'd introduced punched a small hole in his confidence. Doubt again. But there was one thing he felt Freedah needed that only he could provide: To get in touch with the nature she professed to love.

He called her cell phone.

"I know you weren't thrilled with the forest, but I know you're passionate about the earth – " "Majestic Mother Earth,"- she interrupted – "Then I think you should go with me to where the earth really shows its true colors."

"Don't tell me you're thinking about that camping thing again?"

"That's right. I know all kinds of great places where we could camp by streams or rivers or lakes, just you and me, and you can really get in touch with the thing you worship. Seems to me you need to do that if you want to show you have real credibility when you speak about Majestic Mother Earth."

"I understand that you think that, but it seems like a waste of time. I can't spread the word about her imminent demise if I'm out in the woods someplace. And I don't worship anything. I'm not religious."

"Let's just try it. You might just change your mind about its demise." Freedah remained noncommittal.

"You could really get some important, objective facts that might help in your – our – mission."

"This is not about objectivity. It's about a message. A changing-the-world message. A save-the-rivers message. You don't get effective messages by being objective."

"But you do get the facts."

"Facts, shmacts. If there's one thing I know about PR, it's that facts almost always get in your way. Facts dilute messages. They're never clean and easy to understand. Facts complicate things unless you can control them. Facts are much harder to control than a carefully crafted message. And that's my job. To control the message. I'm damn good at it, and I should decide how to deliver our message of saving the rivers. We'd be a lot better off if we toured with Acrid Reins."

"How could a band of morons like Acrid Reins help get the message out?"

"Well, Tony, as you know, is a passionate environmentalist and pro-organic farm activist. And none of them are morons."

"But he is an animal rights wacko."

"A title he wears proudly," she said, quickly and imperceptibly pushing down her rage at the term 'wacko.' "How can it be wacky to be compassionate? How can you say that being against cramming animals into cages and cramped little sheds is wacky?"

"That's not what they do."

"It is. I've seen the videos."

"Have you ever been on a real farm?"

"Yes. Real, organic farms without animals. I can't be in the presence of animal farmers because they're too cruel. Sinful, even, if I believed in that kind of thing."

"Well, now, I don't know all that much about what's sinful and what's not; other than that I know I'm sinful, and so are you."

"No," she said. "There's no such thing as sin."

"What else do you call all the BS that goes on in the world? All the evil?"

"Not sins, just choices. Choices cannot be good or bad. They're just options, and one can't be better than another."

"I don't think that's how it works."

"But it's the truth."

Ty shook his head slowly, glad that Freedah couldn't see it. "There are a lot of farmers who disagree."

"I don't care if they disagree. They're hiding the truth."

"But without objectivity, how can you be sure?"

"Because my truth makes for a better planet. Their truth destroys the planet."

"I don't believe people can have their own truth, but if anyone could, it would be farmers who feed the whole nation. Saving rivers only helps a few fishermen and rich folks who want to build McMansions with scenery to look at. How does that help people more than farmers who feed people?"

"First of all, a clean river benefits all kinds of life within the ecosystem. I know you know that. And the ecosystem is more important than people. No one can convince me that a human is more important than a lichen or a polliwog. We're all in this together, after all, and truth for them is different than truth for us. Second, most fishermen are very aware of the ecosystem's importance to life on this planet. Those people don't pollute on purpose just for their own greed and profit."

"Neither do farmers."

"Our statistics say otherwise."

"Your statistics don't have to deal with real-world conditions on the farms. And your statistics don't show all the dead fish with some dufus lawyer fisherman's hook stuck in their mouths or all the Styrofoam and plastic they leave behind."

"But they show the bigger picture, and that's what I'm most concerned with."

"The bigger picture is only for statisticians. What happens every day on farms is what concerns me. The hundreds of things farmers have to be aware of, from veterinary medicine to government decrees that make it hard for them to do their jobs."

"Their jobs are immoral."

"So I guess that makes you a sinner by eating."

"If I ate factory farm meat, yes."

"No such thing as a factory farm."

Freedah shook her head, wishing Ty could see her. Much as she hated it, she had to compromise. For how long was her most pressing question? At least, she needed to convince Ty that she would compromise.

"Look," she said. "I've got a lot on my plate right now, and on top of the list is Acrid Reins, my biggest client. I've got to get them going on tour. How about if we both go with them on tour for a while and then I'll go camping with you. Just a few days, mind you. I'm very busy."

"I'll hold you to the camping thing, but I'm not going to tour with that band of wackos."

"Not even for me?"

"Nope."

Things had just gotten more difficult for Freedah.

***

Two days later, Freedah arrived in Jovial and went to their casino suite and waited, naked, on the bed. When Ty arrived, with the sole purpose of showering before heading off to the Dogues farm for food, beer and discussion, the inevitable happened.

After that, she announced that she was only there until her flight to Detroit the next morning. She was on her way to DC, she said, to arrange the final details of the Acrid Reins tour's eastern swing. But she couldn't resist seeing him, if only for a few hours. And she wanted an answer from Ty, along with the second hundred-thousand-dollar check he'd promised.

"If we take this tour, I'll be shoved to the background like I was with Kaley Carrumbo. I want to have a role, to make it a celebration," he said as he handed her a check. "You said it yourself. I'm in demand now. People have seen me in the news and they want to see more. I got so many looks on the plane, you wouldn't believe it. But I don't want it to be about me. I want to present the whole picture. I want to thank farmers for what they do. For feeding us, caring for their land, for being the ultimate and only real environmentalists. With the fame and face I have, I'm in big demand. You told me that. If I toured with Acrid Reins, I would want ten minutes before every show to speak and tell the farmers' story."

Freedah took his hand and pulled him close again, kissed him.

"If that's what you want, love, that's what we'll do. Just let me create the buzz around it. Let me handle the PR. It's what I do best, and together, we can really make this happen." She pulled him in and hugged him long and close. He returned her affection, and she could feel it in his crotch. All was OK again.

"Let's do it," Ty said.

***

As he stepped into the shower, Freedah stepped into the dining area of the suite, scanned the check with her phone, transferred it to MELL and called Phoenix.

"We need to change tactics a little," she said. "Did you get the hundred grand?"

"Just got it. Where's the rest?"

"Going to take a little more time. He thinks he's been given some purpose in life by his God. And he wants to promote and congratulate farmers.

"Congratulate them? For what? Killing the planet?"

"Don't worry. I'll get it all taken care of. But I could use a few of our activists for a while. If we can disrupt his message, we can get the press on our side, and our message will be even stronger. If he gets his way, it will all be a huge snooze. We need a hook, a public relations gimmick. A little controversy. A lot of controversies."

"Most of our best rabble-rousers are tied up here in California. We have ballot initiatives to influence."

"I don't need the best. Just ones who will do as they're told."

"Why don't we get Grandy to help? He's close by you, in Detroit."

"Lansing," she corrected. "OK. Send him up. We'll be ready to go in a couple of weeks, I think."

Ty slept well but had a strange dream. He was a mosquito, so sated with blood that he could not fly. But he was satisfied, content even if he were about to be squashed. Then some unseen hand did it, and blood splattered a large stain on the white wall on which he clung. He awakened.

Chapter 28

Ty parked his new Ford, now showing he had driven 1,028 miles, behind what locals had dubbed "bait shop row," and walked the boardwalk to Ernie's Outfitters. With a passing nod to Betty, he went to his mailbox and the postal drop station next to it He filled out the form for a change of address and sent it off.

In his cubby mailbox, he found a note from Coney.

"I'm planting trees today and need a hand. Interested?"

Ty drove to the Dogues farm and parked as far away from every other vehicle between the house and barn as he could. He rough-housed a moment with Pearly and Gates and heard a noise in the farm's workshop. Coney was loading pails full of seedling pine trees in the back of the farm's rusted but functional utility pickup truck, along with long sections of twine and dozens of metal fence posts. Two large containers of water had been secured above the bed and up near the cab, and two long hoses were attached to spigots near the bottom.

"Nice truck," said Coney. "Someone might think you came into some money lately."

"Nope. It came to me."

"Well, then, how about paying me that a hundred bucks you owe me?"

Ty twitched his head. It was entirely possible that he did owe Coney. But Coney smiled, and they both grinned.

With the dogs trailing closely behind, the two men drove slowly to a five-acre patch of lush green grass, which seemed out of place this early in the year.

"Sure looks different without all the pines," Ty said. "How many trees to replace them?"

"Two thousand. About every 20 years, we get to do this. Last summer, we harvested, then ground out the stumps and planted this rye as a cover crop, all while you were indisposed." He grinned at Ty.

"You don't have to be so gentle about it," Ty said. "I was in prison. For trying to make false lottery tickets, and no, I'm not proud of it."

Coney said nothing as they parked the truck at one end of the field, just in front of a small pile of debris.

"Where'd all this crap come from?"

"When we were harvesting, some greeniacs came out with hand-painted signs and placards. Started chanting something about saving the old growth and that I was a carbon monster. Or earth destroyer or climate denier. Take your pick. None of them are original, and none of them are true. Very angry group, that's for sure. I made some calls, and before long, they each had two guns pointing at their butts. So they threw their signs all over the field, for some reason, and scurried off like cats who just heard a pack of coyotes coming at them. They were yelling about having me arrested for assault. Guess they never did. We'll load up all that wasted lumber when we're done. Good for our bonfire on Memorial Day."

Ty laughed, and the two began work. Both knew from experience what to do.

Coney took one end of the twine and walked with it and a five-pound hammer in one hand and several metal fence posts in the other. Ty stayed behind and kept the twine from knotting. When Coney reached the other end of the field, he pounded in his stake and tied the twine to it, about a foot off the ground. He motioned to Ty, moving him left of where he was and yelled to go ahead. Ty pounded in his end, and soon, they had a perfectly straight string along which to start planting the first row.

Ty pulled another stake from the truck, one with another length of string, tied it to the first post and went sideways. Where the string ended, exactly four paces away, he pounded another stake. Coney had retrieved more stakes and string and was doing the same. Before long, they had staked out the entire acreage and were ready to start planting.

Coney had a long, narrow spade for the job that looked like something fishermen use for ice fishing. He'd slice a small opening in the sod, then move four paces along the string for the next. Ty pulled a plant from the clump that was resting in a five-gallon pail half-filled with water. The green pine needles perched on top of a six-inch or longer ball of roots. He pulled individual seedlings apart and shoved the roots deep, pulling the tiny trees back up until about six inches was above the ground, and stepped the hole closed around it. He'd done that about 100 times when Coney stood to stretch his back. Ty was faster than most non-farm boys, and Coney was only ahead of him by a few holes as the two worked efficiently.

"Glad you're back, Ty. Nice to have someone who knows how to work. Guess your new MELL girlfriend would be proud of you for doing this work, huh?"

"Don't know if she's ever seen an operation like this." Ty laughed. "She's a tree hugger, not a tree planter."

"So what's MELL's problem with farmers? We're the ones who plant trees and crops that sequester carbon. Tree huggers should love farmers."

"That's not how they see it," Ty said. "They think farmers use too many chemicals and pollute the water and ground and poison the food. They think cows are more dangerous for the environment than cars." Both laughed and shook their heads. "But they believe they're the ones who will save the planet."

"From what?"

"Haven't quite figured that out yet. Maybe from farmers, I guess. They think farmers are cruel just for the fun of it. All I know is that they're committed to solving all these problems, whatever they think the problems are. You know, the ones that they'll never solve because they're really unsolvable. But they keep trying. At least they're trying. My only problem with them is they're convinced that they know more about the big picture, and that puts them a level above the rest of us in their minds."

"What do you believe?"

Ty paused and stood from his planting stoop and stretched his back. "I believe what we're doing right here is the best thing we can do for the planet, and I believe tree huggers are mostly city folks who believe what they see on the internet."

"Never met a greenie yet who really understands what farmers do," Coney said. "I even hired one a few years ago. He lied about his work experience, and Jenn caught him trying to steal a calf. He was trying to put it in his car. Said he was going to set it free. That's how much sense they make."

"Free?" Ty repeated. "Free to do what? Starve or get eaten by wolves in the woods?"

"Don't know if they ever think about that. When I fired him, he started in on a long speech about nature taking care of itself if we'd just leave it alone. Got so excited that he was spitting on me."

Ty shook his head. "My gal Freedah hasn't laid that kind of crap on me yet. I think she would be willing to listen to the farmers' point of view. She'd just never had the chance, growing up in the city."

"Have her come on out here for a day. I'll put her to work shoveling manure in the bullpen. She'd get an education fast."

"Don't think that will happen." Ty laughed and suddenly realized something he hadn't quite yet comprehended. "She's trying to grow her own brand. Her words. I don't know what that means, really. But I know growing is a good thing."

"How about you, then," Coney asked as they continued their task. "Are you growing in faith?"

"I don't really know what all that means. How do I know I'm growing?"

"Lots of ways. Some people gauge it by things that have fallen away. I already know you've purged gambling from your life, so that's a start."

"That's only because the casino would arrest me if I win." Ty smiled. "I still get the urge sometimes, you know, feeling lucky at times?"

"Do you really want to gamble during those times?"

"Sure. But I know that it's really a stupid thing. Why should I give my money to a casino that already has enough?"

"You're on the right track without even knowing it. Proverbs asks why we think we should spill our water in the streets and answers by saying we should drink water from our own wells."

"But that's not me resisting," Ty said. "It's the casino, or fear of the casino jail, that stops me most of the time. Don't know if that counts as resisting temptation."

"Sometimes God uses people and earthly conditions to help you grow," Coney said. "But besides removing things, what have you added?"

"Well, to tell the truth, I've failed. I forget to read my Bible. I don't pray like the real Christians do. Don't even know where to begin. I haven't been to church since I was in prison. I don't know which church to pick. And then there's the money. It seems like the whole world wants my money. Money seems to be the only thing anyone wants out of me. How do I deal with that?"

"What do you want?"

"I just don't know. Some people tell me I have it made. They say just take it easy. Party. And really, most of the time, that seems to be the most attractive thing. The easiest thing, anyway. I mean, even before the money, I never really had a whole lot of ambition or drive to be some big wig or influencer. I was happy enough just living. I always had a kind of distrust of people who threw their money around to impress people. But this money changed it all. God gave me the money, I suppose, but now I don't know what he wants me to do with it. It's frustrating. My first instinct was to live high on the hog until it was all gone. That would make me an interesting character. Maybe Garit West would even do a story about me to make me famous for a day or two, right? Lots of famous artists and musicians are all messed up. But the whole world seems to think their quirks are what it takes to make a difference in the world. But that seems so selfish and wasteful and, well, insignificant to me now. I think it's important to support the people who need it most, but are they farmers? Are they the poor, the homeless, the addicted? Does Mother Earth need it?"

"Everybody thinks they need it. But what God wants is you."

Ty planted a few trees in silence, doubting that a God as powerful as religious people said he was could want a flea like him.

"Does this count? I'm in demand to speak; at least, that's what my girlfriend Freedah tells me. If I speak to crowds, does that count as giving myself to him? I'm not that important. I can't match Freedah's devotion or her influence, no matter how good-looking I've gotten since Snowmaker punched me around."

Coney consulted his phone. "Here's a guideline when you decide what God wants from you," he said, holding it out for Ty to see. "Colossians 3: 23-24 says that "whatever you do, do it heartily, for the Lord, and not for men."

"So basically, don't be a lazy ass," Ty said. Coney laughed. "That's a good interpretation."

"So how do I know what to do?"

"What's been in the front of your mind? Coney asked. "Sometimes God will keep whispering to you until you get it."

"The only whispers I hear are Freedah's, right into my ear."

"Understood. She's a hottie, huh?

"Way out of my league."

"Yet here you are, playing in her ballpark."

"I have to, Coney. Where else could I be part of her life? I mean, every time we're together, I can't resist her. No one could. She has it all."

"I'm sure. Well, I was thinking about telling you to be careful, that she may be a user, a gold-digger, as they used to say. But I think you can handle it. I just don't want to see you thinking too much with … you know." He grabbed his crotch in his best Michael Jackson imitation.

Ty grinned. "I know. I've been guilty of that before, and to tell the truth, I thought I was doing it with her. But when you meet her, you'll know. I don't figure that there's any way this will last very long, but dammit, Coney, where else will I get a ride like this? I'm going to enjoy it while it lasts."

Coney nodded.

"What's your plan for the money you have left when she's done with you?"

Ty grinned at Coney. No wonder he consulted the farmer whenever he could.

"Well, and I'm just spitballing here, when I was in prison, watching politicians and preachers on TV, I thought that I could do a better job than any of them, particularly the politicians. I thought that so many of them missed the point of what they were talking about or maybe didn't really understand the day-to-day life of everyday people. I had the time, so I even wrote a speech or two, trying to find common sense in all the things politicians seemed to be missing. I never gave those speeches, though. I figured I'd never get the chance anyway. I have no education and no experience with the things they talked about."

"Have you read about Solomon?" Ty shook his head.

"He was and is widely known as the wisest man besides Jesus who ever lived. He wrote in Ecclesiastes 11:1 that we should cast our bread upon the waters, which means trying new things and new investments. You never know which slice will gain you a profit or which won't. Maybe you should try making one of those speeches, but only if your whole heart is in it and you give it all you have."

"And where do I start?"

"Well, you're in luck," Coney said as the two settled into routine planting work again. Soon the dogs walked among them, inspecting their work, then, satisfied, laid down in the shade of the truck and watched their progress.

"The JFA's annual picnic is on Saturday, and we had a speaker cancel on us. I can get you on the docket to speak. It's probably time to clear things up about your property because there are a lot of rumors and tongue-wagging going on. It might be good to talk to that PR gal from NFA. Melanie, I think, is her name. You met her. Good-looking redhead? She'll be there. I think you'd do great."

***

Ty was as nervous as an executive with a dead phone battery as he looked up at the stage. For two days, he'd been preparing, although he was often interrupted by the temptation to cancel the whole thing. No one wanted to hear what he had to say. Why would they? But it was too late now. He was there, and his name was on the one-page program being passed out to attendees.

He didn't feel prepared, but he'd done what he could. He'd bought a new laptop without shopping at all, and he'd studied great speakers as far as the Internet would take him. He read articles about public speaking and watched old famous speeches by statesmen such as Martin Luther King and preachers such as Steven Furtick and Billy Graham. He noted how they structured their speeches, how they drew the audience in and how they held their audiences' attention. He went to the library and studied a middle-school book meant for speech classes. He wrote a speech and practiced it, polished it and refined it. In the end, he wasn't satisfied that this was the kind of effort it took to do a task for the

Lord, let alone himself. Above all, he didn't want to become an embarrassment.

He took the stage at the covered and heated pavilion at the Jovial City Park, under the watchful eyes of the Civil War statue of Alan Jovial, town founder. The statue wore a fading, chipping coat of paint meant to look like underwear, and he smiled. Underwear on the statue was now a hallowed tradition for Jovial's youthful society, replacing annual messages on the tall town water tower.

It was a large crowd, dressed for the still-chilly early spring air, content to listen passively after a marvelous homegrown dinner of seasonal peas, corn, carrots, potatoes, beef and pork, all from the surplus farmers had set aside for this very occasion through the Farmers Own Store. What Ty didn't know as the butterflies built cocoons in his stomach was that, before he stepped to the mic, he'd already charmed most of the women in the crowd based on his new face alone.

"Thank you all for allowing me this opportunity to speak to you and for cooperating with me through all the trials and tribulations of unexpected prosperity," he began. Female voices laughed. So far, so good.

"I feel kind of like one of those lottery winners you hear about who blows their whole fortune in a year. Or like the farmer who won the lottery and kept farming until it was gone." More laughter, but he knew it was a cliche. "But I know you folks have experienced nothing but prosperity because of the government..." He rolled his eyes and waited for the laugh, which came, but he wasn't sure his sarcasm had worked completely. He was still nervous, but it was fading. Time to settle in for the meat of the message.

"For you folks who don't know me, I'm Ty Mooring, a child of an American father and Mexican mother," he continued. "They worked the fields here in Jovial and taught me the value of hard work and the chance it gives you to improve your own lot in life. So, I want to thank you, farmers, for giving my parents the opportunity to make a new life in Michigan and the United States, the land of opportunity. I count just being in the United States –

and being a citizen – as a gift from God, and Jovial, in particular, has been the place where the opportunity presented itself if you're willing to work hard. I've talked to enough of you and other business owners to know that hard work is something the rest of the country has forgotten.

"I will admit that even though I was taught hard work, I made some bad decisions not that long ago. I was looking for a shortcut through all that hard work, and I paid for it. But my time in jail led me to a preacher who introduced me to Jesus, who I still don't quite understand, and I went back to my former employer, Coney Dogues, who hopefully can help me understand.

"But then, just before I got out of jail, I was really baffled to find out that the state wanted to give me land and money just because of who my parents were and because of my Hispanic heritage.

Now, if either of my parents were still alive, they would not have liked that whole development. Without putting in the work, they would have told me, you shouldn't accept anything. Now, that's not to say they would have turned down three million bucks and a piece of the most productive vegetable ground in the country because, despite what some politicians apparently believe, all migrants aren't stupid." The audience chuckled, but it seemed an uneasy laugh, just as he'd hoped. "But they would have told me, in line with their work ethic, to be careful not to squander this, but to put it to good use.

"And that's what I want to talk to you about tonight. Putting my newfound, undeserved and unexpected good fortune to good use."

Ty had the farmers' attention now. He smiled, and many women of all ages sat forward in their seats.

"I've told some of you this before, and I want to make it clear that I will continue to keep this ground I own in farming, and I will lease it at a very reasonable price. That's the least I can do to help farmers, who I respect and have admired just about all my life. You've been kicked around by government regulations and rules made up by people who have no idea what you need, and if I can help, I will. I want what you want. To keep you guys farming. The whole country depends on you." He paused to let the applause die down. "So, if anyone has questions, I'd be happy to answer what I know."

Fulton Gray stepped from the front row of tables and took the mic from the wandering NFA's public relations girl, the thick, pretty redhead. Ty didn't remember her name but noticed that she was dressed and made up differently than that day in Fulton's greenhouse break room.

"We've all just heard about this new bill that has been introduced that would restrict our ability to use pesticides and fertilizer," Fulton said. "Ty, maybe you can educate people about the danger of that bill?"

"I don't know much about the bill, But if you folks will help me understand what's going on, I'd be happy to help. But I don't know how to help. Please give me suggestions, and let's make it about more than just the money. I want to get involved. I want to have a clear message now, and I want to help you feed the world if I can. Just fill me in on this bill. If it hurts farmers, then I'm against it." The crowd cheered, but not as enthusiastically as Ty had hoped.

When the formal speeches were done, and the crowd was milling around, Coney, Fulton and Jenn approached, along with a few more fierce-looking farmers.

"We hear that you've been aligning yourself with some anti-farming group," someone said. "How can we trust anyone who's doing that?" Ty found the voice. It was Rick Frandor, the biggest rock dealer in the state, from nearby Sventon. Ty had hand-picked rocks on his farm a time or two.

"It's called MELL - -Mother Earth Liberation League," Ty said. "But don't be fooled by the name. They're not crazy. Just passionate. And the woman I've been working with is passionate. Dedicated to ending pollution and making the rivers clean and perfect again. But she needs education about what farmers do. I can help her with that. You folks are the example she needs to see."

"Ah, so there's a girl," said Fulton. "MELL's a pretty radical group, has used big-time deception in the past. How do you know she's who she says she is?"

"I just know," Ty answered. "She's not like the other enviros. She has a mission in life, and she wouldn't want to destroy farmers. When she begins to understand that the land and the farmers are inseparable, she'll see to reason. She's just never had any experience with farmers. She's a city girl."

"And you've fallen for her?" asked Fulton.

"You don't even know the half of it," Ty smiled. "And not only that, she's a very hard worker. A little education about farm issues, and she can get stuff done."

"Just beware of hidden agendas," Coney said. "Remember, I was your age once. I understand how easy it is to be manipulated by a pretty face." Jenn playfully smacked his shoulder. "I meant you!" Coney protested. Jenn smiled.

"I'm not being manipulated," Ty defended. "She's sincere, even if she doesn't quite understand all there is to farming. Her focus is rivers, but she's reasonable. She wouldn't do anything to hurt people. I'm sure of that."

"How do you know?" Coney asked. "Most of the enviros I'd dealt with hate people more than they love the earth. Have you been reading the first few chapters of Proverbs?"

"Haven't had much time lately to read my Bible."

"I suggest you do," Coney said. "It's awfully easy to be deceived. And be aware that there are people – mostly farmers -- who will oppose you if you align yourself with MELL."

"I'm one of them," Frandor shouted. Coney continued. "Some people believe they are a sort of terrorist group, out to destroy farming and make themselves rich. There are all kinds of wolves in sheep's clothing out there, Ty. Besides all that, this is our money, our taxes, that made you rich."

"I hadn't thought about that," Ty said, "but I didn't ask for your money. I had nothing to do with it."

Frandor grumbled."But you took it, didn't you?" Ty looked Frandor in the eye. "Yep. But I can use it for your good, I hope."

"I hope so, too." Frandor spit on the ground and walked away, shaking his head.

***

When the crowd thinned out, Ty noticed the NFA's Michigan PR person standing on the perimeter. He wished he'd remembered her name as she stepped forward, a solidly thick, fit woman in her early 40s, put together in balanced proportions and both pleasant and fierce simultaneously. She introduced herself with a two-handed, lingering handshake.

"Ty, I am so interested in your story," she said. "I'm Melanie Swann, director of public relations with the Michigan branch of the National Farmers Association.

"Sure, we met at Fulton Gray's farm."

"Did we? Well, I'm sure I would have noticed you."

"I look a little different than I did then."

"Well, don't change anything more," she said, touching his arm and squeezing. "As I'm sure you know, farmers have been getting a lot of bad press from the media and public that just doesn't have the first clue about what they do, how hard it is, the challenges they face. You seem to have that understanding."

"Well, I grew up around farmers. Can't say any of them ever did me any harm."

"But they did you good?"

"Sure. The farmers up here, at least, offered my parents full-time jobs after they'd been running around the country following the harvests. They told me the farmers here had the best housing, paid a fair wage, and allowed my mother to support her family back in Mexico. And my dad, who was illiterate, found a place to settle down, get a steady income, and provide for his family here, even though it was just me and my mom."

"And you've worked with the fruit, vegetable and field crops?"

"Yes, all of that. I've sprayed pesticides and fertilizer. I'v helped work cattle, sheep and horses. Picked rocks. Even milked cows for a few months."

"Let me run an idea by you, Ty," Melanie said, pausing. She looked into Ty's eyes for an uncomfortably long time. "Sorry," she shook her head slightly as if to shake off stray thoughts. "You're sure we met? How could I not remember you?" Ty didn't respond, even though he wanted to tell her it wasn't the first time he'd heard that since his face had been fixed. "We're going to have a political rally next Saturday, April 8," Melanie said. "Would you speak there?"

"What would I have to do?"

"We'll get you prepared first about this bill because after you read it, I'm sure you'll understand just how bad it will be for farmers. But the most important thing you've got to do is tell your story."

"I don't know. Why would people listen to me about a bill? All I know is what happened to me. I'm not good at politics. I'm too honest." Melanie smiled.

"You're a very charming young man, very charismatic," she said, touching and holding his arm. "People will listen to you because you're young, good-looking, and have a real trustworthy face. Your voice is deep enough to sound authoritative but not harsh or grating. With the right publicity and your looks, media will come to you if they're interested in getting the farmers' side of the story."

"Why don't they go ask the real farmers?"

"It's a trust thing, Ty. Most farmers lost trust in the media decades ago. They're wary of any reporters, mostly because reporters don't have the first clue about ag issues. Worst of all, they don't seem to care. Farming is foreign to them, and it's too hard or time-consuming for them to do any actual digging. If you were to agree with our stances on issues like this, which I think you likely will, we'll give you the facts. The real truth. All you'd have to do is communicate with them. We'll keep you trained and up to date with the latest technology and practices. And we'll pay you. You could become famous as the face of agriculture. It's really up to you how far you can go."

"Don't know if I really want fame. I'm just a plain, ordinary guy who got lucky." Melanie blushed.

"Fame helps you help people. More people than you could imagine. You could help educate an ignorant public, and I think you'd find that it could be a lot of fun, too. You'd meet all kinds of interesting people."

"I meet interesting people now. How could I convince people that what I say is true? I mean, the other side has their sets of facts, too, which would almost certainly contradict your facts."

"Our facts are true. Theirs are lies. Blatant lies, proven to be false. Besides, if you speak at the rally, you're speaking to the choir. Mostly, you'll just reinforce what they already know."

"But how will I know the difference between truth and lies?"

"With hard evidence. We'd give you documentation from scientific data."

"The other side says theirs is scientific and true, too."

"I understand the problem," Melanie said, smiling. She was so close to closing the deal she could smell it. "But only one side can be true. People lie with statistics easily and often, but not us. In contrast to the enviro's history of dirty practices and methods, we admit if we were wrong and try to correct it. Check out our website and you'll see it's true. Enviros stick to their lies even when a problem has already been fixed. Farmers try to fix problems. Enviros and anti-farmers try to keep problems problematic. For example, science says beyond a doubt that the Jovial River – and most rivers, in fact – are much cleaner than they were 20 to 30 years ago. We admit that we were part of the problem back then, but we know we're part of the solution now."

"I can vouch for that. When I was little, my parents didn't allow us to eat fish from the river. Now, even the state has said it's okay. Good thing, too, because those fish are really, really good when they're cooked right."

"Perfect answer from the face of agriculture," Melanie said, stepping into his aura. He didn't step back from her as he smelled her perfume.

"The facts we can document tell you why," she said. "Farmers have decreased pesticide use and use them much more efficiently than ever before. We have sales figures and state statistics that prove it. Enviros won't tell you that. They prefer to cite statistics from 30-40 years ago because, without a problem to look at and cry about, they're out of a job."

"I still don't know if I'm the best candidate for this."

"Are you kidding? You're perfect. Handsome, experienced, modest and appear to speak with passion from the heart. You'd be as charming to them as you are to me. Let's just start with the rally. Speak there for maybe 15 minutes. That's all we ask. If you'll do that, we'll take the next steps. How about we talk about this over a drink?" Suddenly, she was irresistible.

***

If Freedah Forest believed in such ridiculous rituals, she'd have felt like she did years ago, a repentant sinner prepared for cajoled contrition. But now she knew priests were the worst sinners of all, so she was prepared for a fight when she sat in a cushy chair in front of Phoenix Tippin's oversized, 140-year-old oak desk. Phoenix was no priest, although she suspected he and many priests shared the same sins. But she had nothing to repent about.

The cushions pulled her down like quicksand, causing her to look up at the CEO at an angle that strained her neck muscles. She would not relent, but Phoenix had accusations from which she could no longer hide.

She lightly massaged a complaining neck muscle with her left hand. With her right hand, she gripped a copy of a glossy print magazine.

"Phoenix, I wouldn't blame you at all if you called me in to fire me, but there's something you should know," she started. "It wasn't my fault. The farmers up there in Michigan convinced some right-wing nut legislator – a guy with power and influence on the finance committee, for some reason – to stall that bill in committee. His name is Fectid. Something like that. And Grandy is too green to know yet how to get around the SOB. It was beyond my control. I couldn't be everywhere at once, you know. I have too much on my plate."

"But isn't it your job, Freedah, to be aware of anything that could compromise our goals? Didn't you train Grandy well enough? Did you lose your passion for Mother Earth?"

"Don't be ridiculous," she argued, waving off the charge against her with her left hand. "I just didn't have the staff I needed. Maybe I underestimated the farmer groups' power. They actually have a PR division, weak, but it's there. Being so near to Detroit, I thought those polluters would have already been in trouble. But the voters listened to the farmers' statistics, not ours."

"They're the same statistics! You just didn't interpret or present them properly. I thought we taught you well enough that there is always something to ferret out of statistics, something we can use. You didn't do it. And that was your job. And at this point, I don't know if we should keep you in our fold anymore. You didn't exactly remain faithful to us."

"I've been as faithful as anyone and even more passionate," she said, forcing down emotion that she could not let this man see. "I would think my dedication would be obvious to you. I had my name legally changed for MELL. I dyed my hair like this for MELL. I've brought in thousands of dollars over the last 18 months. I haven't betrayed anyone or anything related to the ultimate cause of the Mother Earth Liberation League. I'm guilty of nothing except that one mistake, which was really Grandy's fault, not mine, and one that anyone could make, and I think I deserve another chance."

"Or maybe you need to go to Michigan and help Grandy." Tippin clicked his computer mouse and looked at the screen. Freedah thought she saw his features soften a little, and as she looked at him, she understood why his detractors called him 'pretty boy.' His still-black hair was thick and quaffed in a high-end San Francisco salon every two weeks. His suit costs a couple of thousand bucks, easily. His completely capped teeth shone as if he'd just come from a whitener commercial, and his eyes were a deep, penetrating blue, the result of tinted contact lenses.

"My records show you were involved in seven cases, including the one in Detroit." he said. "Your total fundraising was only $200,000. Maybe a little more. That's terrible, Freedah. That money won't even pay my pension, let alone what's been promised to all those other lawyers on staff. And when I subtract your salary and benefits over the last year-and-a-half, I just don't know if I can, with all good conscience, support you much longer. The board of directors will have my head. I think it may have something to do with that redneck snaggletooth boy. You've gone sweet on him, haven't you?" he smiled luridly.

Freedah ignored the question. "I've earned a second chance. She held up the magazine and struggled to lean forward from the clutches of the chair. "I guarantee you I can raise at least a million bucks in the next few months. Phoenix. Let me try. Go ahead and send me to Michigan. Let me get that bill passed. It's worth more than millions to us. Give me six months. You can fire me if I don't have that bill passed by then. And give Granderson a chance. He can still help. He speaks these rednecks' language. He's one of them."

"Sma," Phoenix corrected. "What do you have in mind?"

"I thought you didn't want to know. You know, credible deniability?"

Tippin leaned back in his leather desk chair, his head resting midway up the chair's back. He pressed his fingertips together and put his two index fingers to his mouth, feigning pensiveness.

"In six months, you'll be vested into our pension system, and then I won't be able to weed you out if you don't perform. But I'm a forgiving, compassionate man."

"I know," Freedah said, leaning forward still more, fighting against the cushion, trying to hold her down. "I've seen the pictures of you with your dog."

"Not my dog," he corrected. "Just a prop. I hate dogs. Always too happy and eager to please. And what do they give back? Big food and vet bills and shit all over your yard. But that doesn't matter. Look. What makes you think you can get this rube to give his money to MELL? And what makes you think you can get that Michigan bill passed?"

"Look at me, Phoenix." She stood, breaking the chair's hold. Her skirt was tight and high, and her bare, tanned legs were long and lean. "You know me and how I work. You even hit on me a couple of times, remember?"

"Don't even try to blackmail me, Freedah. You have no proof of anything, and even if you did, you'd be way out of your league." As if recognizing a flaw he'd been trying to hide, Tippin straightened his tie and smoothed the lapels on his shirt, which was whiter than his teeth.

"As I said, I'm a forgiving and passionate man —er, compassionate," he said. "And I do know that there are very few men who could resist you, let alone some backwoods hick with bad teeth living up in a shithole, Michigan, anal abscess of the world."

"However," Freedah interrupted, producing a second printout and handing it to her boss, "that abscess has a cause. The Jovial River has been named one of the cleanest rivers in the world."

Tippin read a little while from the article printed just six months before in "Pure Fishing Magazine," the official publication of the Pure Fly Fishing Foundation (PFFF).

"Well, I can see your hook, and I can see where you think you can raise funds from the fear that the river might be polluted, but how are you going to correct the problems with this rube, to begin with? He's already gone rogue, and right in front of Kaley Carrumbo. What if he does it again?"

"He won't, and Kaley's show is no problem. Tony Finn's performance glossed all that over. No one will remember Ty. And now that his teeth are fixed, he's a new man. He could really help if I can make him see the light."

"I believe you," Tippin said. "I also expect results. If you can show me a million bucks and get that bill out of committee within the next four months, I'll let you keep going. Four months gets us to the primary election out there. Get me two million, and I'll get you a window office. But you only get four months. Then it's either produce, or you're gone."

"I said I wanted six months," she asserted, but Phoenix didn't blink. She lifted her head high. "Just keep those fishermen on the hook," she said, pointing to the magazine on Phoenix's desk. "That land is just waiting for them. Thanks, Phoenix. You won't regret it. But there is one small problem before I get started."

"Oh?"

"Acrid Reins needs me to get their tour started."

Tippin sighed, then stood to meet her powerful gaze. "Do them both," he said. Her eyes widened and grew quickly steely. She snarled at him.

"I'll do it," she said. "I'll keep you informed."

***

One thing Freedah had always appreciated about Majestic Mother Earth was that she kept her nose out of things. Oh, there was a time when MME had control over her own destiny, but that was long past, and historians had stopped talking about that. Majestic Mother Earth never meddled in the affairs of humans anymore, no matter how much damage they did to her, like some abused and frightened spouse. And that was why Freedah was in charge. MME left all those fine details to people like her, who had the drive to defend her and the talent to change things. Sure, she sent the occasional big storm, but she was just upset and vengeful. But the day-to-day lives of the people MME supported were of no consequence.

Besides, the affairs of puny people like Ty Mooring were up to people like Freedah. It was her duty to get what she could out of life. Mother Earth didn't even care if she was saved or not, eternal or not. She knew her place in the universe, revolving around some random sun star. People were on their own, and as Freedah began planning her next move, she wished that she wasn't.

The plans in her mind were never going to let her sleep that night. Four measly months to get money out of a guy who never had money before. Four lousy months to get a bill through that had more things for farmers to object to than anything she'd ever seen. This was a new challenge. Men who had money to burn were easy. A little attention from her, maybe let some homely millionaire be seen in public with her, maybe even have a picture taken for credibility purposes, and those men opened their bank accounts to her. But Ty was different. He didn't seem to care about the money, which was foreign to her. She never met anyone who wasn't scratching every day, all day, for more money, more power, more sex. He was an enigma, but given enough time, she'd get him figured out. And four months wasn't enough. She'd have to really put on the full-court press on this one. She called him, knowing he'd be pleased to hear from her.

***

"You'll never believe it, Freedah," Ty said when the obligatory 'miss you' words were exhausted.

"The National Farmers Association wants me to speak at a local political rally."

Ty had been right. Freedah didn't believe it. It couldn't be. She had been out of the loop, getting the Acrid Reins tour on track, and Ty had gone rogue, done something on his own, without consulting her. She should have known she couldn't trust him. This was dangerous, and she needed that control back. This was the worst thing imaginable, especially with her tight window of time.

"You sure this is legit? This group supports all the bad things farmers do to their animals. They've fought against MELL on nearly every piece of legislation we've supported."

"I don't know what happens in DC or Lansing," Ty said, "but I do know farmers. Been around them all my life. They're honest and caring. I trust them. How can I trust MELL, a group on the other side of the country who I never met before?"

"Don't you trust me?"

Ty paused. She felt panic but shoved it aside. *Shit. Things just got more complicated. Think Sandra, Think! Don't let this one go! Maybe you can turn this to your advantage.*

"Of course, I trust you, Freedah," Ty said. "But I don't really trust Phoenix or those other phonies I met while I was out there. And you've told me from the beginning to follow my passion. Well, I'm more passionate about the people who farm than a river, and I have no passion for any river other than the Jovial."

"Look, this is not a decision you make hastily. Don't decide until I get back there. Promise me?"

"Okay. When are you coming?" He said it in his most enthusiastic voice, but his conscience was eating him alive. All because of Melanie Swann, who he had let manipulate him when he'd let whiskey see her flesh only and not her soul.

A good sign, Freedah knew from his voice. He missed her. Maybe she was getting her grip back.

"I'll be back as soon as I can, babe."

***

Freedah's first call when she hung up with Ty was to Tony Finn.

"Hey, gorgeous," he said. "Hold on a minute." She heard some music go silent, and Tony's voice reappeared.

"What's up?"

Freedah rested her arm on her desk, pen in hand, ready to make a few check marks.

"Look, Tony, we've been together a long time, right? I mean, who was in your corner and got you out of that mess in California?"

"That was all you, beautiful. Never saw a PR spin done better."

"Yep, and I've gotten even better at it since then. That's why I think we should work together again."

"We're already working on my next tour. What you got in mind?"

"Well, I've been thinking about MELL and how it's changed so much since you signed that contract. They're not about the planet anymore, Tony. They're too busy making money."

"Nothing wrong with making money, honey."

"Agreed, but what are we all in this environmentalism for, anyway? It can't be all about the money. We still have an obligation to defend the planet, right?"

"Absolutely."

"I knew we were on the same page. You and I are too driven, too dedicated to let the planet be killed for profit. That makes us no better than the farmers, and that's why I'm afraid MELL has lost its sense of mission under Phoenix. They're far too focused on rivers, and you know as well as I do that there are more important things. Greater things. Now, your PR contract is up with them next month, right?" Freedah knew it was because the Acrid Reins file was on the screen in front of her.

"That sounds about right."

"Would you consider signing with me? I'm thinking about starting my own company, one that wouldn't compromise with the planet just to make some board of directors rich fat cats."

"I agree. Capitalist assholes. Only after the money. But I can't break my contract. They'd sue my ass off."

"But after this tour, and after you've done all your community service concerts, and your contract is up, you're free. I wouldn't ask you for anything but that. Besides, it might take me a little time to get it all pulled together. Just don't let anyone manage you except me, okay?"

"Well, I think we could do that. After all, you're the one handling everything now. So it would be a seamless transition."

"Exactly. So I can count on you?"

"I'd do anything for you, Sandra."

"It's Freedah now, remember?"

"Sorry. Old habits. Send me a contract, and I'll sign it. My new album comes out soon, so we'll be ready to go."

"Perfect. I may have just the thing to promote it and get your community service over with. A kind of soft promo that will set the groundwork for your bigger, for-profit tour later. But you have to do the community service freebies first. If you don't, you go to jail. It's just that simple. We'll go to farm towns and convince them of the error of their ways. Small venues, but an impact you can't buy in a stadium or fair venue. We'll still get the crowds because of the fireworks, if nothing else. You won't make money off it, but it could be great PR. Shows that you're about more than the money, and we can even convince people that you're doing all this community service stuff out of your own benevolence, not because of a court order."

"I wouldn't make any money? No, no, I trust you, Sandra. Can't wait to see you."

Freedah ended the call and checked the first name off her list. Twenty more clients to steal. That would teach MELL. And she had Ty to thank. He'd shown her what real passion was all about. She could be just as passionate. More passionate. It was her job, her style. No matter the cause. As long as she got what she wanted. That was all that mattered. She'd been looking after herself most of her life, after all, and a self-made woman had to roll with the flow.

She checked the website for information about the NFA. It disgusted her. Everything she'd ever believed in as far back as she could remember was disputed on their site. Examples: They claimed that abusing animals was good for them. Dehorning. Cruelty. Artificial insemination: How dare they take the pleasure out of sex for an animal? Government intervention: They should be regulated. Pollution. They had the guts to claim they weren't polluters. And they supported political conservatives most of the time. Bastards. Gestation crates. Just because sows killed their babies by laying on them? So what? Crates were cruel. The image of them was great negative PR. Chicken cages. Just because they wanted to keep the eggs clean and sanitary. Forced vaccinations. Nope. That was a can of worms that didn't need opening quite yet. She stopped reading. These people were terrorists. Just as she'd always been taught, she didn't have to see for herself. She knew.

But on the good side, their PR machine was not all that sophisticated. She could use this to her advantage and maybe screw Phoenix Tippin at the same time.

***

When Ty ended the call to Freedah, his phone immediately rang again. It was Melanie.

"Just wondering if you've decided anything." She was cheerful.

"I'm not sure I'm qualified," Ty said. "And I won't do it if I can't tell the truth."

"That's all we'd ever ask you to do."

"But how do I know what's truth and what isn't?"

"Let me send you some fact sheets. Farmers would be very grateful to you if you'd do it. They want to see you. Their wives want to see you more. It's just one rally."

"Send me your materials."

Melanie hesitated. "OK, but we only have two days until the rally. I think you can really convince people because you have style. I believe in you, Ty. I mean, I'd never ask this kind of thing from people I don't believe in. We're ready to launch this thing as soon as we can. House Bill 616 – the one you've been studying, I hope, could put us out of business, and we need to fight back hard and fast. It's only in Michigan, and the Michigan chapter of the NFA has been fighting it hard, but there's too much riding on this. If this goes through in Michigan, dominoes start falling. It will empower other states' enviros to take similar action. Part of their effort to save the world from weather, I guess. That's not a big deal on your part. All you have to do is know what's in the bill and why farmers can't live with it. But we want you to be convinced. We don't need any phonies. Farmers can see through it. The NFA board is really watching what happens in Michigan as a sort of first domino. So they've directed me to start an informational campaign. People have to be educated. So that's what we'll do. We'll hit every Michigan county NFA chapter and warn them about this bill. That should be a good start."

**

Ty didn't know why certain thoughts were in his head, but his next call was to Garit West.

"Garit, I wonder if you could ask Aspen to do a job for me."

236

"What's that?"

"I know she's one of the best fact-checkers there is. I have two sets of facts about the Jovial and the way farmers treat the environment. I'll pay her well to sort things out for me."

"Well, I'll ask her. She is very good at it. You can bank on whatever she finds. She has this unique ability to look at things objectively. There would be none of her opinion in it."

"Just let me know how much she wants and how long it will take, and I'll pay for it."

Chapter 29

At the April Jovial World and Sasser's monthly staff meeting, the agenda was unusually long.

The meetings were almost always the same. Owner and publisher Botsdorf tackled the usual items on the agenda, which again included instructing the sports guy to clean up his copy and encouraging ad salespeople to work a little harder. Garit brought up new business.

"You're familiar with Ty Mooring and his story, right? Well, he contacted me the other day and asked if Aspen would fact-check a couple of documents for him. Apparently, he's about to make a speech to farmers to educate them about a bill that's right now in the ag committee" – he checked his notes – "House bill 616. It's being pushed hard by some of the more radical enviros, and the farmers feel that it would end their way of life if it passes. But that's not what he wants fact-checked. It's a brochure that makes some claims about the Jovial River Valley and the property he was given by the state. He has no price limit. But I thought I'd better bring it up in a staff meeting because it's your call, Aspen. Apparently, Ty thinks he can win these groups over with some facts. I told him that's impossible, but he wants to be prepared before he starts his speech."

"How much would he pay?" Botsdorf asked.

"That's not the issue," Aspen cut in. "How am I ever going to find time to fact-check things when I barely have time to fact-check what I have now? I mean, you know how I love doing that work, but I have enough on my plate."

"If it pays well enough, I could free you up for it a little," Botsdorf said. "I need to keep my hand in this business more than I've been doing lately, anyway."

It was agreed that Ty should be billed $10,000, and if that was too much, the deal would fall through. Garit made the call while the two waited. Ty agreed. The deal was done.

***

Aspen was thrilled by the opportunity to roll up her sleeves and do some digging without pressure from her other daily tasks, and set about to make a hypothesis. The question she would answer was a very general one: Do farmers pollute the Jovial River and the 100 acres that Ty Mooring now owned? Had to be yes or no. The facts didn't lie. Not much, at least.

She separated claims from two documents – one from MELL and the other from the JFA. She scanned down to the end of both. Completely different conclusions from the same evidence and facts nearly always indicated that someone was lying.

There were several specific questions that needed answers before the big question, however.

1. MELL claimed that farmers are polluting the Jovial River so badly that fish are dying.

2. MELL claimed that if the pollution continues at the pace MELL insisted it's happening now, it will not be able to support plant or animal life for more than 12 years.

3. MELL claimed that global warming was decreasing the amount of water going through the river.

4. MELL claimed that the river water was warmer now than it was before farmers started double-cropping on the 100 acres of rich black earth.

5. MELL claimed that farmers were forcing enslaved animals to feed in the water, pooping in it, further polluting it.

6. MELL claimed that all these facts had been proven, not only by state DNR scientists and federal EPA biologists, but by citizen samples of river water and soil samples.

7. MELL claimed that erosion of the river banks was destroying the ecology along the river.

8. MELL claimed that all these things were undoubtedly the farmers' fault.

9. MELL claimed that farmers were doing all these things intentionally, out of meanness and greed.

It was all a lot to tackle, and the digging would take some time and some creativity to find the statistics they quoted. Many of the stats were buried in state archives under many layers of computer records. And the citizen stats were impossible to find. Aspen took that realization as a challenge.

She began digging.

***

"How long do you think it will take you to get through your list of questions?" Botsdorf asked the next day.

"If it's all I'm doing, about two weeks, I guess, barring any delays in FOIA requests. Mostly, I can find my way deep into their websites and data, though. All the state water surveys and pollution data are posted going back at least 20 years."

"Well, Garit can help me with the editing while you're doing that. Who knows? This may become a new business. Fact-checking isn't just for news people, after all. Lawyers need them, although I doubt if many of them, besides me, would ever use them. If we establish $10,000 as a kind of baseline price and get it, I'll give you $7,500 per fact check."

Aspen was floored. That was more than she'd ever made in two weeks in her life.

Let's start here and see what the market is," she said. Botsdorf agreed and said he'd start investigating the demand for fact-checkers.

"Seems to me that the market is growing all the time, what with the lies and distrust of social media," he said.

Chapter 30

Grandy waved and smiled from the depths of his soul when he saw Freedah come through the Detroit airport gate. She was different than the last time he'd seen her, likely a bit disheveled because of the long flight. Her makeup wasn't perfect, as it normally was, and her hair was tangled, with reds and greens weaving together like a novices' quilt. Somehow, for her, it worked. She could never be less than beautiful. He watched with growing anticipation as she approached, like someone who'd been watching Christmas cactus buds ever so slowly blooming into a stunning red flower. People would see her embrace him. It would be enough for the moment.

He waited impatiently as she made her way through the crowd of disembarking passengers, then opened his arms as she approached the ground he was defending.

Her embrace reeked of corporate ritual, cold and stiff yet warm for casual observers. Heads turned as they hugged.

"I hear you haven't made much headway," she said, but he chose to believe he heard just a hint of forgiveness in her voice. "What's been the problem? Have you been working with Representative Montenegro out of Detroit?"

"Oh, he's on our side all the way. He introduced it, but there are some farming caucus guys who won't get out of the way. They've stalled it in committee."

"Farming caucus? So what? They have no power or influence. And even if they did, there aren't enough farm votes to sway it."

"Maybe they don't have enough in California, but they do here," Grandy replied. "There's a group of rural reps, led by Chairman Fectid, who don't like the whole thing at all. They want to remove the potential to pollute part, and the parts per trillion are where the hair on their backs really stands up."

"What does that mean?"

"It's what dogs do when they're threatened. Haven't you ever been around dogs?"

"Never cared for them." She waved her hand dismissively. "Never really could understand why people want to enslave them in cages and on leashes. They're descended from wolves, you know. Animals the Native Americans consider sacred. They should be allowed to run free."

"The Native Americans or the dogs?"

She smirked at him in a way that told him she didn't care for the joke. He continued. "Well, these guys are pretty loyal to their constituents so far. I've been hammering on the zero tolerance and the gambling with the river and the environment narrative, but no soap. You might be able to make them see the light?"

"Set up some appointments as soon as you can. I'll stay in your guest room until we're ready to go. Tomorrow would be good."

"I can't tell you how happy I am that we're working together again," Grandy said. "They won't be able to resist you."

She grunted, impatient with his fawning. Of course, he was right, but she didn't want to take the time with this. There were many more important things to do, and she could dispose of the entire matter with a single visit with those climate deniers.

"Let's just get this bill moving out of committee as soon as possible," she said. "I have some work to do in Jovial. The farmers are fighting us there, too, and I need to convince someone to see things our way and get an injection of funds into this thing."

Suddenly, she softened and touched Grandy's arm as they walked to his car. "So, what's so critical in Jovial?"

"You know the kid who got the reparation money?"

"Ty Mooring? Of course, I know him. I saved him in prison."

"Saved him from what?"

"Sin, of course. What a relief. He'll be no problem for you."

"I don't know," Freedah said. "He's got this crazy allegiance to farmers. That's why I have to get this bill out there fast and with very little publicity. Without me to guide him, we might lose him and his money."

***

Freedah's timing had been perfect. The agriculture committee, chaired by Jovial-area state representative Peterson Fectid, was scheduled to meet the next day. Before the hearing began, Grandy had scheduled a few hours for visiting legislators, and Freedah was pleased that he had set up meetings with five of the 11 members of the agriculture committee, where HB 616 was stalled.

The five, however, were all city-bred liberals, the easiest to convince that farmers needed to be controlled.

***

"My concern isn't at all about the farmers," Montenegro said while keeping one eye fixed securely on Freedah in the cramped meeting room. "I mean, I only have a handful of farmers at best as constituents. My people are more concerned with their drinking water. Therefore, I have nothing to say and little concern about how this bill affects farmers. We don't need them at all in my world, so I support the bill without any of your convincing, Grandy. If you and this young lady have done the research and reached the conclusion that this bill is necessary to keep my people's water safe, then that's good enough for me."

"We at MELL appreciate that," Freedah said, "but we need your influence on the other members of the committee. Your constituents have just as big a stake in this as farmers. It's your voters in Detroit who will be damaged if the farmers continue to pollute the river and the farmland around it. So, can you please at least make a few phone calls?" she reached out and touched his hand. He nodded.

The full agriculture committee would be more difficult. Six Republicans took their seats around the raised, horseshoe-shaped committee table, three of whom represented rural districts. Among them were Boyd McCockert, vice-chair, and Peterson Fectid, chair, two farm-loyal officials who, thanks to more pressing matters that affected far more than farm voters, hadn't really considered the bill very closely.

"I know you have agreed with me before in my stance against gambling," started Grandy after Fectid had gaveled the unofficial meeting to order and introduced the speakers. Grandy and Freedah had free rein to answer questions, and they took the speaker's seat at the far end of the table, "This is the exact same thing," Grandy continued. "Farmers are gambling with the environment. The Jovial River is just the canary in the coal mine. How can farmers be sustainable when the very land they rely on is being gambled away by big profits from the chemical companies who don't care about anything but lining their own pockets?"

"But this bill goes too far," said McCockert, the thickest meat-eater on the committee. "My voters will not stand by calmly when the government threatens to seize their property only on the basis of a single lawsuit being filed. That's just theft. Restricting their potential by taking away their ability to protect their crops from disease and insects is like cutting our own throats. The citizens of this state need to know their food supply is consistent and safe, and the farmers who support me have done excellent jobs in keeping the food healthy and high-quality."

"What if we could convince the bill sponsors to tone that down a little?" Freedah asked. "Maybe the state couldn't seize the land based on one suit, but three?"

"What if you took that out altogether and made the state buy the land only if a lawsuit alleging pollution were successful?" Fectid asked. "That's much fairer. And what if the standard were lowered from parts per trillion to parts per billion? That's still stricter than parts per million, as it is now."

"But we have to use the latest science if we're ever going to protect the land," Freedah said. "Parts per trillion, I think you'll agree, is the safest level possible to achieve until more research is done, and it would bring us a long way to preventing any kind of pollution at all."

Fectid gazed into her eyes, and she smiled at him.

"I still contend that our farmers don't pollute at all now," he said after shaking his head to clear it and break the spell of her eyes. "You mentioned a canary in a coal mine, but the canary is singing and happy. Nothing wrong with the river. In fact, it's been named the cleanest in the country by this fly fishermen group, Pure Fly Fishing Federation or foundation, or whatever it is. PFFF should know. The measures and money they've put in place have prevented everything except wild animal and fish poop from polluting the river for years."

"But it's still a gamble," Grandy interjected. "How do we really know how much pollution is too much? We contend that one drop is too much. Betting a penny is the same as betting a hundred bucks when all you have is a penny."

"I'm still not convinced," Fectid said, "and we all have other meetings to attend." He smacked his gavel and dismissed the committee, then walked calmly toward Grandy and Freedah. "Perhaps we could talk this over in more detail over dinner tonight?" he grinned.

"I'd be delighted," Freedah said, smiling the smile that melted men like they were plastic army figurines in a microwave. "Grandy will be working late into the night anyway, trying to get this bill's language refined a little."

Grandy looked at her as if betrayed, but she made eye contact and winked at him. All was instantly forgiven. He shook off the jealousy that was invading his mind. She was out of his league anyway. Just stick with business, he told himself. She liked dedication, and it could work in his favor if he would just be patient. She'd see the light.

246

Chapter 31

A committee had been formed. After consulting the Michigan NFA chapter's public relations staff and Fectid's media relations staff, it was decided to bill the upcoming political rally as an educational session. That would keep the general media away and raise funds that Fectid needed to fight House Bill 616.

Melanie Swann had asked at the meeting to go over the details of the rally and to ask why Fectid needed funds for that. All he needed to do was cast a vote against it, as he'd promised.

She was assured by the NFA board president that it was necessary, and if she didn't understand how politics and money worked yet, maybe she wasn't the right person for the job.

As people began arriving at the Rick Frandor farm, she calmed herself with deep breaths and a few push-ups. Not enough to start sweating, but enough to clear her head of all the scenarios she'd been imagining and to reassure herself that she had an excuse. She was new on the job. A large turnout would purge at least a few of her sins, the mistakes that had left her ineffective. At least, that's what her last job evaluation said. Her boss had also shown a little grace, however, telling her to make this job her own. The problem was she didn't know how to do that. No one had really defined success for her. Was it money? Turnout? Most definitely, success was a moving target.

Her short career as a public relations "expert," as her job description outlined, had been rocky but not bad for someone who'd spent most of the last ten years in human resources. Perhaps she could finally turn the corner in PR, thanks to this anti-farming bill. Maybe by now, it might look like she really knew what she was doing if this, her third fundraising event, was successful. Maybe these people were drawn by the message that had been promised, but she knew deep inside that rain had drawn the crowds. Though it was sunny and warming today, she knew the recent rain had made field work impossible for at least a day or two more, and farmers, anxious after a long winter to get outside, wanted to get out of the house. Most of their wives wanted them out, too.

She pumped a few push-ups beside her company-issued Chevy Equinox, where at least 100 pickup trucks were already parked next to the farm's largest rock pile. The farm owner and host, Rick Frandor, had been prepared and had mowed a pasture just for parking. A few of his best Angus steers had been moved to the next pasture over, a relatively easy task, since he practiced rotational grazing. Besides that, the animals in the spring's first verdant green grass provided a bucolic scene that not even crazy animal rights people could disparage. If they had an ounce of common sense, that is. She was not optimistic about that.

Ty parked his Ranch Farm pickup in the back, near the pasture fence. He gazed at the beautiful Black Angus steers and the large pile of rocks behind them and remembered to thank God for the beauty he'd provided in this part of the country. Something about the first green of spring had always made him grateful, but only recently had he realized who had arranged the whole thing.

He wished Freedah were here to bolster his resolve. If she were here, people would pay attention to her, and he would be out of the spotlight, a place that suddenly gripped him with terror. He reminded himself, as he checked his hair in the visor mirror (and liked what he saw), that he was not the headliner here.

Two state representatives, Boyd McCockert and Peterson Fectid, had their staff do most of the planning work for this, and Melanie's sole responsibility was to get a large crowd to turn out. Both politicians were up for reelection, but only Fectid's handlers thought he needed to press the flesh, and his primary campaign would start in friendly farm territory. What better place to start than amid his base? Farmers had been leaving his side recently, and he wanted to assure himself that the most influential farmers still supported him.

Proposition 616, a bill that no farmer in the area supported, was a perfect fundraiser, although Fectid knew they wouldn't understand why he'd done what he'd done if the subject came up.

He'd thought about avoiding it, but farmers didn't vote for people who ignored their interests. He'd have to be bold and proactive, as his PR handlers called it. He had to address 616 if he were to collect sufficient money for his campaign. He needed to appear confident, an expert on the bill. Farmers were generous, knowing that a little money now to stop such biased and anti-farm legislation could pay off in the future when the bill was killed with great fanfare, publicity and photographers. If it could be killed. If not, he'd find a scapegoat somewhere.

As Ty greeted people he knew in the crowd, he bolstered himself with the assumption that people wanted to look at him now. Everywhere he went these days, his new face turned heads. It didn't hurt that he'd been the subject of a local television story, a kind of hometown-boy/prodigal son returns in victory kind of story. Of course, the report had missed the point entirely. It never even mentioned his future, only his past.

Such bolstering, Ty learned quickly, was usually short-lived. If people didn't seem to notice him, his confidence waned. And in this crowd, mostly male, middle-aged farmers with leathery skin and solid opinions, would not care much about his looks. Perhaps their wives would. But Ty was prepared to do more than just look good. He'd done his research and learned everything he could about HB 616. No matter how many different angles he took, it always came out the same on the bottom line. The bill stunk. It was nothing but a political concession to the environmental lobby, and it ignored unintended consequences.

It hadn't been easy to figure out this bill. Not because it was so complicated, but because it wasn't. It was short and to the point, but his mind was too often interrupted by thoughts of Freedah.

He wanted to think mostly about what she'd taught him, the passion she'd instilled into his brain and nether regions, and how his life had changed since they met. Mostly, he told himself, his life was better. Was it love? How could he know? Now and then, he wondered what life would be like after her. Songs played in his head. All these musicians insisted that they couldn't live without the loves of their lives, yet sooner or later, most of them would. Thousands of people out there lived long after their loves left. How did they do it? How was he to make a difference in the world if he wasn't more passionate and committed, just like Freedah? So he studied all he could about HB 616, examined every nuance and contemplated every "unintended consequence" if the bill were to become law. He consulted the NFA attorneys and lobbyists and consulted Botsdorf often, dissecting every part of the bill as it was written. It still stunk. The more he understood it, the more it stunk for farmers.

***

Melanie met him with a long, tight hug, but her face was showing stress. The news out of Lansing had been alarming. It appeared that their most ardent supporter in the fight against HB 616 was losing some of his backbone.

"Looks like we have to change our tactics on the fly," she whispered to Ty. "Fectid looks like he might be flip-flopping on 616, and we need to get these farmers riled up just enough to put a little steel in his spine."

The weather was nippy again after a short, warm spell. Full-fledged planting season was nearing on the calendar when the political rally began, and farmers were ready to go the moment soil dried out sufficiently. A word about the rally had gotten to the group in the bunker, thanks to Ernie, and Ty greeted all of them individually as he walked from his Ford, thanking them each warmly for showing up.

Fectid was on the other side of the crowd, glad-handing people, putting his left hand on supporters' right hands when they shook. It was one of his trademarks. Staff had told him years ago that it made him appear more caring and more empathetic.

When Ty came behind the stage, Melanie by his side, he was introduced to a number of Fectid's staffers. They assured him that Fectid needed the farm vote, even though they didn't really understand how farmers thought. Their champion had only taken time from his busy schedule, they said, because he was the only politician who had the courage to stand up for farmers and show up at rallies like this. Fectid had stepped in to shake Ty's hand, and as he turned to go toward the stage, Ty heard him ask a staffer who that young man was.

Garit West, camera around his neck, mingled with the crowd to get a feel for what was being said. He paused as he made his way toward the stage to view a text message from a fellow reporter in Lansing, who had agreed to keep Garit up to date on HB 616.

Garit found Ty behind the stage between the barn and house, practicing his speech. He approached Ty and pulled him aside, showed him the text message, then forwarded it to Ty's phone.

After a welcome to his farm by Rick Frandor, some preliminary introductions and short speeches from politicians who were out of the district, but still called themselves farm-friendly, Peterson Fectid stepped to the mic.

"Ladies and gentlemen, we are at a crossroads." He pulled a small card from his suit pocket and held it aloft.

"You all know that I'm a proud card-carrying member of the Michigan branch of the NFA. I've always had your back and supported your causes in Lansing, particularly the things that are very difficult for you to understand. I stand on my record of help for you, and I have to tell you about one very complicated bill. It's been difficult to balance all of our concerns about the environment with this seeming intrusion into your businesses and right to farm. And so I think a compromise is important in this matter. Political reality demands it, and I'm a realist. I will always support your rights, just as I've always done, but we may have to give in on a few of the finer points in the proposal. Farmers cannot move forward unless the general public believes you're doing all you can to protect the water, the air and the earth. Now, I, of course, believe in you, and I won't rest until the doors of communication are open and we get something we all can agree to. I will be honest with you, and I'll do that as I always have, and I sincerely ask for your support in the upcoming primary election."

The crowd clapped a rather mediocre response, but Fectid beamed as if he'd just changed a bunch of minds toward his way of thinking.

"Are you talking about 616?" a voice cut through the applause. "Why don't you just throw this bill out and start over?" Garit took special notice and moved ahead to see if the person who'd asked that question was who he suspected it might be.

As Fectid began his long-winded explanation, Garit saw the man. It was Rick Frandor, the host farmer, who held strong convictions and was never shy about expressing them.

***

Garit remembered a story for which he interviewed Frandor maybe a year ago. Frandor had wanted publicity about a march on Jovial County's office of the Michigan Department of Agriculture. He was planning to protest a new edict that required farmers to put two percent of their proceeds from grain sales into a fund that would pay farmers for their losses if a registered elevator defaulted on its financial obligations and went out of business.

What Frandor had not understood at the time was that the two percent was not mandatory. Farmers could opt out simply by filling out a form online. Of course, opted-out farmers would not receive payments from the state if they opted out, and that seemed unfair to Frandor. It was nothing but socialism, he'd said.

Garit had asked during the interview about that stance, and he quoted the actual language in the act, which plainly stated that after the fund reached a certain monetary level, all assessments would stop. But Frandor still viewed it as government overreach, and while he did pay into it, he continued to speak out against it, preferring that such a hedge against an elevator's bankruptcy should be a private fund, not run by the state. The proposal passed after more than 75 percent of farmers statewide voted, so the issue died. Within a year, the fund reached its limit, and assessments stopped.

Garit didn't quote Frandor in the story. Instead, he did a separate story about the new assessment, which farmers had voted overwhelmingly to approve; and produced a business story about Frandor's rocks. That was the better story, anyway. It had set a new record for local hits on the website.

Garit had learned while on Frandor's farm that it was the rockiest 500 acres in the entire state. Frandor's ancestors had picked them by hand, and he had old photographs to prove it. But Rick, once he'd taken over the farm, had invested in top-notch rock-picking equipment. Every year, those rocks pushed toward the surface, making planting the field impossible until they were removed. Once removed, the land was fertile and rich, and Frandor had built up an impressive pile of rocks beside his livestock barns as well as coming in the top 10 corn yield competition for years, never getting higher than fourth place.

The story became a business story because, as Garit learned, Frandor had begun marketing the rocks to local landscapers, and during the present building boom from people fleeing the city for more pastoral areas, the rocks sold for big money. At least it was big to Frandor. Five hundred dollars each for rocks of considerable size, all the way down to five bucks per rock for smaller, easier-to-handle specimens. But they all seemed to have excellent color once washed, and so Frandor, with the simple investment of a pressure washer, began to make a tidy living on rocks that far exceeded his farming income. He'd even invested in a large rock cutter and splitter, so large it required a building around it. That was where he'd placed the huge sign which read "Frandor's Rocks!"

That largess had launched Frandor and his naturally suspicious nature into a keen interest in politics, and today, he was ready to speak his mind yet again. It was his farm. He deserved a voice.

***

When Ty stepped onto the stage, he feared that his churning stomach would not allow him to complete his speech. But the applause he got in front of the Jovial crowd made him know he could do it. He recognized a few friendly faces, including Fulton Gray, whose skin was already darkening under the spring sun. Coney Dogues's presence calmed him, and his wife Jenn was there too, looking regal as always. Ty waved to his bunker friends, who had congregated at the back of the crowd of at least 150 people. They weren't smiling at him, but many young women were.

Ty told the story of his newfound fame, told the crowd how he'd turned his life around in prison, how he was trying to follow Jesus, and how he was determined never to waste another day. He told the crowd about his intention to keep farmers farming the land he now owned, even though it didn't feel like he owned anything.

Soon, the attention he was getting and the smiles in the crowd allowed him to forge forward about HB 616.

"Every single person I've talked to about this bill who is even remotely involved in agriculture tells me it's a disaster waiting to happen," he said. "With all due respect to Mr. Fectid, I've read the bill and studied it like I should be studying my Bible. It's not as complicated as he thinks, which seems odd since he's been closer to it than I've been. He's been in the committee meetings, and I have not. But I've consulted with people who know more about politics than I do, and they've convinced me that we need to defeat this bill with great force. It doesn't even deserve to get out of committee, they tell me. Knowing that, they've all asked me to urge each of you to call or email your representative – or talk to him here – and explain to them the damage it would bring, the disaster. And that's just what's evident by reading the bill. The groups behind it spout noble intentions, and many of them have great-sounding names. Like this fishermen's group PFFF." He said it as one would describe a fart, which created a stir of contained laughter from the crowd.

"PFFF is a group of lawyers who like to fish," Ty said as attention turned back to him. "Nothing more and nothing less. I've been fishing the Jovial all my life, and I'm here to testify that these fair-weather fishermen don't show by their actions that they really care about the river or the fish. They don't know how to remove a hook, and they leave litter all over the place. I've picked up many a load of trash left behind that was so thick that farmers couldn't get their machinery to make contact with the soil. It's like there are big rocks there or something, but they're not pretty rocks like the ones you see here on this beautiful farm. But there's more to this bill than just big money. It's about what big money wants. How they plan to get it, I don't really know, but I make a promise to you right here and now that as long as I own this 100 acres along the river, farmers will be able to farm it. I will not sell to lawyers and thieves." The bunker group roared their approval, and Ty noticed that even Rick Frandor was nodding his own brand of skeptical approval.

That was going to be the end of his speech, but Ty, after seeing Garit in the crowd, was reminded of one last detail. He held up his hand and continued.

"It's a really horrible bill, one that Mr. Fectid here has said for months now that he would kill as soon as it was introduced. That would be the best thing. But I've just learned something that may not set well with you folks. It's now been confirmed" – he looked at Garit, who nodded to him – "that there is deception afoot here. The state representative who just now told you all he's going to do for you has, in fact, voted in favor of House Bill 616 without much discussion and without any of the compromise you've been promised. If you've read the bill, you know how bad it is. And it was just passed without amendment and will be folded into the budget bill that will be passed along to the full house."

The crowd fell silent for a moment until Frandor, who had moved near the stage on which the two reps sat, shouted, "That can't be true. You're lying, Ty. Pete Fectid has always been honest with us."

The crowd began to murmur, but Ty stepped a bit closer to the mic. "It's on public record now," he said. "Check it out for yourselves. Mr. Fectid has betrayed you! Look at the record. He's voted to move it out of committee to the full house!"

Fectid lept up and shoved Ty aside, spilling him down the stage steps.

"My fellow farmers," he shouted, his hands in the air, "this is no betrayal. There are still hearings scheduled on some of the final points, you know, whether it will stand alone or be part of a different bill. This is a bill that had to pass in order for us to defeat it once and for all."

"That makes no sense," Frandor shouted from the stage edge. "Is it true? Did you vote for the bill?"

"Well, technically, I guess I did, but you don't understand ..."

"We understand that you've betrayed us," cried Frandor, and before anyone knew what was happening or took the effort to stop it, farmers began climbing the steps onto the stage, grabbing for Fectid as McCockert tried to stand between them. McCockert was shoved aside, and Fectid was quickly knocked onto the stage floor as farmers rushed up. Just when it appeared that Fectid would be dragged off for a beating as McCockert fled for his car, Ty stepped to the mic, a bruise already growing around his eye, which had been struck on the stair handrail.

"People, calm down," he said into the mic. "This is not how I learned farmers do things. If we resort to violence, we're no better than the folks who burned down cities a few summers ago. I thought the JFA was all about political action, not violence. You speak your minds with your votes, don't you?"

"Not anymore," shouted Frandor. "Enough is enough!"

With shouts from many people drowning the stage in confusion, Fectid was grabbed and held by a couple of large farmers, who forced his hands behind his back as other people began punching him in the stomach and head. Before long, Fectid had a bloodied face and was doubled over, gasping in pain. Just then, Ernie and four of his followers charged up the stairs and pulled the people off Fectid, who collapsed to the stage floor, gasping.

"Enough!" shouted Coney Dogues, who had run up the stage steps behind the bunker dwellers. "Ty is right. Don't commit crimes here. Stop!"

Coney's authoritative voice calmed the crowd quickly, and as Fectid squirmed on the floor of the stage, the people backed away.

"It's clear what must be done, and it will be tough since the election slate is all but set with only three days to go to announce a primary candidate. We must vote this traitor and liar out on election day."

The crowd roared it's approval as Coney continued. "If we do that, and we should, we have to think one step ahead and put someone in office who will not betray us. Who will step up? Any suggestions?"

A chant began quietly near the side of the stage, led by Ernie and the bunker dwellers. The chant gained momentum until it was a unanimous roar: "We want Ty, we want Ty," it resounded and echoed off the barn and out into the fields. As it grew louder, Coney finally stepped to the mic and raised his hand, silencing the crowd.

"How about it, Ty?" he asked, reaching out a hand to bring Ty forward. "Will you fight for us in Lansing and run in the primary?"

Ty was caught up in the moment. His heart raced, his palms were sweaty, his head was throbbing, and he didn't really know what to think. "Do you think I'm qualified? Because I don't," he blurted to roars of approval from the crowd.

"All we ask is that you are honest and support farmers," a voice shouted. "Can you do that?" He looked at Melanie, who stood adoringly staring at Ty.

Ty, later, could not recollect the thought, even when it came into his head before he spoke. "Well, I can do that." The crowd roared.

Before the crowd dispersed, Melanie had run to her car and produced the paperwork to start a signature drive to get Ty on the primary ballot. By the time Frandor and his hired hands started dismantling the stage, Melanie had gotten 162 signatures, more than enough to throw his hat into the political ring.

Chapter 32

"You did what?" Freedah screeched into her phone from Grandy's lush apartment. "How does someone go from some passing interest in rivers to running for statewide office overnight?"

"I don't even know how it happened," Ty said. "All I did was point out the facts, the truth, that Fectid and McCockert voted for HB 616, and the next thing I know, people were chanting for me to run for Fectid's office in the primary. I don't know if I can beat this guy, but I'm going to give it a try. It's pretty clear to the farmers that he betrayed them and lied to them. The people have spoken. They want me."

"How many people?"

"I guess there were maybe 200 people there."

"Two hundred people having a fly-off-the-handle reaction is not enough."

"But they want me."

"And so do I," Freedah said, her mind churning. She thought a moment, and when Ty asked if she was still there, she said, "I'm here." Her mind was quick, but she needed one answer first. "How did you know it passed the committee?"

I have reliable sources."

"Don't play cute with me, Ty. You know I'll support you in anything you want to do. But I don't think you're ready for this kind of thing. Politics is mean. You're not mean enough. And I encourage you to really understand HB 616 before you make a fool out of yourself. You need to know how to keep control over things, over certain people, but most importantly, you have to control the message. And you can't, can you?"

"Well, the NFA Michigan chapter has a whole team to advise me on things like that. But having you beside me wouldn't hurt."

"I wish I could be, but I can't. I'm too busy with things out here, getting Acrid Reins started on their tour."

"I'm going ahead with this either way," Ty said. "I've made up my mind."

"Be prepared for heartache," she said, wondering where she had failed, where Ty had gotten his independent streak. "Keep your eyes open. I'll be there when I can."

She ended the call and kicked the couch, leaving ripped fabric. This type of thing didn't happen to her. She'd somehow lost control. She didn't know how just yet, but she had to get it back.

***

Melanie Swann was trying to understand what was happening, how it happened so fast, and how it all escaped her control. She'd gone from trying to manage a simple information project to being the person in charge of a political campaign, and it all made her very nervous. She was out of her league, although the board at the Michigan NFA had been quite pleased with the turnout at the rally, if not the outcome. Fectid was acting out of character, going against farmers, and several board members wanted to know why, but Melanie didn't know why.

Ty walked into the casino bar, as the two had agreed, and Melanie was at a table, downtrodden and morose, sipping her third gin and tonic.

"I just don't know how to do this," Melanie said after she kissed Ty on the cheek with a hug. "I just know I'm going to be fired." She sobbed and turned her face away from Ty. "I have no idea how to run a political campaign, but" – she collected herself and sat up straighter. "I suppose I can learn."

"You're not really trained in public relations, are you, Melanie?" he asked softly, compassionately, like an old friend who had arrived to save the day.

"No," sobbed Melanie. "I'm in way over my head. I came from human resources. I only applied for the job because it looked like fun, and I'd gone as far as I could in HR. They gave it to me because of my seniority, but I'm not qualified!" she burst into tears again. "I don't know what to do anymore."

"Calm down, Melanie," said Ty, gently as a purring kitten. "They can't tie my campaign to you. I'm a long shot, at best. If I lose, it's not because of you. If I win, it will be. Don't borrow trouble." He'd learned that from somewhere in the Bible and, finally, applied to something he could understand; it made sense.

"But what can we do now?" Melanie said. "It's all too late. The bill looks like it's going to go to a hearing to the full house next week."

"Where did you hear that?" he asked cautiously.

"We've been watching it," Melanie said. "Our lobbyist said someone in the environmental community has convinced our only two reliable legislators to vote for it. How, I don't know. How could we have lost McCockert and Fectid? It's such a disaster."

"First," he said, "it's not too late until the bill is signed into law, and that's still a long way off. Maybe we just have to get out there more and stir the pot. If I learned anything about PR from my girlfriend Freedah, it's that people don't want to be informed. They want to be inflamed. And we already have the first spark, that riot or whatever it was at Frandor's farm. Media was all over it, doing your PR job for you. What can you do about the fact that I'm a one-trick pony, running on one issue? When that's all you have, you ride that pony until it drops. That's what makes social media live and thrive. And that's all we need to do. We can still inform people about the bill, but it has to rile them up. People don't post on social media unless they're riled up. And that's what you should propose to your board."

"You've really learned a lot in a short time, haven't you?" Melanie asked, placing her hand gently on Ty's. "I don't think many people recognize that about you." She leaned in, kissed Ty deeply, and gazed into his eyes. "Let's go somewhere else," she whispered. Ty said nothing; he just took her hand and led her to his suite.

***

After five straight nights and days in the company of State Representative M. Peterson Fectid, Freedah was ready for the death thrust.

The bill had been quietly and quickly scheduled for a final vote of the agriculture committee, and with the promise that Freedah would be in attendance, each member of the 11-member agriculture committee was determined to be there for final debate and a vote.

Agriculture Committee members took their seats in the huge, ornate chamber of the House, along with a few other representatives who'd bothered to show up. Issues from the ag committee usually didn't draw crowds, even when a vote was scheduled. Full attendance could not be expected unless the debate was over some hot issue, and even then, only if the media were there from their various districts.

Freedah and Grandy were the only spectators in the room. Grandy leaned over and whispered in her ear: "Looks like your hard work paid off. Luckily, no one on this committee is from Jovial except Fectid. And the hundred grand from MELL really put it over the top. The letters and emails have been flooding in. All in support."

Rep. Montenegro banged the gavel.

"I assume you've all read the bill and are ready to proceed?" Nods all around. "Fine. Let's proceed. This bill is a major step forward for our environment. Not only will it restore, preserve, and protect one of the most beautiful areas of the state, but it will, despite arguments against it, also be a boon to tourism in the Jovial River Valley. What farmers fear they will lose in cropland, they will gain back 10-fold in tourism dollars. And we feel that the best use of this land in question is tourism."

One of the last holdouts against the bill, someone Freedah had missed, spoke out.

"You seriously think that growing food is not the best use of the most fertile valley in the state? And how will tourism dollars affect farmers who no longer can do business on a piece of land that's really best suited for farming? How are farmers going to cash in? You're taking away their livelihood." He looked around the gallery to see if he had any supporters, and his eyes were drawn to Freedah, who smiled at him, rendering him speechless.

"They'll just get new jobs in the tourism sector," Montenegro said. "Probably better-paying jobs at that." The holdout looked at the notes he had made, paged through them, and asked: "What about all the food produced by farmers on the land you want to take out of production? Who will grow our food?"

"That's a non-issue," Montenegro said. "We'll get our food elsewhere. It's not like only farmers can grow food."

"They're the only ones who can do it on this scale and with high quality."Maybe we can give some budget considerations to community gardens," Montenegro said. "People in the inner cities can do it, and they can do it just as well."

"Doubtful," the holdout said. "Never seen a community garden yet that lasted more than a couple of years." He looked at Freedah again and sat down.

With little else said, the bill passed with only two votes against it and was sent on to the budget committee, where a more intense fight against it was expected until it made its way to the full House chamber.

Chapter 33

James Snowmaker had been preparing for this day for months, ever since he'd first written the language of HB 616 and convinced a Detroit-area legislator to introduce it. He wouldn't wait for the full House to act. Most of his sources gave the bill little chance of passing the Senate if it ever got that far, but he was nothing if not proactive. His suits had to be in place as quickly as possible, just in case, and he was not a patient man.

To be sure, however, before he would command that his aides send the file to the court, he reread HB 616 very carefully. It read:

Introduced by Rep. Aloiscious, supported by Reps. McCockert, Montenegro, and Fectid were referred out of the Committee on Agriculture.

A bill to restore, ensure, and preserve the pristine quality of Michigan's sovereign water, air, and land and to provide penalties for violation of this bill; to return a specific portion of the Jovial River Valley to its pre-settlement conditions via legal action against polluters; and to remove all potential to pollute from any and all sources.

The people of the state of Michigan enact:

That the word 'pristine' shall be determined by scientific data compiled by the Michigan Office of Environment, Inclusion, and Bigotry, a government agency that shall heretofore be known as MOEIB;

That 'pristine' should be defined as no more than one part per trillion of pollutants based on frequent tests of water quality, air, land, and soil quality;

That Frequent Tests shall be defined as a minimum of monthly tests conducted by individuals and/or entities approved by MOIEB until such time as farmers no longer apply damaging fertilizers or chemicals to the land;

That "pollution" shall be defined by MOIEB based on observations and scientific methods;

The penalties for violating these acts should include no less than $10,000 per day per each day of violation and will include forfeiture of the land to the Michigan Office of Inclusion, Environment, and Bigotry when unpaid penalties accrue to a sum of $500,000;

That MOIEB has the authority to distribute such forfeited property as it sees fit in fulfillment of its authority to create equity and environmental justice;

That farmers, in order to ensure that this standard is met, are banned under penalty that MOIEB shall determine from applying manure, phosphorous, nitrogen fertilizers, any existing and potential future chemical pesticides, or anything that is unnatural;

That Unnatural shall be defined as any substance, organic or inorganic, that is applied to the land by mechanical devices; That any action by MOIEB may be taken against polluters in violation of this act based on three or more lawsuits filed by any governmental office, private citizen or other interested parties, regardless if the suits result in favor of the parties involved.

***

Snowmaker decided he needed a little more. He was on solid ground, and the governor would certainly sign it, so that was no problem. And he thought, since the judge who would likely hear the case had been appointed by the liberal governor, that the Senate was all that stood in his way. A large barrier, to be sure, but it was only one.

He would file two more suits in the next month, satisfying the conditions of the bill and solidifying his office's claim on the land. He sent the suit and a copy of the bill to an attorney on his staff, with instructions to file it with the court ASAP.

He wrote a note to his staff attorney when he sent the bill to him:

"Close any loopholes you may find," the note read. "If this passes the House, we have to be ready to act fast."

***

One the day House Bill 616 was moved to the house and referred to the House Committee on Environmental Relevance and Restoration (SCERR), Aspen noticed significant activity on Twaddle. The Jovial World and Sasser had an influx of 200 new followers, all of whom spent significant time with Ty's story about the bill, which included the bill's entire text.

That California lawmakers and aides had become followers was logical since the case could have nationwide effects, but it was the anonymous accounts that baffled her. What could some Joe Blow from San Francisco care about a minor bill in Michigan?

She dug deeper into Twaddle's demographics and data, but she couldn't get by the surface firewalls. Only people who had willingly identified themselves, such as a politicians, could be found. She tried something new. She put in a request to be a Twaddle administrator, which was denied.

She manipulated her way around that, how, she didn't quite know, and got into the company's personnel files. She discovered that Twaddle had been founded and funded by the same moneyed investors as MELL. Interesting, if not connected to what she was looking for.

She found, in the personnel files, a girl named Debra who had started on the job only a week before. She hacked into the girl's company email, covered the girl's email and text information with her own, and sent a note to the site's second-in-command of information services.

"Please help," she wrote. "I lost my password. Sorry. I'm new here. Can you help me get into the system?"

After about a half-hour, Aspen received a text.

"Don't ever lose this again, Debra. Memorize it and delete this text. Password is Chaos$$5."

Chapter 34

On April 30, Melanie Swann received official confirmation, as was expected, that all but nine signatures in support of Tyson Mooring's candidacy for the state primary election had been verified. Ty was in.

He was now a candidate in the Republican primary, although he insisted and told everyone who was interested that he was, in truth, an independent and that he would vote that way if elected. That could be a problem down the road, but Ty was stubborn. He is too stubborn for his own good. Melanie had been warned.

On her drive from Lansing to Jovial, she spent most of the time on the phone with the Michigan Farmers Union's political action committee director. He told her that the PAC had convened after the rally, but there was no consensus.

"Representative Fectid has a stellar history of supporting farm causes," insisted one board member, betraying the slightest hint of anger. "And if the PAC rejected him, people might wonder why. His voting record followed the Union's policies 99 percent of the time."

"Until now. He betrayed us on 616," Melanie argued. "And 616 is the most damaging bill for farmers in 50 years. We all agree on that. That's why the committee agreed to fight it months ago. I believe farmers want to make Fectid pay for supporting 616, and those are the people you claim to represent in this organization. If you had been to the rally out at Frandor's farm, you'd realize that. I know you don't want to give up Fectid's influence on the ag committee, but he has to pay. Farmers are demanding his head. This one bill can and will undo all the good things he may have done. He betrayed his most loyal constituency. If the PAC supports him, it betrays all our farmer members."

With the assurance that the PAC would stay neutral for the immediate future – a victory all in itself – Melanie finally understood, as she reached the Jovial city limits, that Ty was pretty much on his own. No endorsements, no funds. But she was convinced – after reading her new job description – that she must help him in the primary. Perhaps if he won, the PAC would then support him in the general election. But not before. If he lost to Fectid, things would go back to normal, and the board would deny any support for Ty.

✳✳✳

"Look, we have only a little more than 12 weeks before the election, and no one knows your name," Melanie told Ty. "That has to change and fast."

"I've been thinking about that," Ty mused. "I don't know much about the ins and outs of politics like you do, but I know one thing that will always draw a crowd. Free beer."

"Pretty risky. How are you going to have crowd control? Beer at a campaign rally is only legal if it's on private property. Cops won't be there *because* it's private property. Things could get out of control fast when people get themselves tanked up."

"But they'll remember my name if we connect it to the free beer. The people I know would remember the guy who bought it for them."

"So that's your campaign idea? Vote for the free beer guy? What about your platform and your stance on issues other than 616? What about fundraising?"

"I'll pay the bills. I mean, how much can it be? If I pay my own way, no one can accuse me of being in debt to any special interest groups. I'll do this all on my own if you can find the farms that will host rallies."

"I think I can get a few farms who are mad enough to host an event. But what about the message? You need a slogan."

"I've been thinking about that. How about Ty Won't Lie?"

"No, that could be seen as a personal attack on Fectid. The PAC generally sticks to the idea of keeping on the high road."

"You're kidding. The high road? In politics?"

"That's what they say. They want to see integrity in the candidates they back."

"Again, you're kidding! Integrity in politics?"

"Well, that's what they want, and if they don't see it, they won't throw any money your way."

"Bah! I don't need their money. I have enough to do it all on my own."

"It could run into tens of thousands of dollars, all for a job that only pays about 70 grand."

"They make 70 thousand dollars? Every year?"

"Base rate. More for expenses and stuff."

"They're all overpaid."

"No argument from me. But we have more important things to get figured out. Like your campaign slogan. I suggest we find a focus group to figure that out."

"Well, if I'm going to finance this all on my own, and if I'm going to have to do all the work, then I pick my own slogan."

"I'd advise against that."

"If I'm all on my own, I live and die by myself. That way, you won't get in trouble. And if I fail, I can only blame myself. I think it should be Ty Tells the Truth. Then, we can build on it and change it to keep it fresh. You know, Ty the Truth teller, No Lies from Ty, stuff like that."

"If that's the way you want it. But I think it's a mistake."

"It's the way I want it. Now you just find me a few farmers where we can hold free beer rallies, and we'll get started."

"I can find places, but again, what about security?"

"I have a plan," Ty took her by the hand and led her to his pickup. They drove to the center of the riverfront district and walked down the boardwalk to Ernie's Outfitters.

They ate a sumptuous meal of trout with local potatoes and asparagus from California, for which Ernie apologized.

"I know it doesn't have the flavor of local stuff, but the Michigan harvest is still a little way off," he confessed as he filled their glasses with sweet wine from a local vineyard. "How about dessert tonight, Ty?"

"Sure. How about cheesecake with last year's frozen cherries? And then, come and sit awhile. I have a proposition for you."

Ernie sat down with Ty and Melanie and gave each of them a large piece of cheesecake.

"I'd like to ask if you could put together a little security detail for me," Ty asked. "I'd pay the going rate once I figure out what that is."

"How many guys?"

"Five, maybe? For this first one, anyway, but maybe more if the crowds get bigger as we go along."

"I have five that would do it, I'm sure. A couple of them used to be cops, so they would know what they're doing."

"Perfect. Now, I don't want any interference unless things get out of hand. I'll buy you each black T-shirts with 'official security' printed on it, but no bullying of any kind. And if people get out of hand, you can't be afraid to bust a head or two within the law, of course."

If Ty paid for the insurance for all this, Melanie said, the host farmer's fears would be relieved. That would help.

***

Freedah wondered if the ingrates at MELL knew just how thin they had stretched her. Here she was in Michigan, with leftover gray from winter still overpowering young spring colors, trying to cajole a bill through the legislature. She found herself longing for the ocean smells and the queer sights of San Francisco, and even the scents that drifted in from the south, an odd mixture of human refuse and liberal angst.

But no, she had to control the next Acrid Reins tour remotely, which was regrettable since she was so far away from Tony Finn, who really needed hands-on management. He'd already been complaining to her about working for free.

"Public service is supposed to be for people who committed crimes," he'd said. "You know as well as I do that I was justified in what I'd done. My conscience is clean."

Of that, she couldn't disagree. He was a disciple of the earth, and the people who polluted it with their animals and manure and chemicals deserved what he would dish out.

If she were there to keep him in check, though, maybe he wouldn't do something stupid again. But it was a chance she had to take. As soon as her work on HR 616 was done, she'd have to go back to Jovial. Ty had a lot more to offer her and MELL at this time, and she would not release her grip on him. But he was becoming an aggravation. Ty was thinking for himself, which is always a dangerous step for one of her donors.

***

Freedah had insisted that Tony's mini-tour, as she called it, stay on the West Coast. And even though the tour would bring no money, it would satisfy the judge, who she was certain was keeping tabs on him. The band's first two albums had brought in millions, and the analytics suggested it was mostly people under age 26 who shelled out the money. A free concert for them would practically guarantee future album sales.

If they could get similar numbers for this third album, Tony might gladly agree to a Midwestern free concert to finish his court-ordered public service. It was an odd order from the judge, and she regretted that she hadn't told Tony about that before, but there was no sense in cluttering his mind with such details while he was touring and creating new songs for the next album. His mind had to remain free to create, to convince a young, affluent generation to follow his philosophy, just like the old farts had been convinced by the Beatles so many millennia ago.

***

Acrid Reins' first venue was standing room only. But despite the judges' order to refrain from "inflammatory politics," Tony Finn took a quiet moment to explain his last song.

"This song is brand new, on our new album set to be released this fall," he said as female voices hooted. "Of course, you can buy all of our albums here at one of several booths we've set up. You can preorder the next album there, too. Imagine getting it before the rest of the world. Could be a real collector's item." He smiled, melting sycophants' hearts.

"I wrote this next song in small spurts during one of the band's tours across the country. On those long bus rides, I had the chance one day to really watch the scenery of the nation's heartland. The farm fields, as you know from flying, look so orderly and structured from the air. But get on the ground, and you can really see it. It's not all as neat and clean as it appears from the air. In fact, it's dirty and messy." The crowd murmured a low boo.

"During one stop, when we were gassing up the bus at a place where farm fields – and their unnatural smells – almost completely surrounded the truck stop, I noticed a farm tractor – a weapon against the earth – pulling something I'd never seen before. It was creeping along the ground, and I soon noticed it was picking something up. It seemed to me to be too early in the spring to harvest anything. Just then, the farmer who was driving the tractor, a fat, dirty redneck wearing a red baseball cap and a flannel shirt, stopped and walked over to get a bottle of Coke, so I struck up a conversation with him. He was friendly enough for a stupid rural earth destroyer, and I learned from some well-placed questions that he was picking rocks. Well, I didn't know what that meant. I mean, what possible use could rocks and stones have for a farmer? I mean, I always knew that farmers don't exactly feed their animals the best, but rocks?"

A murmur of offense rippled through the crowd. Tony, caught up in his own thoughts and unaware of the crowd noise, continued.

"Later that day, after we got back on the road, I was scanning through the local radio broadcasts, just to get a feel for what was happening in the area, you know, get a feel for attitudes? I like to do that so I can relate to the crowd, and they can relate to me. It's what I'm all about. And I landed on a radio talk show, which I learned later was a religious show. But the person was quoting something from somewhere, which I later learned was the Bible, but he was talking about the rocks and stones themselves would start to sing. It was as if the cosmos had given me an idea. So I wrote this song. I know you'll like it. It's called "Rocks and Stones."

It was a melodious and catchy tune, a bit of a departure from the head-banging music that had made Acrid Reins its fortune. Tony played it himself with an acoustic guitar as his band fired up a hookah backstage. He sang:

"Mother earth's mountains, solid rock,

push for the heavens steady as a clock.

They cry out in passion, showing the way

As the valleys are raped by polluters who say

the rapists are heroes whose captives belch hay.

Foul machines attack the mountain's majesty

and commit crimes from river to sea.

They throw their captives in piles along their fields,

caring only for profit pollution and yields.

The stones cry out, the rocks protest,

but the raping machines think it's all jest.

Free the rocks and let them sing

Hallelujah to the king."

Then the chorus:

"Stones and rocks, rocks and stones,

we should leave them all alone

or they will rock and rock and roll all over you."

He finished with a chorus repeat, and by the time he strummed his last chord, the crowd began chanting for him to play, "It's all the same." He raised his fist and cried, "Free the rocks," and walked off the stage to boos and hisses.

***

First week of June

Ty's official "Ty-ed to the Truth Tour" began in Sventon, on the farm of Rick Frandor. He greeted Ty with a handshake, enthusiasm, and honesty.

"I don't know if you can win this thing, son," he said, "but we're going to do everything we can to get that bastard Fectid out of there. To be honest, I didn't have much good to say about you at first. I mean, you took taxpayer dollars for yourself. But then I heard your story. At least you're honest about it, and you're using it to help other people. And after you blew Fectid's cover, I've decided that you're the better choice. Otherwise, I never would have offered my farm to your first rally."

"Well, thanks for your confidence in me," Ty said, but Frandor didn't seem to understand the sarcasm.

Melanie had been on the farm since morning and spent a good deal of time shooting phone videos of the gorgeous cut rocks that Frandor had on display. As Frandor and Ty spoke about where the stage would be and where the free beer table would be set up, she walked up, pawing through the footage she'd taken.

"Look what I got this morning!" She seemed confident to Ty, not overwhelmed as she'd seemed before. She showed them footage of the morning mist rising behind the cattle, with the sun splashing new colors across the horizon. She skipped to footage behind the barn, where steers and horses grazed. She had angles from below and above of the huge pile of rocks that had been harvested but had not yet been chosen or cut to a landscaper's desires. How he'd ever piled rocks so high, she couldn't imagine. More footage was close-ups of some cut rocks, one as tall as she was, showing rich veins of colors she admitted she'd never seen before.

"I'm going to post the event live, and I'll have a promo video online featuring these rocks within a day or two."

***

It was 20 minutes past the scheduled start time, and Ty received the crowd's polite applause with a smile and a giant wave. Before he said a word, he held a beer in one hand and a piece of paper in the other and raised it higher than the beer.

"I'm being sued," he said and smiled. The crowd hushed. "I hold in my hand a lawsuit against me, filed by the head of MOEIB (the crowd booed) for pollution that hasn't happened yet and probably never will," he said. The crowd murmured and took long slugs of beer.

"This is the kind of thing farmers can expect from Mr. Fectid." The crowd raised a loud boo. "He supports House Bill 616, which is the brain child of his own ridiculous aim to win support from absent-brained environmental wackos and the other brain-dead and lazy politicians he's dragged along with him. This lawsuit would enforce all the awful things in 616, a bill that isn't even in law yet. It's a land grab, plain and simple, and it's just flat-out wrong, immoral, and a power grab. House Bill 616, which my worthy opponent supported and voted for, even though he said for months that he never would, would make it legal for the state government office known as MOEIB to take all your land." The crowd booed louder.

"I will not stand for it," he said as the crowd fired itself up. "I will fight HB 616 to my last breath, and I will fight to take it one step further. I will fight to disband MOEIB because 616 is a power-hungry bill from a power-hungry office and its power-hungry leader." Melanie looked up from the phone, perched on a tripod in front of the stage, and rolled her eyes, hoping Ty would see. She motioned her index finger across her throat, but Ty ignored her.

The crowd became more agitated as he explained in great detail what was in the bill. He read most of it to them, which inflamed the crowd even more.

"Now, I'm no politician like Fectid," Ty said. The crowd cheered. "I've been told that I'm too nice, too young, too naive to be a politician. But I prefer to look into history a little bit and take my philosophy from the Founding Fathers. They envisioned a people's house, one run by people who are from the people. Now I know many of them were wealthy people, but they still had common sense, mostly because they understood farmers and farming. I am now wealthy because MOEIB made me that way, but much as I'd hate to seem ungrateful, it was all a ruse. MOEIB is trying to use me to grab this river-front farm property away from the farmers. But I will not allow it. I only own 100 acres, and I have already promised the farmers who work that land that I will continue to let them farm it. I will not break that promise, no matter how much the state may sue me and the farmers. And why

277

do they want to sue farmers? Because of their agenda of environmental radicalism. They think they're smarter than the people who keep this country fed through their hard work and devotion to the land. I don't think they're smarter, do you?" The crowd, in unison, shouted, "No!" Ty paused to hear it, to soak it in. The people were in the palm of his hand.

"I think the common man – people like you – know how to do things," he continued. "Politicians in their ivory towers, yes, the ones in Lansing, have lost touch with the people they've been elected to serve. My opponent calls me a populist, implying that's a bad thing. I think devotion to the needs of the common man and woman is where we should be in this state, and if you elect me, I will put your interests ahead of the greeniacs. And I will continue to fight against this high-brow, privileged, and out-of-touch rule-making that benefits them and their money. A vote for me is a vote for truth!" He waved as the crowd roared, and he walked into the crowd to shake hands and answer questions. Ernie and four other young men in black 'security' t-shirts stood by and smiled. No threats were evident, so they, one-by-one, lined up for beer.

***

After the second stop on Ty's tour, the local press got together and took a poll. If the vote were held today, Freedah read on the World and Sasser's daily news feed, Tyson Mooring would win. Fectid didn't stand a chance. She had to do something. But it was all okay. She was a master at manipulation.

Freedah sat for dinner in an out-of-the-way restaurant in downtown Lansing. Grandy had recently discovered it after a recommendation from Fectid, who was beginning to understand that Grandy could be a big help to him, what with his MELL connections and deep pockets. As long as he trusted Freedah, he'd be fine. He didn't doubt her abilities. And he didn't doubt that he, if patient, could connect with her on a deeper level, a physical level. Being with her would be a spiritual experience, and he wanted it more than anything he could remember. It was as if his mind had been blinded to anything else.

Freedah and Grandy sat at a table in a dark part of the very dark restaurant, designed that way so politicians could sneak in after a long day at their desks and never be recognized.

Grandy let his eyes adjust to behold Freedah's beauty. It was something he'd not forgotten, of course. No one could. There could be no doubt that she was the most beautiful girl the world had ever seen. She was indeed a gift from God, and she was even more stunning tonight than he'd remembered. Her eyes seemed different, more fierce than he'd recalled, but he assumed it was the dim lights that created a mood that would not block the penetrating laser beams of mesmerism in her eyes. But she was determined to be all business, even though, as they sat, he told her how beautiful she was, how enchanting it was to see her again, how welcome she was into his chaotic world among politicians.

She brushed aside his fawning as she tossed back her hair and ordered a snakebite for them both, but Grandy changed his to beer.

"So, how's it coming in the full House?" she asked, knowing they hadn't progressed much, if at all.

"That's a really hard sell," Grandy said. "The ag committee members there are a little more anti-MOEIB than the whole House. And let's face it. This bill is pretty one-sided. I know it's designed to end the gamble with the earth, but it's not easy. People think it's too extreme."

"Extreme is what we need," Freedah said after downing half the drink in one gulp. "That's the only thing that will get results. And besides, if you think you have it bad, I'm juggling two sides against each other here."

"What does that mean?"

"I'm on board with the Ty Mooring campaign," she said as if that should be immediately accepted.

"Ty Mooring? The reparations guy? He's a criminal! How could you do that? We promised Fectid our support if he rammed this bill through. He did that. We should be true to our word."

"This is politics, Grandy," she said, touching the top of his hand on the table. "Fectid's a loser. A real flip-flopper. Ty will follow whatever I say on this matter just because..."

"Just because he's in love with you like everyone else?" Grandy interrupted.

"Well ..." she said, and smiled in a way that made her irresistible, like a cold lake on a sweltering day. "That doesn't matter," she said. "What matters is that we can control him. I can control him. We can't control Fectid, but I'll be able to handle Ty. Besides, old Pete is no longer of use to us. He got the bill passed, okay, so his purpose has been fulfilled. He has no influence in the Senate, and farmers hate him for turning on them with this bill. Farmers are Ty's one and only strong constituent base, and if I'm going to keep him thinking our way, the farmers have to turn on Fectid, at least for a little while. Besides, there's no way Ty can beat Fectid in the long run. The farm vote is just too small. Fectid has the weak, easily influenced suburban earth-lovers in the bag as long as he hammers on the environment. But as for Ty, MELL needs his money. If we're going to save the earth from gambling with these chemicals and big-farm interests, we need it. He can feel good about himself if he gets all the farm votes, but that won't get him elected. So let him have his day, his little 14 minutes of fame, and then we'll move on, either with Fectid or Ty in our back pockets."

"Seems a little disloyal to Fectid," Grandy said. "I'd like to show him that we will stand by him the way he stood by us."

"Wake up, Grandy," she spat as she waved for another drink. "There is no loyalty in politics. It's about nothing more than getting what we need to save the planet and future generations. Besides, his loyalty is to me, not to MELL or you or farmers or voters. He'll do what I want, just like every other weak-kneed guy with an over-inflated opinion about his penis size. But again, we don't need him anymore. You need to concentrate on getting House votes for this bill, not some old-world, outdated devotion to loyalty. The earth is the only thing we need to be loyal to. All the people in our way are idiots. Trusting idiots, perhaps, but they're the best kind. They can be manipulated like cards at a one-deck blackjack table. Do you think the casinos care who they manipulate? No. They take the money and run. And that's what we need to do."

"Seems wrong to me."

"What's wrong?" she asked again as the drinks came. "Nothing is wrong when the end game is as noble as ours. Do you think God cared about all the people he killed in the flood or any who will be killed because the environment will choke them all with soot and poisoned water? No. The end is all anyone should care about. I'm surprised you haven't learned that yet. You're being paid well just to learn that, and it's high time you did." He looked into her eyes and held her gaze. But it was different than before. Harsher. Manipulative. Still, she was Freedah. She had earned his loyalty, if for no other reason than that she was sitting here next to him.

"So if you think Ty can't win, why are you supporting him? I mean, his support for HB 616 will be just as damaging as it is for Fectid."

"Have you not been listening? We need his money. And he's against the bill, but that will not help anyway. And, well, he's kind of my boyfriend."

Grandy's face dropped as his fantasies burst apart and burned like shrapnel in his leg. All his dreams, all of his sense of purpose, had been misplaced. He had no shot at earning this beauty's affection, so how could a snaggle-toothed criminal get it? How could he have not seen it before? His hopes had always been a long shot, he knew, but he'd thought that at least she liked him, maybe not as a lover, but as a man who had convictions and a conscience. But as they made eye contact and he saw that her ferocity was the result of mascara and the way her nascent yet adorable tiny crows feet gave her eyes depth and a sense of wisdom beyond that initial attraction, it was enough just to be there with her, in a hideaway for which he would always be grateful. She was right, he decided. But for the first time, he wondered about her motives. And, for the first time, he hated Ty Mooring. He pushed those thoughts out, though, knowing that God had given him a new purpose in life, and he would fulfill that purpose, even if she wouldn't be beside him. God had given her to him as an extravagance, nothing more. But it was enough. She could be used by God just as he had been. And it wasn't up to him to question God's purpose. All he knew was that he was learning, and she was more than he ever could have asked to help him pursue it. People who doubted never accomplished their purpose.

Oddly enough, and in contradiction to his character, he thought later when the four beers had made him think things that had never occurred to him before, he'd never prayed about his relationship with Freedah. Perhaps it was because, deep inside, he knew the answer. She was bad news wrapped in a package of desire and lust. If he prayed to be with her somehow, he was afraid of the answer. If he prayed for guidance, he was afraid he'd lose his job and all connection to the most beautiful girl he'd ever seen in his life. But he couldn't pray for his eyes to be opened. There was too much at stake. Open eyes would make him doubt and reevaluate, and that wasn't what God wanted. God hated doubt. It was a principal on which he had stood for many years. God wanted him to fulfill his mission against gambling, in whatever form that took, casinos or the earth. And the earth was a much nobler goal. Freedah had taught him that if being blinded by her was inevitable, that was his purpose. So, instead, he prayed for success in passing HB 616, and he prayed that Freedah would see the light and dump Ty Mooring. It was a short prayer, said from his Lansing cushy couch. He would not wait for a reply. He would postpone his prayers for God to give her the same desire for him that he had for her. Timing was everything.

***

Freedah was in the air, flying into Los Angeles, when she got the message from Ty. The fact-checker he'd hired had laid it all out quite clearly for him. He would support the farmers. He attached Aspen's findings, which are detailed in nine categories.

"I'm convinced," his message read. "I will run to win, and I hope to have the NFA endorsement. MELL's facts are not really facts. The farmers at least have some documentation – scientific statistics that I know you value. Please read these conclusions. Seems pretty clear to me. I will pursue truth. Apparently, truth is better received from a hotty like me."

Freedah rolled her eyes. She'd created this monster, and she may someday have to destroy it. But for now, she needed him, and in a way she never really contemplated before, she supposed she wanted him.

Satisfied that her decision to put MELL behind her at the proper time had been the right one, Freedah was also pleased that she had not yet informed Phoenix of her decision and still had nearly three months to use MELL's resources.

She read the fact-checker's conclusions about MELL's claims. They contained links to real data from the government and several independent studies. They were:

"Claim 1: fish are dying as a result of farm pollution: False. The fish population has been steady or grown every year for 15 years. There had been ebbs and flows, which, according to the data from the Michigan Department of Fisheries, were due to several factors, many of which could be explained by natural phenomena going back to the first years of data collection. In fact, the fisheries department's own conclusion was that the fish population in the Jovial River was healthier and more abundant now (the most recent data is already more than a year old) than at any time since records had been kept. The department took some credit for that since it had been planting fish for many years, with much success. The department had recommended, five years before, that fish catch limits be raised, but the state government had ignored such requests without comment. Fishermen's clubs, of which the Pure

Fly Fishing Foundation (PFFF) was most prominent, had opposed the recommendation and lobbied the legislature against it, and it had dropped. As a side note, the fishermen's group had contributed more to the governor's and local legislator's campaign coffers than any other single group in the state.

Claim 2: If pollution continues at the pace it is happening now, it will not be able to support plant or animal life in the Jovial and surrounding area for more than 12 years. False. Plant and animal life in and around the Jovial River had thrived despite a level of pollution that was at one time at least 10 times greater back in the 1950s and '60s when pollution monitoring began. Also, pollution levels from two years ago (the last available data) are so minute that they can no longer be found in parts per million. Even measured in parts per billion, it is well below the DNR's threshold for sustaining life and allowing it to thrive and grow.

Claim 3: Global warming has decreased the amount of water going through the river. False. This is hard to quantify since global warming has not been proven to impact water flow. Water flow, according to the DNR's records (see link), changes from year to year, but averages indicate that it holds steady, on average, over the last 75 years.

Claim 4: River water is warmer now than it was before farmers started triple-cropping on the 100 acres of rich black earth. False. River water temperature, on average, according to DNR records, is the same as it was when records first began being taken. Also, there is no scientific evidence that raising crops alongside the river contributes to warmer water. And there have been very few years in which farmers have had the time to triple-crop in this climate.

Claim 5: Farmers force "enslaved" animals to feed in the water, defecating in it, further polluting it. False. First, animals cannot feed in water. Second, while farmers were allowing some animals into the water fifty years ago, farm management practices and prohibitions on animals in the water from the DEQ have ended the practice. The state has no record of citations for animals in the river going back to 1982. Deer and other animals, however, continue to use the river.

Claim 6: All MELL facts have been proven, not only by state DNR scientists and federal EPA biologists but also by citizen samples of river water and soil samples. False. See any and all links cited in this fact check. Also, citizen samples have been thrown out by EPA biologists as unreliable, tainted, and not following a well-prescribed scientific method.

Claim 7: Erosion of the river banks is destroying the ecology along the river. False. Significant erosion has not been documented along the river, in the area claimed, for more than 30 years, during the last 100-year flood. DNR reports credit farm grassy strips for this improvement and showed surprise that the filter strips worked as well as they did during such an unusual flood event.

Claim 8: All these things were exclusively farmers' fault. False. First, the claims are debunked. Second, any minor claims that may be questioned are contributed predominantly by homeowners and other industries, not farmers. See links.

Claim 9: Farmers pollute intentionally out of meanness and greed. False. No one can pretend to know the intentions of anyone's mind and heart, and no one can know a person's motivations unless they are revealed by the person. In this case, the history of farmers' conservation measures and the policies that have been publicly stated and enacted show that farmers are doing more than any other group to improve their practices and, thus, to improve the ecosystem along the Jovial River.

Other notes: I've looked at every reference to laws, bills, studies, and scientific data cited in the documents I've been asked to fact-check. In 12 out of 15 references, MELL's data is at least 10 years old or older, and in 10 of the 15 references, the data was not specific to the Jovial River. – This concludes the report. Aspen Kemp.

* * *

Freedah heard the captain announce the descent into LA and put down the document. She knew at that moment that her time with MELL was short. What was left for her now? What would Majestic Mother Earth have her do?

When Freedah had settled into Tony Finn's lush hotel room, Freedah sent a text to Ty:

"I've looked over your fact check. It all makes sense. You've nearly convinced me. Farmers deserve support IF they're really helping. I'd like to help. Go ahead and run, be a lackey for the NFA. Be the handsome face of ag. It needs someone like you. And don't forget you're MY handsome face. I'm a bit detained out here, but I will be with you as soon as possible. Luv U."

Chapter 35

Garit had been dragging his feet.

"When are you going to do your first-person, eye-witness story like you promised?" Aspen demanded.

"Something has to inspire me."

"Well, get inspired soon. How about this next Ty Mooring rally?"

"Might be boring. We need something exciting."

"Well, do something soon. I need to prove to you that it's impossible to write a story that has zero bias in it."

"You mean just me or anyone?"

"I can do it all day, every day, but I've been working on it."

Garit smirked.

It wasn't long after Garit arrived early at the Ty for Truth tour event that he suspected this might be a good chance to try the first-person story. There was an atmosphere that weighed like a pair of insulated Carharts on him. It was a kind of excitement that bordered on nascent danger, but he couldn't figure it out yet. It reminded him of the feeling on a Big Ten campus on championship football Saturday, but it was heavier, somehow ominous, absent of friendliness.

By the time it was over, he was sure that a first-person account would be worthwhile, and he wrote a story that set a new record for clicks on the Sasser website and added 250 new followers to the Sasser's Twaddle page.

She received Garit's story but put it off for a moment, saving the best for last. Aspen was enjoying her little espionage, perhaps a little too much. She'd had access to the MELL Twaddle page for a few weeks now, and no one over there seemed to know what she'd been doing. Even with her administrator access, she'd been careful. She'd only been monitoring posts they sent out, never adding things, although there had been times when she practically ached with the desire to edit posts. The writing was poor and obviously unedited. It drove her crazy, but she shoved the feeling aside.

She had to dig deeper into MELL's Twaddle page first. There was a common thread between the MELL followers that she hadn't been able to figure out. Some secret, password-protected private communication group, she suspected but hadn't been able to find it. Yet.

Seventy-five new people joined the Sasser Twaddle page after clicking on a different story about the rally on the MELL page, which baffled Aspen, but she'd figure it out. Administrator access could take her anywhere. She just had to be careful that the real administrators didn't find her, but after all this time, she assumed that they weren't paying much attention. She'd put in all kinds of diversions to keep them from finding her, and so far, it worked.

She assumed that Garit's story, if she submitted it anonymously, would be banned from Mell's Twaddle page because of its even, factual content, and she smiled. If her administrator's code kept working, she could eventually post entire stories there, but she didn't want to press her luck. Maybe just a link in the MELL story that brought readers to Sasser and Garit's story might be a good place to start. She'd learned how to get around detection, and her new methods likely would work on any social media site, but Twaddle was easier than most. They were just getting started and hadn't put a lot of firewalls in place. But for now, she had work to do picking Garit's story apart for bias.

For context, she first read what MELL had posted with the byline Freedah Forest:

> *A group of violent animal abusers assaulted MELL supporters in Jovial, Michigan, yesterday.*
>
> *The abusers, who were mostly local farmers who continue to pack their animals in cages so small they cannot even turn around, attacked the passive animal rights*

activists during a political rally that is attempting to block Michigan House Bill 616, which would prescribe specific, reasonable and stringent animal welfare practices and would put into law penalties for polluting the once-pristine Jovial River.

The farmers, angered by a charming chant from environmental activists to stop the pollution, rushed to the stage and began beating the peaceful protesters with their fists. Only after other animal welfare activists stepped in to stop the violence did the bullying stop.

Details are still emerging, but we at MELL continue to advocate for humane animal husbandry and for the Jovial River, an endangered and beautiful stream that hosts some of the best fishing in the nation.

MELL does not advocate fishing, but acknowledges that sustainable fishing groups such as the Pure Fly Fishing Federation can have a positive impact on the environment when done in a sustainable way.

MELL will continue to monitor the progress of HB 616 and encourage its members to advocate for the defense of the earth.

Aspen shook her head. The story was awful. Biased, poorly written, and not even a hint of objectivity. It was a press release, no more and no less.

She leaned her office chair back, anticipating Garit's style in this new context of first-person, eyewitness reporting.

Here's what Garit submitted:

Noah Brenner trusts very few outsiders, so it was, he admits, out of character for him to agree to invite anyone – least of all politicians – onto his farm.

He'd been burned before.

"I was scammed by a young man posing as a milk inspector," he told me when I arrived on his farm to cover the Ty for Truth rally. "He and his confederates, who, thank

God, are now in jail somewhere, broke into my computer system and plugged in a hack that showed manganese as PBB. I killed several high-quality heifers because of that."

His eyes look downward at the recollection. He's sad, he admits, although not angry. He's forgiven those he calls "bad actors." But he is determined that no one will scam him again. So why trust and host a bunch of political wannabes?

"Because we've been deceived," he said. "Mr. Fectid said one thing and did another. In my book, liars should never represent the people. And it is up to the people, isn't it? So we need an alternative, someone who will walk the walk, not just talk the talk."

It is that conviction alone, he said, that convinced him to open his farm for the event. He trusts Tyson Mooring, he said, "because the boy worked hard for me for a couple of summers, and I found him to be honest and trustworthy. I think he'll tell the truth."

And so it was that the Brenner farm, with its rolling hills and content, grazing dry cows accented by a background of distant fruit trees and a lengthy stretch of the Jovial's tributary, Brenner Creek, was made available for the first political rally in its 144-year history.

Brenner and candidate Ty Mooring had arranged for the stage to be set up at the western edge of a large flat space, an acre, maybe a little more, under which rest the cattle Brenner shot to save them from the ravages of PBB. He didn't know then that it was all a lie, so having the truth told over their bodies, he said, seemed appropriate.

I arrived for the rally in the late afternoon, a couple of hours before it was to begin. People were already lining up on the east end of the flat space, enjoying its close-cut grass and the smell of newly-mown alfalfa wafting in on a southwesterly breeze. He'd cut the hay this morning, Brenner said, because it was ready to cut and to give people a lingering scent of what he describes as the best smell on earth.

Where the people gathered, Brenner had set up large grills and tables. People were already lining up for free burgers, hot dogs, brats, potato salad, and coleslaw, all paid for by Mooring, the recent beneficiary of the first 'reparation' in the state's history. He paid for several kegs of beer as well, and rally-goers wanted to take advantage of the offer before it ran out, several early-arrivers told me.

It's the first weekend after Independence Day, and it's hot and humid here, though not sticky enough to keep people away from free ice-cold beer.

Candidate Mooring is here too, mingling with people, shaking hands as most political candidates do, and his smile invariably brings smiles to the people he meets. Young women, in particular, tend to linger in his presence and assure him that he will have their votes on election day.

I recognized a few people from interviews I'd done before. The first one who agreed to an interview was Ernie Cook, a local businessman who arrived wearing a black t-shirt with 'Security' printed in red across the chest. Behind him were five other men in identical black shirts.

"I've volunteered to help Ty keep the peace," Ernie said. "As you remember, I have experience with security from my time in the military, and these men with me are former police officers who know more about crowd control than me."

"Why?" I asked. "Is there a threat of some kind?"

"Don't really know," Ernie replied. "But we'll be ready if there is." I learned soon after that the "security" detail was on Mooring's payroll.

As Ernie and his so-called peacekeepers lined up for food and beer, I recognized Rick Frandor, owner of the state's largest rock business and host of Mooring's first rally on private property. Political candidates cannot offer free things on public property, so Ty, he told me, decided to hold events on willing farms.

Frandor was followed in by about 25 people, all of them farmers, he told me. Frandor agreed to speak for them all as they gathered around to be sure they agreed with him. Many said they'd interrupt quickly if he said something amiss. I encouraged them to do so.

"Oh, I'm here with more than a little skepticism," Frandor told me. "I like the fact that someone is standing up against HB 616 and MOEIB, but I'm not sure this get-rich-quick kid is the one who can stop it, even with all his government money. However, he seems to really want to help farmers if he's elected. On the other hand, I know for sure that Fectid is not the man we need in office. He's a flip-flopper and basically lied to farmers about this bill and his position on it. He must pay for that."

As people ate and drank, I spoke to several other rally attendees. And everyone spoke of their opposition to HB 616, and about half spoke of their betrayal by Rep. Fectid.

Mooring was on his way up the stage's stairs when up the farm driveway rolled a Trailways Motor Coach, kicking up dust and backfiring twice. I turned to see this, as did most people in the crowd.`

The first person off the bus was rather androgynous but soon showed by his whiskers that he was male. He quickly set up a small folding table and a shade umbrella and began distributing t-shirts to the people disembarking. I moved closer and saw that the man was selling Acrid Reins Rocks and Stones Tour shirts and shirts with the capital letters MELL on them, and everyone received a small sheet of paper with a small type on one side.

I noticed that people could also buy t-shirts with many other slogans printed on them, such as "farmers rape the land" and one that depicted a cartoon scene of a little boy throwing a rock at a straw-sucking man on a tractor.

I saw Rick Frandor passing by the MELL crowd, perhaps 30 or 40 people, no more. Frandor made eye contact with a young man wearing one of the busy rock-depicting shirts and, in what I thought was a rather non-threatening way, asked the young man what the shirt meant.

"Rocks must be free to be rocks," the young man said, a bit of a drunken slur in his voice. "Leave nature alone, and it will take care of us."

"Really?" Frandor said, his voice containing a mixture of contempt and curiosity. "How can a rock be free? It's just a rock. No feelings like humans have. Humans are here to control rocks, not give them some sort of anthropomorphic properties."

"I don't know what that means," said the young MELL supporter, "but I do know that anything we do to disrupt nature will come back to bite us."

"You're insane if you think nature isn't a cruel bitch," Frandor said and walked away to join his own crowd; to position themselves near the stage for Ty's speech.

I followed the young MELL supporter back to his group. He was sputtering something I couldn't decipher completely about rednecks and planet killers, and he gained the attention of many of his fellow MELL folks, who were passing a bottle among them, washing it down with free cold beer.

By the time the contents of the bottle – and two more – were drained, Ty appeared on the stage and began giving his pitch against HB 616. The entire crowd was polite until Ty made his point about farmers having no financial incentive to pollute the Jovial River.

Ty finished asking the sound crew to open up two mics near the center of the crowd for questions.

"So you're saying that planet-killing huge farmer profits are more important than preserving Mother Earth?" demanded an Acrid Reins-slogan-wearing young man who grasped the mic in both hands.

"First," Mooring said, *"why do you say that farmers are planet killers? They're on the front lines every day preserving the earth, adding back the nutrients the earth needs to grow food for us all."*

"Bullshit!" shouted someone behind the questioner. *"The earth doesn't need farmers. Just leave it alone, and it will take care of itself!"*

"Do you have any scientific basis for that theory?" asked Mooring. *"I mean, do you have a degree in earth or soil sciences, or have you ever farmed?"*

"Only evil land rapers farm," shouted someone else, grabbing the mic and knocking over its stand. *"You and your type are stuck in the last century, slaves to the big corporate fat cats that own all the farms now."*

"That's just not true," Mooring said. *"All official government statistics show that farms in the United States are upwards of 85 percent family-owned."*

"Lies," shouted someone else, who then turned around to face the growing mob behind him. *"Are we going to put up with these lies?"*

The drunken part of the crowd murmured a guttural 'no' and started shouting, *"Save the planet. Save the Rocks!"*

As if suddenly spurred on by an unseen instigator, the crowd from the bus started chanting, *"Save the planet, save the rocks!"* Then, seemingly led by a bobbing head of red and green hair whom I couldn't see for long, the 30 or so people surged forward toward the stage, their chants now no more than a desultory cacophony.

As the first ones reached the stage and began jumping up and shouting epithets at Mooring, Rick

Frandor leaped onto the stage and grabbed the mic away from the candidate. As it screeched from the closeness of his mouth, the crowd quieted a bit, mainly to wait for the squawk to end.

"Do you want a rational discussion here about the issues, or do you want to riot?" he asked aggressively.

"Riot, Riot, Riot," the crowd began to chant.

"You're all a bunch of ignorant trans-morons," Frandor said gutteruly. "Ain't no use trying to reason with crazy people." The subsequent roar taught Mooring a lesson about what really cranked up a crowd to a fever pitch, he told me later. "People are far too easily offended," he said.

Frandor began to walk stage left toward the steps when a MELL-shirted young man jumped on the stage and charged him, his head low as if he'd had some football training. But Frandor was not knocked down by the attempted tackle. He pushed the boy aside and waited. The boy charged again, but Frandor landed a right hook on the boy's nose, spurting blood onto a couple of other boys who also were storming the stage.

Frandor was standing his ground, whupping two or three of the boys at once, when the five security people leaped on state and pulled Frandor off of them. They formed a barrier around Frandor and shoved all those who had jumped onto the stage off it. The boys dusted themselves off and scurried back to the bus, Mooring's security detail on their heels.

Soon, the bus backfired and rolled back off the farm. Frandor calmly walked back to get another burger and beer, and Mooring blended into the crowd.

He had gained support, he said. But he knew he had to to more than hold a rally to beat Fectid in the primary. But that's another story..."

***

There was another part of the story that Aspen would not see. Garit told himself that it wasn't important to the story and Aspen didn't need to know about Sandra.

He'd seen her in the crowd, at first because of the red and green painted hair, but as he got closer to her, the months he spent on tour with the Acrid Reins came to the front of his mind. He'd had such promise then. His cover story about the band in Rolling Stone had been his best work at the time. But he'd left the tour when his parents committed suicide. And he remembered with both regret and fondness the girl who had convinced him to be with her on the tour. He had loved her then. At least, he'd thought so.

He milled around the crowd, finally coming up behind Freedah. He was still working, but as Garit tried to move around and get photos of the most vocal opponents of Ty's message, he saw her next to him. Sandra, the gorgeous woman with whom he'd traveled with Acrid Reins. She was slinking about in the crowd, encouraging people to keep shouting. She was moving smoothly, almost floating with the grace she'd always possessed, and Garit, before he had time to pull his camera away from his face, knew he couldn't move very quickly in the mob. She was looking elsewhere when she moved sideways, bumping her shoulder into Garit's chest.

She turned, startled for a second, and her still-beautiful eyes met his.

"Hi, Sandra," Garit said. She allowed a second for her vision to focus, a look Garit recognized as cocaine eyes, and suddenly stepped back and frowned.

"It's Freedah now," she said, then suddenly pulled him close in an embrace that made him remember just how irresistible this girl had been then. He knew she still was, on a superficial level, but he'd seen inside her and realized that below the surface, there was plenty of ugliness.

She turned to follow her crowd as it moved toward the stage when she looked back. "Let's catch up sometime," she said, then turned away and was lost in the crowd, or at least as lost as a woman like her could be.

***

Aspen called Garit into her office.

"Look, I spotted a couple of instances of your bias in this story, but I've run it anyway, but only on Twaddle. Your story tells a very different point of view than the MELL story, but maybe it's time to let the readers decide which is true."

"Which one do you think is true?"

"That's not for me to decide. All I know is that your story has increased Sasser's followers by 2006, and those people mostly read the whole thing. A lot of them clicked the link I put into MELL's story. Don't tell anyone I did that. Anyway, this story, from someone called Freedah, only got 100 views. Only 50 read the whole thing, and it was a lot shorter than yours."

"Maybe people are waking up," Garit said. "Show me the bias."

"First, how do you know the cows are content?"

"They're not bellering."

"Doesn't mean content."

"It does."

"Well, then, how about this: You say it was hot but 'not sticky enough to keep people away from free ice-cold beer.' How do you know?"

"Because people told me?"

"That's not in the story. If it's true, we can add that."

Aspen scrolled a little. "How about this major bias? You say, 'I thought was a rather non-threatening way' about Frandor. Your bias shows."

"It was non-threatening. He didn't raise his voice. It was the protester who was threatening."

"If it was for the daily publication, I'd remove it. But bias is OK on Twaddle. People expect it."

"Twaddle."

"You also say the boy spoke with a drunken slur. How do you know?"

"I know drunk when I see it."

"Maybe he had a speech impediment."

"Yep. From half a fifth of whiskey."

"Did you see him drinking?"

"Yep."

"I'll add that."

Aspen scrolled and frowned a few times.

"All in all, a good first attempt. But I win the bet. You showed bias."

"I disagree. Besides, you show bias by inferring my bias."

"Let's not start that again."

"We've agreed before that bias is inherent. If we're human, we have bias. However, the difference between this story and the purposeful bias of the mainstream press is that this one tries to be objective. And it's as objective as I can make it."

"And it's good enough. For Twaddle, anyway."

"I don't care one spit about Twaddle."

"Then your career will be a short one."

"At least I'll end it with a clear conscience."

Aspen had almost forgotten about the photos.

"Did you shoot any photos of the protesters?"

"All that I could," Garit said.

"Send me all you have. I may be able to figure out who they are and what they're doing. I inserted a facial recognition program into their follower's administrative page. And don't you dare tell anyone?"

Garit nodded.

***

The penultimate Acrid Reins venue of the California mini-tour was in Modesto Park, and after securing all the necessary permits, the show ended with a spectacular fireworks display, one the local news reported was nearly as good as the city's annual Fourth of July celebration spectacular.

The next day, Tony Finn received a text from Freedah: "Nice fireworks, as always. But you're not done yet. You still have one more rural stop to complete your public service. How about coming to Jovial, Mich?"

Tony replied: "Okay, I guess, but why should I let a bunch of rednecks view my fireworks? They're not worthy,"

Freedah replied: "I don't really care about the fireworks. Just be here Aug. 1, two days before an election we need to win."

Tony replied: "Glad it's almost over. After Vegas and your new gig, the public service is over, right? The album will come out in the fall. Then we get a real tour going."

Chapter 36

There was only one private property rally left before the debate, scheduled for two weeks before the primary election. Fectid's camp had been quiet, at least from what Ty could see. But then, Ty's information about the political race and the issues it addressed was limited to broadcasts and what Melanie said. He told people he met that he was proud to have never, ever, not even once, participated in anything on social media, including the newest sensation, Twaddle.

Melanie arrived at Ty's room promptly at nine a.m. She walked past him when he opened the door and, without a word, sat at the kitchen table, opened two laptops and her phone.

"You look worried," Ty said.

"Try frantic," she said. "The rallies aren't working. Sure, we're getting some press coverage, but it's because of the fights, not your message."

"I've heard that no publicity is bad."

"Maybe for celebrities who have nothing to lose, but we're talking issues here. Your message seems to be lost in the controversy."

"So how do we get the message out?"

Melanie sighed. "I know you're going to be against this, but we have to have a bigger social media presence. And, we need more funds. You haven't ever asked people for contributions. You have to start doing that. Fectid is outspending you about two-to-one right now."

Ty frowned. "How does being a celebrity on some ridiculous place like Twaddle that's not even real help get the message out?"

"It's about extending your reach. You can't go out and speak directly to 100 thousand people in your district. You can't bribe them all with beer. But if you go on social media – and Twaddle is the newest, hottest platform – you can reach them all. And some of them will contribute. That's where Fectid concentrates his efforts."

"Really? How many of my 100 thousand voters are on Twaddle?"

"I don't know. Probably not that many. It's a new platform, but that's the best place – the hippest place – to start. If you can convince some of those influencers, maybe your message will spread."

"And what is an influencer?"

"Well, let's see." She pulled up some things on one laptop screen and twisted it into Ty's sight.

"Here's Fectid's Twaddle feed. He's influential."

"But only because he's a public figure, and he was that before Twaddle came along."

"Just read his posts and look at the comments below them. And don't get all pissed off. You're new to social media, and it takes some getting used to."

Ty read the most recent Fectid post about the primary, which was a mere two weeks away.

"All these fights and violence from my primary opponent is proof that I earned your vote. Do you want a dedicated, long-trusted public servant or some pretty-boy novice who's spending your tax dollars running on only one issue?"

Ty scrolled as he spoke.

"So what? It's what I expected from him. And it doesn't make any sense. How do fights at my rallies prove that he's earned a vote?"

"We should ask that question on Twaddle."

Ty frowned. "What you haven't read yet is previous posts where he accuses you of promoting the riots."

"Again, so what? Does he ever talk about why he voted to betray farmers and to promote stupid flavor-of-the-day environmental restrictions?"

"No. And he won't. It's his one weak point. You have several."

"Like what?"

"You're new to politics."

"So I haven't been corrupted."

"Put that on Twaddle."

"People around here – your potential voters – know his name and face. And sometimes they just vote for the status quo."

"The status quo that will ruin the farm economy around here?"

"Put it on Twaddle."

"I think my website, which you developed, Melanie, states my positions clearly."

"But it's not enough. Your face needs to be recognized, too."

"It's been all over the publications and broadcasts around here."

"Only because of the fights, and well, maybe because your face is clickbait. At least in your publicity photos. They publish the worst of you in the pro-Fectid publications, you know, with your eyes half shut or yawning."

"I thought publications were supposed to remain neutral." Ty was scrolling as he spoke. Suddenly, he stopped and read, still on Fectid's Twaddle site.

"Listen to this. This guy – doesn't give his name other than 'smart boy' – says I'm the devil who has fun torturing kittens, and I should be killed for the sake of the planet. Do the police know about this?"

"I alerted them after the first rally when all the threats

against you started. Some have even described how you should be killed. Not very creative, but at least they're brutal."

"Should I be worried?"

"Well, the cops know about it, and you have that bunch of your security buddies at the rallies, and remember that people who make threats like these are mostly cowards and would never confront you to your face."

"Well, if Twaddle is full of cowards and liars, why should we get involved with it?"

Melanie sighed again. "Because that's where the people are."

"People who could vote for me are on Twaddle?"

"Well, again, probably not many. I mean, the people making threats could be from anywhere."

"Then why listen to them instead of the people here who could vote? Why do I care about people who I wouldn't represent, even if I win?"

"Because people need to see your handsome face. Might make them want to vote for you."

"People who vote based on appearances alone aren't the type of people I want to appeal to. I want to represent people who think, who know the issues, who have strong, informed opinions."

"Good luck. Those people don't exist. And even if they do, there aren't enough of them to win you the election."

Ty kept scrolling through the comments.

"You know what amazes me?"

Melanie grunted.

"There is very little original thought on these comments. Mostly, they repeat Fectid's line of bull, saying that the river is nearly extinct and that anyone who says otherwise should be silenced or eliminated. Do they not know that the river is perfect the way it is? That it doesn't need politicians?"

"They don't know that, and no one but you can tell them. Or will tell them. So tell them on Twaddle."

"Seems like a waste of time if they're not eligible to vote in this district."

"But we still need it."

"Then you do it because my time would be better used knocking on doors."

"Yeah," Melanie grunted. "You do that. And are you also going to pay your own way for the next two weeks?"

"Yep. You tell me how much we'll need for my campaign ads, and I'll put them in the campaign account. So far, it's been what? Is it only about 50 grand? Is that enough to buy an election?"

Melanie glared at him, frowning. "That's completely inadequate. Let's start with another 200 grand, and we'll go from there."

"As good as done."

"All this stress makes my stomach churn," she said. I don't know how I'll ever get through these next two weeks." She quickly rushed to the bathroom.

Ty left to transfer funds, but Melanie was still in panic mode, perhaps now more than ever.

She went through a stack of papers on Ty's desk and found a business card.

She called the number on it.

"Is this Freedah Forest?" she asked when the call was answered.

"Yes. Who's this?"

"This is Melanie Swann, Ty Mooring's campaign manager." She gulped. "I know we're on different sides of some of the issues here, but I also know Ty needs help, and I'm in over my head. Would you be willing to help me a little bit, just for Ty's sake?"

"Let's start with the money," Freedah said. "How much is in the campaign fund?"

Melanie gave her best guess.

"You'll need more. Give me access to the account, and I'll send it to the right places."

"I'm desperate," Melanie replied. "Just spend it wisely."

"Always."

***

Aspen had put the daily news to bed, and since Garit was working overtime to catch up after all the time spent at the Ty for Truth campaign, she began to catch up on some photo filing.

She checked her office computer and looked over some of the photos Garit had sent from the last rally, and one caught her eye quickly. On stage, speaking with Ty as workmen set up the stage instruments, was one of the most stunningly beautiful women she'd ever seen. She called Garit.

"So, who is this woman I see everywhere? Is that your old girlfriend?"

"I told you all about that before. You know all about her."

"You didn't tell me how gorgeous she is."

"It's all for show. Inside, she's moldy and rotting."

"Like that makes a difference to men. You all think with your groins."

Garit sighed. "Believe me, Aspen, I have no interest in her."

"But you did once."

"A very long time ago. It's been over for years. And I'm committed to you."

"You better be. I'm going to check her out, just to be sure."

"Check ahead," Garit said. "I don't even know anything about her in the time between the Acrid Reins tour and now. And be sure to see if she's manipulating the MELL group. I have a queasy feeling that she might be stirring up some of these activists."

Aspen went to the MELL website and found that Freedah Forest was irresistible and ubiquitous. Her image was on nearly every page, and for good reason. Aspen couldn't turn away from the images, even though she already hated this Freedah woman. She was the embodiment of clickbait, and it appeared as though she knew it. Aspen checked into Freedah's recent postings on all the MELL social media sites. And she knew some fact-checking would be appropriate.

With Garit's latest story on the violence at Ty's last rally printed out next to her, Aspen read the story from Freedah on the MELL website:

> *Events that should concern all defenders of Majestic Mother Earth are reaching a fevered and violent peak in Jovial, Michigan.*
>
> *The polluting farmers' champion, a rather dull Mexican boy named Tyson Mooring, gets befuddled easily by the well-reasoned arguments from a group of local MELL members, who, at a recent political rally, silenced Mooring's claims that farmers don't pollute. We all know better.*
>
> *The group of peaceful protesters, led by MELL legislative counsel Donald Granderson, argued that Mooring's attempts to undo a recently passed bill that would put reasonable limits on farmers who pollute along the once-pristine Jovial River would, in fact, contribute to global warming and destroy the world-class fishery forever.*
>
> *Throughout his desperate campaign to rescind the bill and unseat incumbent earth warrior Peterson Fectid, Mooring has trotted out supposed experts from the state's fisheries and environmental division, which recently was made more efficient by folding it into one department, the*

MOIEB, headed by MELL board member James Snowmaker. That long list of so-called experts is, of course, in the pocket of the farm lobby, which desperately wants to continue polluting the river for their own obscene profits.

The MELL supporters, of course, saw through this deception last night, and as they began slowly and peaceably marching toward the stage, a small but vocal and violent group of farmers stormed to the front of the stage, where they began beating MELL supporters with sticks and baseball bats. Because the MELL supporters were unarmed, they defended themselves the only way they knew how: by throwing small stones at the farmers. Those tactics quickly dispersed the violent and cowardly farmers, and the show went on.

To be fair to Mooring and his misguided campaign, he has allowed the other side to be heard, but speculation is that he's only doing that to raise the profile of his campaign against Majestic Mother Earth through violent means.

MELL is fighting this fight all over the nation for you. Help us protect the planet. Contribute today to MELL at MELLsavesearth.com.

Befuddled by the report, Aspen rubbed her eyes and decided to take a break and look at her Twitter feeds, among others. One posting caught her eye, and she dug deeper and looked up news reports about Tony Finn's new tour, all writing in glowing terms about the man's talent and passion. An obscure story popped up, and she dug deeper into Tony' most recent arrest, and found it in the archives of the Los Angeles Beat:

Rock star Tony Finn was arrested today and accused of "Eco-terrorism," destruction of property, and trespassing after he attempted to free farm animals from their cruel conditions at a local dairy farm.

Finn, most famous for his number one hit "It's all the same," is a long-time animal rights activist known for songs that point out the cruel conditions to which farm animals are exposed on factory farms. He's also an accomplished master pyrotechnic and produces some of the most amazing post-concert fireworks displays since lightning itself.

Reports from the LAPD said that Finn was caught on surveillance cameras committing vandalism on the farm by spray painting 'MELL' on the walls, along with slogans such as Milk is Murder, Keep Kow (SIC) Families Together, and Stop the Cruelty. Finn is also accused of breaking down gates and herding the cattle out of their barns and onto a busy road adjacent to the farm's barns.

Four of the animals were struck by vehicles on the road and were later euthanized by local authorities.

A spokesperson for Finn and the band said the police jumped to conclusions by arresting Finn, insisting that the videos were too dark to tell who was caught on camera. Police, however, said surveillance videos allowed them to identify Finn, who was dressed in black but left uncovered a tattoo that spelled out Acrid Reins.

Finn was released on a personal recognizance bond.

Aspen searched for a follow-up on the story and found only one entry five months later. Finn had been fined $500 for trespassing and ordered to pay for the four cows that were killed. He was also ordered to conduct several free concerts, at least one in rural America, as part of community service. A small story was buried on page 27, near the bottom.

***

It started raining about an hour before the Ty for Truth rally at the Frandor rock farm. A placid, gentle rain fell that refreshed the earth and made fish bite in the Jovial River.

Under such conditions, the MELL counter-rallyers didn't show up. But CNN did.

CNN sent only a cameraman, who stood back and took no footage of Ty's speech, which congratulated farmers in his usual manner.

But after the speeches were done, a man in the crowd slipped in the mud near the draining beer keg and hit his head on the side of the ice tub that held the keg. A crowd of people rushed over to help him up, and he was helped to his car as he held a borrowed white towel to his wound. The camera caught the rich red blood soaking into the towel before the man was taken by his heckling wife to get three stitches.

The CNN headline the next morning proclaimed

"River stakes rise as violence draws blood at a dark-horse political rally."

Aspen recorded the story and read follow-ups on Twaddle. She labeled it a lie from the first word to the last.

***

After she read the CNN lies, Aspen received, in a blanket email to every TV station and so-called news outlet in Michigan, an official statement from the Pure Fly Fishing Federation (PFFF). The top teaser said, "The Jovial River is a dangerous place." It read:

> *"Recent climate-related historic rain, and the rain that's expected to continue in the long-range Upper Midwest forecasts, will soon destroy the flora, fauna, and aquatic life in the Jovial River.*
>
> *"Forecasters say if the predictions hold true, the river is in great danger. The greater problem, of course, is that farmers and other planet-killing entities will continue their polluting practices after the flood subsides. PFFF calls on all fishermen who care about the river and the planet to organize and stop at least one practice that ruins the future of fishing for everyone. During such rains, fish*

are likely to escape from a local factory fish farm. If that happens, the genetic diversity and health of the river will be damaged beyond repair. So please, fight against the factory farmers. Contribute today at PFFFcares.com."

Every "news" source Aspen checked in the next few days ran the story, but she refused.

"This is all speculation and brings no hard evidence to the allegations of future events." she told Garit. "I will not run it. No one with any journalistic integrity would."

It ran in 750 media outlets across the nation.

Chapter 37

Lawsuits from the Michigan Office of Environment, Inclusion, and Bigotry had been thrown out of court, according to a letter Botsdorf sent to all members of the Jovial Farmers Association, including Ty.

Two days later, Garit received a blanket email to all media announcing a press conference in Jovial about the issue. A contact of Garit's in Lansing told Garit that MOEIB head James Snowmaker was simmering in his typical stews over it all, and he was prepared to malign this travesty of the judiciary. It was the best political move when it looked like he'd failed, which, he told staffers, he never did.

Garit and two local TV station cameramen represented the only media at the event. Aside from MOEIB staff members and a few young interns who were allowed to attend as a reward for their volunteer work, Tyson Mooring, with Melanie and a handful of farmers, also attended, as did four of Ty's five bodyguards and four armed fellows with Rick Frandor.

After being introduced by a young, sycophantic staffer who looked as distressed as the pimples on his face, James Snowmaker stood on a hastily constructed platform just off the main bridge over the Jovial. The river flowed peacefully behind him, and crops on the black earth were perfectly aligned in straight rows, a picture of peace and order. Before the small crowd's murmurs subsided, he felt for the mic, a typical scowl on his face.

"The earth has suffered a horrible and devastating blow today," he read from notes. "A partisan judge has erred in ruling that the critical lawsuit filed by my office, which was established to bring equity and inclusion to the people and the ecology of Michigan, had no legal basis. This judge has shown that the conservative party's goals are to destroy the earth and provide obscene profits to farmers who have repeatedly polluted the land without regard for the future of their children. But the children are who my office keeps at the front of our minds every single day. The judge used false information to decide the case, and I will appeal. We must stop the destruction of the Jovial River and the pristine land around it, and I will not stop until we stop this devastation of our land, water, and people."

He paused for questions. Snowmaker looked past Garit and pointed to a local TV guy.

"Just how devastating is the pollution you speak about?" Garit rolled his eyes. Leading questions were, apparently, the norm now.

"Well, I'm glad you asked," Snowmaker said, smiling at the young reporter. "That's a very good question. We all know how devastating pollution is, and we at MOEIB are committed to stopping it for the sake of our children, who deserve a clean river and unpolluted land."

Garit, who had turned off his recorder because the question was so ridiculous, turned it on again. He'd done his homework and was familiar with the judge's decision, unlike, obviously, the rest of the press there. Garit raised his hand, and Snowmaker reluctantly pointed at him.

"Mr. Snowmaker, you mentioned that the judge – who, despite your accusations, has no known political affiliation – used false information in his decision. Will you explain what is false about the data? It was provided by the former DNR and EPA studies by scientists that you often cite as the most reliable source of science. Every piece of data the judge considered was from state agencies like yours, and you would ask that the people believe your data."

"The information did not consider several factors," Snowmaker replied and looked to find another TV person, who blankly stared. Garit pushed ahead. "Such as?" he asked.

"Just because the data did not show pollution from farmers at levels that would trigger fines and penalties does not mean they have not made every attempt to destroy this river and the land that they illegally control around it."

"Why would they intentionally destroy the land they need to make a living?" Garit said. He was ignored.

"And it did not consider that most of the farmers that do the polluting are white and prevent people of color from having access to the area," Snowmaker spit.

"First of all, race and what you call equity was not a part of this suit," Garit said. "The way I understand it is that the judge ruled on a very specific and focused topic, which was whether there has been damage to the environment due to the farmers' practices. The data that your office supplied as evidence of your suit shows pesticide and nutrient traces in the soil well below the levels that state and federal agencies have established as any danger to people, the river, or the soil. So why do you still think they're polluting?"

"Any level of pollution is harmful, devastating," Snowmaker said, smiling again at the now slack-jawed TV reporter, who was obviously lost in the facts. "I established this office with the goal of zero tolerance because that's what the people want. I won't rest until there is zero pollution, zero farming, and zero worry about the consequences of inaction."

"But your own data shows there is already zero environmental damage," Garit said.

"Zero is a relative term," Snowmaker said. "Who's to say that the level of pollution found in parts per million won't be damaging when we look at the parts per trillion level?"

"Your own departments, or the ones that were folded into yours, accepted those levels years before MOEIB was in existence," Garit said. "If it's not harmful at six parts per billion, why would it be harmful at six parts per trillion? And it seems a bit specious to say that zero is a relative term. Seems pretty clear to me."

"'Are you a scientist?" Snowmaker asked, snarling.

"No, sir. But I can read data, and I can count. Zero means nothing. Always has and always will. The judge was very clear that this was a frivolous lawsuit that should never have been filed to begin with."

"That's your interpretation," Snowmaker snapped, his face beginning to redden. Garit held up the decision printed in his hand.

"It's the judges' interpretation, sir. I'll quote directly from his writing: 'This is a frivolous action, full of arbitrary and capricious claims, and should never have been filed.' End quote. Then he warns you, by name, to stop wasting the court's time and resources."

"I'm not going to stand here and listen to some so-called journalist who's trying to make a name for himself by questioning authority," Snowmaker said. "My official and last word on the subject is that my office will protect this endangered river and land, no matter the cost."

"I was not aware that the river or land was declared endangered," Garit said.

"I just declared it," Snowmaker said, smirking. "But we still have to settle the issue in the courts, and that's what we'll do."

"The cost of the lawsuit is estimated at just under ninety thousand dollars by your own office estimates," Garit said, but Snowmaker had stormed off the podium, five young staffers and interns in tow.

Before Snowmaker had one foot down the first step on the right side of the unsteady stage, Ty ran up from the left and grabbed the mic.

"Why don't you tell people your true motivations?" he cried into the mic. "Why don't you tell them you covet this land and are abusing the power of your office to get it?"

Snowmaker turned around and sent Ty a look that would have killed an alligator. "You're a low-life scum," he shouted but did not step back toward the stage. "You're in bed with these greedy farmers, and you hate the earth!"

"Why don't you come back here and back up that claim?" Ty asked. "Why don't you come up here right now and try to beat me up just like you blindsided me in San Francisco?" Snowmaker's face turned white. He walked away, his minions behind him with their heads on swivels.

Rick Frandor nudged his closest compatriot in the ribs. They suddenly charged Snowmaker's group. One of the young staffers saw them coming, and they all picked up their pace and began to run toward the safety of their large, roomy SUVs.

"You better run," Frandor shouted behind them, and he and his posse began raucous laughter like justified heroes.

***

Snowmaker waited until he was in his limo, on his way to the airport, headed to his leased private jet, to call Grandy.

"What the hell are you doing out here?" he demanded. "If you'd been able to pass that bill when I wanted you to, this suit would have us suing these hick-ass farmers one by one by now. What's the hold-up?"

"It's the senate," Grandy whined. "I'm afraid I can't *make* people vote our way."

"Freedah doesn't seem to have a problem doing it."

"Freedah has charms I don't possess," Grandy said. "She got it through to the House, which is farther along than anyone could have thought just a month ago. And if you knew how she got it through, you wouldn't want it made public."

"I don't want excuses, dammit, I want that land!" Snowmaker shouted. "Either do your job, or I'll find someone who will!" He ended the call, wishing he could still have the old satisfaction of slamming the phone on a cradle. Damn cell phones. Just an unsatisfying button to push.

***

Grandy watched the full video of the press conference from the World and Sasser's website, including the shouting match between Snowmaker and Ty, and his stomach lurched with his worst fears. Land! What had that to do with anything? From the beginning, this was about preventing greedy people from gambling with the environment, right? How was wanting a prime piece of real estate bringing MELL and its supporters toward that goal? No, Snowmaker must have misspoken. He wanted the bill to pass, not possession of the land, right? What good would the land do him? No one person could afford it even if it were for sale, and the heavy muck would likely never perk enough to build a house. Besides, it was Snowmaker who gave the land to Ty, and Ty had already told the farmers that he would lease it to them come hell or high water. Or was Ty conning them all? How well did he really know Ty, anyway? Always thought he was a nice kid, but he had met him in prison, after all. And what did he really know about Tony Finn? Or Freedah?

Freedah. Thoughts of her sparked a drip of saliva, a precursor to nausea. She was pure, right? Driven? Passionate? No one who looked like her could be a deceiver, right? She was nothing if not passionate and sincere. She liked him. He liked her. He'd looked deep into those luscious eyes, and he'd remembered nothing but pure, honest beauty. But for the first time since he'd met Freedah, he asked himself why he was so enamored by her. How could someone not love a sunset or a beautiful mountain range? He appreciated God's work of creation, and Freedah was one of his best works. She was evidence of a loving creator God and, as such, should be followed. Not falling for her would be like spitting in God's face, just like not opposing gambling was an assault against God's intent for people to manage their money well.

What was Ty doing with all his money, anyway? Blowing it all on Freedah? Who could blame him? No, he could not have doubt. Not again. He had to do what was right. And keep his job. What was the key? What would God want him to do? He'd put him here, in this position, after all. For what purpose? He thought back to how it all started. He traced his memories forward. Was it the church he'd founded? Was it his stance against the casino? Were they involved? No. It was when he'd met Ty. Ty was the key. A saved man who could be in danger of losing his salvation if he kept down this path. Ty could put a stop to the whole thing.

These were all good reasons to confront Ty, but as he thought about it, certain thoughts kept invading his mind.

Why should Ty be hooked up with Freedah, anyway? What did he have? Why couldn't Grandy have it?

He resolved, after a sleepless, agitated night, that he'd have to confront Ty with his sin. He was the only pastor Ty knew, after all. God had chosen him.

For once, Grandy should get what he wanted, what he deserved. He was sick to death of undeserving people getting all the grace. Ty was certainly undeserving, but he was getting not just ordinary grace but Freedah-level grace. That was a sin; Grandy was certain of that. Ty was sinning and enjoying it. Only he, Ty's pastor, could correct the error and convince Ty of his sin. If he could do that, God would open the window of his grace and bring Freedah back to Grandy. He deserved her.

***

On top of everything else, Freedah fussed; she was being asked to write a press release for Peterson Fectid. She was obviously stretched too thin, and her bosses back in San Francisco should have known that. Obviously, they didn't care. They were using her. But by the end of the day, she had written and posted on Fectid's social media pages:

> *In spite of the recent violence and threats of violence promulgated by my political opponent, I have decided to accept the offer by Mr. Mooring to participate in a debate scheduled for seven days before the primary election.*

Young Mr Mooring's ongoing violent actions have no place in our political system, and even though I have received death threats against myself and my family's persons, I will courageously confront my opponent's violence on the debate stage.

All voters of this district should know that I have never condoned violence, and I never will. I have been steadfastly committed to peaceful discussion of the issues, and even though that seems impossible with the political climate my opponent has cultivated, I will get it done. My firm stand on the issues surrounding HB 616 remains intact. I will fight for the environment and against violence at all costs.

I call on my friends to do what my opponent will not do and calm the crowds during the last dirty and manipulated political rally of this campaign, and as always, I will stand for the people, the majority of peace-loving citizens whose only desire is to save the earth and the Jovial River.

Chapter 38

Tony Finn relaxed after his Vegas show on a reclining leather couch. He held a firm grip on a half-gallon of whiskey while the remains of an eight-ball of cocaine sat on the coffee table in front of him. Beside him, in the early stages of undress, sat two cute blonde young girls with severely painted eyes he'd picked out of the front row. He'd not asked them their ages. Experience taught him that was a question that should never be asked.

Tomorrow, he told them, he could go home to San Francisco, where he could dive into his Olympic-sized pool and chill in his cool theatre room. The girls were invited to stay the night, but he made clear they were not invited to San Francisco. His cell phone rang. It was Freedah.

"I've heard about how great the tour has been," she said. "You're knocking them dead. You're almost done."

"I am done," he snarled into the phone. "No more of these morons who try to sing with me during the show. No more trying to remember where I am."

"But you have one more stop," Freedah said. "One free show, and your community service is finished. Then you can do whatever you want."

"I'll do what I want now," he said, chugging whiskey like it was water.

"Look," Freedah said, exasperated. "I got you out of jail time in California. I got you a judge who happens to be a fan. Do you know what you could have gotten with a different judge? Third offenders generally go to prison, not to mention the civil cases I paid off. So the least you can to is come to Jovial for the last show."

"Where?"

"Jovial, Michigan. You know, the place with the river MELL is so interested in? You don't have to play more than five songs or so. But come here. Kaley Carrumbo is coming to do a piece on the Jovial River, and I want to have her interview you. This was just a warm-up, remember? After Kaley gets done, we'll plan a real tour. You know, the west coast, where people really appreciate you."

"Don't wanna," he sulked. "I already did my signature finale. The fireworks were the best I'd ever done."

"Don't worry about that," Freedah said. "This is your last freebie. No need for fireworks. Save that for the paying customers."

"But I'd be breaking my pattern."

"Look, honey, sometimes you have to do things you don't want," Freedah said. "You killed those cows in California, and you got off easy. Do this one little thing, and you're free. But get here asap. Your interview is set for a week from today at an outdoor arena in Jovial. It's not a bad venue for a bunch of slavers. Kaley will interview you on stage, and then you will play a couple of songs, bang some groupie, and go home. Then you're free."

"Bah," he grunted, then relented. "You'll be there?"

"Yes, I'm here now, getting things arranged."

"I'd rather bang you," he said.

"We'll see," she said and hung up.

Tony, the next morning, after he'd taken too much hair off the dog, decided to check out this Jovial gig. Five songs and a hookup with Kaley? Seemed worth it, he supposed. First, though, he had to remind himself of just how hot Freedah was. He went to her MELL social media page and clicked on a video she'd posted with a warning: "Here's what the corporate farmers do when there's no watchdog group to keep them in line. Damn, profiteers."

The link led to a video: Melanie's coverage of Ty's first rally at the Frandor farm. He watched as the camera scanned the rock piles, the cut rocks on display with streaks of color hidden since they were first taken from the ground. He recoiled at the gaudy sign out in front that advertised Frandor's rock farm with 1970s style lettering, which read "Frandor's Rocks!!. He replayed it several times, then made a cell call.

As he waited for the call to go through, he opened his wallet and pulled out a worn card. When the phone was answered, he applied his professional voice.

"Tony Finn here, pyrotechnic license number C435691-5. I need a special order. Double the last order and add three interconnected cell phone triggers. I need it all delivered in the fastest way possible to Jovial, Michigan." He gave the address Freedah had given him, which was at the Jovial casino.

"I need it all there in no more than three days," he said. He gave his bank account number, received his confirmation, and called his crew.

"Get things set to go," he said. "It was all my bad. I forgot about this last gig in Michigan. We're heading out as soon as we can to some god-forsaken place over by Detroit."

Chapter 39

The Acrid Reins tour coach spit heavy plumes of diesel exhaust as it barreled east on interstate 80. Tony awakened somewhere in Illinois and made himself a Bloody Mary with extra hot sauce.

He examined the latest sales figures for his various songs and was disappointed. Resting his eyes from his phone's glare, he noticed, in the vividly colored farmland, a sight that angered him. Stones at the edge of fields were crying out to him.

Some farmers had piled the stones neatly in rows as if to make fences or boundaries, and others just piled them up in a heap, like bodies that had been stacked up by Nazis. He'd never believed the Holocaust was real until he'd seen the black-and-white photos on some Jewish website. One image was the same as another in those archives, which brought his mind back to his first giant hit, "It's all the same." That song was still selling nearly four years after it hit the top 10 nationally. Nothing like at first, but the cash was still good. But what baffled him was the poor sales from Rocks and Stones. Sure, it had just been released, first in California and later across the country, but it should be selling better. Sometimes, it took time for his followers to realize the importance of his work.

Rocks and Stones was an evolving masterpiece, and as such, he should have expected that the common folk out here in flyover country didn't quite get it. On the bright side, he was still adding verses as he traveled around the United States and now Michigan, which was even less important than the Plains. The Plains were on major highways. Michigan required a drive out of your way to get there.

He pulled up the video of Frandor's farm, searching for even more disgusting and immoral displays, and another verse came into his head. He recited it, and it steeled his resolve to take the message wherever it needed to go. Farmers needed to learn that removing and piling rocks was wrong. They were taking them away from their natural habitat and away from their families in the same way farmers tore calves away from their mommies. He'd heard them crying on videos. The same goes for rocks. Tony knew he was one-in-a-million. Very few people in the world could really understand what calves were saying, and even fewer could hear the rocks as he could.

He'd never heard rocks speak audibly, of course. He heard them cry in his spirit. It was a talent or a gift that he'd first realized when he'd heard a Christian talk about how he knew God was speaking. Seemed like a good practice to cultivate, but he wanted to be more down-to-earth than those religious fanatics. And he had almost given up on it until those pebbles jumped into his shoes in California. And now he heard rocks speaking to his spirit anytime he wanted. If he kept practicing, he'd be able to call them to speak. He and rocks were like-minded, which wasn't a bad song title. Rocks understood him.

With such thoughts, he prepared for a phone interview. Kaley Carrumbo was scheduled to call to get up to speed on his brand-new masterpiece before the taped event coming up in Jovial, planned for maximum effect, with the Jovial River trickling and singing in the background.

The call came, and Tony made himself enthusiastic.

"Tony," Kaley began, "Just tell me about the rocks and stones tour and your motivation behind it. You've told me before about how it started with the pebbles, but take me deeper."

"They were called pea stones," Tony said. "That name in itself tells you how most people disrespect what Mother Earth has hidden inside her. Pea stone, like urinating. It's an insult, and I want to educate people and let them know that rocks and stones are not inconveniences but are as necessary as teeth for us earth-bound human animals." Kaley asked him to continue.

"Who can really say for sure if rocks are just inanimate objects," he said. "Sure, the radical conservatives, the profit-mad farmers, say they're nothing more than things that get in their way, but if they said it, it deserves to be questioned. But the point of

Acrid Reins has never been just to question things. Sure, that was the point of the entire first album, but the band and I were quite a bit younger then, unsure about our ideals. But we've grown. I knew if I were ever to make an impact on the world with my self-developed talent and brilliant lyrics, I'd have to take the next step. Action."

He'd been warned three times against action ever since the dairy farm incident in California. First, it was done by Freedah, then by his lawyer, and then by the judge. But he hadn't gone to jail in that incident, which was too bad in a way, because a jail term would really be a PR windfall. Freedah could take care of him again, probably to keep him out of jail, and he appreciated her efforts almost as much as he appreciated just how fabulously that girl was put together. The universe really collided with the right genetics to make her. Funny how accidental circumstances could create a woman as perfect as her. Even a well-conceived plan wouldn't have done as well.

"Who's to say that rocks don't have specific genetic proclivities that were just as lovely to other rocks as the two young groupies I'd been with in Nebraska had been to me," he told Kaley, trusting her word that this interview was for background only, to help her prepare for the Jovial interview. "It's still a mystery to me how species are not attracted, necessarily, to species apart from their own. Seems a little racist to me. A little bigoted. And quite a bit arrogant. These farmers actually think they know for sure that rocks are not anything to be valued. They just rip them up out of their homes in Majestic Mother Earth and pile them up like cadavers in World War II. It's obscene, really, but very few people share this questioning, and even fewer agreed with me that rocks must have feelings, too. Just because they were ancient – meaning old soul – doesn't mean that humans shouldn't try to understand them and care about their welfare. That's where I can help."

The latest song was a start, he told her, but he, as an artist, should be able to do more. He should be able to make other people question things the way he did with his opulently open mind.

"The smart ones follow my lead, which is obviously more enlightened than mere consumers of my art can comprehend," he said. "Especially these rural hicks with rocks piled up randomly just to get them out of the way. These people are too stupid to open their minds, too closed-minded to understand that rocks and stones are as vital a part of this world as mosquitoes and rats. And while the hicks limit their understanding to accepting the notion that humans were created equal – a theory I've never really accepted, I mean, just look at me and you, Kaley – I need to make them understand that all things were created equal, if they were ever created at all. More likely that Mother Earth just got out of the way of the cosmos and let it all happen without her help. That seems to be her pattern. That all led to the facts that are now obvious, at least to people like us whose minds are open. Birds and insects and rocks and animals could never have more intrinsic value than any other accidental creation of the universe. My theory is that humans, while arrogant enough to think they're on the top of the food chain and rulers of the world, are, in reality, on the bottom. A rock, animal or insect or even a virus could kill them, but they can't see it. They just want control. Well, it's time to show them who really is in control. And it's time to create a campaign that shows people that opens their eyes. And that's why I wrote Rocks and Stones."

He did not reveal his ultimate goal to Kaley or his surprise that would finally open blind eyes, awaken them as he had been awakened by that little escaping stone in his shoe. Freedah would handle the fallout later. It was why she represented him and the band. She'd gotten him out of scrapes before, so often and so well that he had been freed to be himself, a free spirit without restraint. It was all about living life to its fullest.

He was still a little angry, though, about how the California thing had all fallen apart. So, a few cows had been killed. Death was a small sacrifice to save a whole herd from being milked against their will. He was sure they appreciated being martyrs.

Well, obviously, people – hicks – who didn't understand why people called farmers slave owners – would never understand the inherent rights of rocks. It baffled him. Even the folks in California – Freedah, Kaley Carrumbo, Phoenix Tippen –understood his point of view, and they'd never even been out of the city, as far as he knew. Why couldn't these hicks, who were working among the animals and insects and rocks, see it? Rocks pushed ever upward, and despite these pseudo-scientists who said it was freezing and thawing that moved them up through the earth, Tony knew better. Rocks consciously pushed upward, year after year, millennium after millennium, to escape their dirty captivity and free themselves from manure and chemicals that farmers doused them with year after year. Rocks had been content in their homes deep under the earth until farmers started using Roundup.

As Tony pondered such things, a new phrase came into his mind, and he tried to fit it in with the tune and the new lyric. It would be something that could make a big splash in Jovial.

He was humming the tune Rocks and Stones when he fell asleep, and when he awoke, it was dark, early in the morning, and there was very little traffic. He'd gotten the tracking info, so he knew the fireworks were already in Jovial, waiting for his expertise to make the Jovial fireworks the best and most impactful he'd ever done.

The Jovial finale, his ultimate convincing argument for the poor rocks and stones, would have to be brighter and more explosive than ordinary fireworks. He had to make a lasting impression if he were to sell more albums. How he would arrange the explosions was not yet set in stone, so to speak, but he'd get it figured out. The polished rocks in his pocket helped him clarify his mind and ground himself with the earth as he fondled them. What could have more impact than his music? Now he knew. Freedah had told him long ago. News coverage. He needed to make some news.

He was starting to write down the next verse: "You expose our colors, hidden from the first, our connection to our brothers washed away like dirt." ... Maybe he worked a little too hard for the rhyme.

But then, a sign zipped past his view: Frandor's rock farm. Home of the rockiest fields in America. Landscape with us!

What arrogance! Exploiting the natural environment for personal gain. This Frandor must be stopped. Tony hated that man. Never met him, but it was a fact that this man must be stopped.

Tony had learned to trust his feelings about such things. His feelings were fact, mostly. Besides, if there was anything illegal about what he was planning, it shouldn't be. He had to open eyes.

*＊＊

Tony and the band arrived late in the morning, and he slept in the casino room Freedah had arranged in Jovial. He awakened as the sun was setting, and he immediately felt the adrenaline he'd need. He'd been dreaming about Rick Frandor, so he was angry as he sleepily planned his actions.

He picked up his fireworks and all the triggering devices from the casino's mail room and loaded them into his rental car. It was well after dark, his time to shine. He drove toward the Frandor farm, and the gasoline smell of the car fueled his anger as each mile went under him. Frandor might as well be a pimp. Not like the benevolent pimps he knew, but more like inner-city tough guys. Frandor liked to expose bare rocks' colors for his own amusement. Selling those pretty rocks as if they were common prostitutes and not related to all of creation and, above all, humanity. Rocks were stable, firm, and hardened. They were better than humans. More reliable. Far more eternal, like one of his songs.

Tony Finn stopped the car under a tree about a hundred yards from Frandor's driveway and sat for a few moments. He undid the seat belt and reached into his pockets. He fondled the smooth rocks in each pocket, then took them out and rubbed them against his chest and neck, then pressed them against his temples. The rocks were angry, too, but it was only anxiety. "calm down, little ones," he whispered. He kissed them and put them back in his pockets. Even martyrs for the cause could be excused for a little apprehension. "Yours is a noble sacrifice."

He donned a furry outfit, his favorite, a fox, and started walking, backpack overflowing with explosives heavy on his back. After a few yards, he decided it was too hot for the full costume, so he went back and removed it. He kept the foxhead hat, though, for luck. He'd worn it when he did the California dairy thing, and he'd never gone to jail. Freedah helped a little, but good luck was good luck. He would not jinx it.

All was quiet, as it should be in the back country at 3 a.m.

These country bumpkins always had to live in out-of-the-way places for some reason. Idiots.

He stopped at the driveway approach and made sure all the lights in the house and barn were out. It had stopped raining earlier in the day, and with the smell of cleansing moisture still heavy in the air, he noticed by moonlight that animals contentedly walked around a pasture above the hill from the farmhouse and barns, and things seemed peaceful enough. He walked stealthily, cautiously, since stupid farmers usually had mean dogs, kept as slaves, hanging around, but he heard none. He shifted the fireworks, heavy but secured in his Acrid Reins Rules logo backpack. The burden would be lighter soon. With a smallish flashlight, he walked behind the barns toward the pastures and found what he'd seen from the highway the day before. Rocks. A huge pile, bigger than any he'd ever seen. They seemed sad to him, and he wondered what would finally make them break their silence if he did not act now.

He picked up a small rock from the base of the pile and kissed it gently.

"You're a martyr," he said. "You are honorable, and your death will shout louder even than this explosion. Thank you, rock. May your soul be released by your actions."

It didn't take long to unload the gunpowder-filled explosive devices. Tony climbed about halfway up the pile and removed small rocks until his arm was up to his shoulder. He was careful to avoid a cave-in, but these rocks were solidly packed and stable. He pushed as much firepower as he could into four such holes and connected five long wires around the pile and back to the first explosive – something that ordinary fireworks aficionados – the ones who only cared around the fourth of July would have called an M-80, a quarter stick of dynamite. It was the smallest thing he'd packed into the hole. It was the trigger.

He hooked up a lead wire to what looked like a cell phone, only with two wire ports on the underside. He carefully placed it where he thought it would be unencumbered by trees or other obstacles that would block reception, and calmly walked past the house and barns again, oblivious to the presence of two video cameras on the house and two on the barn. He walked back to the car, stashed the furry head in the trunk, and drove out toward the highway on-ramp. Traffic was almost non-existent, and he pulled off the highway where, in a moonlit sky, he could make out the shape of the rock pile. He pressed a key on his cell phone when his eyes had adjusted to the night sky, and the concentrated fireworks blew up – four explosions in quick succession – with a force that even Tony hadn't expected.

Rocks shattered and scattered and flew what seemed like miles into the air. He heard windows breaking as the rocks fell back from their flights. He heard them land on roofs and vehicles, and as the lights in the house came on and people rushed out, he heard animals bellowing. Horses whinnying. Friendly fire was never a pleasant proposition, but it was unavoidable, if not necessary.

He watched as shadowy figures rushed around the barns and headed for the pastures, screaming in agony. Soon, he saw the lights of emergency vehicles miles behind him. He pulled out his pocket rocks again, kissed them, thanked them for their sacrifice, and sped, lights off, toward Jovial.

***

Garit was glad this election was almost over. He'd covered it well, he thought. But what was all this really for? Sure, he'd reported on one of the most unusual political campaigns Michigan had ever seen, but what was really happening? He could understand if there was really a lively political debate going on at each event, but no one in the last few had really had the chance to sit calmly with Ty and debate the issues.

Ty had lost the ability to tell the large crowds about the betrayal of their political leader or the dangers of PA 616. He had been shouted down and pummeled with rocks at the last place. What had been accomplished? The election polls were still favoring Fectid, and Ty seemed destined to be a footnote, however colorful, in political campaign history.

He was loading his camera equipment into the car when his phone rang.

"How far are you from Sventon?" Aspen asked.

"I'm in Sventon now.'

Get to the police station as quick as you can, then over to the Frandor Rock Farm, whatever that is. A big explosion overnight. Potentially have a suspect in custody."

"I'm on it," Garit said. He was familiar enough with the area to know that the Frandor farm was on the other side of town. The police station was closer.

He approached the front desk and identified himself to the dispatcher, asking if anyone would talk to him about the mysterious explosion late last night. She asked him to wait, and a few moments later, a Sventon deputy sheriff appeared.

"The police report isn't done yet," he said without introducing himself. "It's still under investigation, is all I'll say on the record.

"Was there really an explosion?"

"Yes."

"Property damage?"

"It appears so, but mostly to a pile of rocks."

"Rocks were blown up?"

"It appears so, but that's off the record."

"On the Frandor farm?"

"Yes. Listen, that's all for now. I'll send the report over to the World and Sasser when we get it done." He turned and walked away.

Garit drove through town and soon arrived at the Frandor farm, and, seeing Rick on a large front-end loader, he approached and watched as dead cows were scooped up and dumped into a deep pre-excavated hole.

When he was done and Garit had counted three dead cows and two dead horses, Frandor shut down the machine and approached.

"If you write this up, Garit, make sure it's on the front page. Whoever did this is one crazy son-of-a-bitch."

"Any idea what happened and who did it?"

"On the record?"

"Yep."

"Okay, Garit. You haven't ever turned on me before, and you need the facts.

"Police say they don't have all the facts yet,"

"I do. It was about 4 a.m. I'd been home from the Mooring rally about a couple of hours or so, I guess, just about asleep when I got rocked nearly out of my bed. My wife woke up screaming, and then I heard the sound of moaning animals. Come around to the rock pile, and you'll see where it all happened."

They walked together past his 'rocks for sale' sign to the pile, which was still sizable, but the top and sides had been blown off toward the highway as if it were Mount St. Helens.

"How much force does it take to do this much damage?" asked Garit, taking pictures of both the rock pile and the flying rocks' damage to the house and barn.

"I'm no munitions expert, but I've used enough dynamite to dislodge big boulders to know that this was no prank," Frandor said. "This was a big explosion."

"Any idea who would do it and why?"

"I'll tell you exactly who did it," Frandor spat. "That idiot Tony Finn."

"How do you know?"

"Want to see the video?"

Chapter 40

Grandy had encountered faithless thoughts from his tainted mind before. He had hated his doubt about God's grace, but he'd gotten over it himself with hard work. This time, his faith in Freedah fading far too quickly, he prayed that one last close interaction with Freedah would restore it. He likely had only one more shot at her before this stupid, confusing political campaign was over, and she went back to San Francisco. He had a bad feeling that when that happened, he might never see her again. But, and he hated this doubt, it could be a relief when she was gone. She'd changed. Maybe she didn't have all the answers. But then, who did?

She'd been his focus, he had to admit, ever since he first met her. He'd gladly let her instruct him despite her youth. He'd feigned interest in everything she said, even the stuff he didn't understand. Had Ty ever done that? Had Ty even tried to earn the privilege that was embodied in her? Had Ty worked as hard to gain her favor as he had? Or was he just manipulating her? He'd never told her or himself, but she was authority personified on this Mother Earth stuff. It was almost as if he'd made her an idol, a thought that had never occurred to him before. Idolatry was wrong, of course, but this was the real world now, not some tiny church with a few lost sheep. Freedah was the expert, and he would follow the one who had the authority, just as he'd learned in his online lay-pastor training.

He knew she'd still be there at Ty's finale in Jovial, where he planned to finally tell her how he felt, consequences be damned. An old line from his church days reinforced it. "Obey God and leave the consequences to him." But how could he obey a far-away God when Freedah was right there, within his reach, a temptation that could not be wrong when he felt love in his heart? If that's what it was. He just couldn't tell anymore, and God wasn't giving him any answers. Not that he'd consulted him.

He'd practiced a line about asking her if she had ever considered the benefits of being with an older man, and in his fantasy, she smiled sweetly and told him she had, and he was that one. Together, he would tell her, they could be a real force in changing how stupid, apathetic human animals cared for the earth and the rivers and the wildlife. She'd know it to be true, would tell him she'd been waiting for his change of heart, his conviction to her and Majestic Mother Earth. They'd then hold hands and launch a separate entity, aligned with MELL but more focused on the earth of northern Michigan. He'd raise the funds, and she'd charm everyone into seeing the truth. A perfect partnership. Gambling with the planet had to stop. The ends justified the means. She would agree to that, right?

But, alas, no. She was out of his league. No doubt about that. She was with Ty Mooring now, dedicated to trying to be a one-man woman. At least that's what she'd told him, but, to his increasing shame, he doubted her. He hated doubting her, as he hated doubt of any kind. It showed weakness and a lack of determination. God would not honor the efforts of those who doubted, so he could not doubt. What was the verse? Somewhere in James, he thought. "Let not the man who doubts expect anything from God." Something like that. He didn't look it up but knew he had to expel doubt, not just for Freedah, but because Freedah, whether she knew it or not, was doing God's work. And so was he. He could never doubt that.

As was his custom, he checked his news feeds on his phone frequently, but today, the day of Ty's last pathetic rally, he saw something he didn't expect from the Jovial World and Sasser website.

Garit's bylined story featured the headline: "Explosion kills animals on Sventon-area farm:"

> *Police are searching for a suspect in an explosion Tuesday night that killed three cows and two horses on a well-known and unique Sventon-area farm.*

The blast, heard for an estimated five miles away, according to Sventon police reports, was allegedly intentionally detonated.

"There is no evidence to suggest there was anything accidental in this incident," said Sventon Police Chief Benjamin Lundgren. "The explosive force was set in a rock pile, and when it blew, rocks struck some animals and did extensive damage to a nearby house and other outbuildings. Some shards of rock were also cleaned up on the highway, nearly a quarter-mile away."

While police declined to positively identify the suspect, surveillance camera footage shows a figure dressed in dark clothing passing between the barn and house, after which the person climbed halfway onto the large pile of rocks, dug several holes, and set something inside. The video shows the man, who, during his escape, was tattooed with the words "It's all the same."

"It was unmistakable," said Rick Frandor, owner of the farm on which the explosion took place. "Only one man has that tattoo. I know because I've seen it on this man many times in the last few weeks. It's Tony Finn of Acrid Reins."

Police would not confirm that claim.

Finn arrived in Michigan within the last week, according to his publicist. He'd been touring to promote his band's latest release, entitled Rocks and Stones. His last stop on the tour is set for Friday, on the same stage as the final rally for candidate Tyson Mooring's campaign to become a member of the state House of Representatives.

Finn and the Mooring campaign are on opposite sides of the political fence, particularly over House Bill 616, a bill that would restrict farmers' legal right to farm land along the Jovial River. Mooring owns 100 acres of that land after having been deeded it as part of a "reparation" from the Michigan Office of Environment, Inclusion and Bigotry (MOEIB). Mooring is running for office based on his dedication to fighting that one issue and Finn supports the bill.

They will appear together Tuesday night, according to Mooring, as a way to show that people on opposite sides of any single issue can discuss it rationally. However, that has not been the case with Mooring's political tour. At every stop, violence took place as bill supporters clashed with farmers and others opposed to the bill. Fist-fights have broken out, and more than 50 people, according to compiled police and hospital reports in towns where the tour has gone, have suffered injuries from thrown rocks.

Police have not issued an arrest warrant for Finn at the time of this publication, and Finn has not been seen in public since performing with his band last Tuesday night in Las Vegas. Friday night's rally and concert, the last before the primary election next Tuesday between Mooring and incumbent Boyd McCockert, is expected to go on as scheduled.

See our exclusive video of the explosion incident on our website here.

Grandy watched the video. There could be no doubt it was Tony. He watched further as the cameras captured both the sight and sound of the cattle, dying painfully, moaning as they lay on the ground, trying to get up but unable to with broken legs and blood gushing from their heads. Nothing made sense anymore. He tried as he might for two hours to push down the doubt he was feeling about his mission, and he asked God why? No answer. Should he know? Were newfound doubts something he should listen to? Could he have been wrong? Could he have been deceived? Could he have ignored or misunderstood God's mission for him? He remembered the last time he had such strong doubts. But he had long ago convinced himself that blowing up the casino was what God had wanted him to do. How could he be sure?

He checked the MELL social media account. On top was a story with the byline Freedah Forest.

Recent violent attacks and misinformation by farmers supporting a Michigan state representative's bid for office were taken to the next level yesterday when the local press wrongly accused Acrid Reins singer Tony Finn of a senseless act of violence.

An explosion amid a large pile of rocks on the Richard Frandor farm, near the last stop on the tour, remains a mystery as to why it occurred. But Finn, in an exclusive interview with MELL's independent news team, said he was too busy writing music to have done the act.

If he had, Finn said, it would be commendable.

"This farmer has a long history of exploiting rocks and stones (the title of Finn's new album) for his own obscene profits," he said. "He yanks them from the ground, where they have been content for millennia, and sells them to wealthy homeowners at a significant profit. Sometimes, he even splits them in half quite violently. I think it's time to realize that the earth is not designed for people to exploit."

The Acrid Reins tour will have its last performance on Friday night, and the election is slated for Tuesday next week.

***

Grandy pulled into the driveway of the Rick Frandor farm as dusk was approaching.

"Pastor Grandy," said Frandor, his voice absent of joy or dismay. "What brings you here? I thought you were working with the idiot earth wackos."

"No, I've been trying to end the gamble with the earth," Grandy said defensively. "But I thought you might need someone to talk to after the explosion."

"Well, you were my pastor," Frandor said. "But that's a long time ago now."

"About two years," Grandy said. "But I still feel some sort of obligation to my former fellow believers, even if they did cast me out."

"Cast you out?" exclaimed Frandor. "Who did that? My family and I couldn't wait for you to get out of the prison ministry. We were told you decided to make that your full-time occupation. And then we learned that you'd gone to be a lobbyist, and we just assumed that you'd lost the faith."

"Faith comes in many different forms," Grandy said. "The board decided, based on a consultation with a PR agency, that I was a liability because of the rumors about me blowing up the slot machines."

"That's not what we were told," Frandor said. "Most of us respected your decision to stay with the prisoners, but we also lost that respect when we found out in the World and Sasser that you'd gone in with the MELL group out of California. We can't respect that, obviously."

"That's something I'm still trying to work out in my own mind," Grandy said. "First things first, though. I saw the videos from your farm, and I've read in the Sasser about the violence at Mooring's rallies. You've been there. What's the truth?"

"That's the first time I ever heard you ask that, pastor," said Frandor. "I thought you knew all the truth because of your closer connection to God."

"Maybe I should have asked that question more often," he said.

The two sat at Frandor's kitchen table late into the night. Several people, all with cell-phone videos to show, came and went, and by the time Grandy left, making his way down gravel roads to the highway in a driving rain, he had seen footage of the violence at the rallies from a dozen different phone cameras. He'd seen Freedah in many of them, working in and out of the crowds, and in one, she was energetically working the crowd, spurring people to move forward as the violence on stage erupted. As the commotion shifted and the camera angle changed, she was still in the picture, her lovely face contorted in anger, shouting with her piecing eyes darkening, so it seemed, with vitriol.

***

The next morning, after Garit had caught up on a little sleep next to Aspen for the first time in far too long, he opened his email, which contained a file with dozens of videos.

It was from an anonymous sender with the tag line "compromised election". Each showed Freedah, and each with a different man in very shady places. She was kissing McCockert in one, straddling Finn in another as he held her up by her fanny. Another of her necking with Ty in the casino bar. More photos came from San Francisco, where she was strolling down a crowded street with Phoenix Tippin. There was one showing her and Tippin snorting lines of cocaine in a darkened bar. There were even a few, much less graphic, of her and Grandy walking down the streets of Lansing, gripping his arm like an old debutante in a civil war movie, and then the last one on the list. A surveillance camera video from the day before the explosion. Freedah with two MELL-inked young men paying Frandor in cash, then loading rocks – mostly bowling-ball size and smaller -- onto a pickup truck's bed.

Chapter 41

Garit was putting on his rain jacket when Aspen asked where he was going.

"Following a lead," he said. "Check out these videos I left on the table, and we'll discuss it when I get back."

He received Ty's room number at the casino front desk, took the elevator up, and knocked on the door. There stood Sandra, with newly dyed hair, both green and red, dressed in only a plush hotel oversized towel. A new nose ring was too large for her face, but she still looked pretty. When they first met at an Acrid Reins concert on the University of Illinois campus, he'd thought her the most beautiful girl he'd ever seen. She hadn't lost one speck of that attraction.

"Sandra," Garit said coldly.

"It's Freedah now," she said. "Come in, and we'll reminisce about all the good old days."

"I'm really looking for Ty," Garit said. "And I'm not interested in yesterday." He stepped into the room as Freedah shut the door and stood with her back to it.

"He's gone fishing for some stupid reason," she said. "Probably thinking ahead to after he loses the election."

"You seem pretty sure about that. It's as if you have some sort of inside information."

"So what if I do?"

"You have no right to manipulate an election. It isn't right."

"I've heard that phrase from you way too many times. Just like on the Acrid Reins tour, you got all judgmental on me. Some thanks for me getting your story on the cover of Rolling Stone. And here you are again, years later, trying to make me the bad guy."

340

"You are the bad guy," he spat. "And you had nothing to do with that story."

"Really," she said icily. "Who got you on the tour? Who gave you everything you wanted anytime you wanted?"

"That was before I realized just how ugly you really are on the inside," She stepped back, staring at him as if she'd never heard such words before, and her face contorted into pre-crying pain.

"How dare you call me ugly?" she screamed. "I am the best you've ever seen by a long shot. You're just jealous that I've moved on after dumping you."

"Were you so coked up that you don't remember that I left you and the tour when my parents died?"

"That's not how it happened."

"You remember the past any way you want to, Sandra."

"Freedah!" she shouted, her face turning red with no hint of tears that he would have expected just a moment before.

"Whatever. I'm concerned about you manipulating Ty for some reason that I still haven't quite figured out."

"And by the time you do, I'll have control. I will get the bill passed. I will get Fectid elected. And I will do whatever I wish with Ty. It's all for the greater good."

"We'll see," said Garit as he stepped back toward the door. "Just keep in mind that I'll be at the rally tomorrow, watching everything you do."

She stepped toward him, her face softening back into the glorious beauty he once knew. She placed both hands on his chest and let her towel fall to the floor.

"Don't be like that," she whispered as she moved her lips toward his. "Nothing unusual is planned anyway. Just the last event of a failed political campaign. And by next Wednesday, it will all be over. The earth will be cleaner, and the river will stop being violated by farmers and Ty Mooring."

He pushed her away. The first man who had ever done that to her.

"You can't stop what karma does," she said, her look of hurt seeming genuine this time. "It's out of all our hands. It will be up to the people to decide, and Ty can't win. He shouldn't. The river deserves better than him or you. My mission is to the earth, and I will be remembered for that long after your little hometown byline is long forgotten."

"That doesn't matter to me at all anymore," he said. "Fame is for fakers. That's you."

He stepped out of the room and closed the door. She screamed gutterally.

Chapter 42

The day of the debate

Rain continued to fall as the final campaign event stage was set up. Crew members of Acrid Reins wore raincoats and boots for the first time on the tour, and they struggled with the wind. The rain was warm and bothersome, but they finally succeeded in getting up an extra large awning to keep the electronics and instruments dry.

Garit arrived, camera set to video, at the same time as a pickup truck backed to the front of the stage and unloaded, carefully placing rocks into a pyramid-shaped pile, the top stone, a large rock with veins of pink, red, and blue sparkling in the rain and lights from the stage. A chip on one side, showing the sparkles, was placed facing out toward the potential crowd, which, despite the rain, was expected to be quite large. At least that's what the radio had said after interviewing the event's coordinator, Freedah Forest.

"So come on out tonight, folks," the radio personality said to his listeners. "The politics part doesn't take long, and then you get a free concert from Acrid Reins. Besides that, getting to see Freedah Forest instead of just listening to her is well worth the trip to the Jovial County Fair Grounds." His co-host agreed. "She's definitely a looker," he said, and the pair moved into a commercial.

By the time the folding seats were set up, the rain tapered off a little, and fairground employees quickly slid down the aisles, wiping the chairs dry. People started filling them, and Garit took an inventory. There were plenty of farmers in the crowd, many of whom he recognized from various interviews. Filing in, yet seemingly segregated from the farmers, were dozens of young people, solemn, or so it seemed, as Garit heard beer cans popping open and noticed several bottles being passed around. He looked past them, and his suspicions were realized. Three touring coaches were idling in the far side of the parking lot.

The crowd had barely reached their seats and hadn't had time to get listless when Freedah stepped on stage, holding hands with Ty and Tony on either side of her.

"Welcome to the most unique political and musical event you'll probably ever witness," she said, flashing her iceberg-melting smile as the rain fell a bit harder, sticking her white t-shirt to her body, unencumbered by underwear. At least three-quarters of the young people, Garit noticed, had quickly held up their phone cameras to get a lasting memory of that sight.

"This is the last stop in Tyson Mooring's Both Sides Tour and the Acrid Reins Rocks and Stones tour," she said, motioning to the pile glistening in front of the stage. "See, Ty is running for state office so he can stop House Bill 616 from passing into law." A raucous group of young people began booing, but they seemed to Garit to be in a jovial mood. Freedah raised her hands to silence them.

"And Tony Finn is here because he thinks HB 616 should be passed because protecting the earth is so important. He's dedicated his entire musical career to Majestic Mother Earth, and he's giving you this rare chance to see him and the band perform for free." The crowd cheered liquidly.

"He's here for free to fulfill his court-ordered community service!" cried a voice from amid the farmers. Garit looked carefully. It was Rick Frandor. Garit looked his way and saw him surrounded by three of Ernie's armed bodyguards and, tucked in behind them, Reverend Donald Grandersma. He looked back to the stage, where Ty stood, and noticed two more rifle-bearing guards behind him. He's safe, at least.

"So first," said Freedah, "we'll hear from candidate Tyson Mooring, who wants to be a politician for some reason." She waved her gorgeous arm and turned so the boys got a profile view of her effortlessly tight body as Ty stepped forward. "Ty?" she said, "come on up and give your misguided opinions."

Ty looked at her as if he hadn't expected such a comment at all, as if he'd been betrayed. But he stepped to the mic.

"My position is not misguided at all," he said as rumbles of grumbles began in the back of the crowd. "HB 616 doesn't protect the earth; it attacks farmers." Boos began getting louder. He raised his voice. "I would ask each of you who apparently don't want to hear anything you may disagree with that you would step into a farmer's shoes for a minute. In fact, if you worked on a farm for just one day, I bet your attitude would change. You farmers out there know it's true." He motioned to the farmers he recognized, most of whom were still seated in their chairs. "Ask any of these farmers here if they would ever purposefully injure the ground where they get their living from. Would you bite the hand that feeds you?"

"Farmers bite," someone shouted, and laughter erupted. It was not an affable laugh but sarcastic and mean-spirited, like a stereotypical evil genius's laugh from every action movie.

"Farmers are the backbone of the entire nation," Ty said, still louder as the crowd grew restless and began pushing forward. "You bunch of paid protesters don't even realize that you have the privilege of your brainwashing in college and your trust funds because farmers work their tails off to feed you, even if you don't seem to appreciate it at all. And I intend to support them in the state house in every way I possibly can."

"You support murder!" someone shouted. Someone else: "Farmers are killing the planet!" More murmurings, louder. The crowd pressed forward again.

"Let the man speak!" shouted Frandor, jumping onto a wet seat nearer to the farmers. "How can you learn if you won't listen?"

"Don't let him speak!" shouted someone again. "He lies! He lies! He lies." The chanting began, and it was louder with every rhythm. The crowd surged forward a little more, and Ty's closest bodyguards stepped forward, their rifles now held in front of them, appearing much more menacing than before.

Suddenly, Frandor ran up the steps and to Ty's side, his pistol evident from the rain that had pushed the wet fabric of his shirt between the gun and his body.

"If you knew what lies really are, you'd know that your hero, Tony Finn ..." he looked behind him, but Tony was not in sight. "Where is that son-of-a-bitch? Tony Finn is a liar. He's the one who killed my animals and blew my rock pile all to hell!" he shouted, but the crowd still chanted, "he lies!" and pushed toward the stage, a massive crush of bodies that ran toward many of the farmers, who were by now on their feet, taking defensive postures.

The human-crushing wave forced all Ernie's men to retreat and take defensive positions on the stage, and along with the flow came Grandy, who arrived onstage just as the first of the shouting crowd started picking up rocks and throwing them at Ty and whoever was near the stage. As Grandy rushed to the mic, Ty's two bodyguards blocked him and redirected him backstage, where Tony and Freedah were holding hands, peeking through a curtain break, grinning. Tony pulled back to be hidden behind the curtain and turned on his mic.

"Free those rocks and stones!" he said. "They can't fight for themselves!" Freedah ducked off backstage and disappeared as stones landed with increasing force, breaking speakers and band instruments.

"I know that voice," shouted Frandor. He looked to find Ernie. "Ernie!" he screamed. "We need to make a citizen's arrest!" Ernie raised his hand to signal with a circular motion, and three armed men dashed onto the stage and behind the curtains. They grabbed Tony by the arm and dragged him toward the curtain and the crowd as he and his band mates flailed and resisted. Grandy was heading that way, too, arms in the air as he tried simultaneously to calm the crowd and Ernie's men. Tony broke free as Grandy reached Frandor's side.

"Stop, you evil son-of-a-bitch, or I'll put you down!" Frandor screeched, reaching for his sidearm. Ty rushed from behind the curtain, calling for Freedah. He jumped up to where Tony was reaching for a handrail on the stairs. Grandy shouted, "Don't! And reached under Frandor's hand to push the gun up and out of the threatening position, but Frandor was too strong. He squeezed off three rounds, each one missing Tony as he ducked and escaped. Grandy looked back at the crowd, which moved as one and ran helter-skelter toward the fairground exits, trampling some slower and smaller people into the mud. Knowing there was nothing more he could do, Grandy looked back. Tony was gone, and lying on the floor, covered in blood, was Tyson Mooring, grimacing in pain and clutching his chest.

***

Aspen was trying to reach Garit on his phone when she heard the emergency calls on the paper's police scanner. She received an alert on her social media feeds that MELL had issued a breaking news alert. She opened it. Byline Freedah Forest:

A toxic political speech from Michigan House primary candidate Tyson Mooring led to gun violence tonight as farmers rushed the stage at his last rally and fired multiple shots into the crowd.

While casualties have not yet been assessed, eyewitnesses at the scene say Mooring was shot and taken to the local hospital, a victim of his own hate speech.

What began as a peaceful rally, attended by a few farmers who support Mooring's earth-destroying policies, quickly turned violent when supporters of HB 616 tried to make their voices heard and hoped to settle in to hear Acrid Reins play tunes from their brand new album, Rocks and Stones. When armed farmers leaped to the stage and began threatening the concert goers, they quickly and peacefully dispersed into the rain-soaked night.

State Rep. Peterson Fectid, Mooring's political rival in the primary and a supporter of HB 616, luckily had not arrived at the rally, even though he had been invited to debate Mooring.

"I know just how radical these farmers can get when they find themselves victims of false information that they want to hear," he said. "They'll do anything to protect their obscene profits. But I wasn't afraid of them. I was

simply delayed in traffic due to the driving rain, by the grace of God."

Police are looking for the shooter or shooters. MELL will keep you informed when more news develops.

Chapter 43

By the time Freedah came out of the motor coach where she and Tony were hiding, a team of medics were working to get Ty loaded on a gurney. She saw the blood from his lower abdomen soaking through the bandage already, and his shoulder was also bandaged and bleeding through. She watched them for a few moments, saying nothing.

As they were moving him to an awaiting ambulance, a group of three television cameramen, their heavily breathing reporters close behind, approached. She was fortunate. She'd been schmoozing each of them. She waited until she was sure they were filming, then started screeching, "They shot my boyfriend, guys!" Then she trotted to catch up to the medics.

"She has a boyfriend?" one reporter asked another.

"Sounds like it, dammit," the other replied. Then the third added: "I'd shoot someone for her, no hesitation. All she'd have to do is ask."

Garit checked his camera to see if the video he was shooting clearly showed the shooter. It did not. So he rushed off the stage, trying to find Frandor. He couldn't. He started interviewing farmers. since the crowd that had thrown the rocks had formed a shoving mob by the entrances. The four farmers who were willing to talk confirmed what he had seen with his own eyes. The crowd had started shouting and throwing rocks before Frandor jumped on stage along with many of Ernie's men. But none could say who fired the shot.

Freedah ran to her rented car and slipped it in the traffic line behind the ambulance, checking to be sure the TV cameras were still following her. They were. When she followed the ambulance out of their range, she took the first right and traveled at the speed limit to her casino hotel room, the one she'd been sharing with Ty.

She slept fitfully for a few minutes at a time. She'd startle awake, check her laptop for news, then settle back in. It was too late at night now to expect the TV reporters would have anything to report yet, but she sent emails to about half a dozen reporters whom she'd gotten to know and mesmerize.

By 7 a.m., the first reports were coming in. She smiled. They bought her line of reasoning.

"A violent end to a violent campaign," the graphics on the screen said as a reporter, one whom she'd smiled at before the hubbub began last night, began a live feed from outside a now-deserted fairgrounds.

"Reports from credible sources who were at the rally told us that the farmers who had gathered to protest HB 616, many of whom were armed, created a riot when Tony Finn appeared on stage. Finn has been wrongly accused of blowing up the rock pile at the Rick Frandor farm the night before. No evidence of that allegation has been confirmed, the spokesperson said."

"Dammit," cursed Freedah. "I warned him about saying I was a spokesperson. That implies that someone is controlling the news here."

She shrugged off the thought. These guys were too stupid and too concerned with their own celebrity to really check out any claims. She was still in control.

She watched until she saw footage of herself screeching that 'they'd shot her boyfriend' and smiled. She was about to shower and get ready for her day when a political ad popped onto the screen. It was Peterson Fectid, appearing like a talking head, solemnity painted on his face.

"We are all saddened by the senseless violence that occurred in Jovial last night," he said. "There can be no doubt at this point that it was the opponents of a bill I supported to save the Jovial River from extinction that caused all this mayhem. I will not stand by and tolerate any of these underhanded, dirty campaign tactics sparked by a man who was only recently released from prison. He's been promoting violence throughout his whole campaign. It was only by providence that I was delayed in getting to debate my opponent last night, or I may have been the victim of this uncalled-for shooting, which left one person nearly dead. And now we have an election coming up next Tuesday. Who will you vote for? A public servant who wants to see the river saved for the future of your children, or a violent criminal who only knows one issue – and supports farmers who want to destroy the river for the sake of their own obscene profits?"

The screen phased out to a graphic. "Fectid for you!" it read in red, white, and blue letters.

Freedah prepared herself, dressed in tight jeans and a white v-neck t-shirt, then pulled a clear raincoat over the top. It was raining even harder than during the last three days, and she noticed a local weatherman warning about flooding along the river, but dismissed his report. It was great timing, this rain, and she'd ultimately use it to her advantage in her own time.

She parked beside three TV news trucks and pulled the rain hood over her head, double-checking to be sure her hair was positioned properly, falling down over her breasts. All three cameramen saw her and started filming. She waved at them without smiling as they asked her questions about the shooting and her boyfriend's condition.

"I can't say anything right now, men," she said and rushed past them, making sure they had a clear view of her face before she crossed through the hospital doors. Always leave them wanting more.

She went into Ty's room. He was out of intensive care but still hooked up to many bottles of fluids and machines constantly whirring and beeping. He was unconscious. She pulled up a chair next to his bed and waited, keeping herself busy with something on her phone. She didn't notice when his eyes fluttered open.

"Hey, love," he said weakly. "When did you get here?"

"I've been here all night. You were just in no condition to notice me."

"Oh, that's not possible," he smiled again weakly. "I'd notice you no matter what, just like everyone else."

She smiled and took his left hand in hers.

"So, I hear you're going to survive," she said. "None the worse for wear."

"Did anyone else get hurt?"

"No. Just you. You took all the bullets. How soon before you get out of here?"

"They're waiting for the feeling in my legs to come back," he said. "One bullet rested next to my spine, but they said they got it out. Hopefully, there is no paralysis. Won't know for a couple of days."

"Election day's coming," Freedah said coldly. "I don't think this is helping you."

"I'm a victim, ain't I? Voters seem to like victims."

"Fectid's been saying you can't serve from a wheelchair," she said. "Not sure he's wrong."

"So what happens if I lose? What happens to us?"

She stared at him, her eyes as intense as he'd ever seen them, the crystal spackle in them pulling him deeper into her aura.

"There is no us." She released his hand. "You've done all you can to save the earth, misguided as you may be. But it's over now. We've got your money, which is all we really wanted, after all. We can really do good things with that last half-million you donated to MELL."

"When did I do that?"

"When you paid the bill for the campaign expenses," she said. "Don't you remember? You're a card-carrying member of MELL now, which will do you pretty well politically if you are elected."

"But I was fighting MELL."

"How do you figure?"

"By being against that bill."

"You never were really against it," she said. "You financed us, and we got it passed in the House. You wanted, just like me, just like when we first started this, to save the earth. Now you will."

"It's all bullshit," he spat, then coughed weakly.

"No, it's the future," she said. "And if you're against the earth, you're against me. I can't take that anymore. You betrayed me when you ran for office. You were just playing at this thing and should have known that I play for keeps."

"What does that mean?"

"It means that you've been on the wrong side all this time," she said. "It means that with you gone, we can do right by the earth again. And it means I can go back to saving the earth and promoting my clients."

"Clients?"

"Yep. I'm the sole representative now of Acrid Reins, soon to be the hottest band on the planet again."

"So it's never been about you and me, even from the start?"

She hesitated. It was time to lay things on the line, once and for all, but something told her she shouldn't hurt this man. All the others had been healthy when she dumped them. But this man, for some reason, in his pitiful state, brought out some sympathy in her. But, she'd learned that quick, sharp cuts healed easier than dull poking. The scars on her arm testified to that.

"Face facts, Ty," she said. "You're an idiot. You've never been able to see what was happening right in front of your face. Do you really think a snaggletoothed hick like you could last long with me?"

His eyes narrowed. The blood pressure monitor started making noise.

"So all that talk about loving me was just a lie? You were just using me?"

"I never loved you," she spat. "You've always been nothing more than a tool in my hands. It was a nice ride, sure, but I've used up that tool. Time to throw it out and get a new one."

"So I really meant nothing to you but a check?"

"Don't make me out to be the bad guy," she said.

"But you *are* the bad guy," he said, coughing again. "You're a user and a bitch!"

"But I'm the best one you'll ever see," she said. "And you'll never see me again."

Ty forced himself into a state of calm. But there was one more question. "I have to admit to my naivete," he said. "Didn't see this coming. You've never shown this before, Freedah. What turned you so mean?"

"This is the way your god made me," she said and stood.

"No, your god did this," he spat. "Because your god is you!"

"Who better to be?" she said, flat as a whetstone.

She shoved her chair, scratching it against the floor, and walked out. He watched her leave, then broke down and wept as the machines made furious noises.

Ty could still hear her steps when he reached for his phone. He dialed his bank and asked for the manager.

"This is Ty Mooring," he said. "I need to put a stop order on any funds that have been taken out of my account as far back as you can go."

Chapter 44

It was early afternoon when Garit mooned Freedah and her crowd. Immediately, he made his way to Ty's room, but Ty was asleep. Garit decided to wait and looked out the window, but the crowd had dispersed in the rain. He knew it would drive away these fair-weather protesters, but he didn't think it would have happened this fast. It had been raining non-stop for three days, or so it seemed, so paid protesters should have been accustomed to it by now.

He asked the nurse when she entered the room if Ty had regained consciousness since the shooting, and she said he had been conscious, talking, and doing fine. Until ...:

"Some hotsy-totsy girl with green and red hair was here this morning, and when she left, he was agitated and sorrowful." She smiled but not cheerfully. "I don't know what she said to him, but we needed to sedate him, or he'd have blown a gasket. And he's too weak to survive undo stresses, so we gave him some powerful stuff. He'll be out for eight hours or more, likely."

Garit left the room and headed back to the office, but when he drove near the Jovial Police station, he jerked the steering wheel right and pulled into a parking spot near the front of the building. He'd almost forgotten. Perhaps the cops had an official report on the shooting by now. Maybe he could even help, having been an eye-witness of sorts to the event.

As he walked from his car to the police station, he made eye contact with a man who was also walking in. The man tried to hide his face with his hand, but Garit recognized him.

"Sir?" Garit called. The man stopped. "Aren't you Reverend Grandersma?"

"Not a reverend anymore, son."

"I know, Mr. Grandersma. You're a lobbyist with MELL, right?"

355

"I'd rather not say, and I'd just as soon not talk to any reporters."

"How about off the record? It would help me try to make sense of all that's been going on."

"You're West, right?"

"Garit West. Of the Jovial World and Sasser." He held out his hand, but Grandy did not take it.

"I read your stuff. You're not as biased as most, so maybe later. I've got things to do right now."

"What are you doing right now?"

"I'm turning myself in. I shot Tyson Mooring."

"No way," Garit interceded. "I saw you run on stage, and you didn't have a gun."

"I used someone else's."

"Really? I saw you running toward the stage. You were trying to stop Rick Frandor, weren't you?"

"No comment. Now leave me alone."

Suddenly, a siren began howling. Police came running out the front door, causing Grandy and Garit to push themselves to the side of the wide cement stairway that led to the entrance.

"What's going on?" asked Garit to a group of three police officers.

"Ask us later," one said, disappearing into a police car.

Garit grabbed Grandy by the arm. "Let's go." Grandy followed. The two ran outside and got in Garit's Jeep. He waited for police cars to get in front of him and followed.

The train of police cars led to a farm above the river, which was running higher than just the day before. But it was far from the flood stage as the rain continued. When they arrived, Garit pulled up his raincoat and tucked his camera under it.

The farm, as Garit knew, was Olie Hansel's Fish Farm, a century-old place that operated by taking river water in through a small barrier about 20 feet from the shore to its end. Olie used it continually because of its efficiency and clean water, and it would continue to operate under a grandfathered and long-standing permit to divert water into fish ponds. If he stopped diverting water, the grandfathering would be void, and the business would be shut down.

Olie, the largest fresh fish supplier in the state, was standing on his front porch, waving to the cops. He pointed toward a barn used for storage of tools and equipment. It was on fire, and in front of the barn were 20 to 30 people, all shouting and chanting "earth killer." Freedah Forest kept the chant going with a bullhorn.

Garit stepped as close to Freedah as possible in the rain as firetrucks pushed their way through. The protesters were yelling, "Burn it down!" and "No river, no mercy," but they scattered when five firemen began to spray water on the fire, and one turned the hose on them, spraying fresh river water until they were drenched.

As their chanting drowned in the spray, Garit yelled at Freedah: "Why burn down a barn? What's the point?"

"I don't talk to biased, hateful reporters," she yelled back and began chanting, "River killer!" as two television reporters drove up.

Garit stepped aside, knowing there was no arguing with Sandra/Freedah, but he stayed close enough to hear some of the interviews Freedah was granting to the television boys.

"This farmer caused pollution that will destroy the Jovial River," she said, the emotion in her voice either genuine or not. Garit couldn't tell. "This fish farm releases diseased and inferior fish to the river all the time, and now, just go look at the river. There's fish feces floating down all the way below the city!"

As the reporters gazed at Freedah and asked no questions about how this farmer did anything wrong, Garit walked down to a point where he could look at the water flowing. Freedah had been right. There were feces floating in the river. But they were human feces.

He walked back up and approached Olie.

"What happened, Olie?"

"Nothing," he said. "I looked up from harvesting some fish for the market in pond number 4 there, and the shed was on fire. That's all I know."

"Have any fish escaped?"

"Nope. I have monitors in every pond, and every fish is right there, right where they're supposed to be."

"Any waste storage ponds or septic tanks flooded?"

"Nope. It can't happen. I spent a year's income making sure it doesn't."

The protesters continued their chants as the fire was put out, and the police herded them back to their rented cars as they screamed epithets at them.

The real story, Garit knew, was still to come. He drove down to the river to speak with Ernie.

***

The next morning, the fire was long quenched, and the protesters were nowhere to be found. Garit was walking the river from the downtown dam when he saw three "official scientists" – at least that's what their jackets had printed on the back – from MOEIB by the river's edge, taking water samples every 100 yards upstream. Most of the visible pollution had been washed away by then, but they took samples anyway.

It didn't take long for the samples to be collected, and before the group of three left, Garit shouted at them.

"When will you have results?"

"Shouldn't take more than a couple of days," a young man shouted back and was quickly hushed by another member of the team and pushed toward their waiting black Escalades.

Garit called the department the next day. Nothing has come up yet, he was told by an official spokesperson who would not give her name. Off the record, she said, the test results would not be released until MOEIB director Snowmaker had a chance to review them.

***

Snowmaker, later that afternoon, saw the results clearly in a print-out. E-coli was present, not at illegal levels, but it was human waste that had caused it. A relatively small spill, about 500 gallons, by estimates. It was really hard to say definitely, the report said, because it was all gone and diluted by the river and the rain. It had been a one-time event, the report's chief investigator had written, lasting maybe three hours. Snowmaker read the statistics and scrolled down to the cause. He cursed. This was a complication he hadn't foreseen. But the numbers were pure science, void of anything but facts and numbers collected at various sites. He resolved to keep the tests quiet until an opportune time.

Chapter 45

The rain had been falling for almost three days straight, but not even traditionally alarmist television meteorologists were too concerned. The river had risen an inch or so but was still an inch or more below flood stage. The flood stage in and of itself was of little concern to farmers, who would simply wait until it receded, as it always did. The need to replant after a flood was common enough to keep extra seed on hand, just in case.

The rain had put a halt to most of the water-related businesses for a time because the river was just too fast, and at Ernie's Outfitters, business was slow. The restaurant was still seeing steady tourist traffic, but the fishing and outfitting, bait and tackle, were practically non-existent.

Garit found Ernie under an awning on the riverfront boardwalk, cleaning and repairing rental poles. A damaged canoe leaned against the wall under the awning, waiting for a 50-cent-piece-sized hole in the side to be repaired. Ernie had found a small rock in the canoe.

Garit and Ernie knew each other, but not well. Garit had done a story on Ernie's Outfitters a couple of years back as part of a series on local businesses. Garit reintroduced himself, and Ernie was amiable.

They talked about the weather, the flood, and the protesters until Garit thought it was best to get down to business.

"I was out at Olie Hansel's farm the other day when the protesters were out there, and I noticed human turds floating down the river," he said. "The protesters were blaming Olie, but I know for a fact that there is only one place near enough to the river that has septic tanks for human waste. It's the only place that could have been under the water in this flood. Did your camp's septic system fail?"

"Are you going to write a story?"

"Not immediately. Anything I saw or smelled would be nothing more than an educated guess. I'll wait until the official results come in, and that could take days."

"I won't comment," Ernie said, cautious about anyone from the press, even though he knew Garit, read his stuff, and considered him a fair reporter.

"Will you comment when the MOEIB gets results?"

"I trust you to tell the truth, Garit, so let's just wait and see."

***

Three hours after Garit left Ernie's place of business, a white-haired man walked into the store, wearing what Ernie thought was a very expensive suit.

"You the owner?" the man demanded. His demeanor was blunt and, Ernie thought, more than a little confrontational. Ernie's first impression was that the man was arrogant and trying to throw his weight around. He'd seen them before. Rich tourists who thought the river and all the businesses around it should cater to their every whim and solve every complaint.

"I am," Ernie said with what he hoped sounded like boldness to match this man's.

"Do you also own a multi-room facility that once was a survivalist training school that has been shut down by the state?"

"You must know I do, or you wouldn't ask the question."

Snowmaker reached into his coat pocket and produced a folded stack of papers. He unfolded them with what Ernie considered extreme pomp and ceremony, snapped them, and peered at them.

"This is evidence that the spill earlier this week came from your septic tanks," he said. "But I'm not concerned with that right now. Sure, you're on the hook for at least $100,000 in fines plus the cost of fixing the tanks, which I've been told shouldn't have been there to begin with. So we've got you from all kinds of angles. Falsifying records, illegal environmental activity, illegal operation of a racist club on state land, should I go on?"

"Ain't nothing racist about anything. I also had a permit to start the survival training school. And we're not on state land."

"That schooling permit expired years ago. This whole thing could cost you millions. You really want to lose this business?"

"I guess the state will do what it wants. I have lawyers, too."

Snowmaker laughed derisively.

"You can't hope to fight our legal team. The fact remains that you've violated numerous laws, and I guess you're right about one thing. You're not on state land yet. We'll get it eventually because this idiot kid named Mooring can't fight us, either. We need to have this land to protect people like you, with businesses downriver. As long as Mooring owns it and lets the polluters farm it, it's a danger to you and everything you stand for."

"Maybe that's a risk I'm willing to take."

"Maybe you don't have to. I can make this go away."

"And who are you?" The man reached out his hand. "I'm Jim Snowmaker, director of MOEIB."

"Sure," said Ernie, refusing to shake the hand. "The director would come out over a little septic tank failure?"

"In this case, yes. See, we know from the records that you've had this facility for about nine years now. But we've just learned that the spill was from a septic tank and that it flowed across Mooring's property and, eventually, into the river. That makes Mooring's property an accessory to this environmental crime. And, we suspect that the septic tank, due to inexact surveys, really is on the 100 acres that Mooring got as his reparation."

"So what?"

"So here's the deal, one that you'd be a fool to ignore. Suppose you've been there nine years, even if illegally, that makes you a squatter. And if you've been squatting for nine years, that makes you the legal owner."

Ernie said nothing.

"As a legal owner, you have the right to sell it. If you sell it to the state for, say, a reasonable sum, I will make the fines and penalties go away. Just sign it over to the state, and that will be that."

"And what about Mooring's legal deed?"

"We can make that go away, too. MOEIB gives, and MOEIB takes away. He'll be out on his ass so fast he'll never know what's going on."

"So you want to steal his land?"

"If it wasn't for MOEIB, he wouldn't own it to begin with."

"Sounds pretty shady to me."

"That's none of your concern. You should be concerned with saving your ass because I have the power to hand it to you on a paper plate!"

"I'll need some time to think about it."

"Fine. I'll give you three days."

He walked out of the store.

Chapter 46

Three days before the primary election

Peterson Fectid was not happy with the latest poll numbers. He called Freedah.

"We have to do something more." She recognized panic when she heard it, and she smiled. Fectid could not break her grip now.

"I know just what to do," she said. "Leave it to me."

"I can't. We have to be proactive."

Freedah sighed. "Just relax, Pete."

"It looks like there's been a surge of sympathy for Ty Mooring since he'd been shot," Fectid said. "We're only two days away, you know. I cannot lose this election. Let's do something!"

"Don't panic," Freedah said. "This farm spill is just the thing to get you over the top. It's the perfect tool for getting HB 616 passed, too. If this bill had been in place, you should say on camera, the farmers would never have been able to farm property so close to this river, the most valuable resource in your entire legislative district.

"And if word gets out that it wasn't a farmer at all?"

"That little bit of information will be delayed until after the election. You just keep on pounding the environmental message for the next two days. I'll write you some copy for a final ad for a huge local TV and radio blitz, not to mention social media. We'll film it tomorrow, and by Tuesday morning, when the polls open, you'll be the hero, and Ty Mooring will be just another schmuck in the hospital who's too stupid to know his money is financing your last election push."

***

The ads started Sunday night and ran once an hour on three different local TV stations from 10 a.m. Monday through 8 p.m. Tuesday, the same time the polls closed.

The opening shot was footage of the river, swollen from the rain, which had now subsided to almost normal summer levels.

"You think this is a peaceful scene?" said the voice-over, back-grounded with thumping, doleful bass-driven notes from an Acrid Reins song. It was Fectid's voice, which continued as his face appeared. "Well, it should be. A peaceful river and a restful environment have been my goal ever since the smart people of Jovial elected me eight years ago. But lately, the environment, an issue we all agree on, has been turned into an extremist battleground."

The video melded into a still shot of Mooring on the campaign trail, his face contorted into a scream and his finger pointing into the camera. It melded again into video footage of the MELL supporters screaming and throwing rocks.

"Scenes like this are what you can expect if Ty Mooring is sent to the state House," Fectid said as the video morphed into a shot of him appearing somber and shaking his head as the river flowed in the background. The music turned more melodious, but still ominous.

"Tyson Mooring supports the farmers who created this recent disaster," Fectid said. "He was given property along the river under false pretenses. He's not really an American, after all. He doesn't reflect your values. He's a polluter, a convicted criminal, and a con-man."

A soft song – an instrumental -- from Tony Finn played as Fectid's somber face came back onto the screen.

"If you care about saving the river from criminals, you'll vote for me!" He smiled as the video faded away and up flashed the obligatory legal disclaimers and voice-over. Finally, in bold letters, a graphic was displayed. "Peterson Fectid. Giving it all for you!"

***

Garit and Aspen were enjoying a rare Sunday together, snuggling on the couch in front of the television as they prepared to watch something, anything, to pass the evening without any of the pressures they had both felt so closely over the last few months.

When Fectid's ad was done, Garit jumped up.

"That ad is almost solid lies!" he said. "It's malicious and slanderous!"

"That's just the way politics is," Aspen said. "Let's just let it go for today."

"How can you say that?" Garit barked. "You've done enough fact-checking to know how false this is. Ty is an American citizen. He doesn't support polluting farmers because that spill was not from farmers. He's never polluted. Yes, he was in prison, but Fectid's the one who should be in prison. I have to stop this!"

"It's too late," Aspen said. "The election is Tuesday, and there's nothing more you can do except report the facts impartially."

"I can report all the facts out there, but they're just manipulated and turned into lies!"

"That's not your call," Aspen said. "Your job is to be objective."

"Isn't it my job to expose lies and tell the truth?"
"You've done that," she said. "What more can you do?"

"I can get off the fence and fight for what's right!"

"And that means taking sides in an election? That's against your ethics."

"Ethics is just a buzzword for people who want to substitute what's right for their own preferences," he said. "You can say all day that something is legal, but I prefer to ask what is right?"

"We can't discern that," she said. "It's up to the people to decide."

"How can they decide when they don't get anything but lies?"

"Again, that's not your job."

"Well, maybe it should be."

He sat back on the couch, leaning forward, so upset that he was shaking.

"Relax," she said, stroking his back. "There's nothing you can do about it!"

"Maybe not as a reporter," he sulked.

"What does that mean?"

"It means that there comes a time when we should stand up for truth, not just try to report it and hope people believe it!"

"Standing for things is not a reporter's job," Aspen said. "Objectivity is!"

"Well, then, maybe I shouldn't be a reporter anymore. It's time to take a stand for the truth!"

"What does that mean?"

"Not sure," Garit replied. "Maybe it means I should change professions."

"You're not thinking straight," she said. "Writing is all you've ever wanted to do. It's what you're called to do."

"And why did we – you too, you know, become reporters? It was to expose lies and tell the truth."

"Things have changed from that idealism, " she said. "I check facts, and I don't find them. I reveal the truth, and so do you. You can't change how people think."

"Why not? It's what PR people do all the time. The only difference is that they lie blatantly, without conscience. The only thing I change is people's information. They're still more influenced by pretty lies than the sometimes ugly truth."

"So you think PR people have more influence than a well-written, fact-based story?"

"Yes, unfortunately."

"That's just your frustration showing," she said. "Can't you just be satisfied with your own objectivity?"

"Objectivity may give a certain perspective, but it doesn't make people do the right thing," he said. Aspen sighed.

Chapter 47

The day before the election, Ernie walked down the bluff behind his house and surveyed the damage the now-receded flood waters had left behind.

The lone septic tank that accepted the survivalist's waste was half-exposed, and the pipe that should have connected to a drain field was now connected to nothing. But there was still hope. Ty's offer to pay for a new system still stood, and that could bring him new hope. A new system would allow him to open the camp again, all legal and permitted. Maybe, in a decade or so of operating, he could recover the cost and break even. If he didn't have to pay a huge fine for the pollution that he now knew was his fault. But what was the big deal? A 500-gallon spill was nothing compared to what cities dumped through their wastewater treatment plants, and, although unreported in the at-large media or social media, he knew a flood – one much worse than the tiny one that just happened – would require the city to dump solid waste or risk an even greater spill. He could not afford such fines, even though by now, all the pollution had been diluted by the river's powerful surge and its God-given ability to clean itself.

He decided to survey any damage that may have been left behind, so he went back to his house and dragged down a small kayak. As he dug it out of his garage, the radio that came on automatically when garage lights were turned on featured a new ad from the Boyd McCockert campaign.

"… And why has Ty Mooring, the convicted criminal, been afraid to debate me?" the voice said. "We don't even know where he is right now. What is he afraid of? I'll tell you, and I'm a trusted public servant. He knows it was the people who he supports that all but destroyed the river during the recent flood. He couldn't justify it, so he ran and hid. He has no accountability to you, the smart voters of District 6. I do. Vote for Peterson Fectid."

Ernie fumed as he carried the kayak to the river. That lying bastard knew full well where Ty was right now. The man was a bigger liar even than most politicians, and that was really saying something.

He stuck to the edge of the water, which was still slightly muddy but flowing peacefully. He saw herons fishing at the edges, and he saw eagles soaring above. He saw fish jumping. The river carried no feces smell, no rank odor of manure, human or animal. In fact, it smelled clean, as it usually did after a long-awaited gentle shower on the land.

He floated past the piece of property that so many people wanted to control, and he felt somewhat powerful. He had a choice in how to retain that power. One way was easy, and one way was hard. A few farmers had pulled equipment to the edge of the heavy black-earthed fields and left them, waiting for perhaps a day or two before they could work it. The grassed buffer strips were intact, greener than he'd ever seen them. The earth smelled rich and ripe. Ernie thought it was one of the most pleasant smells on earth, behind only fresh-cut alfalfa.

He remembered that he'd agreed with Olie to provide some of his survivalist boys as protection against the protesters and reminded himself to give them all a call when he got to his store/restaurant. But it was difficult to know their plans, and they were crafty. They always seemed to be one step ahead of the law, and that was frustrating. But Ernie had to make a more personal decision first.

The decision, however, was not about him. It was about right and wrong. It was about his community and the outsiders who seemed to want to take it all away from the people who, for generations, had been here and left the land, river, and community better than it was before them.

By the time he docked the kayak at his riverfront dock, he'd made up his mind. Right was right. Wrong was wrong. No middle ground.

***

An ominous-looking man and a smaller, bookish, younger man were already in Ernie's restaurant, sampling a huge breakfast, standard fare, served up by Ernie's wife. When Ernie walked in, they both rose from their tables and invited him to sit with them.

"We'll get right down to business, Mr. Cook," said the larger, harsher man. "We represent MOEIB and, more particularly, Mr. Snowmaker, who has a particular and personal interest in your decision. We have all the paperwork here to get you started filing a legal claim to the property on which you've been squatting for more than nine years. It's done under the state's adverse possession law. It's all quite clear and quite legal. Just sign, and we'll get things started."

Ernie glanced at his wife, and the eye contact they made steeled Ernie's resolve.

"I've decided that I will not file any such claim," he said, pushing the papers back toward the two men.

"That's a very foolish decision," said the larger man. "We've offered you an easy way out, but rest assured that MOEIB and Mr. Snowmaker have both the will and the ability to ruin you. You'll be labeled a polluter, and we'll have you so tied up with lawyers that you'll never recover. We'll take your house, this restaurant, your reputation, everything. I suggest you rethink your position. Why would you jeopardize everything you have?"

Ernie looked the man squarely in the eye. "I'm willing to pay the fine for the pollution," he said. "But I'm not willing to be a part of this shady deal that will give you and your sham of a department any leverage to steal this property from a good man, a friend of mine, in fact, and turn it into some private playground for corrupt lawyers and government shysters."

The large man motioned, and the smaller man stuffed the papers back into his briefcase. They stood to leave when Ernie's wife walked up with the check. "No one dines and dashes here," she said. The large man dropped a $20 bill on the table, and the pair walked out.

***

Garit was working on the election story, getting a framework set up in which he could fill in the final figures and quotes from the candidates when the results came in. Aspen called him into her office.

"I've done it," she told Garit.

"Done what?"

"I've broken the MELL protesters' firewalls. I can now get the same messages they get in real-time. Now you can be on the spot to report what they're doing almost before they know it."

"Why? I thought you were committed to reporting, not being proactive."

"I hate that phrase, so don't use it again. Look, it doesn't matter why. Let's just say I've given you the tools you need to be the first reporter on the scene anywhere in this part of the state."

"Don't con me, Aspen." Ty grinned at her, then reached out to embrace her. "You really want to take these idiots down too, don't you?"

"My dedication is to the news. Only the news. And you getting scoops on the competition is good for our news and our bottom line."

"How'd you do it?"

"That's my secret. Just know it is and will be accurate. Trust me."

"Getting to be quite a hacker, huh?"

"A good fact-checker has to be. Too much is hidden by these folks. We all want government transparency, but every other group should be transparent, too. That's just fairness. But don't tell anyone else I can do this."

"That's not very transparent."

Aspen laughed and rested her hands on Garit's chest.

"There's an exception to every rule."

Chapter 48

Three days after the election, the Jovial World and Sasser featured a front-page story with the byline Garit West, headlined "The rise and fall of a political novice":

> *Two bullets were removed, one a mere fraction of an inch from his heart. The other had rested against his spinal cord. He may have back pain – spasms – for the rest of his life.*
>
> *Besides that, doctors say, he'll be fine, eventually. There is nothing physically wrong that would stop his contribution to society. There is still a little internal bleeding they think will repair itself. Ending the bleeding is a hope that Tyson Mooring has for his hometown, too, but he isn't really up to the effort. Not yet.*
>
> *"I had no idea just how dirty and blood-thirsty politics really is," he said from his hospital bed, three days after losing the primary election that would have made him a candidate for the state legislature, potentially representing about 100,000 people in Jovial and surrounding areas.*
>
> *"I thought I could change things," he says weakly. " I'm naive, I know. But I had faith that by presenting facts and common sense on this particular issue, people would consider what was at stake and come to the same conclusion I had. You know, the right conclusion."*
>
> *He smiles at his own self-deprecating joke. "But that didn't happen. I thought we could have rational, calm discussions about anything if people would just listen first and talk second. I thought that's part of what makes America great. Maybe that time has passed."*

Even though it's all over now, there is no apparent bitterness in Ty Mooring, neither toward the voters nor the as-yet-unnamed assailant who shot him.

Still, he fears that he may have caused more harm than good.

"I got into this political stuff for what I thought were good reasons," he said. "People don't seem to understand just how valuable farmers are, how much everyone depends on them. And it seems that people just don't have much regard for living free anymore, either. House bill 616 quite obviously takes freedom away from individuals and hands it over to the state bureaucracy. Truth seems to have died here, like that canary in the coal mine. What happened here, all the violence and nonsense of chanting worn, dull phrases just to silence someone on the other side, is the first death of free speech, the warning that we need to protect the right of the people to decide what they want. If the forces that silenced me gain strength, as it seems is happening, then we're all in danger of losing our freedoms, just like House Bill 616 does. All you have to do is read the bill, and that becomes plain. But we still have a chance. We can still defeat HB 616." He smiles at the thought but weakly. Before he was shot, and even before he dabbled in politics, he smiled easily.

House Bill 616, which is currently stuck in the Senate, was the one-trick pony Ty used to get as far as he did. It was the reason a young, inexperienced young man came so close to defeating an experienced politician based on a one-issue campaign.

It all started when Tyson Mooring received correspondence from the Michigan Office of Environment, Inclusion and Bigotry (MOEIB), informing him that, due to the policy changes that came when the office consolidated departments of the environment, natural resources, equity, and racial relations into one, he would receive a 'reparation' of river-front property. He was the only remaining ancestor of migrant laborers who had been 'oppressed' by farmers, the official paperwork said. The office also paid him around $3 million in taxpayer money just because of who his parents were. The budget for reparations was $5 million, but $2 million was spent elsewhere, mainly on legal fees. See the related story here.

"I didn't deserve any of that, and I never asked for it," Mooring said. "I still don't really understand any of it. I just figured, at first, that God was blessing me for some reason. Now, I'm not sure it was a blessing at all. And maybe there's no blessing at all when things are handed to you for free. We just don't appreciate what is given to us. At least, mostly, we don't. I will always appreciate the land that was given to me, and I will not use it for my own purposes. I want to use it for the good of society. That's what I think God wants me to do."

Those efforts will have to find another road, he said, because   Mooring's political career ended with a bullet. Three, actually. One missed the mark and was dug out of a panel of the Jovial Fairgrounds stage.

"I have every intention of fighting to keep the land now and use it for the good of society," he said. "And that means helping farmers feed the world. That starts with defeating HB 616."

Working behind the scenes is best for him now, Mooring said.

"Honestly, I don't know why anyone would want to be in the public eye," he said. "It all seems so self-serving. I know it's not supposed to be that way. I went into it, on the good advice of a trusted Christian advisor, to be a servant. But serving isn't what happens anymore in politics. I hope to fight against that."

It's difficult to fight these days, Mooring said, at least in part because of social media's influence.

"Twaddle followers seemed to buy all the lies," he said. "I never cared for it before, and I really hate it now. It's hollow and one-sided and rejects common sense. To me, *it was worthless. To people who believe it without question, it's dangerous. Until it strikes some balance, it will drag society down."*

Mooring's opponent in the primary election, Peterson Fectid, won the vote by a narrow margin, the closest of his political career. (See the final tally here) He didn't so much win. He told the World and Sasser that Mooring lost.

"Many voters just don't understand that being a lawmaker is about the art of compromise," Fectid said. " And it was obvious that Mr. Mooring was unwilling to compromise. I think in the end, the people voted for me and HB 616 because they knew the importance of the environment, and they voted for their opinions. They voted for me because they knew I knew how to compromise. It's what politicians do. It's just like democracy is supposed to work."

Mooring, however, doesn't see it that way.

"Democracy works when people see at least two, if not more, sides to an issue and actually consider their options, not just from their own perspective, but from others," he said. "How can people consider things if only one side is presented? That's how it was with me and my campaign. I was continually shouted down by protesters. I was threatened, called every name in the book from places I'd never even heard of before, out in California." He pauses as if contemplating the irony. "I don't think California can rightfully speak for people in Jovial, Michigan. The culture is too different. Environmental issues are not one-size-fits-all. Did you know that 99 percent of those opponents, at least among those who were willing to speak to us and pollsters about it, admitted that they had never read the bill and never really knew what the campaign was all about? That baffled me. It only takes about three minutes to read the entire bill, and that's at the most. It was printed in the World and Sasser, so there's no excuse for not being able to find it without the internet.

Twaddle around here is about getting rid of political speech that gives people all the information they need to make a decision. If they can't do it with Twaddle, they'll do it with the police, lawyers, or lawsuits. This is not how our system is supposed to run. We need to get back to a society that is willing to listen and contemplate, not run their whole lives on emotions that change with the prevailing political winds."

Soon after receiving the reparation, and less than two months after he'd gotten out of prison for trying to produce false lottery tickets, Mooring was thrust into the political limelight when a crowd that had gathered in opposition to HB 616 learned that Fectid, despite having vowed in his speeches to stop the bill, voted in favor of it and moved it from his agriculture committee to the full House. Amid the scuffles and thrown punches that followed, Mooring was swept into the primary race.

"I never expected that either," he said. "I guess I was swept up in the emotion of the moment. People were angry that day. Maybe that's not really a good state of mind to be in when you choose a political leader."

Mooring's campaign soon got the attention of the national press, however, not because of his principles but because of his connection with Acrid Reins, a band that toured to promote a new album and to fulfill a public service requirement from lead singer Tony Finn, a long-time radical animal rights activist who had been convicted in California of trespass and malicious destruction of property, for which he served no jail time. Acrid Reins` took the position opposite Mooring's, arguing in a song that the environment is too valuable not to pass HB 616.

"That was my fatal mistake," Mooring said. "I didn't anticipate that the drawing power of a rock band would soon overwhelm the crowd who showed up to listen to the issues and get a little free beer. But keep in mind that Acrid Reins is from California, and Tony Finn has some

problems with reasoning. The protesters, at least the most violent among them, are not from this legislative district." That claim has not been confirmed by the World and Sasser.

While the political experiment ended in failure, Mooring said, he hopes to be successful in helping farmers against political foes. How he does that, he's still not sure.

"Right now, I have to heal up, then find a new direction," he said. "I just hope and pray it's the right one."

***

Freedah was lounging with a drink in Grandy's Lansing apartment, reading Garit's story on her phone.

"That S.O.B.," she muttered when she was done. "Not one mention of me in the whole story."

She heard Grandy drop something in one of the bedrooms.

"Did you see this, Grandy?" she cried. "What a crock of crap."

He peeked his head out of the room and grabbed another box from the hallway.

"I saw it," he said. "Seemed pretty well done to me."

"But I was the brains behind his whole candidacy," she said. "If not for me, he'd never have gotten this far."

"If not for you, he wouldn't have been shot, either," he said as he filled a box with books.

"Shot, schmot," she spat. "It's all part of the game. But I will admit that I wasn't prepared to come into gun country. Your people back in Jovial are really a bunch of redneck dumb asses, aren't they?"

"Well, at least they know what they believe in," he said.

"So what, I don't?"

"No, you don't, Freedah. You drift in the wind, latching onto whatever can satisfy that sick ego of yours."

She walked into the room and looked at him with rehearsed misty eyes.

"Is that what you really think of me? After all I've done for you?"

"Everything you've done for me has been for your own benefit." He looked into her eyes and melted, just like always, and he hated himself for it, just like always.

"I'm sorry," he said, embracing her. Her reciprocal embrace was cold and stiff. "I know you're doing what you think is best. I just don't happen to agree with it anymore."

Freedah took a step back. "How can you not agree? I'm right! I thought you believed that, too."

"Maybe once, but not anymore. I was not listening to the right sources."

"Seems like a pretty weak reason to abandon your job, your salary, me!"

"No one can abandon a place that's already empty." He stopped and looked around the place.

"Guess that's it," he said. "See you back in Jovial someday."

"Sooner than you think. We have protests at the farm again starting tomorrow."

"I won't be there."

Her eyes went from mist to ice.

"You will be there, you jackass! You're being paid until the end of the month. If you don't show, I'll stop your pay and take back what you've been given already."

"Do what you have to do." Grandy carried his last box out of the room.

***

Grandy went back to Jovial and checked into a room in one of the downtown area's cheaper motels, which he had rented for a month for $3,000. Tourists had already booked all the good hotels and paid double their price for a mere week.

He'd decided what to do, but he had doubts which bothered him. He couldn't pray, and he knew why. God no longer listened to him, but he deserved it. He had been wrong all along about God's real mission for him. But he knew God hated gambling. He decided to move forward by faith.

Two days later, he walked into the casino bar, making sure to lower his chin to his chest when he walked through the entrance. He wore a cowboy hat pulled down to his eyebrows. Cameras would surely send each clear face to the casino's facial recognition app, but he tried anyway.

He walked into the casino bar, and, as he expected, a large group of MELL activists was reveling over flowing alcohol.

Freedah was leading the meeting, and although it was hard to hear over the cacophony, he got the gist. Tomorrow, a farm would be ambushed. Select news outlets were already on high alert. This, Freedah said, would be the final, definitive answer to river pollution. If it didn't convince the state to take Ty's land back, they'd take the fight elsewhere. The group had to be flexible and open-minded, she said.

Chapter 49

The next morning, when Garit checked his phone for morning news leads or tips, he noticed a large file containing several videos. He opened each one. The first one showed Freedah holding the arm of Peterson Fectid, the date stamp of three weeks before the election. Several videos showed her and Ty, with more involved kissing and plenty of passionate butt-grabbing. Another showed Freedah with Snowmaker. Another showed Freedah with Grandy. One showed her and Tony Finn holding each other close as they walked down a street. Most videos were a bit fuzzy, having come from surveillance cameras. Others were clear, taken from a phone held by a steady hand.

Many of them showed her inciting the crowd at one of Ty's rallies. One even had audio, which revealed Freedah telling the crowd's leaders to storm the stage, throw rocks, and put on farmer-looking flannel shirts, t-shirts, overalls, and John Deere hats.

One video that seemed a little out of place showed the Frandor farm's surveillance video of the night of the rock bombing. Clearly, it was Tony Finn. His gait was unmistakable, as were the tattoos all over his arms and neck.

And then there was one last video, about four minutes long. It showed the moment when Frandor charged the stage, gun still in his holster, strapped to his right leg. It showed Tony running away and Ty running forward. And it showed Grandy running onto the stage. Then things got blurry as the camera was jostled, and then immediately, the sound of three shots. It was impossible to see who fired the gun. And then it showed Ty falling to the ground, struggling to breathe.

Garit's first instinct was to post the videos on the paper's electronic feeds, but he knew Aspen would likely nix the whole thing. Without context, she'd say, where's the real value of posting them? What was the use of getting into a fight with her at this point?

He forwarded the videos to the Jovial Police Department with a subject line that read: Who shot Ty Mooring?

Chapter 50

One of the many fallacies taken as fact by young, passionate, and emotion-driven people is that their code can't be broken. They believe their key phrases and agreeable innuendo are unique to them, much the same way a teenager believes his parents will never know about the cigarettes or the smells associated with other youthful experiments. But the group of protesters in Jovial was even more secure. No one, they assumed, could find the apps they used to communicate. They were too clever, and outsiders were too stupid. Especially rural people.

They were a very tight-knit group, communicating via programs that deleted messages quickly and finally. But they were getting a bit cocky, too, Garit thought as he read their latest instructions.

Aspen had found their network, and despite her protests about objectivity, Garit had forwarded the information to the Jovial County Police. He also forwarded them to Botsdorf, Frandor, and each member of the Jovial Farmers Union without comment. The next and perhaps final violent protests would be at Olie's Fish farm. Garit would never reveal the source of this information, but he smiled just the same. Aspen, despite her devotion to objectivity, still knew right from wrong.

Freedah did not. That was clear. And she didn't know her Twaddle account was open to many more than just her group of protesters.

Every day since the spill that was now long gone, diluted so far downstream that no traces of human excrement could be found, Freedah said through her Twaddle messaging that the spill was the worst environmental catastrophe in the history of Jovial. The group of 20 or so well-paid followers agreed with a simple check in a box. Another box indicated that they would all go where she told them. They would carry kerosene and Molotov cocktails. Who wouldn't follow Freedah Forest? Even to the slaughterhouse?

For all that blindness, Freedah seemed to have some sort of sixth sense about missions and their shelf-life, and she warned the group that their time was short and they had to go out with a bang, just like the fate she saw for Majestic Mother Earth.

But that bang was no longer secret. News outlets knew it was coming. Police knew. Farmers knew. But they wouldn't tell. Rick Frandor, in particular, had given the protesters enough rope now that they could, indeed, hang themselves, and he'd be immensely pleased to see it. He had to play his part. It was the right thing to do.

***

Today, as Freedah had demanded, the protesters were ready for one large event and one quick getaway.

They parked their rental cars – not an electric or hybrid in sight – along the gravel road below Olie's gate and unloaded their trunks. Garit, watching from his spot in the loft of Olie's 150-year-old barn, counted 21 protesters in all, not including Tony Finn, James Snowmaker, and Freedah Forest.

They picketed for an hour or so on the road, careful not to trespass, carrying signs that said 'fish farms are murder,' 'stop killing our river,' 'polluters must pay,' 'save the earth, save the river,' and even one 'Join MELL' sign.

But the sun was hot on this early August day, and soon the protesters became weary. By then, police had set up a line along the perimeter of the fish ponds and stood firm in front of Olie's house with sawhorses painted blue and red.

On a "secret" command from Freedah, the protesters began moving onto Olie's property. Suddenly, on their right flank, popping up like minutemen, about 50 persons appeared, varying in gender and age from teens to white-haired, beer-bellied men. On the other side, the left flank, another group of jeans-clad, t-shirted men and women stood boldly and lined up, each one armed with a rifle or shotgun, and most with sidearms too. Some carried long-handled shovels. Slowly, they took single steps forward behind the protesters, forcing them almost imperceptibly into a tighter group. They pushed the protesters up the driveway like cattle being pushed into a corral.

Suddenly, as if it were a silent snap count from quarterback Freedah, the people – all except the three leaders – charged the old barn and began throwing Molotov cocktails toward it. One even sailed through the window where Garit was sitting, so he fetched it and threw it back at them, knowing that Aspen must never know about that.

Confused and befuddled when other incendiary devices also started coming back at them, the protesters ran closer to the barn and began dousing the large sliding barn doors with kerosene. When a match was lit, the police moved in.

The flanks of farmers pushed harder now, moving the protesters away from the barn as more armed citizens worked quickly to douse the fire with shoveled dirt. As the protesters pulled back, the citizens pushed them ominously toward the police, who began grabbing protesters and handcuffing them. Confusion and lack of vision due to smoke from their Molotov cocktails and the fire caused several protesters to wander about in their new surroundings, trying to hear directions from Freedah's bullhorn. But it was silent.

Garit saw Freedah, Snowmaker, and Tony run away toward the river, and two young men with varmint rifles stepped in and separated them from the others. They each ran in a different direction, and Snowmaker joined a small group of protesters who seemed to know where to go. He heard a voice that he thought came from behind the barn, although it was too smokey to really tell.

"Come on this way, everybody," the voices insisted urgently. "We'll get you out of here and away from these rednecks!"

Snowmaker joined about 10 of the protesters who also heard the voice and ran in that direction and safety of the group as police hustled the arrested off to their cars. The armed farmers continued to squeeze the remaining rioters into a sort of funnel, moving forward in what appeared to be a coordinated effort of movement. Herding skills sure come in handy sometimes,

Garit couldn't see well through the smoke, but he knew the voice he heard. "Into the trailer there!" Ernie shouted to the 10 or 12. They were moving too fast through the smoke for Gait to count. Ernie and several other people herded them into the cattle truck and slammed the door shut. Ernie jumped into the truck's driver's seat; two of the other three truck doors slammed, and the truck rambled off down the gravel road, hitting every pothole Garit saw.

As the men in the truck rode into some very heavy woods, it was time for Grandy to make his next move known. He turned from his shotgun seat and spoke to Rick Frandor in the back seat.

"I'm going to do this," he told him. "It's only right that I pay for my sins and take one for the team. You need to testify, if need be, that I grabbed your gun and tried to shoot Finn but missed and hit Ty."

"But why not just let it all die down for a little bit?" Frandor asked. "Nobody was killed, so they might not even come after anybody. I mean, look what they let these protesters get away with."

"It doesn't matter," Grandy said. "I have to do what's right, and I think this is it."

"Why?" Frandor asked. "Why would you take the fall for me?"

"Just following the example of my lord and of Ty Mooring."

Chapter 51

On his way to the police station, Grandy stopped at the Jovial Community Hospital, which, without protesters on the street, had once again become a quiet place.

Ty Mooring was out of intensive care and off sedatives.

"Mr. Mooring, my Christian brother!" Grandy exclaimed as he walked to the bed where Ty was sitting up reading a novel called "The Organic Underwear Conspiracy."

"Grandy!" Ty said enthusiastically. "Haven't seen you since we were both in casino jail."

"I'm here to confess and encourage you," Grandy said. He sat in a chair beside the bed, turning it around so he could lean forward on its back. His leg pain diminished a bit when he sat that way.

"Confess? You have sins to confess?" Ty asked, grinning.

"I've been a fool, deceived," Grandy started. "I was so blinded by my own ambition, which I thought was really a service to God, that I didn't see just how wrong I really was."

"What are you talking about? I knew when you became a lobbyist that it was a risky business for a man of God like you, but I guess I never thought that in and of itself was sinful. Usually, it's in practice where the sin comes in, right?"

"Oh, there may be a few lobbyists who are trying to keep things on the straight and narrow, but I've never met one, " Grandy said. "Maybe a lot of them are like me, thinking they're doing right when they've been blinded to the truth by philosophy or greed or selfishness. That was me."

"Are you sure it's not just passion? You told me once that passion is what God wants. That's not a sin."

"That was before I understood doubt," Grandy said.

Ty remained silent.

"See," Grandy said, "I always thought that doubt was one of the biggest sins. I always went back to James 1:6-7. I abhorred double-minded people, not understanding that I was double-minded. I deceived myself. I'd decide something on my own, then demand that God support my decision. Then, I'd get angry and confused about it all, leading to doubts, which angered me more. I wanted no doubt in my life, but I didn't know how God could use that doubt. I should have figured out what God wanted first, then asked Him to bless His mission through me."

"I don't really understand," Ty said, "but what changed your path?"

"A few things. Freedah led me astray. I fell in love with her, or rather, lust. I didn't believe that someone that beautiful could carry such rot and ugliness around with her."

"Funny," Ty said. "My eyes have been opened about her, too."

"I guess we all see things a little better now," Grandy said. "But the second thing was that I understood that doubt can be a tool God uses to make us question. I've learned that questioning can lead you where God wants you, and that's why I'm here to tell you that I've learned from you, too. Seems to me that even before you gave your life to Jesus, you knew to do the right thing. You went to jail to protect your friend Todd. So I'm going to take the punishment for the man who shot you."

"It wasn't you?" Ty asked. "That's what all the media are saying."

"Let's put this another way," Grandy said. "I shot you. That's all you need to know or believe. Maybe I was trying to shoot Tony Finn, and my aim was bad. That's my story. That's what will become the truth. I'm going to turn myself in when I leave here, confess to the whole thing. My prayer is that I get sent to prison so I can do what God really wants me to do, which is to save the souls of prisoners."

"But only the Holy Spirit can save souls," Ty said.

"Thanks for reminding me. Old, selfish attitudes are not easy to get rid of. You're right. I am not the Savior. But the Savior can work through me. And I believe it's what he wants for me."

"Any doubts about that?" Ty asked. Grandy grinned.

"Sure," he said. "And I'm not going to reject those doubts like I did before. When they come up, I'm going to ask God to let me know for sure. I'm positive he'll guide me. But I have to read my Bible more and take it deeper into my heart. Maybe he wants some doubt in me so I can relate to the people he wants me to reach."

"Sounds like you're on your way to change," Ty said.

"What about you?" Grandy asked. "What are your plans for the future?"

"I don't really know. The only thing that's certain is that I won't get involved in politics again. Too much drama."

"I'm afraid that may be something you can't avoid," Grandy said. "You're in too deep. Running for office? I understand why you're giving that up. Politics is a cesspool. Best avoided. But you have money. Power and influence. You must remain active in the fight for the river and the farmers. Fight against the evil, though, Ty. Help the farmers who are doing it right. Study and see through the lies of the activists. Remember that they're just like me, or rather, how I used to be. Too passionate to see clearly." He paused as if doubt was hitting him right then and there.

"Anything else?" Ty asked.

"There is one thing. The reason I came back for your last rally. I was going to confront you about your sin."

"Which sin is that?"

"Your fornication."

"What?"

"You were sleeping with Freedah and Melanie. That's against God's law."

"What? Why? I'm not married."

"You never learned that God hates sexual sin?"

"I thought that was for homosexuals and weird, kinky things."

"Guess you haven't read your Bible enough. God meant us to be in deeper relationships. Your relationships with those two girls were shallow and physical. I know those girls both probably gave you a thrill, and it seemed pretty good, right?"
"Good, but short-lived."

"God wants you to find the best rather than just the good. And the best is a one-on-one relationship with just one woman."

"I'll have to study up on that. First I've heard of it."

"Just one more thing," Grandy said. "Grow."

He stood up, shook Ty's hand, and began to walk out.

"Just one thing for you, Grandy," Ty said. Grandy turned.

"I forgive you for shooting me." They both grinned.

***

Three days later, a letter arrived at MELL headquarters in San Francisco with a return address that gave only a post office box number from Lansing, MI. It sat on Phoenix Tippin's secretary's desk for another day because snail mail was always the last thing opened at MELL. When Phoenix read it, the color drained from his face despite a morning tanning bed session. It read:

"To whom it may concern: Ten of your paid protesters are experiencing Majestic Mother Earth first-hand today. They are totally inept and likely will die because they have no skills in dealing with nature. Instead, they've chosen to destroy, criticize, and condemn things they know nothing about. We will, however, rescue them and send them back to San Francisco on the following conditions: First, MELL will abandon all interests in Jovial, MI, and never meddle again in local politics. Second, Mr. James

Snowmaker resigns from his position with the MOEIB. Third, none of this agreement will be leaked to the general public or press in perpetuity. This offer is good for three days. If we do not hear from them via the USPS, we will leave them to fend for themselves, and that would not be good for any of them. The choice is yours. Reply to PO Box 48765.

***

Freedah was booked into the Jovial County Jail, but only after the arresting officer agreed to let her brush her hair and fix her makeup before the mug shot. To this day, it is agreed among the police that Freedah was the best-looking woman they'd ever booked. A couple of them, a man and a woman, got copies of the photo and hung them where they could see it when at their desks.

"You're accused of vandalism, trespassing, general mischief, attempted arson, inciting a riot, and resisting arrest," the judge said, his eyes fixed on Freedah's classically chiseled cheekbones and her seductive figure. Even in baggy prison clothes, she couldn't hide it, nor did she want to.

"As hard as it is to keep a woman who looks like you out of the public eye," the judge said, "I'm going to try. This may sound like the old wild west, ms. Forest, but I'm telling you to get out of town. And don't come back, or I will hear these same charges again, which could lead to real prison time. Do you understand?" Freedah nodded, and it appeared that perhaps she was contrite. She was led out of the room, and by the afternoon, she was on a plane to San Francisco.

Tony was arraigned right after Freedah.

"Looks to me like you have a warrant or two against you out in California," the judge said. Tony stood stone-faced. "Well, I'm perfectly happy to let you be their problem. I'm recommending extradition and warning you, Mr. Finn. Don't ever come back to Jovial County."

Tony ended up on the same flight to San Francisco as Freedah. They sat together on the plane.

***

Phoenix Tippin had five copies of the letter made and handed them to the executive board of directors at MELL, who had assembled quickly at Phoenix's request.

The directors read the letters, then sat silently for an unusually long time. Phoenix broke the silence.

"They think they have us by the short hairs," he said. "I need suggestions about how to get them back and not make it look like we were financing arson and violent protests," he said.

"I say screw 'em," said one director. "We'll just sick Snowmaker on them. He'll bring them to Jesus."

"Maybe," Phoenix said. "But there's a problem. We haven't heard from Snowmaker for days. He might be one of the hostages, and they might not even know it."

"How about Freedah and our lobbyist there – what's his name?"

"Granderson," Phoenix replied. "Grandy's no good. He quit three days ago. And Freedah was arrested and basically kicked out of Michigan."

"That can't be legal," said another director. "But we need to put first things first. How does this impact the potential for us – and by us, I mean MELL and PFFF – to get that hundred acres?"

"I'm afraid we might have to abandon that," Phoenix said. "All Snowmaker's suits have been thrown out of court, and it turns out that legal action over that little spill is way off. But it's okay. We still own enough property upriver to build the golf course."

"But what about my fishing?" shouted another director. "I told my PFFF members it was in the bag! They're not gonna like this!"

"I don't like it either," said the fifth director. "But we'll get through it. We can still go out there and fish that stream."

"It's not the same!" shouted a director. "I want to fish from my own land, on my own riverfront. I'm not going to go out and fish some public river that's polluted by all these rednecks and crackers." He slammed his fist on the table. "And now you tell me that all we've been doing is going to hell because some Mexican kid outsmarted us?"

"Please, gentlemen, calm down," Phoenix said. "We'll bide our time. Start building the golf course. There's no problem there. But the first thing we need to do it figure out how to get our people out of there, wherever they are."

"I say screw 'em," said the most upset director. "I mean, we've covered our bases, right? I mean, no one knows what's happened, and we don't have any of these protesters on the payroll, right?"

"No, they're all paid out of a separate, secured, foreign account," Phoenix said. "They can't be traced back to us."

"Then I propose that we have no knowledge of any of this, don't know what happened to whom, and this meeting never took place."

They voted in favor of that proposal unanimously.

**

Ernie and his cohorts had not left the protesters without a safety net. For the three days and nights since they'd been dropped off in the forest, at least two men had been assigned to watch over them. Most of the time, they videoed them from tree stands, if for nothing more than a laugh later.

Protesters, of course, didn't know that and had been fighting with each other far more than they spent time trying to find food or water.

Ernie and five of his followers, including Rick Frandor, drove to where they had dropped off the protesters. From a distance, they saw the people scatter when they heard the truck. All of the Ernie cohorts put on medical face masks and sunglasses before they left the truck,

"Come on out, little tree huggers," Ernie called like he was calling dogs. "We won't hurt you. We're here to rescue you."

"Like you rescued us down by the river?" a voice called, then a young man peeked from behind a tree.

"Nope, we're going to take you back to Jovial, but only if you give up this earth worship crap."

"Never," said the young man.

"Haven't you had enough?" Ernie asked. "I mean, look at you. You're all dehydrated. Didn't you know there is a stream only about a tenth of a mile away?"

"We were afraid," said another voice as more protesters managed enough courage to come into the open.

"Afraid of Ma Earth, who sustains you?" Ernie asked mockingly. "I thought you folks would know more about what you worship."

More people came from behind their trees and bushes. A few already had rashes on their arms, and many raised bug bites.

"You should have left us some food, at least," a voice said.

"You should all just shut the hell up," Ernie snapped. "But don't worry. We'll take you out. Where is the one who calls himself Snowmaker?"

Snowmaker could not really hide. His trademark white hair and sizable midsection exposed him, but Ernie said nothing. The protesters were silent, and so was Snowmaker.

"All right, then," Ernie said. "If he's not here, we might as well go home and leave you idiots to fend for yourselves."

"He's right there," said a voice. A young man pointed. Snowmaker sheepishly came forward.

"James Snowmaker?" Ernie asked, knowing.

"Who wants to know?" Snowmaker was amazingly arrogant, considering his circumstances and the fact that he and Ernie had met.

"Read this." Ernie held out the letters between himself and MELL. Then he read MELL's reply. It said only this: FU.

Ernie waited for Snowmaker's blood to return to his face, then took the letters back, yanking them from Snowmaker's hand.

Ernie handed him another piece of paper.

"This is your official resignation letter," he said. "Not only do you resign, but you also recommend that your entire department be disbanded and put under their old departments."

"Why should I do this?" Snowmaker spat, still defiant and proud.

"Maybe you should look at this," Ernie said and handed him a cell phone set to play a video.

It was footage of Snowmaker walking down an unidentified city street with a woman. She was very young and thin, almost the opposite of Snowmaker's wife. After they stopped walking, the video clearly showed Snowmaker's right-hand rise and fall. Fist hitting cheek made a very loud sound, after which the girl crumpled to the ground and began crying while holding her arms in front of her face like a boxer who knows he cannot win.

"This goes to whoever wants to see it; if you refuse, you braying jackass," Ernie said. He tapped the paper in Snowmaker's hand. "Now or never, man."

Snowmaker held out his hand, and Ernie produced an ink pen. Snowmaker signed it, and Ernie's group of followers opened the cattle trailer door. They all climbed in, found a case of bottled water in the front corner, and sat until they disembarked unceremoniously in front of the Jovial hospital.

Chapter 52

Aspen was trembling when Garit came into the office. One look brought Garit's memories back to when she was struggling just a few years ago, before she and he had exposed editor Wally East and several others for selfish, dirty deeds. She'd just lost her job because of her dalliance with East. Her undercover actions had beaten Garit up. She was unsure of herself, something she never revealed to anyone but him, as far as he knew. But over the last couple of years, she'd grown, and it wasn't necessarily for Garit's good.

"Garit," she said, motioning him into her office.

"Sit," she said. He did, and she walked behind him to shut the door. "I have something big to tell you. I've gotten an offer to be a fact-checker for Senator Canon in Washington, D.C."

"And?"

"And I think I'm going to take it."

Garit looked deeply into her eyes. He'd known their relationship could be changed at any time, but he hadn't seen this coming.

"You know I don't want you to go," Garit said, pulling her close. "But you also know that I don't want to go to DC."

"That's what makes this so hard. I don't want to leave you, either, but this is a chance to really make a difference. And the pay is phenomenal."

"Have you checked with Botsdorf? Maybe he can match the salary."

"No way he can even come close. I love this job, but both of us are kind of at the top of our field here. There's no room for advancement. In DC, there will be. You know how long I've wanted to make a difference in the bigger world. You know I'm that good. I can do this."

"You can play your part, there or here; it doesn't matter. If you're that good, and I know you are, what difference does it make if you're benefiting a thousand people or a million?"

"A million is better. I want to make a difference in the world, not just Jovial."

"You'll be working for politicians. After all you know about them from the last few months, how could you retain your integrity?"

"I just won't let them influence me. That's part of the deal. All I do is check facts. Cold, hard, straightforward work. And you know I'll be good at it."

"No question there. " Garit stared into her beautiful eyes again and knew he could not hold her back.

"I'll miss you. Can we try to make this work long-distance? You can fly home on weekends."

"And you can come to DC on weekends," she replied, turning away her eyes as if trying to separate herself from her present world and step into the next.

"Sure."

"You know this means you're going to be the new editor," she said. "If you want it."

He leaned in toward her because if he had waited or thought about it very much, he would have begged her to stay. He prayed quickly and silently for direction, and the word came into his head as he was moving toward her.

He kissed her softly, tenderly, and looked into those gorgeous eyes.

"Goodbye, Aspen."

Chapter 53

Two weeks later

Tony Finn picked up his phone when he saw the incoming call was from Freedah.

"Where have you been, gorgeous?" he said as he put the call on speaker.

"Just clearing my head. And thinking about your next concert tour. When do you want to start?

"I got one more song to finish for the next album, so after that," he said. "I'm still pissed at you, you know. Those concerts I just did weren't worth a thing. It's not like you, Freedah, to plan things so imprecisely. I only made about a hundred grand on that stupid tour. And that trip to Michigan? Completely worthless."

"You weren't supposed to make money. It was court-ordered, remember? I got you out of real community service work, didn't I?"

"Yeah, but I had nothing to sell, really. I will pretty soon, but I won't go back to the Midwest again. I'm going to stick to the west coast, where people understand me and love me."

"They might have loved you in Michigan if you hadn't blown up those rocks."

"Don't be bitter. I had to do it. I had to free those rocks. And I picked up some nice, beautiful shards from it all. Going to start selling them on my website as pocket rocks."

"You really think that's smart? I mean, it seems like a creative prosecutor could use them as evidence."

"That's all behind us, right? Sure, we shouldn't go back to Michigan, but no one will care if we do. I sent a check to that Frandor guy just yesterday to settle the civil suit he filed."

"How much?"

"A pittance. A couple hundred thousand. I'm still getting that much twice a year from the It's all the Same album. The Rocks and Stones will probably outdo that if you can spin the explosion into a quirk of my character, a deed done out of my overabundance of passion. People like that."

"I'll see what I can do. When can we meet and plan the next tour? You still got your steady supply of coke?"

"Doesn't really matter, does it?" Tony asked. "I mean, my tours are not your concern anymore."

"What do you mean?"

"Phoenix didn't tell you? I hooked up with MELL again to manage my tours."

"What?"

"Sorry, I thought you already knew."

"After all this time, you're throwing me away?"

"That's just business, Freedah."

Finally, he remembered her new name. But too late.

She dressed in her finest, knee-high boots, an extremely short skirt, and an opaque blouse and strutted with all the confidence she could feign into Phoenix's office.

"Well, look what the universe dragged in," Phoenix enthused, although Freedah knew his real side was about to show.

"Cut the crap," she snarled. "You took Acrid Reins management away from me? They're mine, Phoenix. You can't do that!"

Tippin sat back in his giant desk chair when he realized he would not get a hug from Freedah. Then, he assumed his CEO posture.

"You got the guts of a factory farmer," he said, his face turning stern. "You tried to go behind my back and steal them. Almost got away with it, too, you crazy bitch."

"That was only an attempt to keep them under my guidance while I was sequestered up there in Michigan. I had dozens of things to multitask, and I did it well."

"Well? You failed at every turn. First, you didn't get the whole three million from that hick with the bad teeth, and then you tried to steal the Acrid Reins contract, then you let our activists get kidnapped and get someone shot. That's bad PR for us, Sandra. It can't be tolerated."

Her face began a slow slide into crimson. "Damn it, Phoenix. How dare you call me Sandra? You don't remember why I changed my name? Do you not remember that I single-handedly freed that forest from the lumber barons up in Oregon? I freed a forest, Phoenix. You told me at the time it was the greatest act of manipulation of the courts you'd ever seen. And I changed my name just to celebrate and show my commitment to Majestic Mother Earth. You can't just throw that all away because I fell two million short with one bumpkin."

"I have to admit that the Oregon deal was good work, but when I weigh that good work against the horrible work in Michigan, they don't balance. Your sins outweigh your good deeds. No doubt about that. In my opinion, you've lost your focus and your commitment. I think maybe you should take a little time off to reconnect with Mother Earth up at our retreat center."

"That place is a shit hole," she snapped. "All that primitive living, getting back to the earth. It's a great con for your little sheep dues-payers, but I'm well past that, Phoenix. I'm much more useful to our cause than anybody else in this whole organization, and you know it."

"I'm not saying I'm going to fire you right away. But the board has my head on the chopping block. Just go there for awhile. All expenses paid. No longer than a year. Then we'll reevaluate."

Freedah hung her head. "I'll let you know," she said softly. "And don't you dare watch me walking away!"

He did.

Chapter 54

Coney Dogues arrived at the hospital to take Ty home to his casino hotel room. The pain in Ty's back was caused by muscle spasms, something he should expect, doctors said, until the scar tissue sealed up the holes where the bullet tore away spinal disks.

"Once you heal up a little, there's a job for you on our farm," Coney said.

"I might just do that."

"I have some paperwork from Botsdorf for you to sign. Believe me, each of these 12 farmers appreciates what you're doing. I mean, selling them your property for a buck each?"

Ty smiled and remained silent.

Instead of taking Grey Road around downtown Jovial to the casino, Coney turned right onto Jovial Bluff Road and the ascent that led to the abandoned county park. He slowed near the park's entrance and stopped in front of the closed gate. A new no-trespassing sign hung in contrast to the rusted iron bar that blocked the entrance.

"What's up?" Ty asked.

"Thought maybe you hadn't heard since you've been lounging around in a hospital these past few weeks. The county finally put up this property for sale. Closed bids. Today at 5 p.m. is the deadline to send them in."

"How much do they want?"

"Highest bidder."

"So it's just a guessing game. Anyone could overpay if they want it bad enough."

"Oh, there's a couple of people – organizations, really – that want it bad."

Coney opened the truck's console between them, pulled out a piece of paper, and handed it to Ty.

"I would suggest if you still want this acreage, that you match this top bid."

Ty read the list of bidders. MELL had bid $350,000. Under them was the name PFFF. Bid $400,000.

Ty smiled. "Amazing. I would have paid half a million. How did you get this?"

"I have friends. And some inside information that could save you a hundred grand if you have that much left."

"Oh, I have that much," Ty said, grinning. "After all, Freedah never got that last payment. I put stop orders on everything. She still conned me out of about two million bucks, but I just put that down as learning for me."

"And what did you learn?"

"That Freedah is just an extremely high-priced hooker."

"Good enough. Remember it. Nice packages don't always have nice things inside."

"Agreed."

"But I have more good news for you, Ty."

"What's that?"

"There's a little-known stipulation in the law when the county sells public land to a private person. It went through as a minor amendment to the county charter back when I was on the board. If the top bids tie, the property must be sold to a citizen of Jovial County."

Ty grinned, winced as his back spasmed, and grinned again.

"Take me to the county offices? I have a form to fill out."

***

Early next spring

Ty stepped across the park road's barrier and walked slowly to the grassy area where people once sat on picnic tables and gazed at the majestic views of the Jovial River. Now, it was overgrown with sapling maple, sumac, and pine trees, and the view of the river was blocked by brush. Not for long. The lawsuit that MELL and PFFF filed to have their bids for this land accepted had been thrown out of court. Not only was Tyson Mooring a citizen, which gave him deference for the sale, but he had bid $410,000, ten thousand dollars more than they had bid. As he walked toward his potential building site, he looked at the GPS map he'd printed from the county offices.

The map revealed in official terms what Ty had expected: that the park land was adjacent to his 100 acres of farmland. He had already been approved for construction on the only building site along this high bluff, and so, with a chainsaw in his hand, he cleared the house site and the smaller brush that blocked the road. A bulldozer would be there soon to clear the road, smooth it, and add gravel.

***

Two weeks later, the day before his building contractor was set to start drilling deep into the massive rock below the surface to put in footings, the first fine day of spring arrived.

Ty launched his boat from the dock at Ernie's Outfitters. The boat, in large block letters on both sides, said "Jorgen Fishing Co.," and he cruised upriver at a slow pace. He could see his building site, but casual tourists likely would never even look up to find it. They'd be too mesmerized at the spring growth down here, on the surface, where the Jovial was putting on her multi-colored finery.

As he went past his property and saw the bulldozers working, there was another sight he wanted to see. Ernie had accepted his offer, and workmen were there with heavy equipment, installing a brand new septic system just below the survivor school building. Ernie had paid his fine and applied for permits to open the school again as long as the septic system could hold up.

Ty motored past the work as far as he could until he heard the noise of more heavy equipment. Where the river was getting too narrow and small to continue, he tied up to a tree on the bank and walked up onto what he thought was state land.

He crested the hill and saw three middle-aged men dressed in expensive suits, watching as a bulldozer leveled a hill. Ty yelled a greeting to prevent them from being caught unaware. The men waved back, and Ty walked to them.

"Hey, fellas," he said cheerfully. "What's going on here?"

"Who wants to know?" said the shorter of the two men as he took a challenging posture.

"I'm a fishing guide from down in Jovial," Ty said. "Just checking out any changes in the river since the spring flood, and I heard the equipment. I thought this was state land."

"Nope," said the shorter man. "This is the property of PFFF, the Pure Fly Fishing Federation. We're building a golf course on this property."

"But we exist primarily to fish," said the taller, friendlier man. "We had hoped to get some property closer to Jovial for the golf course, but some Mexican has it all tied up in court."

"You don't say. I thought all that was resolved and finalized. The property actually belongs to the farmers."

"The polluters, you mean," said the shorter man. Ty ignored the comment, but it took great effort. Fortunately, he had been reading Proverbs that morning and remembered that it said not to argue with a fool or you could become one yourself.

"Did you get a good price?" Ty asked.

"No," said the taller man, "but that doesn't matter. It's ours now. We're going to put up condos here with a view of the river. Members only."

"Too bad you couldn't get something up higher," Ty said. "Better views."

"Someday," said the shorter man. "We're mostly lawyers in this club, and so we'll get it one way or another."

Ty had heard enough.

"If you need a fishing guide, just go down to Ernie's Outfitters on the river, and he'll get in touch with me," Ty said. "Name's Jorgen." he reached out his hand and shook the men's hands.

"We're pretty damn good fishermen ourselves," said the short one. "Only the beginners need guides."

"Do the beginners know how to remove a hook without destroying the fish's mouths?" Ty asked.

"Time for you to get off our property," the short man said. Ty smiled at them and walked back down to his new boat. He floated back down toward Jovial, noting mentally a few new holes that could be fish magnets left over from the spring runoff.

"Those boys will never find you," he said as he passed a deep hole behind a large rock and saw a large crowd of fish jumping at bugs on the surface. "Not if I have anything to say about it."

***

Garit had been getting various videos and information from an unnamed source for a couple of weeks, but he knew it was Aspen holding onto her connection with him. This morning, he received a link to a story out of Berkeley, California. Tony Finn, reportedly, was injured after the first stop on his Rocks and Stones

Redux tour. Another link took him to a video interview. The Kaley Carrumbo Show.

Kaley was on the edge of her seat, wide-eyed and apparently full of empathy.

"So, how did you end up in the emergency room?" she asked but didn't wait for the answer. "You know, I was a victim, too, for the sake of the cause of Majestic Mother Earth. For my viewers who may have missed it, I was in the wings, preparing for my interview with you up in Michigan – somewhere around Detroit, as I recall – when that madman tried to kill you. I was afraid for my life, and all because we took an unpopular stand against the evil that is farming. I had come to Michigan all for nothing because of that. I had to wait two hours and never got the interview. It was one of the worst days of my life. But you continued to raise awareness, which is what I'm doing now. So please, Tony, tell us your story."

Tony shifted in his chair, looked for a split-second into the camera, then fixed his eyes on Kaley.

"Well, Kaley, as you know, I've been an advocate for Mother Nature's defense against polluters and right-wing farmers – also polluters – for years. I've also been carrying rocks in my pockets for years. They ground me, calm my spirit, and lead me to a higher plane when I touch them and caress them. They deserve that because rocks and stones have been so abused and taken for granted ever since recorded time. My mission on this tour has been, from the start, to offer this peace and, hopefully, open eyes to the fact that rocks are a sort of metaphysical bridge between the earth and the spirit.

So, as part of that, I had piled a large number of rock shards on a platform in front of the stage here at Berkeley and invited people to come down the aisles and take a stone for themselves, put them in their pockets and experience the love the earth can bring them just by being in contact with another victim of violence against Mother Earth. It was all quite benevolent of me."

"And where did the stones come from?" Kaley asked, knowing the answer.

"All of the shards were ones I picked up in Michigan when that rock farmer exploded his already licentious rock pile. But I don't blame him. His mind is clouded by greed. It's a shame, really." Kaley nodded into her camera with her best sad eye face.

"So anyway, I had done a couple of old songs – you know, the old favorites like It's All the Same – and started talking about the value of rocks, about their abuse, about the crimes committed against them, when some idiots – likely right-wingers – near the back started shouting for me to shut up and play my music. But I stood firm. They needed to hear this for their own good. So I kept talking. I mean, how are people going to find rest for their souls if they don't know the truth?" Kaley nodded, her shining, oval eyes peering into the camera lens. "Then, suddenly, some of the people – I think they were right-wing, anti-rock people, rushed up and began throwing the rocks toward the stage," he said dramatically.

"My goodness!" Kaley gasped. "You must have been terrorized."

"Oh, yes!" Tony said, wiping a practiced finger under his eye, though it was dry. "I barely escaped with my life."

"And is that how you ended up in the emergency room? What were your wounds that you can now wear with pride?"

"Well, my physical wounds were luckily limited, but my spiritual wounds will always be with me because one of my roadies – I don't remember his name – was hit in the head and took quite a little cut. I rushed him to the emergency room and waited for him."

"So you *were* in the emergency room?"

"Yes, for almost two hours!"

Kaley turned to the camera. "How sad. When will people learn that violence is not the answer?"

"I know. I think our founding people would be ashamed of an America where people will take rocks against people they disagree with. I mean, it never crossed my mind that a pile of beautiful, innocent rocks could be used as weapons! Who does that?"

"We'll try to figure that out after this message," Kaley said.

Garit turned off the video and laughed, forwarded it to Ty.

***

One week after Ty moved from the casino hotel room into his new house on the bluff, he received mail. Amazed at how quickly it had been forwarded, he noticed one letter with a hand-written address line from the Jovial State Prison.

Dear Tyson:

You'll be happy to know I am still doing God's work up here in the prison. Something about being a real inmate and not a chaplain helps me connect with them. So far, in the three months I've been here, 12 young men have given their lives to Jesus.

As for me, I've been changed by God too. I've had lots of time to think about my doubts. See, I always looked at doubt as a weakness, something that could never be acceptable in the life of a Christian. But now I know that doubt can lead to growth. Doubts are to be reasoned out, fought, sure, but God seems to want me to ask Him questions these days.

I hope you know that my taking the fall for shooting you was my choice, one that God approved, I think. I still doubt it sometimes, but I'm going to persevere. You took the fall for your buddy, and God used it to develop our relationship and lead you to His son. Jesus took the fall for all of us. So I wanted to be more Christ-like, and this seemed like a good bit of penitence for my crimes, too. In a few years, after I've paid my debt, I hope to come and see you, as long as you're not still living in the casino. I'd be arrested again if I came anywhere near it.

You may wonder why I was in Jovial the night you were shot. I had been fuming, in my selfishness and pride, because I had learned about your intimacy with Freedah. I was envious of you, a deadly sin. I had fallen for her, just like everyone seems to do.

Then I learned that you and Melanie Swann from the farmers union were committing fornication, and that was my opening. I thought it my duty to confront you with your sin, but I had become blind to my own. You're still a relatively new Christian, so maybe you don't know this yet, but God hates adultery, even if it's only in the mind.

I pray you find one woman, as God intended, who you can spend your life with, someone you can devote yourself to. Remember, love is not a feeling but a commitment. A choice. Choose to love even when you don't feel like it. One-on-one, exclusive devotion is the most satisfying relationship humans can ever imagine, and even better, you can have a one-on-one relationship with Jesus. Grow in that.

Last year was certainly an adventure, wasn't it? I pray for you daily, and I hope you pray for me too. God has blessed me, and I pray he blesses you, too, with salvation and success.

Sincerely,

Reverend, Repented.

P.S. Because I'm a prisoner, the state has paid to have the last of the shrapnel taken out of my leg. I can walk again without pain!

***

James Snowmaker's bitterness was his daily morning greeting. He had awakened with a snort of derision most mornings since he was taken out of the woods of Michigan. He'd been manipulated, out-smarted. And when his thoughts immediately turned to revenge, he thought about the videos of him with Freedah and other people in various compromising positions. Not that he'd done anything wrong, after all. His bank account still proved to him that he was powerful, smart, and innocent.

He'd gone back to San Francisco and started working lawsuits for MELL again. Then, during the winter, a board member of the University of California at Berkeley died, leaving an open post. An alumnus, Snowmaker ran for the post and won by a narrow margin in a special election.

He was driving his Cadillac Esplanade across campus to get to a board meeting when he tossed his McDonald's breakfast meal bag out the window. A campus police officer pulled him over.

The officer's body cam recorded the altercation. It took four officers to pin him to the ground and arrest him.

As Ty moved into his new home, Snowmaker was in police custody, charged with environmental crimes.

Chapter 55

Tourists had left Jovial and the river, and Ty's new business was slowing as winter threatened.

Ty was relaxing on his spacious deck overlooking the river on a bright, warm, and birdsong-filled fall morning. Business for his fishing guide enterprise had been steady and good, but he was determined to enjoy a day with nothing to do but sit in a massage chair to silence his barking back.

About mid-morning, as they'd arranged, Garit West walked onto the deck.

"Got to admit, Ty, this is the most spectacular view of God's creation in the whole county," Garit said. "But I have another thing you might find interesting."

He hooked up his phone to Ty's large laptop, and as he clicked around, a video report from some TV station in Seattle popped up.

The story was identified as one in a series of reports on environmental heroes who had been discriminated against in various other parts of the nation and had fled to Washington for protection amid like-minded people.

"Here it comes, turn it up," Garit said. Ty cranked up the sound just in time to see a large group of people in a meadow – maybe it was just a lawn that hadn't been mowed in a while – holding hands and chanting as they danced in a circle, "Hail, Majestic Mother Earth. We honor you for your beauty" several times. Their unison was amazing because Garit and Ty could hear the words of the chant clearly. The footage played as they danced, and suddenly, Garit said, "Freeze it right there." Ty did.

"What are we looking at?'

"Look closer." Garit pointed at one woman on the screen.

Ty leaned in. Did a double-take.

"Can't be," he said.

"But it is," Garit said. Ty looked again. The woman was rotund, her face plain and round, but her eyes stood out, sparkling, yet somehow dull, as if they had been painted onto her face. Her oversized dress was simple and frumpy. Ty resumed the video and watched the circle move. The woman was chanting the loudest and seemed quite enthusiastic.

Ty paused it again to look at that face.

"Freedah?" he said. "Can't be."

Garit laughed. They watched the video a few more times, even when the footage of the circle dance was done. The film cut to an interview with the woman.

"People need to understand that Majestic Mother Earth is all there is," she said. "But if they choose to disobey, to ignore her, she'll take her retribution. And it won't be pretty."

The video ended, and the two young men sat in silence for a moment.

"Is that what you call justice?" Ty offered.

"Maybe," Garit responded.

The pair sat in silence for a few moments, then played the video several more times. Their laughter receded with each one, replaced by sympathy, maybe.

A delivery man arrived with a pizza, hot and loaded with meat. They dug in, occasionally noting what a shame it was that Freedah had let herself go.

The pizza was gone; they sat back in their chairs and gazed at the river and her fall colors, the fading greens turning yellow, then brown, and thousands of colors that neither of them could name.

"You know," said Ty, "you should write a book about all this stuff that happened, you know?"

"I just might." They watched the video again.

"I guess her influence is gone," Ty said. "She's a part of Mother Earth now. She always said she wanted to be of the earth. Guess that's where she's stuck now. In the earth and of the earth."

Garit agreed.

"The real shame of it all," he said, "is that she always was."

THE END

Made in the USA
Middletown, DE
05 November 2024

63651872R00230